Rise of the Moon

By

Nicoline Evans

Author: Nicoline Evans – www.nicolineevans.com
Editor: Emily Kline – www. ekediting.com

To my beta readers and everyone else who has offered support (in all ways, shapes, and sizes) during this entire process—thank you!

The Solarpunks of Quintessence

Thermapunks

Element: HEAT
Location: Fyree
Hearts contain the Source Flame
Gears made of Gold
Veins filled with Magma
Lead Family: The Dawes

Thermapunk Sub-faction(s):

• <u>Pyropounks</u>; fire faction within the Pyro-Argo Militia. They combat the moon monsters.

• <u>Steampunks</u>; work at the Steamery and collect water for Fyree.

• <u>Welders</u>; specialize in repairing metal structures with fire.

• <u>Thermadocs</u>; medical mechanics who specialize in healing/repairing Thermapunks with ailments.

Aeropunks

Element: GAS
Location: Gaslion
Hearts contain Helium
Gears made of Copper
Veins filled with Liquid Nitrogen
Lead Family: The Holloways

Aeropunk Sub-faction(s):

• <u>Pilopunks</u>; aviators of the sky.

• <u>Argopunks</u>; gas faction within the Pyro-Argo Militia. They combat the moon monsters.

• <u>Gas Spinners</u>; conservationists of the solar shield.

• <u>Aerodocs</u>; medical mechanics who specialize in healing/repairing Aeropunks with ailments.

Terrapunks

Element: MINERALS
Location: Terra
Hearts contain Uranium
Gears made of Chrome Silver
Veins filled with Petroleum
Lead Family: The Horrigans

Terrapunk Sub-faction(s):

• <u>Tinkerpunks</u>; gadgeteers who maintain the geared world of Quintessence.

• <u>Revopunks</u>; they skate in continuous loops atop the giant Terra gears, keeping them turning.

• <u>Digipunks</u>; miners of Terra.

• <u>Terrapunk Guards</u>; patrol the basic workings of Terra.

• <u>Stone Patrol</u> (Stoneheads); serve and protect the Horrigan family.

• <u>Terradocs</u>; medical mechanics who specialize in healing/repairing Terrapunks with ailments.

Hydropunks

Element: WATER
Location: Hydra
Hearts contain Ocean Water
Gears made of Zinc
Veins filled with Octopus Ink
Lead Family: None

Hydropunk Sub-faction(s):

• <u>Nautipunks</u>; pirates of Hydra.

• <u>Watermen</u>; specialize in channeling their water hearts and dousing fires with ocean water.

• <u>Hydrodocs</u>; medical mechanics who specialize in healing/repairing Hydropunks with ailments.

The Lunarians of Mōnalene

Lepidos – monarch butterfly royals
Odonatas – dragonfly and damselfly warriors
Orthops – grasshopper astronomers
Formies – ant builders
Macrotermes – termite engineers and builders
Anthos -bee gardeners
Mantos – praying mantis scientists
Vespas – hornet engineers
Coccinellies – ladybug medics

The Gods
Solédon – god of all suns
Lunéss – goddess of all moons
Incarna – goddess of souls and reincarnation
Matrigaia – goddess of all mortal life
Marlodon – god of the seas
Kólasi – god of mortal death and chaos
Mortacia – goddess of death and mischief
Obscuro – god of darkness
Lumine – goddess of light

Dimidivinus – half divine
Dimidivinus describes mortals who have received a divine touch from a god, a divine progeny, or a totumdivinus mortal. The touch must be blessed by a god to take effect. This level of divinity makes them nearly indestructible and grants them access to some of their god's powers at reduced strength.

All Solarpunks are given dimidivinus status at birth from Solédon.
All Lunarians are given dimidivinus status at birth from Lunéss.

May we discover the value within our differences

Chapter 1

Silver grit and stardust rose in a plume around Emmeline as she gasped for air.

Panicked and desperate, she fell to her knees and clutched her throat.

The moon had no oxygen, no air for her to breathe.

She hadn't thought this through. She was in foreign territory where her body could not survive.

Wheezing as she expended the last bits of air in her lungs, Emmeline collapsed to the ground, shaking violently on the dusty terrain.

This was it.

This was how it ended.

Was she wrong to trust Luna? Had she been led into a trap?

Why did Luna tell her to use the portal if she knew Emmeline could not survive the moon's atmosphere?

Darkness blanketed her vision, cradling the corners and creating a tunnel veiled with shadows.

She could see straight ahead—gray craters on this desolate moon—but nothing else. Left, right, above, below; everything dimmed as her breath thinned.

Is this what she deserved?

Perhaps it was.

Perhaps her brush with infamy was stolen from her with good purpose—her greatness was built on a foundation of lies. Her potential stemmed from a debilitating illness. If she led her people to mirror her as she was, they'd fall victim to similar obsessions. They'd go mad trying to emulate her. To mimic her was impossible; they could never match her abilities without touching a moonstone.

Her ascent to excellence came at a cost—a curse she wouldn't wish on her greatest enemy. If this was her time to die, perhaps it was a blessing to remove impossible feats from the imaginations of her people.

They could not fly without sacrificing their lives.

It was a trade only fools would make.

Emmeline's eyes closed as delirium set in. The faces she loved most flashed across the backs of her eyelids: her parents, her brothers, Gemma, Avery, Clementine. Louie's face appeared last. Silver-blue eyes gleaming, smile endearing, he whispered, *"Come back to me."*

I can't, Emmeline thought. Her mind's voice sounded as weak as she felt.

"Come back to me," he repeated.

Aware that she may never see him or anyone she loved ever again, Emmeline surrendered to her sorrow. Sobbing hysterically, the few remaining wisps of oxygen fluttered from her lungs. She was wasting her breath, wasting her energy—both of which she had little to spare.

Mourning replaced with panic, Emmeline squinted through her darkened vision for help. Sight tunneled, she scanned the barren wasteland.

Not a soul in sight.

"Come back to me." Louie's words rang inside her head.

The stone.

Emmeline raked the dusty ground, searching for the moonstone. If the incantation she had used worked both ways, she could teleport back to Quintessence.

Where had it landed? Why wasn't it still in her hand?

"Come back to me."

Emmeline's heart sank—she had left the moonstone with Louie.

This solution was not viable.

She could not save herself.

Clinging to her dignity, she prepared to surrender with grace when a set of sharp talons snatched her waist. Nearly unconscious, she hardly felt the pain as they cut into her flesh and carried her away.

With no energy to wonder what was happening or where she was being taken, Emmeline instead thought of Solédon. Though she had her doubts about His governance, He was the only one who could grant her final request.

Please honor my life, she prayed in thought. *Grant my soul passage to Incarna. Allow me the chance to try again in a new vessel.* Though her mind slipped as her life faded, she was able to make one last wish. *If you grant me this, please also let me remember this life in the next. I do not want to make the same mistakes.*

As the prayer left her mind, so did her final breath.

Choking on nothingness, Emmeline's eyes shot open in horror as her lung gears stuttered to a stop.

"Hold on a little longer," a familiar voice urged.

Emmeline opened her mouth to respond, but no words came out. No air, no energy; she was at the mercy of whoever held her now. She looked up to identify the voice but could not see clearly through the haze. Death-induced shadows and clouds blurred everything, allowing her to see only a generic outline of the individual.

Dragonfly wings and long dark hair—Emmeline hoped it was Luna.

Together, they tore across the moonscape, rocketing at wild speeds toward the unknown. As they reached a giant crater, distorted figures emerged from the crevice.

"Let me pass!" her savior shouted.

"She is not welcome here," one of the figures responded. Another familiar voice Emmeline could not place.

"I have permission from the Monarchs."

"We say otherwise."

"You would go against Lepido Dione?"

"She is misguided on this matter."

"Be careful," Emmeline's savior warned.

"Send her back to the sun," a different opposer said.

"I am tasked to bring her to the Monarchs."

"Do not test us, Luna."

Hopes confirmed, Emmeline could hold on no longer and fell limp in Luna's grip.

A moment of tense silence lingered between Luna and those who opposed her.

Time was running out.

"If this Solarpunk dies, the war between the sun and our moon will intensify, and the Monarchs will have you to blame."

"It's your fault for bringing her here."

"I brought her here to save her from a curse *we* caused and to form an alliance between our people. The Monarchs know all of this. You need to let me pass."

Half of the group moved aside, while the other half stood firm.

Cèla stood among the dissenters.

"Your father would be standing beside me if he wasn't paralyzed from his time spent imprisoned on the sun."

"When all of this is over, you both will understand my reasons. For now, you have to trust me."

"An alliance will never work!" Cèla argued.

"It has to." Luna glanced down at Emmeline, who was unconscious in her grip. "If I waste another minute, she will die."

"I hope they all die!" Cèla shouted before she charged at Luna, aim zeroed in on Emmeline.

Luna dodged moments before Cèla could rip Emmeline from her grip, then nose-dived toward the crater. To her relief, she had a giant lead on Cèla and none of the others gave chase.

She flew faster toward the crater. As soon as she entered the inside world of Mōnalene, Cèla would have to cease her attack—the Coleo guards would be there to protect her delivery of Emmeline to the Monarch fortress.

Luna transferred Emmeline to her arms and then came to a screeching halt as she hit the ground. She darted to the nearest doorway, which was camouflaged by gray moon rock, and entered the inner world of Mōnalene.

Inside the moon was a massive world of floating meteors connected by webs of black cords. Within these meteors were homes, training centers, and various establishments that served their society.

She could not fly here—the lack of gravity was less than above and too volatile for the strength of her wings—so she ran. The magnetic cords coursing through her body kept her bound to the equally magnetic cords zigzagging across this space. Luna navigated the intricate maze of webs, careful not to shake the cords too much as she raced to the fortress. Too much movement could cause the delicate arrangement of meteors to ricochet into a cataclysmic mess.

When she reached the Monarch fortress, Lepido Dione was standing on the upper balcony, orange wings spread wide. The entire building was made of jagged meteor rock sculpted into an opulent castle. Though it was regal, it held the grit of its origin.

"Get the oxygen ready," Luna called out.

Two scientists, known as Mantos, appeared at the main entrance, rolling out a breathing contraption. Their extra-long arms and legs moved with meticulous leisure.

Luna raced toward them, repositioning Emmeline in her grip. Once they were close enough, she dropped Emmeline into the arms of the largest scientist, Manto Maldi, who caught her and pressed the breathing mask onto her face. The other scientist, Manto Bogo, cranked the tank levers, allowing oxygen to pour through the tubes and into Emmeline's mouth.

While the machine worked, they waited.

Minutes passed.

They fidgeted uncomfortably, afraid for the worst, when Emmeline opened her eyes.

Mask still strapped to her head, she sat up and gasped.

"Where am I?" she asked

Luna smiled.

"Welcome to Mōnalene."

Chapter 2

Quintessence

"Emmeline!" Solís shouted from the rooftop.

Tears welled in his furious gaze.

"Emmeline!" he shouted again, his voice cracking with desperation.

"She's not with the Aeropunks," said a voice from behind. It was Helix, stumbling toward Solís in a locomo high. Though his chemist toolbelt was fastened and loaded with his most prized tools, the rest of his appearance was a mess. His knickers were covered in black soot, his tweed vest was unbuttoned, and his golden hair was unkempt.

Solís ignored his brother's disheveled stupor.

"She had some connection to the sky. I saw her talking to someone up there."

"Do you think it was a gas spinner?" Helix asked.

"I doubt it. Raven and Remington swear they have nothing to do with her disappearance, nor did their fellow gas spinners." Solís paused. "Though they did mention her magic many times. And I heard her speak of magic once in the hallway. Her and Clementine were bickering about it."

"Have you talked to Clementine?"

"Not yet. She's in Hydra, along with the rest of my top suspects. Dad won't let me visit until I *calm down*," he said, emphasizing his words with a mocking tone.

Helix shrugged. "I don't blame him. You look like you're ready to combust."

"Am I the only one who cares that Emmeline vanished with no explanation? She's been missing for two weeks!"

"We all care," Helix retorted, "but we aren't about to destroy all of Quintessence in the process. You are too rash, too impulsive. We have a search party going, too, which we have invited you to join—"

"It's the laziest search I've ever seen," Solís spat. "They spent an entire week *talking* about where she might have gone. No action, no investigation—we lost valuable time!"

"We needed to gather all the facts. There's no sense running around like maniacs, searching locations she'd never be."

"If she's not somewhere up there," he said, waving his hand at the sky, "then she's in Hydra."

A gush of wind swirled around them and Avery landed beside Helix in a crouch.

"Louie swears she isn't in Hydra," she said as she removed her goggles and relocated them around the brim of her aviator cap.

"Who is Louie?" Solís demanded.

"If you had attended the search party meetings, you'd know," Helix said, fidgeting within his high.

"Louie is Emmeline's boyfriend," Avery said.

"Boyfriend?"

She nodded. "True love forms in the most unlikely of places."

"Is he a Nautipunk?" Solís demanded.

"He is."

Solís's face sweltered red as his anger grew. "He is the only punk we should be questioning! Of course, he knows where she went. For all we know, he drowned her!"

"He would never—" Avery said.

"He is a scoundrel! A rotten pirate! Nautipunks cannot be trusted."

"You're wrong. I know Louie well. He would die before allowing any harm to reach Emmeline."

"I need to speak with him," Solís demanded.

"You're not allowed in Hydra at the moment," Avery reminded him.

Solís growled.

"Just chill out," Helix advised. "We're all on the hunt. We will find her."

"My gut says she's up there somewhere," Solís said, his attention returning to the sky.

"Do you think the Holloways kidnapped her?" Avery asked, her tone disbelieving.

"No," he answered. "They aren't that stupid."

"Agreed," she said. "Not sure how Emmeline could be up there without help from the gas spinners."

"Me either, but my intuition keeps pulling me toward the sky."

"Part of me wishes the Holloways were involved," Avery said. "It would make everything so much easier."

"What do you mean?" Solís asked.

Avery hesitated, then asked, "Can I trust you both?"

"Yes," they answered in unison.

"Before Emmeline left, she was helping me with a really important mission. The Argopunks and Pilopunks want to break free from the Holloway rule."

"I've overheard whispers about this at the base," Helix confessed. "The Morrells should be reinstated as a noble family. I'm all for it."

Avery grumbled, annoyed that their secret mission wasn't so secret after all. She let it slide. "Emmeline was going to champion our cause on behalf of the Thermapunks. She was going to use her leadership role and choose the Morrell family over the Holloways."

"Surely, not without some sort of plan," Solís commented. "Switching teams for no reason would start a civil war."

"She was certain that Raven and Remington would spy on her again, ultimately breaking the alliance and giving my family an opportunity to rise into a leadership role again."

"Good plan, except we can't catch them spying on her if she's not here," Solís quipped.

"I know. But if the Holloways are involved in any way, you two could act as champions for our cause, at least until Emmeline returns."

"I hate the Holloways, so you have my vote," Helix stated.

"Mine, too," Solís agreed, though he was distracted.

Avery sensed his dismay.

"Our priority is finding Emmeline, of course," she said. "I only bring this up because if the Holloways are involved in any way, we can use that to help my people."

"I understand." Solís was distracted. "I need to speak to Louie. He might have answers."

"He knows nothing," Helix said.

"He must know *something*."

"Well, if you can relax and act like a rational punk, perhaps Dad will lift his ban on your presence in Hydra."

Solís nodded, determined to speak to Louie.

"I need answers, and I think Louie knows more than what he's told you."

"Those are some big assumptions, considering you've never even met Louie," Avery noted.

"It's just a feeling I have."

Avery shook her head and placed her goggles back over her eyes. "I need to get going. If I discover anything worthwhile, I'll report back."

Solís and Helix nodded in appreciation as she flew away. Her copper wings gleamed beneath the swirling solar flare shield.

"Dad is coming home for dinner tonight," Helix informed Solís. "If you want to prove you're stable enough to join the search, you should do it then."

"Fine. I will."

Helix coughed. "I need another hit of locomo."

"You need to stop huffing that poison."

"I'm dealing with a lot, and it's the only thing that helps. Actually, you're so high-strung, you could probably use some, too."

"And become addicted like you? No thanks."

Helix shrugged and stumbled across the roof, leaving through the open attic window.

Solís was alone again.

Conflicted between anger, concern, and despair, his emotions were volatile. He had to learn to control them, or else he could inadvertently make this huge problem worse.

"All that matters is finding Emmeline," he reminded himself. "All that matters is her well-being."

The scent of moon lily ripped Solís from his thoughts.

His head snapped toward the sky, nostrils flared to investigate the aroma. Honeyed magnolia, crisp cosmic zephyr, untouched stardust—the prettiest smell with the most ominous implications.

Solís fueled his fire heart instinctively and spread his titanium wings. Prepared to fight whatever moon monster lurked, he scanned the sky for invaders.

No one was there.

The smell lingered.

"Where are you?" Solís demanded, his voice clear and confident. "Show yourself!"

Though the scent persisted, the sky remained empty.

A strong breeze lashed his face, carrying the scent and a soft whisper.

Ad lunam lu. Accipe me.

Solís swatted the air, trying to escape the whirlwind and locate the source.

"Who are you?" he asked, agitated as the breeze dried out his golden eyes.

He rubbed them, coaxing out a few tears to alleviate the dryness, and when he returned his attention to the sky, both the scent and the breeze were gone.

Alone on the rooftop, he repeated the words.

"Ad lunam lu. Accipe me."

His stomach churned in warning as the words left his lips.

Chapter 3

Mōnalene

Emmeline was strapped to a table made of moon rock. Strong black and silver threads constrained her to the slab of basalt while wide-eyed hellions poked and prodded at her head.

In and out of consciousness, Emmeline could not distinguish reality from her nightmares, as the hellions starred in both. She searched for familiar faces, anything to lessen her terror, but Luna came and went as frequently as Emmeline slipped in and out of her dreams.

The tools the hellions used to examine her were terrifying. She caught sight of them a few times between eye flutters—thin rods covered in tiny spikes, pliers with metal teeth, and a circular saw they had yet to use.

"What does that one do?" she asked during a brief moment of consciousness.

"The spherical blade?" one of the hellions responded, pointing at the circular saw. His silver eyes bulged out of his face.

Emmeline nodded.

He picked it up and spun the crank that tightened the rubber bands attached to the saw. When he released the lever, the serrated blade revolved with deathly speed, whirring so fiercely she was sure it could cut through gold.

The terror blurred Emmeline's vision, and she slipped into a place between sleep and awake.

Metallic dust flurried over her, landing on her lips with a golden tang.

Heart contracting as her gears pushed forward, a quick glance upward revealed her greatest nightmare—the hellions were sawing her skull, slicing it open, and tinkering with her mind's gears. They rearranged them in a way that made her docile, made her forget who she was and where she came from.

"No," she mumbled. "Let me remember."

Their black eyes swirled with silver ink, creating hypnotizing spirals.

She stared too long and the walls disappeared, leaving her in blackness. The only light came from streaks of silver, which coiled in circles above.

Entranced by the monotonous rotation of silver ink, she forgot about the nightmare and recalled the comfort she found in this space.

She had been here before; it was the same place she visited each time she lost consciousness.

This room became her home—it was the safest place to hide while her fate beyond slipped from her control.

Lost in the familiar darkness, Emmeline had no sense of time. She was trapped here until the silver sparks allowed her another peek into the outside world.

The swirls flickered with light.

Pain gone, worries subdued, Emmeline was captivated.

"Wake up," a familiar voice said.

Emmeline looked around and saw nothing but the silver-stained darkness.

"You have to wake up!"

A skinny hand with long, pointed fingernails reached through one of the silver streaks, snatching Emmeline by the waist and pulling her into the light.

Emmeline's eyes opened.

She was back in the medical room, surrounded by unfamiliar hellions. Moon threads weaved through her nose and mouth, rendering her mute.

Panic set in.

She squirmed beneath her restraints, fighting the threads that held her in place.

"Calm down."

Her eyes darted all around until they landed on Luna, who wore a kind smile. She held Emmeline's hand and sat patiently beside her. Dressed in her warrior armor made of leather and Lunarian metal, this visit was a pit stop between tasks.

The giant, bug-eyed scientist pulled the last cord out of Emmeline's mouth, allowing her to speak again.

"My head!" Emmeline exclaimed.

"What about it?" Luna asked.

"They sawed it open!"

"Nope. You're still in one piece. Must've been a nightmare."

Emmeline began to sob. "I can't tell the difference between what's real and fake."

"Just stay strong," Luna encouraged as she applied grease to Emmeline's geared joints. "Paranoia and nightmares are part of the healing process. The curse is being extracted from your mind in slivers. Slow and steady is the only safe way to help you."

"It's torture."

"You have a skilled team of Lunarian scientists and medics working on this. You are in good hands."

"Lunarian?" Emmeline asked.

"You are a Solarpunk. We are Lunarians."

All of Emmeline's fears were replaced with shame. After all she had endured, she was still shortsighted.

"I'm sorry," she expressed.

"For what?"

"Despite all you've done for me, I still saw the scientists and medics as hellions. You have a complex and advanced society here—I need to stop seeing those I don't recognize as monsters."

Luna smiled. "Awareness is the first step. Be patient with yourself. You have a good heart."

Emmeline nodded.

Luna added, "If it makes you feel any better, the majority of Lunarians still see the Solarpunks as monsters."

"They see *us* as monsters?"

"Funny how things look from the other side, but yes. Many believe that Kólasi got into the ear of Solédon and turned Him against us. Many Lunarians see Solarpunks as servants to a devil."

"Kólasi? The god of death and chaos? That's not true."

"I'm not sure what's true anymore. I just know we are supposed to work together, and you are the first Solarpunk to see us as more than monsters."

"I'm useless like this," Emmeline said, still strapped to the slab of moon rock.

Luna corked the small vial of grease. "We're almost out. I'll need to return to Quintessence to get more grease and marbles."

"Have you been feeding me?"

"Yes. Just enough to keep your gears turning."

Emmeline hesitated. "How are things in Quintessence?"

"Your family is searching for you, but they haven't figured out that you're here yet. If we can get you healed before they figure it out, we can show everyone how beneficial an alliance between our people could be. It will take time and patience, though—both sides hold deep-rooted hatred for each other."

"Why were there threads in my nose and mouth?" she asked, wriggling her nose to relieve a lingering itch.

"Those are from the Weaver, specially designed to pull the curse out of your body."

"Who is the Weaver?"

"The arachnid of life—the threads within every Lunarian were woven by her."

Emmeline took a deep breath as she absorbed this information.

"She builds you?"

"Partly. The mating of two Lunarians makes the shell of the body, the Weaver provides the threads, and Incarna delivers the soul."

"Solarpunk souls are delivered by Incarna, too."

"See, we aren't so different."

Emmeline considered this as she scanned the other Lunarians in the room, none of whom looked like Luna. "You all look so different," she commented.

"Our bodily designs are modeled off of arthropods found on the planet that we serve."

Emmeline recalled distant memories from the time her soul lived inside the mortals of Earth.

"Bugs," she recalled. "Insects."

"Yes," Luna confirmed.

"But why?"

"Lunéss believed that mixing their exoskeletons and segmented bodies into our design would make us stronger, which it has. I can lose a limb or part of my body, and it'll grow back. Many of us have torsos and skulls with built-in shields for battle. I am built in the image of a dragonfly, as are all the other Odonata warriors."

"I recognize the scientists as praying mantises," Emmeline commented. "But none of you look exactly like your arthropod counterpart."

"Correct. I suppose we are a blend of insect and human, with a large dose of moon magic."

Emmeline gave Luna a half smile. "It's nice to learn about where you come from."

"One day, this knowledge will be known by all of your people."

"If I ever get to go home," Emmeline said, her tone defeated. "Are you sure I will heal?"

"We were uncertain when you first got here, but so far, the procedure has worked well and they've extracted a good percentage of the curse." She pointed to a shelf with two glass jars filled with silver liquid. "This is a first for us, too. Hopefully, there's not much of the curse left to expel."

Emmeline sighed, then asked, "What will happen to my body once the curse is gone? Will all my gears grow back to their normal sizes?"

"No, I suspect you will stay just as you are. Maybe over time they'll grow—hard to say—but to start, your current appearance will not change. The migraines will go away, and you'll be able to refuel without pain."

"And I'll still be able to fly."

"I suppose so."

Emmeline's tense shoulders relaxed.

She'd be able to finish all the projects she left behind.

Luna noted, "If that thought makes you happy, hang on tight to it. You still have a long journey of healing ahead of you, and keeping your mind right will help see you through."

"I'll try to dream of flying instead of monsters the next time I'm trapped in the dark room."

"Good idea. Learn to master your subconscious."

Emmeline exhaled loudly, prepared to try.

"I'll do my best. I want to go home. I have a lot of unfinished tasks I left behind."

"You'll have a new one to add to your list when you go back."

Emmeline thought for a moment, her mind fuzzy, before responding. "Facilitating the alliance between the moon and the sun?"

"Yes. I'll be helping on my end, too."

"It won't be easy. We'll need a solid plan."

"In time. For now, rest."

Luna turned to leave the room.

"Where are you going?" Emmeline asked in a panic.

"While you heal, I'll be searching for any avenue that leads to peace."

"Don't leave me," Emmeline begged.

"You are safe. I promise."

As Luna departed, Emmeline closed her eyes, wishing to sleep through the remainder of this process.

Time passed quicker when she was lost within the dark corners of her mind.

Luna exited the medical ward, which was situated within one of the many floating meteors inside the moon, then bounced and swung from cord to cord until she reached one of the exits hidden along the outer wall. With a hearty recoil and a single, cautious flap of her wings, she launched herself onto the dusty rock platform and landed in a graceful crouch. A small hike through the cave would lead her onto the moon's barren surface.

She began the short trek, stressing silently about the progress she had made thus far.

As soon as Emmeline had arrived, Luna began her hunt for a secure strategy that would unite Quintessence with Mōnalene. To date, she hadn't found any leads worth pursuing.

Talon to rock, she climbed upward and out of the cave. The expansive sky decorated with stars greeted her. It was a sight she saw every day, yet it still left her in awe. Gratitude filled her heart—endless beauty graced this life. And though conflict plagued them, there was still much to be thankful for.

She looked to the west and observed the planet they served: Earth. A giant globe of greens and blues, swirling with white clouds and swarming with various forms of life. The mortals there lived blissfully unaware of all that the Lunarians and Solarpunks did to keep them alive.

Life across this galaxy could not exist without the sun, and the moon's gravitational pull provided the earthlings with survivable weather. Without the moon, the Earth's tilt would drastically change, causing ice ages and lethal, unpredictable seasonal shifts. The ocean tides would diminish as well, killing many coastal ecosystems.

Worst of all, and still undiscovered by the smartest earthlings who studied space, nighttime would become too cold for their mortal bodies to survive. The Lunarians stole flames from the sun in order to keep the earthlings alive in the darkness of night. Without those flames, without the small, undetectable traces of heat radiating off the moon, life on Earth would perish the moment night arrived.

The sound of talons crushing moon rock and rattling armor approached.

"What is your end game?"

Luna turned to find Cèla and her crew of Odonata outlaws slinking toward her. Though they were still part of the Odonata

17

warriors sworn to serve the Monarchs, they actively disobeyed the orders given under the claims that their insubordination served the greater good of Mōnalene.

"Peace," Luna answered. "I aim to form an alliance with Quintessence. Acquiring fire should not be so perilous for our people."

"You'll never succeed. They hate us as much as we hate them."

"With Emmeline on our side, perhaps this is a rare chance for change."

"You are delusional," Cèla seethed. "Have you been sniffing devodils? Bringing her here will get us all killed."

"I disagree. Saving her will form a bridge between our moon and the sun."

"The moment they find out you brought her here, the war will be brought to Mōnalene. They will come for her, and we will suffer far greater casualties than we've ever seen before."

"They won't find out until she is healed, returned, and can tell them herself. When she tells them how we helped her, the tides between us will shift."

"You are overlooking the countless variables that could go wrong between now and her return. One tiny misstep and it's over."

"You and your crew of insurgents are the greatest threat to the success of this mission," Luna said, her patience waning. "Stop interfering. Let me handle this."

"We will not sit idly while you risk everything. We will train. We will be ready for the worst."

"Fine. Keep training. Just stop bothering me and the Monarchs. We have it under control."

Luna spread her wings and lifted into the sky. Tired of this conflict and eager to discover an infallible plan, she grasped the amulet hanging around her neck and muttered the incantation that would teleport her to Quintessence.

"Ad solem quin. Accipe me!"

Chapter 4

Quintessence

Thick, salty air gripped Luna's arrival.

The portal landed her in Hydra.

Though she did not know exactly where her moonstone was, every time she used the portal, it brought her here, which meant the stone was somewhere in Hydra.

The change in atmosphere forced a wet cough, which she muffled with her arm. Invisible beneath her shield, no one could see her hovering above Red Fang Ralph's ship.

Luna was beginning to take notice of which Nautipunks were on the ships the portal brought her to, as she suspected one of them was in possession of her stone.

Emmeline hadn't been coherent long enough to tell her the last known location of the stone, but as long as Luna's ability to travel back and forth was intact, she could wait on that answer.

She flew lower and circled the pirate ship, admiring the gruesome decorations bolted to the sides of the hull. Thousands of skeletons swayed with the wind as the breeze turned their geared joints. Mirrors fastened in random order reflected the blinding light radiating from the source flame deep beneath the waves. A few times, the reflected light caught Luna's eye, forcing her to squint in pain—her eyes were built for darkness.

Large disced irises swirling with black and silver ink, Luna blinked a few times to clear the light from her eyes. The silver consumed the black, leaving only a small pupil at the center.

Sea water splashed her face as her vision adjusted. Cool, refreshing—a foreign sensation not found on Mōnalene.

The sound of arguing came from above, removing her from the bliss of the sea. She lifted her flight and peered onto the ship's main deck from where she hovered.

Luna recognized the faces—Louie, Avery, and Montgomery. They formed a circle around Solís, who Luna last saw outside of Hydra. It appeared he was finally granted permission to enter the watery underworld of Quintessence.

"He knows more than he is telling!" Solís barked, pointing at Louie.

"I told you all that I know," Louie insisted. "She said goodbye, then vanished. I don't know where she went."

"What did she say during that goodbye?"

"That she would be back." Louie's silver-blue eyes held tearful hope. "She was going someplace to heal."

"To heal?" Solís said. "From what?"

"Solís," Montgomery interjected. "If you had attended the original meetings like I had asked you to, you'd know all of this. According to Louie, Emmeline found a way to relieve her migraines. I don't know why she didn't tell us, or why the remedy is such a secret, but that's the information we are working with."

"She is somewhere above," Solís stated.

"Above?"

"I'm sure of it."

"The Aeropunks have nothing to do with this," Avery assured him.

"I know," Solís griped.

"Then how could she be in the sky? The Aeropunks are the only ones, besides Emmeline, who can fly without assistance," Louie noted.

"She had access to magic," Solís said.

"Magic?" Montgomery asked.

"Yes," Solís answered his father. "And I caught her talking to someone in the sky. I couldn't see them, but she climbed the roof often to talk to them."

"A gas spinner?" Montgomery asked.

"I don't think so."

"Then who?"

"I've been trying to figure that out," Solís answered.

The Devil of Delusion released a gear-rattling screech from its fiery cage.

Montgomery groaned. "We need to find a way to kill that one."

"Have you finished studying it?" Avery asked.

"No, but the noises it makes drive me mad. It never stops. I haven't slept in days." Montgomery's golden eyes held dark circles beneath.

"Neither have the rest of us," Avery commiserated.

"Head home for a few nights," Solís suggested to his father. "We need your wits sharp if we hope to find Emmeline."

"I need to stay here. That devil has already proven it is stronger and more conniving than first believed. Despite the fire, it almost broke free the other day."

"How?" Solís asked.

"Somehow, its poison reached a welder while he was working on the Beast of Panic's cage. In a delusional trance, he began absorbing the fire, removing it from the devil's cage. I imagine he might have melted the hinges off the cage door if we hadn't stopped him."

"If fire keeps it contained, maybe fire can kill it as well," Solís suggested.

"Why haven't I thought of that?" Montgomery said, slapping his forehead.

"Because we are all exhausted," Avery chimed in. "No one sleeps ever since that monster arrived."

"This is something to investigate. Let's add small injury tests to the research. Time to see how much fire the devil can withstand."

Luna turned to observe the fiery cage. She, too, saw the creature as a monster, but knew it by a different name—it was a Marzan from Deimos, one of the two moons orbiting Mars.

The Marzans often attacked the Lunarians for lunar dust and moon flowers. Their only lines of defense against the Marzans were their magnetic moon threads and fire—another reason they needed access to the source flame and why an alliance with the Solarpunks was so important.

Hidden within her shield of invisibility, Luna flew toward the burning cage.

The Marzan cowered in the center, clutching the cold floor bars—the only part of the cage not set aflame.

After a careful scan of the area, Luna lifted the shield from her face, allowing the Marzan to see her.

"You deserve worse," Luna seethed.

It turned its head, crystal blue eyes bloodshot with rage. Its tiny stature and soft facial features indicated it was a young female Marzan. She cowered as the strobing source flame beamed upward through the waves and reflected off of Luna's scaled Lunarian metal armor.

"You don't deserve to fly free," the Marzan hissed.

"Yet here I am," Luna countered. "Unbound and free."

The Marzan screeched in protest, her anger so loud the flames dancing along the bars of her cage flickered ominously.

Luna lifted her shield instinctively, covering herself mere seconds before Montgomery and his crew whipped their attention toward the devil. Montgomery covered his ears, his expression one of utter contempt, then retreated into his captain's quarters. As the crew resumed their work, the Marzan stopped screaming.

"My capture won't stop what's coming," the Marzan said with a hiss. "In fact, it will only quicken the process."

"Why is that?"

"My father is King of Deimos. He will rescue me and display his full wrath in the process. No one standing in his way will survive."

"All of Quintessence stands in his way," Luna replied, then asked, "Is that the plan? To eliminate the Solarpunks?"

"I cannot say." A wicked grin stretched across the Marzan's chapped lips.

"Give me a hint," Luna provoked, aware that Marzans struggled to resist devious games.

"Let's just say that fire will soon be a weapon of the past."
This forced Luna to halt.

A statement like this held heavy implications.

"We could build an alliance and work together," Luna lied. "Tell me more."

"You will see soon enough," the Marzan replied before expelling another horrifying shriek.

Luna retreated and lifted her shield. As she departed, a group of Thermapunks latched hooked ropes to the cage and swung to the scene. Armed with clamps and long needles, they seized the royal Marzan by the arm and attempted to plunge a syringe into her neck. The thin metal needle cracked upon contact—they weren't skilled enough to penetrate the tightly woven chainmail beneath the Marzan's flesh. It took excruciating precision to hit the miniscule spots of soft flesh.

Though Luna hated the Marzans, too, she couldn't help but think of how her brother and father suffered when they were imprisoned here—her father, a prisoner like the Marzan, and her brother, killed in combat beneath the sea. The Solarpunks dissected his corpse like his life meant nothing, then draped his defiled carcass for her father to see.

Cruel and demented, their research was just torture in disguise.

Luna turned away. Though the Marzan deserved the punishment she received, she did not wish to think worse of the Solarpunks than she already did. She was still determined to help her people by forming an alliance with them.

The Marzans were a common enemy.

This was a lead she could work with.

Chapter 5

Mōnalene

"How is Emmeline doing?" Luna asked upon entering the laboratory.

Two of the lead Mantos were huddled around Emmeline's head, lacing black and silver threads through her nostrils and out of her ears. Seven corded tendrils hung from her mouth. Both of the giant Mantos wore spectacles over their bulging eyes, flipping between the various magnification lenses as they worked on their patient. Their long, lanky limbs moved with meticulous precision beneath their formfitting silver lab coats, and each wore a single, arm-length black glove that was strapped from their shoulder to their torso with a leather belt.

"It's possible this might be the last extraction," Manto Bogo finally answered as he threaded cords through Emmeline's nose and mouth.

"Great," Luna said. "I stole more grease and marbles from Quintessence before leaving. She will wake up to a feast."

The medics were there working on Emmeline also. Known as Coccinellies—or ladybugs, as the earthlings would describe similar-looking creatures on their planet—these Lunarians had red back shields decorated with black spots that could spread wide and umbrella over fallen warriors on the battlefield, keeping them safe as the Coccinellies healed them and carried them to safety beneath the shield.

The shields weren't needed here and remained flat against the medics' backs as they created tonics for Emmeline. Gray aprons held on with three belts fastened over their silver medic uniforms, which had multiple pockets to carry their ointments and tools.

Luna stood in a dark corner of the laboratory, watching intently as the Mantos and Coccinellies worked.

Three more cords were carefully looped and laced through Emmeline's golden skull. They joined the seven cords hanging from her mouth, and Manto Maldi braided the ten cords together with rapid precision. As he worked, Coccinelli Katica mashed five moon lilies into powder while Coccinelli Marietta added star oil and cosmic dust to the bowl of powder.

"We need more saliva," Coccinelli Marietta said to Luna, handing her a vial.

Luna spit into it—since the curse came from her moonstone, her unique fluids were a necessary ingredient to the remedy.

Coccinelli Marietta dumped Luna's saliva into the bowl and stirred all the components together until it formed a paste.

Manto Bogo dipped his long fingers into the bowl, scraping and collecting the paste with his pointed fingernails.

He then coated the ten-stringed braid flowing out of Emmeline's mouth.

The opposite ends of the ten threads were knotted beneath Emmeline's nostrils.

Once thoroughly caked with the paste, the scientists and medics placed a single finger each on the thick braid and recited an incantation.

"Levare, liberare, sanare."

They repeated these words in unison: to relieve, to free, to heal.

When the paste slathered onto the threads, they glimmered a brighter silver. Manto Maldi untangled the knots beneath Emmeline's nose and pulled the cords free one by one. Each cord slithered from the braid and spread the medicinal paste through Emmeline's skull. By the fourth cord, Emmeline's cheeks resumed their normal golden blush.

The cords were covered in silver slime—the curse in liquid form.

With delicate care, the medics excreted the curse into glass jars, sealing them as they filled.

The fifth cord was extracted, along with a heaping glob of silver goo, and Emmeline's appearance further improved.

Luna stepped closer, her excitement tangible; the timing was perfect—Emmeline was healing before the Solarpunks learned where she was, and Luna had a solid plan to unite the sun and moon. This could work. Everything was falling into place.

The sixth and seventh cords released slick mounds of the curse, and by the eighth, the silver slime had lessened. The ninth cord was clean of any silver. Manto Bogo pulled the tenth and final cord through her nose, which was also devoid of silver.

"Is that it?" Luna asked to confirm.

"Yes. Two clean cords confirm full extraction of the curse."

Luna stepped closer.

Emmeline's golden glow did not return and her eyes remained closed.

"When will she wake up?"

"Hmm," Manto Bogo hummed while gently prodding Emmeline's eyelids. "She should wake soon."

The giant hourglass mounted to the wall counted the seconds. The final grains of lunar dust trickled into the bottom orb, indicating a full rotation around the earth was nearly complete. As the final speck fell, the weight of the bottom orb triggered the mounted mechanism and the hourglass rotated. Top orb full, bottom orb empty, a new day was upon them.

Emmeline's eyes did not open.

"Is this normal?" Luna asked.

"No. We need to run some additional tests," Manto Bogo said.

"The lunar curse is fully extracted," Manto Maldi added. "She must have a second affliction."

"We need to heal her," Luna insisted, "and soon. We are running out of time. The Solarpunks are starting to look to the sky and she needs to heal before they figure out she's with us."

"Let us work," Coccinelli Katica grumbled as she retrieved the testing kit. Countless vials, swabs, scalpels, and syringes clanged against each other, creating a clinking symphony as she carried the crate across the room. The beautiful, chaotic sound ceased as she set the materials on the counter.

Luna resumed her spot in the corner of the room, unwilling to leave until she learned what continued to ail Emmeline.

The medics poked her arm with needles, swept the inside of her mouth with swabs, and put the samples they collected into vials. As Coccinelli Marietta took a magnifying scope to Emmeline's nostril, she gasped.

"I don't know how we missed this earlier," she said as she carefully inserted her scalpel into the nostril and began to scrape.

"What is it?" Luna asked.

"Marzan poison."

Luna's mind replayed all she had learned over the past few months.

"The Solarpunks call them Devils of Delusion," she revealed. "They caught one in Hydra. Emmeline mentioned smelling its poison a few weeks before coming here."

"She more than just smelled it … she inhaled copious amounts. It is caked like cement to the insides of her nostrils."

"I had a feeling it was playing into her sickness."

"I'm shocked you were able to convince her to heal," Coccinelli Marietta noted, still attempting to scrape the hardened poison out of Emmeline's nose.

"It wasn't me," Luna confessed. "I'm not sure what changed her mind. I'm just grateful that she finally caved."

"I can't remove it with the scalpel," Coccinelli Marietta expressed in frustration, lowering her tool. "The infection is too mature. We will need fresh Marzan blood to dissipate the hardened infection."

"How will we acquire that?" Manto Bogo asked. "They are our greatest foes."

"We cannot ask them for a friendly favor," Manto Maldi added in agreement.

"Nor would we want to," Coccinelli Katica said. "We've been enjoying unusual, prolonged peace. The Monarchs would rise with rage if we instigated their return, especially if their return came by our invitation."

They all looked to Luna, whose racing thoughts showed on her concentrated expression.

Her wide, silver-specked gaze lifted, alight with an idea.

"I have a plan," she revealed.

"What is it?"

"There is a captured Marzan in Quintessence," she explained. "I will return to Hydra and steal some of its blood."

"It is that easy to access?"

"No—she is imprisoned in a burning cage—but I will find a way."

"The fate of our alliance with the sun depends on it."

"So does Emmeline's life," Luna added, realizing that while her driving force was the alliance, she truly cared for Emmeline as well. "I will do my best. Take care of her while I'm gone."

"We will," Coccinelli Marietta promised.

Luna left the laboratory in a hurry, talons digging into the dusty terrain and launching her forward with assertive strides. Her long, thin legs lunged deeply with each step, helping her progress with speed. She exited the meteor within the moon and embarked on the netted world of Mōnalene. A maze of black cords held the inner meteors in place, and she swung and bounced from cord to cord until she reached an outer exit. She made the small ascent into the dusty wasteland above, plotting her next move as she traversed.

The Marzan sat in a cage doused with flames.

If she wanted to succeed in extracting its blood, she needed tools; she needed a fail-proof plan.

Odonata warriors trained in the distance. They practiced in a deep crater lined with moon lilies. While half the group engaged in duels, the other half studied the flowers with help from the Anthos—the gardeners of Mōnalene, created in the image of bumblebees. The Anthos carved detailed summaries into the rock terrain near each flower patch, noting the specific strengths and weaknesses of each blossom. These reports were invaluable when conflicts arose unexpectedly—warriors, explorers, researchers, and engineers alike could briefly skim the notes and determine which flowers would best serve their needs. This

28

proved most useful when the Marzans attacked without warning.

Luna turned away from the training crater, aware that she would not get help from the Odonatas.

She needed engineers.

With strength and agility, she raced halfway around the moon, moving at dizzying speeds as her talons dug into the terrain and propelled her forward.

On the light side of the moon, three clicks north of the Mesial Axis, sat Macrotermes Mountain.

Within the inconspicuous formation resided the Termes and Formies, who designed and constructed all Lunarian weaponry, housing, and transportation. They also were responsible for maintaining the threaded inner world of Mōnalene.

The Termes were created in the image of termites; they had pinchers adorned to the tops of their heads and at the joints of their wrists. They were tall, plump, and skilled at building—and demolishing—infrastructure. Whereas the Formies resembled ants and focused their skills on building gadgets and contraptions.

Luna located the camouflaged door at the base of the mountain and knocked three times.

No one answered.

She knocked again, this time adding a verbal request.

"Please open. I am here on task for the Monarchs."

A rectangular strip of metal slid to the left, revealing a set of silver eyes.

"What's your business?"

"I need help building a tool to assist in a mission approved by the Monarchs."

The man behind the door grumbled before unlocking a myriad of locks and opening the door.

The hollowed interior of the mountain was massive. Dripping stalactites hung from the ceiling, shimmering with crystallized stardust. Rocky platforms were carved into the walls, creating various levels for the engineers and architects to work. The center of the mountain was wide and hollowed out all the way to the mountain peak. Here, their largest creations were stored. Some on the ground level, others suspended by cords from jagged moon rock jetties.

"We are in the middle of building new airships," the Formi explained to Luna. The antennae on top of his head furled together and then untwisted as they continuously listened far beyond their immediate radius. He wiped his jointed fingers against the sides of his gray cargo pants, cleaning off the soot from his current project.

"I need help designing a new tool," Luna revealed.

"Our senior Formies are busy, but we have a few trainees you can enlist for your project." He waved his hand toward a group of younger Formies huddled around a glowing contraption in a dark corner of the mountain.

He added, "That's the best I can do for you."

"That'll do."

They parted ways.

Luna stood tall as she made confident strides toward the trainees.

"Who wants to build me a medicinal weapon?" she asked.

Their heads snapped simultaneously in her direction, eyes alight with curious excitement.

All at once, their hands raised as every single trainee volunteered for the project.

Luna grinned.

With so many engineers on the job, it wouldn't be long before she had a vial of fresh Marzan blood to heal Emmeline.

Chapter 6

Hydra, Quintessence

"Did you hear what Solís said?" Avery asked as she pushed Louie into a vacant cabin to talk privately. "Emmeline was talking to someone in the sky."

"Are you sure it wasn't a gas spinner?" Louie asked.

"Positive. The only gas spinners who leave the upper stratosphere are the Holloways, and they wouldn't hide to talk to her."

"Who then?"

"Come on," Avery encouraged, her patience waning. "All of this chaos started with that moonstone."

"You think she was talking to a hellion?" Louie asked, his chiseled features creasing with alarm.

"Nothing is out of the realm of possibility at this point. Did she ever mention a friend in the sky to you?"

"No. As far as I knew, you were her only flying friend."

"Think harder. She must have said something before leaving."

Louie's expression tightened—he still hadn't told anyone the true nature of Emmeline's disappearance. The more time that passed, the more worried he became.

"If I tell you everything about the day Emmeline left, do you promise to keep it between us? No one else can know. Not yet, anyway. I promised to give Emmeline some time before chasing after her."

"Hold on, I thought you said you didn't know where she went."

"I don't, but I saw *how* she left."

"What do you mean?"

"She vanished right before my eyes."

"Impossible."

"She held the moonstone in her bare hands, spoke in a foreign language, and then disappeared."

Avery's copper eyes widened. "The moonstone is a portal?"

31

"All I know is that she made me promise to keep the stone safe, that it was her only sure way back to me."

"She's on the Moon of Fixation," Avery mumbled to herself. "She is in enemy territory."

"We need to trust her," Louie insisted.

"What if it's a trap?" Avery's voice rose, her horror heightened.

"She wouldn't have left if she didn't trust whoever was helping her."

"A hellion? Are you dense? You saw firsthand how they consistently tried to kill her. Now, they lured her onto their territory—only Solédon knows why—and we have no means of rescuing her. Our militia has never left the sun."

"I trust her," Louie stated. "If we interfere now, we might mess up her plan."

"How long will you trust this plan of hers before beginning to wonder if she was misled? How long must she be missing before you wake up and realize you let the monsters take her?"

Louie's brow furrowed as he repeated. "I trust her. And you should, too."

"You're wrong. She needs our help."

"You will start a war worse than any we've ever known."

"It seems that war has already begun."

"What if *you're* wrong?" Louie asked. "What if she has it under control and our intervention wrecks everything? She has sacrificed so much … we could ruin it all."

Avery groaned, conflicted by her doubts. "We should not trust the hellions."

"But we should trust Emmeline," Louie countered. "Let's set a timeframe. If she hasn't returned by a certain date, we take more serious action."

"How long do we wait?" Avery paused. "How long did *you* plan to wait?"

Louie appeared unsure. "I thought it would become clear once it had been too long."

"She's already been missing a little over two weeks."

"I don't think it's time yet."

"Where is the stone?" Avery asked.

"I keep it on me at all times." Louie patted the pocket of his britches.

The cabin door flew open and Solís barged through.

"Give me the stone," he demanded.

Louie stepped back as Solís lunged at him.

"Have you been eavesdropping?" Louie asked.

"I heard everything," he seethed, then repeated. "I knew you were no good. Give me the stone."

"I can't." Louie shook his head. "You don't understand how it works."

"It's a portal."

"It's also a curse," Louie said. "If you touch it, you will become just as sick as Emmeline, Gemma, and Clementine." Angry tears filled his eyes. "Or you could die like Ruthanne."

"It is our only means to find Emmeline, and if she really is on the Moon of Fixation, we cannot waste another second!"

Avery stepped in. "You need to calm down, Solís. Rash action will not help."

"What is rash about it? She's been missing for weeks!"

"You could start a war worse than the one we already fight," Avery repeated Louie's warning.

"Also, we don't know how the stone works or where exactly it will take us. Everything you overheard was speculation," Louie added.

Solís paced the cabin. The thick soles of his combat boots hit the golden floorboards with rhythmic precision as he contemplated his spinning thoughts.

"This is the only way to help her," he mumbled to himself.

"Have a little faith in her," Louie countered. "When she left, she said she had a plan."

Solís shook his head. "She was ill." His golden gaze narrowed on Louie. "If you really cared for her, you wouldn't have let her go alone."

"I hardly had time to process anything before she disappeared!"

"You should have followed her," Solís insisted.

"How was I supposed to do that? She didn't leave me instructions on how to use the stone."

"You said she spoke a foreign language before disappearing?" Solís asked, recalling all he had overheard.

"Yes," Louie confirmed, exhausted by the interrogation.

Solís resumed pacing as he pieced together all the clues he had collected thus far. He replayed the countless hours he had spent on the rooftop, searching for signs of Emmeline's whereabouts.

Long nights, early mornings, arid afternoons, breezy evenings.

Thoughts of the voice in the wind halted his anxious pacing.

He remembered the words.

Without thought or consideration of the ramifications, he spoke the words aloud.

"Ad lunam lu. Accipe me."

Solís lurched backward by the abdomen as if punched in the gut, then disappeared.

"You have got to be kidding me," Avery groaned.

Louie grabbed a piece of parchment and quickly scribbled the incantation before he forgot it again.

"He didn't even touch the stone," Louie said, confused.

"Maybe you just need to be in close range for it to work," Avery theorized.

"Should we follow him?"

"No. Not yet. We have no idea what's waiting on the other side." Avery's concern was heightened. "Now two of Montgomery's children are missing … I don't know how this doesn't end in war."

"What do we do?" Louie's panic matched Avery's—they both understood the dire nature of this development.

"Let's give it a minute … maybe he will come back."

Louie groaned. "Let's just hope he doesn't arrive swinging and initiate the war Emmeline was trying to prevent."

"I suppose we should prepare for that possibility."

Louie reached into his pocket and pulled out the satchel holding the moonstone.

It seemed the trouble the stone brought was far from done.

Chapter 7

Mōnalene

Solís burst through the portal, blipping onto the moon with a stumbling crash. He landed on his hands and knees, kicking up gray dust as he fell.

The hard landing quickly became the least of his concerns — the air here was unbreathable.

Coughing, gasping, golden eyes wide with panic, he choked on the lack of oxygen.

He needed to return to Quintessence immediately.

Between strained breaths, he repeated the incantation.

"Ad lunam lu. Accipe me."

Nothing happened. He remained on this barren, unlivable hellscape.

Was he on the Moon of Fixation? Or had the stone brought him somewhere else? Was Emmeline even here, or had he risked his life for nothing?

His titanium wings were locked into his shoulder gears and he still wore a helium tank, but neither served his current needs—he couldn't fly home from here. Countless knives, daggers, and fire pellets were strapped to his torso and leg harness, but nothing to help him breathe.

Desperate to survive, he held onto his last remaining breaths and scanned his surroundings.

To his left was a giant crater lined with flowers.

To his right was expansive nothingness.

He crawled toward the only sign of life: the colorful blossoms to his left. Still a long distance away, Solís prayed to Solédon that this decision was the correct one.

His pocketed trousers ended just above his knees, which left his knee gears dragging against the terrain. They made a trail of two ruts in the dust as he inched forward. He had to find help; he had to find a place on this desolate moon where he could breathe.

Air running thin, he did his best to conserve what little he had left.

The nearest side of the crater dipped lower than the opposite side. Solís set his sights on a lavender blossom at the top of this ledge. Inch by inch, he pulled his body through the dust, conserving as much oxygen within his geared lungs as possible.

He wasn't sure what he hoped to find once he reached the flowers, but if they could survive this harsh terrain, perhaps they could help him survive, too.

One more giant push up the side of the crater and the flowers were within reach.

He stretched his left arm, wrist gears churning and fingers extended, ready to snatch the nearest blossom. As his fingertips touched the lavender petal, sight of a nefarious scene appeared over the ledge of the crater.

A swarm of hellions battled each other at the base, fighting with ferocious speed, agility, and accuracy. Leather and scaled metal armor, black hair braided in warrior knots, expressions grave and inked with rage—it was a terrifying sight to behold.

Solís gasped, losing more of his precious oxygen.

The nearest hellion sensed his arrival and twisted its head toward him, its long ink-black braid snapping like a whip.

Solís ducked, praying he hadn't been spotted.

As he hid behind the edge of the crater, awaiting his fate, he noticed the flowers had notes etched into the stone near their stems.

Written in a language he did not understand, he read the words, hoping any of them might look familiar.

Venenum. Oleum. Somnum. Crepitus. Oblivisci. Debilito. Oxygeni.

Solís paused and read it again.

Oxygeni.

He scrambled to the cerulean blossom labeled *'oxygeni'* and pressed his nose to its fuzzy pistil. It tickled his nostril, but provided no relief.

A quick glance over the edge revealed the hellions had paused their training and were climbing the crater wall directly beneath where he hid.

Unsure what else to do, Solís ripped the flower by its root and slid down the side of the crater. As he made his getaway, he shoved the flower in its entirety into his mouth and chewed.

As his teeth demolished the petals, stem, and roots, chilled liquid filled his mouth and slicked his throat. Instead of entering the inner workings of his geared gut, it lubricated the gears of his fleshy lungs and seeped inside. The moment the liquid meshed with his lungs, a burst of air escaped his mouth as a gasp.

He could breathe again.

Solís ran faster now, aware that he needed to hide before the hellions saw him, but as he glanced over his shoulder to check on his progress, he faced the grave realization that they were already deep in their chase. Half of the hellions raced toward him in low lunges while the rest flew with their dragonfly wings spread wide.

He'd never outrun them.

Though the blossom had filled his lungs with oxygen, there was no guarantee it would last. Nor did he have an escape route.

He kept running, refusing to surrender without a fight.

Solís ripped the daggers off his torso holster one by one and began lobbing them back over his shoulder with only a quick glance before each shot to aim.

"Ad lunam lu. Accipe me," he repeated continuously, hoping if he said it enough, it might work.

The farther he ran, the closer the chasing hellions became.

He tossed his last dagger.

It hit the nearest hellion in the chest, bouncing futilely off its metal armor.

The fire pellets were small and meant for close-contact combat, but it was all he had left. Solís tossed a handful of pellets into the sky and sent a quick blast of heat in their direction, causing them to detonate and singe the exposed flesh of his nearest pursuers.

It wasn't enough.

There were too many hellions chasing him and he had no weapons left.

The hellions were closing the distance between them. It wouldn't be long before they snagged him as their prisoner or worse, murdered him without a trial.

Golden eyes set on the never-ending horizon, Solís scanned the dusty moonscape.

In the distance stood a docile hellion. Tall and unexpectedly beautiful, her black hair hung to her waist and the random braids mixed into her long locks sparkled with stardust. Her large black and silver disced eyes glimmered with grave concern.

She wore the same armor as the others, but showed no signs of aggression.

She did not budge as he ran toward her.

Why hadn't she lifted her defenses? Why hadn't she joined the chase?

Solís continued toward her, muttering the incantation with each shortened breath, curious if this calm hellion might help him.

"Ad lunam lu. Accipe me," he said between furious gasps; the oxygen the blossom gave him was depleting. The harder he ran, the quicker it drained.

The docile hellion stepped forward and extended her hand. Starlight from above illuminated her facial bone structure, highlighting her exquisite beauty.

Solís had only ever seen hellions in fight mode—fanged teeth bared, black threads tangled with fury beneath their semi-translucent silver flesh, dark veins protruding around their circular black eyes, and expressions twisted with demonic intent.

She was different.

She was calm.

Her flesh, though semi-translucent, was radiant, and the cords beneath weren't black, knotted, or tangled; they were dark silver and weaved in and out with meticulous grace, creating fluid braids that revolved beneath her skin. Her eyes weren't dark with rage; they were bright with black ink swirling peacefully within her silver irises.

She was beautiful.

Solís scowled as he found himself fawning over a monster.

"Ad lunam lu. Accipe me," he said again. This time, the energy expended was too much and his speed slowed. He tripped over a moon rock and stumbled to his knees. Crawling frantically, he pushed himself onto his feet and resumed his run, but the gang of hellions chasing him were even closer now.

The docile hellion before him extended her wings and lifted into the air.

"Leave him be!" she called out to the others.

"This one is not protected under the treaty," a lead hellion in the sky shouted in reply.

"He is under my protection," she countered. "Hurt him and the Monarchs will retaliate."

"*You* are not a Monarch. *You* don't make the rules."

Solís groaned—her interference only angered the other hellions, and now their motivation to catch him was heightened. He wasn't sure how much farther he could run.

His boot snagged on a medium-sized boulder, forcing him to stumble again.

The docile hellion flew forward and screeched. Her rage created a soundwave so strong it halted the pursuing hellions.

Solís glanced up and found her appearance had transformed. Black eyes, bared fangs, braided cords frayed—she now looked like a familiar monster.

Her scream echoed, giving them a few seconds alone without the other hellions resuming their chase.

Though her rage was settling, her beauty took a moment to return.

"Give me your hand," she said. The black veins around her darkened eyes were prominent against her pallid flesh.

"You're a monster, just like the rest."

She took a deep breath, attempting to calm her rage and resume her natural appearance.

"You need to accept my help or they will kill you."

Solís did not budge.

As her echo faded, the hellions began recollecting themselves, preparing to resume their chase.

She shook her hand at him. "Take it! We are running out of time."

Solís gasped for air. His fingers clutched his throat as he choked.

The blossom's magic had run out.

She grabbed his hand.

"Don't betray us!" one of the opposing hellions shouted as she marched toward them.

"I am saving us," she countered, then placed her hand on an amulet hanging from her neck and whispered an incantation. "Ad solem quin. Accipe me."

They disappeared in a whirlwind of lunar dust.

Chapter 8

Hydra, Quintessence

A blast of gray dust camouflaged their emergence into the cabin where Louie and Avery waited for Solís's return.

Aware she had left in too much of a hurry, Luna quickly dropped Solís and engaged her invisibility shield.

Louie coughed as Avery swatted the lunar dust away.

As it dissipated, Solís's huddled body was revealed; his torso rose and fell dramatically as he caught his breath.

"Are you okay?" Avery asked. "Where'd you go?"

Solís's golden gaze lifted, murder in his eyes.

"Where is she?" he seethed, his energy revitalized.

"Who?" Louie asked.

"The monster!"

"You came back alone … "

"She is here! You need to leave. It isn't safe."

Solís stood and began grabbing at the air.

Louie and Avery watched as he searched for an invisible enemy.

"Are you sure?" Avery asked. "Looks like you're fighting nothing."

"I still smell the moon lily," he insisted, sniffing the air like a rabid animal. "She's here."

"I don't see anyone—" Louie began.

"Leave!" Solís barked.

"You're going to have to tell us what happened," Avery said as she backed toward the door.

"I will—after I take care of the monster."

Avery and Louie left Solís to his strange quest. Once the door closed behind them, Solís ceased his frantic search and glared at the nothingness above him.

He rolled his shoulders and extended the titanium wings attached to his back.

"Show yourself," he demanded.

He was answered with silence, but the distinct scent of moon lily lingered.

"I know you're still here."

"You need to calm down," Luna finally replied in a whisper.

The sound of her voice reignited Solís's rage. He lifted into the air and grabbed the spot her voice came from. To his luck, he managed to seize Luna's neck.

She coughed as he tightened his grip.

"Show yourself!" he repeated.

Luna dropped her shield.

Though she was wincing in pain and gasping for air, her beauty shone through her struggle.

"Show your true form," Solís barked. "Show the monster that you are!"

"This is my true form," Luna managed to mutter through strained breaths.

"Lies!" Solís snarled, pounding his wings and slamming her into the nearest wall. The impact forced her to squeeze her eyes shut in pain. When she opened them again, the silver was overtaken by black.

"There it is," Solís said. "The monster within."

"I'm trying to build an alliance," she explained, though her calm tone was now agitated and her patience was visibly waning. "I'm trying to save your sister."

"Where is she?" Solís demanded, his fury refocused on the most important issue at hand.

"Let me go and I will tell you," Luna bartered.

Solís squeezed tighter.

"I don't need you," he threatened. "I will return through the portal with an army. I will slaughter every hellion living in that wasteland and rescue my sister myself."

His threat awakened Luna's rage.

Eyes black, fangs protracted, cords knotted, Luna could no longer feign submissiveness. If he wanted a fight, she would deliver a fight.

Fingernails extended into tiny blades, she dug them into Solís's wrists, tearing at his golden flesh and forcing him to release her.

He growled in pain, shaking his hands to minimize the lingering sting.

"Killing you will be a delight," he seethed.

Luna charged him before he could make a move. Finger blades dug into his shoulders, she pushed him into the ceiling of the cabin, denting the iron boards upon impact.

Solís retaliated with a golden fist to her face. His knuckle gears tore the translucent flesh covering her cheek and silver blood dripped down her face.

Luna tossed Solís across the room. The hit against the iron wall was so hard it took him a moment to lift himself off the floor. Luna took this opportunity to deliver a swift kick to his ribcage and pin him to the ground.

"Have you had enough?" she asked, ready to refocus and get back on track.

"Not even close."

"You need to hear me out," she implored.

"Never," he said in resistance. Though he was no match for her strength, he had fire on his side. He channeled his source flame heart and heated his body to a scorching temperature.

The rise was slow, but Luna felt the heat simmering beneath her forearm.

"You need to stop," she said.

"I want you dead."

"I am the main Lunarian advocating for your sister."

"The main what?"

Luna ignored him. "If you kill me, you'll kill her, too. My death will end the protection she has on my moon. She still needs my help."

"You are the reason she is cursed. You are the root of her suffering."

The temperature increased.

Luna fidgeted and readjusted her arm over his sweltering flesh.

"She needs you, too," she said.

"Of course, she does! But you won't let me help."

"I saved you so that you *could* help. You just didn't give me time to explain that to you."

"I don't trust you."

"What other option do you have?"

"I'll bring an army through the portal."

"Solarpunks can't breathe on Mōnalene. You won't stand a chance."

"We will find a way."

"Or, you could hear me out."

"You've got a few more seconds before the heat burns your arm to ashes. Speak."

"You can retrieve the blood needed to save Emmeline."

"Blood?"

"Yes. With it, we will create an ointment that will soften the poison leeched to the insides of her nostrils."

"Whose blood do you need?"

"The Marzan's."

"The what?"

Luna shook her head, recalling that the Solarpunks referred to all moon beings as various forms of monsters.

"The devil," she clarified. "The devil's blood will save your sister."

Chapter 9

"You want me to let that *thing* live?"

"Just long enough to extract some of its blood."

Solís stopped the rising swelter of his heart. His temperature cooled as he considered Luna's plan.

"Why does Emmeline need its blood to heal?"

"If I let you go and explain, will you stop trying to kill me?" Luna asked. Still in fight mode, her eyes were solid black.

Solís narrowed his gaze.

"For now," he agreed.

Luna accepted this as progress and lifted her arm from his neck. He sat up, rubbing his neck where her forearm had left a bruise.

"You have until this pain goes away to explain everything," he said, still massaging his neck.

Luna quivered slightly as the rage dissipated from her body.

"The good news," she began, silver streaks infiltrating her black irises, "is that we have healed her of the moonstone curse. Bad news is that we learned she suffered from a second curse. The devil's gaseous poison leeched to the insides of her nostrils. Lunarian scientists scraped and chiseled at the hardened resin, but its adhesion is too strong. They need a tonic of Marzan blood and lunar dust to remove it."

"Lunarian … Marzan … what are these things?"

"The proper names for the moon beings you call monsters," Luna explained. Dark veins around her eyes receding, sharpened teeth retracting, and the cords beneath her translucent flesh untangling—Luna was beginning to look less like a monster and more like the ethereal creature Solís struggled to detest. She continued, "I am a Lunarian from the moon that serves Earth. The Marzan, who you refer to as a devil, is from Deimos, one of the moons that serve Mars."

"I think I'll stick to hellions and devils."

"Whatever suits your tiny brain. I just need your help getting the blood."

"If I help you, you will take me with you when you return to Emmeline."

"Only if you promise not to tell a soul where you are going."

Solís considered this for a brief moment before complying. "Fine. But you get one chance. If the blood doesn't heal her, I will bring an army of Solarpunks dressed in diving suits to your moon."

"It won't come to that," Luna promised, her transformation from warrior to docile state complete.

Her beauty radiated.

Solís tried not to notice.

A fiery crack sizzled outside the cabin window.

Both Luna and Solís raced to the small circular cutout to locate the source.

The entire crew of Thermas and Nautis were preoccupied with the scheduled extermination of the Marzan.

Nautipunks glided atop the waves on zinc foot blades, propelled forward by hydro-powered jetpacks. Tubes fastened to their ankles sucked in the ocean water and filtered through their backpacks. The water spun the cranks and gears and was released through two tubes as a forceful mist that pushed the Nautipunks forward. With handheld hoses, they kept the cages neighboring the devil misted and free of fire.

The Thermapunks latched hooked ropes to the fiery cage and swung from Montgomery's ship onto the flaming bars that kept the devil contained. With them was Gemma, sicklier than ever, but prepared to play her part in this mission.

She clung to Avery's back, who was perched on a fire-free cage next to the devil. Arm extended with her wrist exposed, Gemma was ready to donate her petroleum blood to help kill the devil with fire.

"You have to stop them," Luna insisted. "They can't kill the Marzan yet."

Solís silently assessed the progressing task force. They would have the devil exterminated within the hour. He needed to act fast.

"Will you help? Or no?" Luna asked, aware that their time was limited.

"Will you take me to Emmeline?"

"Yes, if you insist."

Solís nodded, took a deep breath, and then marched out of the room.

Luna restored her shield of invisibility and followed him.

The moment he touched foot on the top deck, he loosened the knob on the helium tank strapped to his back, spread his wings, and lifted into the salty sky. He rose until he reached Montgomery, who was overseeing the project in the high-above crow's nest of Red Fang Ralph's pirate ship.

"I need you to halt this mission," Solís requested of his father.

"Why?" Montgomery barked, his patience as absent as Emmeline.

"I need a sample of its blood."

"What for?"

Solís hesitated—he couldn't yet tell Montgomery about Luna.

"Research," he stated simply.

"That monster is the biggest nuisance, and despite all our efforts, its poison still seeps beyond its confines."

"I have reason to suspect its blood might help cure the infected," Solís revealed.

"Excuse me? How could you possibly know that?"

"It's just a hunch. And without performing research on the monster, we will never know if my suspicions are correct."

"We tried performing research on that insolent beast. Not only was its armored flesh impossible to penetrate, but it also infected every punk that got too close."

"One last try," Solís requested. "We need its blood."

"I'm not letting you anywhere near that thing."

"If the blood is the cure, I'll be healed soon after."

"But you don't know that it is."

"I need you to trust me."

Montgomery grumbled under his breath, golden eyes darting left and right as he contemplated his son's sudden request.

"The gears are in motion," he said, mostly to himself, "but perhaps letting the devil live another day or two for research purposes would be wise. So many punks have been infected … so many could die without a cure."

Solís said nothing, allowing his father to organize his thoughts without interjection.

"Okay, fine," Montgomery said, finally coming to a decision. "I will delay the extermination."

Montgomery lifted the brass foghorn attached to the inside wall of the crow's nest and pressed it to his lips. With a mighty breath, he blew into the horn that called the attention of every punk below. Thermas and Nautis paused what they were doing to look up at him.

"Cease fire!" he bellowed. "We must reschedule this mission."

"Why?" Red Fang Ralph shouted in reply. He was perched on the end of the bowsprit, eagerly awaiting the death of another monster.

"We need its blood."

"Can't we get it after it's dead?"

"There will be no blood to collect after we incinerate it."

"Argh, I hadn't thought of that," Red Fang Ralph said, tapping the handle of his tankard mug.

"Withdraw your crew."

Red Fang Ralph chugged what remained in his mug and then called off his crew. The Nautipunks redirected their ocean blades and skied back to the ship.

The devil howled with delighted victory as its oppressors abandoned their attack. The gear-rattling screech sent a shiver down Montgomery's golden spine.

"I despise this monster," he said with a shudder. He looked to Solís. "You have two days to get what you need."

"That should be plenty of time," Solís said, though he was not yet sure how to get blood from the devil without risking his own well-being.

Montgomery shoved the ends of two handkerchiefs into his ears and exited the crow's nest. He grumbled to himself, wholly irritated by the devil's unrelenting wails. Solís followed him down the ladder.

He detoured to Edwin Doyle's medic station first and when no one was looking, snagged a vial of healing ointment for his new hellion wounds. It was an easy steal—the ship was in a state of chaos.

The top deck had punks scattered all over: Nautipunks were disrobing and cleaning their gear, Thermapunks were cooling their torch guns, and the only Terrapunk on board, Gemma, was stitching the wounds she had slit into her wrists. She'd save her petroleum blood for the rescheduled extermination.

While the scene was busy, no one was within earshot of Solís.

"Are you still here?" he asked in a furious whisper.

"Yes," Luna replied from within her shield.

"How am I supposed to extract blood from the devil?"

He was answered with the clinking clank of Luna fussing beneath her shield. A moment later, her long skinny fingers holding a slingshot syringe appeared. A hand with no body, floating midair, she extended the tool to Solís.

"What is it?" he asked, taking it from her. Her hand disappeared from sight.

"The threads are elastic. Pull them back, aim, and shoot the syringe into the Marzan. As soon as it is injected, a lever within the contraption is activated, creating pressure that will draw blood."

"They have steel chainmail beneath their flesh—it's why our researchers haven't been able to collect any samples yet."

"There are soft spots between the metal links. But even if you miss the soft spots, this needle is made of lunar metal. We use it against the Marzans in battle. It will break the link and do the job. You only get one shot, though. If the needle is triggered and

50

you miss the devil completely, the Formies will have to build another. Could take a few days for them to do that."

"We don't have that kind of time."

"Then your best shot is to get close and constrain the Marzan so you don't miss."

"Will I get infected in the process?"

"Most likely. Just make sure you fill the syringe, and we should have enough blood to heal you, too."

Solís groaned. Trusting a hellion felt wrong.

"Fine, if that's what it takes to save Emmeline," he conceded. "Just know that I will have assurances put into place to guarantee that any betrayal by you will result in consequences far greater than your worst nightmares."

"Your concerns have been noted. Retrieve the blood and you will quickly see that your hatred is misplaced."

A giant gush of wind slapped Solís across the face—a calculated maneuver by Luna—and the pretty scent of moon lily disappeared.

She was gone, leaving Solís with a dangerous task and a curious inclination toward the monster he once claimed to despise.

Chapter 10

Solís growled under his breath.

He would not let the monsters win.

Luna was no better than the demons imprisoned in Dawes Detention Center. He could not let her swoon him into believing she was somehow different from the rest of the monsters.

She would lead him to Emmeline, and he would resume control. The hellions would not worm their way into the hearts of the Solarpunks, not if Solís had any say in the matter.

"I need a crew," he announced, garnering the attention of the punks bustling around the top deck of Red Fang Ralph's ship. "You," he said, pointing at Gemma. "You'll be working for me now."

"What do you need from me?" she asked, her tiny frame shaking with nerves.

"Relax," he said. "I know we never got along while Emmeline was around, but she needs your help and I'm not so prideful that I can't admit my initial judgment of you was wrong. You've been a good friend to my sister and have proven time and time again that you can be trusted."

"You know where she is?"

"Yes, but I can't reveal that information just yet."

"Is she okay?"

"So I am told. There is one final step to her healing, and it lands on us to assist."

Gemma stood a little taller.

"How can I help?"

"I need to extract blood from the devil. I have a source that tells me it will help cure Emmeline."

"The devil's blood will cure her? How?" she asked.

"In addition to the curse from the moonstone, which we've learned is linked to the hellions, Emmeline suffered a second curse originating from that devil."

"Seems a lot of punks have suffered at the hands of that monster."

"If the blood works as a remedy for Emmeline, it'll work for the rest of them, too. We just need to get close enough to take some samples."

"They've been trying to collect blood, flesh, and hair from the devil since it was captured. Everyone who gets too close falls ill."

"I know. Being concealed in the diving suits wasn't enough. The poison seeped through the fabric and left acid burns on their flesh." Solís paced, golden brow narrowed as his thoughts spun. "The suit needs a protective layer, something the devil's poison cannot penetrate. I was thinking clay."

Gemma looked at her hands, fingers wiggling.

"I can help with that," she offered.

"I suspected you could."

"You really think it will bring Emmeline back?" Her silver eyes sparkled with deep concern.

"Sadly, it is our best chance. We need to work fast, though. We only have two days before my father resumes the execution."

"I'm ready when you are. I want my friend back."

Solís nodded, confidence in his choice to work with Gemma solidified. He thought of Clementine, who should have been the more loyal friend to Emmeline, but when he had approached her hours after Emmeline's disappearance, she had been more consumed by her obsession with the sea than her missing friend.

"Has Clementine rusted yet?" Solís asked Gemma as he pulled a diving suit over his clothes.

Gemma shrugged. "She's a fiend for octopus ink. She's done some pretty deplorable things to get her hands on it."

"Like what?"

"Well, only Hydropunks can produce the ink," Gemma said with a shudder. "Use your imagination."

"She hasn't given them fire, has she?"

"Wouldn't surprise me if she has. She's been caught engaging in illegal trades."

"I'll talk to her. She cannot share fire. It is a betrayal to her faction, a breach of the Thermapunk standards."

"Good luck. She'd risk it all for that damn octopus ink. She could dive with a suit, but she refuses."

"She's obsessed with the sea."

"No, she's been consumed by the moonstone," Gemma corrected him. "The curse is the reason she behaves as she does. It's the reason I am so reliant on the firestones. I need the heat because the curse makes me cold. Clementine chooses submersion because the curse makes her feel like she's drowning when she isn't under water."

"It's all so backward."

"If Emmeline is healed, I hope the same can be done for us."

"The craziest part is that all three of you managed to make the curse look like a blessing. Emmeline can fly. You can withstand great temperatures. Clementine can dive without a breathing suit. Solarpunks across Quintessence still believe in the Superpunks. They still hold hope that Emmeline will unite the factions whenever she returns."

"Let's hope she holds the same confidence and influence upon her return."

"The longer she is gone, the more they lose faith in her," Solís said.

"Zipper up then and let's get to work."

Solís pulled a string attached to the back zipper. Suit sealed, he placed the helmet over his head and attached the many tubes to a tank strapped to his back. He scanned the sky, looking for Avery.

"What are you two doing?" Louie asked as he approached from the starboard.

"You had your chance to help," Solís said.

"You still owe us an explanation."

"Where is Avery?"

"She's in Terra, negotiating a deal with the Horrigans," Louie answered. "Your father wants an alternative for locomo dust."

This caught Solís's attention. "Is Helix okay?"

"I didn't ask questions."

"You are useless."

"Where did you go when you disappeared?" Louie asked, his tone demanding.

"I cannot trust you."

"Why not?"

"For two weeks, you held the stone and the key to helping Emmeline. Yet you did nothing and told no one. You are a spineless rat."

"First of all, I did not remember the words to make the stone work. But now I do, and if you don't tell me what's going on, I will find out for myself."

"Do what you wish, though it will likely end in your death."

"How so? You came back the same, though, arguably more arrogant than before."

"I got lucky," Solís said, his admission jarring Louie into silence. Solís continued, "If you want to help, stay out of my way."

Louie's piercing blue eyes held great frustration as he left.

"Emmeline won't be happy to hear you treated him that way," Gemma said.

"Emmeline will have greater problems to face when she returns. Once Avery gets back, we will begin."

Solís marched toward a rope ladder that hung from his father's ship hovering above. Still dressed in his diving suit, he climbed, focus shifted momentarily to finding an alternative for locomo dust.

Gemma watched as Solís ascended. Her fingers raked the palms of her hands, practicing the creation of clay for when it came time for her to perform.

"I want in," a voice hissed from behind.

Gemma turned and found Louie leaning against a mast. A tall shadow covered him, but his piercing gaze shone like a blue beacon in the darkness.

"It's not my mission," Gemma replied. "Solís is in charge."

"Tell me the plan, at least."

Gemma sighed, aware that Solís would not want her to share, but compelled by her allegiance to Emmeline.

"Solís thinks the devil's blood will cure Emmeline," she disclosed.

Louie quietly absorbed this information before responding.

"He knows where she is," he stated.

"Yes, but he wouldn't tell me where."

"She's on the Moon of Fixation," Louie revealed.

"What? How? That's terrible!"

Louie nodded. "The moonstone is a portal. Solís cracked the code and traveled through it. I have to assume it led to the hellions' moon."

"Why did he come back without her?"

"I don't know. When he reappeared, he was in fight mode. Something happened over there. And now he says the devil's blood will cure Emmeline. It doesn't add up."

"I think we should follow his lead," Gemma advised. "He seems to know something we don't."

"And he chastises *me* for keeping secrets," Louie said, anger scathing.

"If letting him be the hero brings Emmeline back, let him have his glory."

"She trusted *me* with her secrets, not him. She came to me, and only me, before leaving. I should be the one to bring her home."

"Don't let your pride get in the way."

Louie's zinc-hued flesh flushed red with frustration. "I don't trust him."

"Why not? He is her brother. Though I agree that his personality is pompous and infuriating, I don't doubt for a second that his intentions are good."

"Let me help," Louie pled.

Gemma pursed her lips in contemplation. "Your best bet is to talk to Montgomery. Don't tell him about the portal, though.

Not yet, at least. We need to get Emmeline back on home turf before Montgomery is provoked to initiate an offensive attack on the Moon of Fixation."

"I won't make things worse," Louie assured her. He looked toward the airship hovering above. The muffled sound of Solís and Montgomery arguing echoed. Louie said, "I'll wait until Solís isn't around."

"We are starting the mission as soon as Avery returns."

"Is Helix okay?" Solís asked Montgomery as he climbed over the railing.

Montgomery's golden eyes were grease-shot and streaked with black lines.

"No," he answered. "He is not okay. He almost overdosed last night. Thank Solédon your mother sensed something was wrong and checked on him in the wee hours of morning. She had to drill two holes into the sides of his temples to release the excess fumes."

"He took that much?" Solís asked, appalled.

"Yes. He almost died."

A tall task for any Solarpunk; they were dimidivinus—half divine—and designed to be nearly indestructible.

"I can't save them both," Solís said, more to himself than his father. Their worried gazes locked. "I hope the Horrigans can help."

"It's not a question of whether they can or can't. It's a question of whether they will or won't. Locomo is made of minerals and gas. It affects Hydros and Thermas more than it does Terras or Aeros, as they are better built to process the chemicals. Locomo is a weapon used against us; it weakens any Therma or Hydro who falls victim to the addiction. It's an upper hand I doubt they want to lose."

"After I save Emmeline, I'll see to it that the Horrigans give us a locomo replacement to help wean Helix off the drug."

57

"How is it that I have children built to live countless lifetimes, and I'm facing the grave reality that I might lose two of them before either reaches their semicentennial?"

Solís shook his head. "Their disregard for their own well-being is not your fault."

"I don't even know where Emmeline is! I can't help her if I can't find her."

"I think I have a lead on that."

Montgomery's energy lifted. "What have you learned?"

"You can't help them both simultaneously. Focus on Helix, and I'll focus on Emmeline. If I need help, you're the first person I'll turn to," Solís promised.

"Just try not to get yourself in trouble along the way," Montgomery pled. "I can't handle another lost child."

"I won't. I'm solid."

"Speaking of solid, Cyrus is on his way to Hydra to help with your mission. I figured you could use a little extra muscle."

"Yes, I will need help. Any chance assigning Helix a task would give him some direction?"

"He is in no shape to leave the house. Anytime he tries to stand, he throws up."

"I need a third helper."

"Recruit Louie."

"Absolutely not."

"Why not?"

"I can't stand him."

"He's a good kid," Montgomery objected. "And for better or worse, he loves your sister. He would be a trustworthy pair of hands to have on your team."

Solís crossed his arms over his chest.

Montgomery continued, "You don't have many other options. My Thermapunk crew is tied up with replanning the execution, and there aren't many dependable Nautipunks. Many will abandon your mission at the first sign of trouble."

Teeth clenched, Solís flexed his jaw muscles. His irritation rose as flames beneath his golden cheeks.

"Fine," he stated. "But I'll scorch him if he gets in my way."

"I won't get in your way," a voice replied.

Solís turned to find that Louie had climbed the ladder to Montgomery's ship.

Solís clenched his fist, knuckles red with heat.

"Why are you here?"

"I was planning to ask Montgomery to assign me to your mission, but it seems that has resolved itself," Louie said with a sly smile.

"Get in my way and it will be my delight to incinerate your smug grin to ashes."

Louie's eyebrows raised. "A bit harsh, considering our end goal is the same."

"When the mission starts, just do as I say," Solís commanded before climbing down the ladder.

Louie turned to Montgomery. "He's a prickly fellow, huh?"

"His emotions, good and bad, always seem to materialize as anger," Montgomery stated with a sigh. "He means well. Show him how hard you work and he'll come around."

"Solís can hate me. I don't care. I just want Emmeline back."

"We all do."

Louie nodded. "I'll see to it that she gets home safely."

Louie knew he wasn't the only one with this goal, but with so much time passing and drastic developments unfolding, he began to realize that his passive measures were no longer acceptable.

He needed to take action.

Chapter 11

Light from above, light from below, clashed where water met air.

From above, through small crevices where the pipes of Terra did not fully touch, light from the solar shield twinkled like stars as the turning gears above rotated and rhythmically blocked the light.

From below, the source flame raged, casting light through the many cracks of its obsidian casing. The light filtered through the ocean, reaching toward the sky. Waves blocked a straight path to the stars and refracted the light, weakening it before it hit the ocean surface. Dim and strobed, this light warped its surroundings; combined with the distorted twinkling from above, the moody, carnival ambiance of Hydra was formed. Only those who lived full lives here could see clearly in such conditions.

Solís liked to believe that he could come and go from Hydra without enduring significant adjustment times, but as he stared out to sea, waiting to start his mission, the mind-bending effects where the ocean met the sky had him spinning. When he turned his head, his surroundings jolted forward at unrealistic speeds, leaving him dizzy. He gripped the railing and closed his eyes, annoyed that this was happening before such an important mission. When he reopened his eyes, patches of darkness flickered across his vision. Hopping spots of black blocked him from clear sight.

He looked up, futilely swatting at the dancing darkness.

Adding to the shadows was a giant pair of wings soaring above. Solís squinted, golden brow creasing and heart gears churning faster. Was it a new monster? Or had Luna decided to reveal herself? Did she come with an army? He examined the approaching wings closer. They weren't dragonfly wings; they were metallic dragon wings.

"Ahoy there!" a familiar voice shouted.

Solís shook his head, forcing the dark spots away. Another glance upward revealed the return of Avery with Cyrus in tow. His brother hung over the basket of the helium balloon with a wide smile on his face. The metal dragon wings attached to the basket pumped the salty air with furious might.

Cyrus waved at him.

"I heard you needed my help," he shouted, a smug grin on his face.

"I thought it might be you. Are you ready to play doctor on the devil?" Solís asked.

"Doctor?"

Avery lowered the balloon onto the elevated landing pad.

"I'll explain after you've landed," Solís said.

He scanned the deck, searching for the rest of his crew. Gemma was sitting on a barrel holding a firestone to her forehead. Clementine sat beside her, massaging the sides of her neck.

Solís walked toward them.

The red glow of her stone had dimmed to orange and an oily tear ran down Gemma's face as it lost its heat. Clementine was oblivious to her friend's suffering, as she currently fought her own demons. A sudden gasp left Clementine breathless—the curse was getting the best of her again. Fingers clutching her throat, she stood, raced across the top deck, and tossed her body over the gunwales. She landed with a loud splash.

"I think she drew the short straw," Solís commented as he sat next to Gemma.

Gemma looked up, silver eyes gleaming with anguish.

"Who?"

"Clementine," Solís said. "Did you not see her dramatic exit just now?"

Gemma shook her head. "Everything goes dark when the coldness takes over. This stupid firestone lost its heat quicker than usual."

"Hand it here," Solís instructed.

Gemma placed the stone, which had already simmered from orange to yellow, into his palm. Solís curled his fingers around the cooling stone and then closed his eyes. Heat from his heart coursed through his body. He channeled the source flame and directed it to the hand holding the stone. As he heated his heart, his flesh glowed red and became translucent, revealing the golden bones and gears inside of him. Within moments, his fire recharged the stone and it resumed its brilliant red glow.

Solís opened his eyes, which now also glowed red from his activated heart.

"Here you go. This should last a while."

He handed the stone to Gemma.

Her entire body relaxed as she took it from him. From rigid and tense to tranquil, Gemma found incomparable relief from the firestone. She pressed it to her forehead and released a heavy exhale.

"Thank you," she said.

"That curse really has a hold of you, too, huh?" Solís noted, his flesh and eyes cooling off and resuming their golden hue.

"Of course, it does. Look at me," she responded, waving her free hand at her skeletal legs. "It almost took everything from me. I am desperate to learn that Emmeline has healed because if she found a way, then so can I."

Solís nodded. "Our mission with this devil will get you one step closer to healing."

"I hope so."

"What's the plan?" Louie shouted to them as he descended the ladder of Montgomery's ship.

"Join us," Solís offered, though the strain within his invitation was apparent. "I'll explain once Cyrus and Avery get here."

Louie jumped from the bottom rung of the rope ladder, then took his place near Solís and Gemma. He leaned against the cabin wall they were congregated in front of, picking at his fingernails as he awaited their next move.

Cyrus approached in a light jog while Avery lagged behind.

"Excellent," Solís said as they joined the group. "Let's get started. The mission is a blood extraction—we need a vial of the devil's blood."

"Why?" Avery asked.

"It could be the key to saving Emmeline."

"You know where Emmeline is?" Cyrus asked, utterly out of the loop.

"I have a hunch."

Avery eyed Louie, who shook his head, indicating he knew little more than her. She furrowed her brow and glared at Solís. "And how, may I ask, did you come to the discovery that devil blood will cure Emmeline?"

"It's also a hunch."

"It is certainly worth a try," Cyrus chimed in, oblivious and optimistic.

"My sentiments exactly," Solís said. "Avery, you will fly us to the cage in the helium balloon. Gemma, you will coat our suits in clay. Cyrus and Louie, you will hold the devil while I take its blood. I only get one shot, so I need to make it count."

"Why only one shot?" Louie asked.

"The tool I'll be using only works once."

"What tool?" Avery inquired.

Solís pulled the slingshot syringe out of the satchel slung over his shoulder, showing it to his crew.

"I've never seen metal like that before," Cyrus commented, his concern growing.

"That's because that contraption is not of this world," Avery sneered. "How could you leave her there?"

"Don't do this," Solís said, his tone a forced calm. "Not now."

"What is going on?" Cyrus asked.

"Nothing," Solís barked. "They have no idea what they are talking about."

"You were on the Moon of Fixation," Avery said. "Louie and I saw you leave through the stone and return empty-handed."

"I barely survived. I spent the five minutes I was there fighting for my life. I didn't even see her."

"Then how do you know this devil's blood is what she needs?"

Solís wasn't ready to reveal his source, so instead, he said, "Based on what I saw there, it's a very educated guess. I need you all to trust me."

"I trust you," Gemma chimed in.

"This is all news to me," Cyrus said. "You've never led the Pyropunks astray. Of course, I trust you."

"I just want Emmeline back," Louie said. "And if this is what it takes, so be it."

Avery grunted, glaring at Solís. "You're a sketch ball." She shook her head, then added, "Let's go."

Solís was already suited up. After Cyrus and Louie grabbed diving suits and put them on, the crew of five boarded the basket attached to the balloon. It took Avery a moment to refill the balloon with a combination of oxygen and helium—a long day of flying had left her depleted, but she used the last of her energy to fuel this flight.

Solís heated the pan beneath the balloon's base, giving Avery the extra lift she needed to carry the weight of five punks.

As they took off, Gemma began raking her fingers against her palms and producing clay. She slathered it onto their diving suits. The trip was short, they didn't have much time, so Solís, Cyrus, and Louie helped spread the clay, covering as much of the fabric as possible.

The devil greeted them with a horrifying scream as they reached its cage. Avery stayed a safe distance above the flames.

"This is as close as I can get," she informed Solís.

"That's fine. We will descend on ropes."

Fully lathered in rapidly hardening clay, the guys each grabbed a rope, secured one end with a knot, and threw the other end over the basket.

"The devil may look small, but it is fierce," Louie warned Solís and Cyrus.

"We've fought worse," Solís stated, unafraid.

"You haven't," Louie countered. "This is the first of its kind, and it didn't enter through the shield; it rose from the sea—how, we still don't know. I helped capture it. It is calculated and manipulative. If it chooses to speak instead of scream, don't listen to a word it says."

"If you do your job, we will be in and out of there before it has a chance to talk," Solís said.

Louie shook his head. There was no use battling Solís's obstinate ego.

Solís jumped over the basket's edge first, lowering himself with speed. Cyrus and Louie followed armed with clamps and chains to hold the devil in place.

The flames were tall and whipping extreme heat in all directions. Fueled by petroleum, they reached temperatures far greater than those of a natural flame.

While Solís and Cyrus had no issues with the heat, Louie struggled. Sweating profusely within his suit, he breathed heavily and blinked rapidly to keep the sweat out of his eyes.

"Let's be quick," he said, voice muffled by his helmet. "It's too hot for me here."

"When we land, hold the devil still and I will work fast," Solís replied.

Their bodies lowered through the flaming bars of the cage.

The devil sat on the floor bars—the only part of the cage not devoured by flames—watching their descent. There was no place for it to run, so it sat in place, quietly calculating, cautiously strategizing. Its furious blue gaze revealed its malintent.

Solís landed first. The devil shifted its attention to him. Squared off with the monster, Solís held a firm stance.

"This is the beginning of the end," Solís stated, hoping to keep the devil distracted while Louie and Cyrus made strategic moves on the other side of the cage.

"Indeed, it is," the devil said with a smirk, its voice smooth and feminine.

"Why are you smiling?"

"Because your end is coming, too."

"Your poison won't work on me this time. We've strengthened our defenses."

She shook her head, long red hair wet with the petroleum that dripped from the top bars of the cage. "You misunderstand," she hissed. "Your end is already on its way."

"Is that so? Tell me more," he goaded her.

"And how you treat me," she went on, "will determine the speed with which you meet your demise."

"Lies," he spat, losing patience with her vague and empty threats. "You've been in this prison for a while now and no one has come to save you. There's no one out there who cares what happens to you."

As the sharp words left his tongue, Louie and Cyrus snatched the devil from behind. Clamps fastened tightly to her skinny arms, pressing them to her sides, she was detained. They used their size—which was double hers—to make her kneel. She flailed in their grip, fighting the restraints they held her with, but their combined strength was too much. She could not break free.

Cyrus knelt behind her and wrapped his arm around her neck while Louie stood in front and pressed against her shoulders. Body locked between Louie and Cyrus, she was securely bound.

Solís stepped forward, pulling the slingshot syringe out of his satchel.

The flames all around them caught the reflective metal, refracting a beam of light in sporadic directions as Solís walked forward.

The devil stopped her fight upon sight of the tool.

"Lunarian metal," she said to herself, her fear apparent.

"What did you say?" Louie demanded.

The devil's blue eyes met his. "What is your intent with that contraption?" she asked, wriggling within their grip again.

"We are taking your blood," Cyrus answered with a grunt as he battled her resumed fight.

"Why?"

"To remedy the damage *you've* caused."

"That metal will poison me," she said.

"Like you've done to our loved ones?" Louie countered. "Sounds like a fair deal to me."

"No!"

Solís scanned her neck, looking for a prominent vein. He pressed his fingers into her burnt-orange flesh and found a bulging purple vein near her ear. His fingertips felt the chainmail resting below the thin layer of flesh. It was coarse, but consistent; the steel bumps rolled like a wave of armor covering the vein he needed to penetrate. He pressed harder and the dark interlinking pattern of the chainmail became visible through her flesh. He could see the breaks in her armor. He could see the soft spots.

Needle tip pressed to a soft spot overtop of her vein, Solís took a deep breath and pulled back the elastic threads. He only got one shot.

He released the threads and the needle plunged into the devil's neck.

Though she howled in agony, the syringe remained empty— blood did not fill the attached vial.

"I am so close ... how could I miss?" Solís said to himself.

"Is it working?" Cyrus asked, unable to see the syringe from where he held the devil.

"Where is the blood?" Louie asked.

"I don't know! It's inserted into the vein."

Louie transferred his weight, pinning the devil to Cyrus with his left forearm, and then used his free arm to assess the positioning of the needle. He placed two of his right fingers around the insertion point and pressed on the devil's flesh.

Solís looked on, desperation in his eyes and his faith placed in Louie to help figure out what went wrong.

Louie massaged the vein with his fingertips, and within moments, goopy purple blood began filling the vial.

Solís exhaled with relief.

The devil shrieked with a fury so loud the entire ocean shook. Huge waves rocked Red Fang Ralph's boat, and a ferocious gust of wind blew Montgomery's airship south, dragging its heavy anchor along with it. The helium balloon was blown up and away from the cage, taking their escape ropes with it.

Solís glanced up at the disappearing balloon and noticed that the pipes lining the ceiling of Hydra vibrated. The rattling of their nuts and bolts rang like a warning bell.

Chaos consumed Hydra.

The devil continued screaming.

"We have enough," Solís said to Louie and Cyrus. "Let's go."

The ropes they had climbed down on were carried away with the helium balloon.

"How do we get out of here?" Cyrus asked.

Diving into the ocean wasn't an option—they could not fit through the floor bars. Plus, countless cages holding various monsters were stacked below.

"I wish we had Pyropunk wings attached to our diving suits," Solís griped.

While Solís complained, Louie took action. With a swift chop, he punched the devil in the throat, smashing her vocal cords.

The wretched screaming ceased.

"That should buy us time," he stated.

"Good thinking," Cyrus commended him.

Solís glared at Louie, unable to hide his dislike for the pirate.

Three ropes dropped from above. Avery had returned and maneuvered her ship as close to the burning cage as possible.

"Hurry up!" she called down to them.

They each grabbed a rope and began their ascent.

The devil's scream turned into echoing whimpers as they departed. Though the chaos had calmed, her crying sent shivers into the spines of every punk within earshot.

Solís tried to shake the chill, but it lingered, latching onto his gears like a wounded leech. The sorrow seeped into him, emphasizing its power, and he couldn't help but wonder how far beyond Hydra the devil's cries reached.

Chapter 12

Deimos

"I can hear her," Daeva, Queen of Deimos, announced as she channeled the frequency only Marzans shared. Her fingers were clawed into the dusty red terrain, and her bloodshot gaze glared in the direction of the sound.

"Deánira?" her husband, King Helmer, asked.

"Yes, our daughter. I hear her cries." Daeva's fierce blue eyes held both contempt and grief.

"I've heard her, too," Helmer confessed. "They are torturing her ... I can feel her distress despite the lightyears between us."

Daeva scowled. "Yet our militia sits, waiting for your order to strike."

"You know why I wait."

"She isn't coming back with intel," Daeva reminded him. "She isn't coming back at all if you don't intervene."

Helmer smirked. "You aren't listening close enough."

"What do you mean?"

"Her cries are coded. Every scream, screech, and bellow holds encrypted messages."

Daeva's eyes lit up. "What has she told you?"

"The Solarpunks are divided. Their leadership is focused on a missing punk girl. Now would be an advantageous time to strike."

"So why haven't we?"

"I was going to, but Deánira told me to wait."

"Why would she delay her rescue?"

"Because there is a Lunarian lurking in Quintessence, attempting to forge friendships with the punks. Deánira suspects she is planting the seeds of an interstellar alliance."

"The punks will never accept."

"They might. The Lunarian is saving an important Solarpunk girl and rallying her friends and siblings in the process."

"We cannot let our enemies band together."

"They still don't know our plan. We have the upper hand."

"The gears of the sun churn too strong, producing fire too vicious to fight. And those infuriating magnetic moon threads— if the Solarpunks team up with the Lunarians, we won't win."

"Calm down."

"How am I supposed to calm down? Solar fire is our greatest foe, and those lunar threads latch to the metal beneath our flesh, constraining us like pathetic animals."

"We have the gods on our side, remember?"

"Are you sure?" Daeva questioned.

"Yes, I am sure," Helmer countered. "Stop worrying. With the gods on our side, we will defeat them both."

"Or perhaps, we ought to prevent them from ever teaming up at all," Daeva suggested, her expression ravaged as strategies ricocheted within her mind.

"Go on ..." Helmer encouraged.

"You said the Lunarian is helping save the Solarpunk girl they are desperate to find?"

"Correct."

"Perhaps it is time for another raid of Mōnalene."

Helmer's confident expression gained a devilish smirk, then he agreed, "Perhaps it is."

Deánira's cries became louder.

Echoing across the universe, she pled in code for rescue.

Helmer's furious, bloodshot gaze narrowed as he listened.

"What is she saying?" Daeva asked.

"Things have taken a drastic turn," he answered.

"Tell me!"

"They tried to execute her yesterday, but it was halted," Helmer revealed, still listening intently. "The Lunarian gave them moon metal."

"No," Daeva said with a gasp.

"The Solarpunks used it to extract some of her blood."

"They injected her with lunar metal?" she asked, horrified.

Helmer nodded.

"We have to bring her home," he concluded, lifting his gaze and turning it toward the sky. An infinite starscape lay before him. Far, far away, the sun shone brightest among them.

He sneered. "Perhaps a truce with the Lunarians is in order."

"Anything to get our daughter back."

Helmer stood tall, extended his long arms, and howled. Bereaved yet inspiring, the summon beckoned his army. Led by hardened Marzan generals, they marched in rows toward the royal garden.

The king and queen scaled the columns of their castle like insects, using their adhesive tarsal claws to ascend. When they reached the balcony, they sat on their thrones, waiting for their ferocious army to arrive.

The Marzan soldiers moved with a distinct march—in flawless unison, they swept the terrain with deep lunge-stomps and precise elbow jabs.

A menacing sight to behold, they tore across the land with fierce intent. Their bloodshot blue eyes peered over their lifted arms. Their right toes dragged along the red dust as their elbows lowered. Then they repeated the motion on the opposite side.

While they performed this march with synchronized perfection, they chanted low-humming hymns that vibrated with terrifying force.

Helmer watched, delighted, as his intimidating army approached. They would save his daughter; the Marzans would emerge victorious once again.

The lead Marzan general unleashed a three-note whistle, and the fleet of ten thousand Marzan soldiers came to an abrupt, unified stop. Silent, despite the sea of bodies, they stared up at their king, awaiting direction.

"My devoted soldiers," King Helmer began, "it is time again to strike. The Solarpunks have imprisoned your princess, and Deánira needs our help."

The massive swarm of soldiers grumbled with displeasure. They adored the royal family and perceived strikes against them as personally as the royals.

"Though it is the Solarpunks who have our beloved Deánira, it is the Lunarians we must infiltrate. But this time, we will not visit to attack or steal their resources—our intent is to form an alliance with them."

The soldiers grumbled again, but this time, the collective feeling was confusion.

Helmer explained, "The Lunarians think they will beat us by aligning with the Solarpunks, but we will find cracks in their resolve and sway them to our side before that happens." Helmer paused, eyes gleaming with mischief. "And if we can't find cracks, we will make them."

The soldiers murmured with excitement.

"The generals will take the lead on finding, or creating, the cracks. But most importantly, remember, the Lunarians will never be our true allies. This is a farce, one to distract them long enough for us to enact our greater plan. They are the only moon beings standing in our way, and once their defenses are lowered, we can finally claim this section of the universe."

The soldiers cheered, as eager as the royals for the day they no longer had to fear fire.

"Soon," King Helmer concluded, "fire will no longer be our greatest foe."

The Marzan soldiers resumed their war hymnal in support of their new mission, echoing their excitement into the universe for anyone paying attention to hear.

Chapter 13

Quintessence

"Where are you?" Solís barked from the rooftop of his home, vial of devil blood in hand. He flipped the skinny tube between his fingers, waiting for Luna to arrive.

It took a few moments before her voice appeared.

"I was waiting for you in Hydra," she said, out of breath and invisible. "Why'd you leave Hydra in such a hurry?"

Solís squinted, searching for the monster with whom he had reluctantly aligned.

"I thought it would be safer to talk here," he answered, then demanded, "Show yourself."

"There are too many punks floating around."

Solís scanned the late afternoon sky—she was right. The workday was done and Aeropunks were everywhere, floating leisurely, as they did every day before twilight. Elderly Aeropunks toured the sky on propeller umbrellas, younger Aeropunks on airscrew unicycles, countless others donned copper wings—it wasn't safer here.

Solís crouched low, then spoke. "Wrap me in your shield of invisibility and take me with you."

"You don't even have shoes on," Luna noted with a scoff.

"I'm more agile without shoes."

"We ought to talk this plan through first."

Solís tapped the tank attached to his back. "It's usually filled with helium. I replaced it with oxygen and connected a breathing tube. I won't be a burden this time."

He placed the vial of blood into the pocket of his tight leather jacket.

Luna's silence lingered.

"Take me with you," he said, voice quivering with warning.

"I will. We just need to set some ground rules."

Solís's golden eyes flickered with annoyance. "Like what?"

"You are there to observe, to see that your sister is alive and in good hands. You will not interfere with her healing. You will not interrupt their attempts to save her. You will trust and respect the process."

"Fine, but the promise is null and void at the slightest hint of foul play."

"There is no foul play. We are trying to save her."

"Then there should be no issues. Let's go."

Luna grumbled under her breath, loud enough for Solís to hear.

He smirked, delighted by her displeasure.

Without warning, her cold hands cupped the sides of his face. He wanted to protest, but her gentle touch soothed his defiance.

"Ad lunam lu. Accipe me," she said, and they were sucked into a vortex.

Similar to his last trip, the few seconds spent rocketing through the portal were nauseating. Luna assisted him with his breathing tube while he struggled to retain his bearings.

One second they were in the portal, traveling at warp speed, and a blink later they were on the dusty terrain of Mōnalene.

Dizzy, queasy, and disoriented, Solís wobbled in place. He pressed his hand to the mouthpiece situated securely between his teeth, ensuring he would not suffer as he did during his last visit. He scanned the empty landscape for the monsters who had tried to kill him.

Luna saw the panic in his eyes.

"They won't hunt you as long as you're with me," she offered.

The panic in his eyes shifted with hostility, indicating he was ready to fight.

He removed the mouthpiece to speak.

"I'm better prepared—" he said, then quickly returned his breathing apparatus, unable to finish the rest of his thought.

Luna smirked. "I prefer you this way."

He removed it again.

"If I have something to say, you better believe I'll—" Solís coughed, choking on his saliva as he ran out of breath. He shoved the mouthpiece between his teeth and took a long inhale.

"Ah," Luna said with a smile. "Silence."

She charged ahead, her long black hair billowing. Her speed and the lack of gravity had her long locks floating.

His bearings restored, Solís found himself admiring her figure. Tall and thin, with slight curves in all the right places. His heart pounded as his heart fluttered. Was he attracted to the monster? Why did he find her so desirable?

Luna sensed his lack of movement. She paused and turned to face him.

"Are you coming?" she asked.

Her beautiful silver eyes sparkled in the starlight.

Solís clenched his fists and shook free from this forbidden feeling of desire. He would kill her before he ever allowed himself to love her.

He marched forward, following her lead, but keeping an eye on the horizon. Luna monitored the horizon as well, shoulders tense as she led him toward a tall crater.

Her hand dragged along the jagged rock, fingers searching for a specific, unseen alcove. Upon finding it, her circular pacing ceased. She looked to Solís, a mischievous sparkle in her eye. If he didn't know better, he'd assume she was flirting.

He removed the breathing regulator.

"What kind of trouble are you leading me into?" he asked, then returned the mouthpiece.

"No trouble, just very curious to see your reaction when you see firsthand that we aren't an inferior race of unevolved monsters."

Solís rolled his eyes, choosing to say no more.

Luna curled her fingers under the alcove. They disappeared behind the gray rock, followed quickly by her arm, then shoulder. Soon, she was crouching and fitting her body into a crevice Solís still could not see.

"Follow me," she said before vanishing.

Solís approached the tall crater wall, hands pressed against the section that seemingly swallowed Luna whole. A quick search led his geared fingers to the alcove, and a deep reach beneath revealed a wide opening that was camouflaged from the outside. He ducked beneath the rock overhang and entered a small tunnel with a downward slope.

Luna waited for him there.

"You're moving awfully slow for someone eager to assess the wellness of his lost sister," she stated before trekking onward.

Solís didn't waste any breath responding. Instead, he saved his energy for whatever nightmarish nest of chaos she was leading him into. This was enemy territory—he needed to remain alert and prepared.

Luna waltzed down the path. The stress she carried above ground disappeared beneath. The scent of moon lily wafted behind her, smacking Solís in the face. Lovely and sweet; everything a monster shouldn't be.

She was a few paces ahead when she paused to look back at him.

"Are you ready?"

His golden brow furrowed.

"You'll see," she said, answering his unspoken question.

She took a step forward into the light and it engulfed her in an ethereal glow.

Solís trailed her warily—a monster den should not yield heavenly radiance.

As he exited the tunnel and entered the world within the moon, his mind fought the sight displayed before him.

It wasn't a nest of death, or a dark dungeon reeking of despair—it was an organized society filled with light and order. It defied all his preconceived notions; it was a place suitable for distinguished living. Thousands of moon threads crisscrossed the massive space, anchored to floating meteors that held living quarters within. Hellions—Lunarians—traveled the threads, scaling and swinging from them with agile grace. To and from the meteors, they used the threads as guides.

Solís removed his mouthpiece.

"I thought you could fly," he said before replacing the regulator.

"We can, just not in here. There is no gravity within the moon—the magnetic threads are the only rooted objects. The threads coursing within us keep us grounded—we control when they are magnetic and when they are not." She pointed to her exposed ankles, which had thinly woven silver threads revolving beneath her flesh. She continued, "A single, careless flap of our wings inside Mōnalene, and we'd catapult to our deaths, our bodies crashing against the interior rock walls. I've seen it happen. It's a horrifying sight." She glanced at the titanium wings strapped to his back. "Heed this warning," she cautioned.

His eyes widened with alarm.

"Yes, you're right," she said, understanding his worries. "Gold and titanium—neither are magnetic." She extended her pointer finger, closed her eyes, and then slowly extracted two silver threads from her fingertip. She then wrapped each around Solís's ankles, twisting them tightly above his ankle gears to prevent any snags. Her touch was gentle and soft; it was considerate. She did not live a life bound by gears, yet she took care not to tangle the wires into his cogs.

"That should help," she said as she coiled the ends together.

She gave him a piece of herself; a gift he suspected he did not deserve.

Solís turned his ankle gears and rotated his foot. Everything was in working order.

"Thank you," he mumbled with the regulator still in his mouth.

Luna nodded, then walked until she reached the ledge of the rock. Two giant threads, which looked more like giant cords up close, were attached—one was large enough to walk on, the other was thin and would require more skill.

"Different routes, but they lead to the same place," she informed him.

"Emmeline?" he mumbled without removing the regulator.

Luna stepped onto the thicker thread. "This path will lead to her."

She took the easier route. Solís followed with careful steps; the metal anklets kept him firmly planted to the magnetic thread.

Eyes down, Solís was hyper-focused on each step. When he bumped into Luna's back, he looked up for the first time since mounting the thread.

A castle made of meteor rock floated before them. Attached to the thread they stood upon, this jagged fortress dwarfed everything around it.

Luna rapped her fist against the front door three times, then took a step back.

The doors swung open, revealing no answers, just more darkness.

Before Solís could ask what this place was, two regal figures emerged from the shadows.

They were unlike Luna and the other hellions he had met in the past—they were taller with a heartier build, and they donned different wings.

"Those are the head Monarchs," Luna explained in a whisper. "Our queen, Lepido Dione, and her king, Lepido Elir."

As they approached, Lepido Dione spread her wings wide, displaying their full glory. Bright orange and yellow, with streaks of purple outlining spots of black. She commanded attention, she demanded respect, both of which she received. Solís found himself shaken with awe and bent a knee without provocation. Luna bowed as well.

"What is this?" Lepido Dione asked. "Another Solarpunk in need of rescue?"

"No," Luna answered, standing tall. "He is the brother of the injured punk. He has just as much influence in Quintessence as Emmeline."

"I see. You want me to show him kindness so he'll spread the word when he returns home?"

"He doesn't deserve your kindness," she answered bluntly. Solís shot her an offended glance. Luna continued, "He just needs to witness our strength and benevolence. I brought him here to show him why an alliance with us would be prudent."

"Well, your timing is impeccable. The Marzans unleashed a wretched war cry. An attack is coming. Let him see how we handle our enemies. Perhaps it will influence which side of our kindness he wishes to reside."

Though their wings, coloring, and builds were different, their inner threads and silver disced eyes were the same.

The queen glared at Solís, no mercy in her shimmering gaze. She grabbed Lepido Elir by the wrist and dragged him back inside, waving her free hand for Luna to follow.

"Be on your best behavior," Luna warned Solís.

He removed his regulator.

"You were supposed to take me to see Emmeline," he barked, then shoved the mouthpiece back between his teeth.

"I never said we wouldn't make stops along the way."

Luna turned and entered the castle.

Out of his element and vulnerable in enemy territory, Solís had no choice but to fall in line—at least until he learned where they were keeping his sister.

Alliances, enemies, battles that did not involve Quintessence—none of it mattered to him. Emmeline was his only concern.

He needed to bring her home before war reached this place.

Chapter 14

The Monarchs led the way into the dimly lit war room. There, Cèla and two other commanders of the Odonata warriors waited.

"No," Cèla barked the moment she saw Luna. When Solís entered the room after, Cèla spread her wings and bared her fangs. "Why is he here?"

"Lower your defenses," Lepido Dione calmly commanded.

"You've allowed another Solarpunk to exist here without consequence?"

"We must keep sight of the bigger picture." Dione took her seat at the head of the table.

"For centuries, they have slaughtered our people for sport! They built a whole religion around hatred for the moons."

"We have Solédon to thank for that," Luna interjected. "His rivalry with Lunéss has done us no service, and who knows where She is … "

"I don't care who is to blame. *They*," Cèla spat, pointing at Solís, "carried out the evil. My beloved—" Cèla choked on her emotions, eyes glaring at Luna, "*your* brother—is gone because of them. If your father hadn't escaped, we'd still be wondering about his fate, too. Your foolish quest to befriend the enemy is a betrayal to the family."

"Enough," Dione roared, her voice booming. Their bickering ceased, and as her echo faded, she stood from her chair. "We need fire—not only for the well-being of our mortals on Earth, but to protect ourselves from the Marzans. We need to inspire radical change between us and the Solarpunks."

"Have you asked *him* how he feels about that?" Cèla challenged.

Dione turned her attention to Solís, who stood in Luna's shadow.

"Step forward, young man," Dione instructed.

Solís hesitated.

Before Dione had to repeat her request, Luna pushed Solís into the light. The room was filled with monsters, all of whom had their mistrusting gazes locked on him. His golden eyes darted between them. His instinct told him to fight—his muscles were conditioned to engage and years of training had engrained a deep hatred for these beings.

Solís restrained his primal reflexes.

He removed his mouthpiece.

"I know nothing of what's going on," he said, took a deep inhale from the regulator, then added, "I only came here to bring my sister home."

"She told you nothing before leaving?" Cèla interrogated.

Solís shook his head.

"I don't believe him."

"Believe him," Luna said. "Emmeline told no one of her friendship with me. She planned to tell them after she returned healed. She felt they'd be more receptive to an alliance once they had us to thank for healing her."

"We need to finish healing her," Solís pled.

"He is right," Luna said. "Solís acquired Marzan blood to help us eradicate the poison cemented inside Emmeline's nostrils."

"That will have to wait," Dione stated.

"Why?"

"As I stated before, war is coming. I need every Odonata on the field, and as much as you resist your calling, your skills as a warrior are needed."

Luna clenched her fists. "There are better ways to win wars."

"I agree, and we still plan to try it your way, but with a physical attack imminent, we must resort to the tried-and-true method of direct combat."

Luna's inner threads writhed ominously, threatening to break their smooth flow and tangle into furious knots.

"Contain yourself, dear Luna," Dione advised. Though her tone was calm, her words were a warning.

"I'm tired of fighting," Luna said, fists shaking. "I want a better life for all of us."

"You are doing good work, but until we can make your vision a reality, we must continue to defend ourselves the best way we know how."

Luna's jaw muscles clenched as she swallowed her aggravation.

"I understand," she finally conceded.

"As I knew you would." Dione turned to the Odonata generals. "The Orthops have been keeping a close eye on Deimos from their astronomy tower. Early this morning they saw vibrating frequencies among the stars. The Marzans are getting close."

"Should we involve the Weaver?" Cèla asked.

"No, not this time. Let her stay in her den. If we cannot handle it on our own, she will sense the dismay in our threads and emerge."

Cèla nodded, then asked, "From which side of the moon are the Marzans approaching?"

"The northern near. Prepare the majority of troops along the arctic axis. Assign a few teams to the near side mesial in case the solar winds carry the Marzans a little bit south."

"No troops along the polar axis?" Cèla asked.

"I don't foresee them landing in the far south." Dione then addressed the commander wearing magnified spectacles. "Odonata Arche, I need you to enact the veil. Block the views of all mortal satellites and telescopes. Our existence here must be concealed from the earthlings at all costs."

Arche nodded, then adjusted the strap holding the glasses to his face. His amplified silver eyes shifted back and forth as he exited the room.

"Odonata Isone," Dione said to the female commander standing next to Cèla. As a damselfly, she was slightly smaller in size. "You will consult with Termes Terrell and herd all remaining Lunarians into whichever stone mound he advises. I suggest a mound on the far side, ideally Vesparian Mountain, but follow his lead."

"No matter if the Vespas protest?"

"I will speak to Vespa Zeruah myself. She will oblige Terrell's counsel and allow the masses into whichever mound he deems the safest. I doubt there will be damage to her hornets' nest within the mound, but if there is, I will make assurances to see to its repairs. If you receive pushback from her, or anyone else, report back to me immediately."

"Understood," Isone replied before fluttering her petite wings and vanishing.

"Luna," Dione continued. "Please join Cèla in organizing the troops."

"Shouldn't I stay with him?" she asked, pointing at Solís.

"I will see to it that your solar friend stays safe."

Luna had no choice but to oblige. Begrudgingly, she followed Cèla to the battlefield.

Only Dione, Elir, and Solís remained in the room.

"You," Dione said, looking at Solís, "will be coming with us."

Dione led the way. Elir followed silently. Though he hardly spoke, his confidence radiated. Beetle guards lined the cocooned corridor, and though they stood firm, their energy trembled ever so slightly as the Monarchs passed.

Solís observed the long rows of guards—they were different in appearance than the hellions he was accustomed to. They were shorter, rounder, and had pincers attached to their faces. Some on their foreheads, others near their mouths. Their backs were rounded with hard shells, and it wasn't until Dione beckoned one of them forward that he saw that their shells hid wings beneath.

"Coleo Scara," Dione beckoned. "Step forward."

Scara separated her shells and a pair of iridescent wings colored yellow and blue carried her to the royals. It was safe to fly within the castle, unlike the netted chasm outside these walls.

"Your Highness," she said with a bow of her head. Two long black braids were pulled tight to her scalp.

"Take our visitor to the astronomy tower. He will observe the battle from there."

Coleo Scara nodded her head in understanding, then made a sharp left and marched down an adjacent hallway.

"Follow her," Dione ordered.

Solís exhaled into his regulator, then obliged.

There were fewer guards in this part of the castle, and oftentimes, he was alone with Scara, who did not speak to him. She simply charged ahead, leading him up countless web-covered staircases and through long, cocooned halls. Fuzzy silk strands covered every inch of the stone castle's interior, and Solís was constantly getting his foot and ankle gears snagged on the fibers. As he knelt to untangle himself for the tenth time, Scara finally spoke.

"You need to lift your feet when you walk."

Solís grumbled through the regulator as he unknotted a particularly bad snag. Scara tapped her foot impatiently as she waited.

"You do realize the Marzans could arrive at any moment, right?" she scolded. "We need to get to the tower before they do so I have time to lock the gates and put the shields in place."

Solís yanked the last of the fibers out from between his toes and stood up. He nodded, indicating he was ready to resume, and Scara huffed.

"Stop dragging your feet," she instructed before carrying onward.

Solís did his best to avoid another tangle.

While walking, he took a quick glance through one of the slitted corridor windows—they were high up now. In fact, they were closer to the rock ceiling than the maze of moon threads below.

"Are we almost there?" Solís mumbled through his mouthpiece.

"We have to cross the threshold."

Solís's golden brow furrowed.

Scara further explained, "This astronomy tower is one of six that crosses between the inner and outer world of Mōnalene. They are stationed at the midpoints of every axis on all sides of the moon. Termes and Vespas built mounds around them so they blend in with the other moon craters and mountains. From our vantage point within the tower, we will have a full view of the forthcoming fight."

They reached a set of stairs with a locked door preventing them from climbing higher.

"This is the threshold," Scara explained as she carefully slid the stone tiles in a specific pattern. Each of the tiles was locked to the board by interlinked edges and could only move in certain directions.

As she slid the final tile into place, the interior mechanisms of the door churned loudly, concluding with a resounding click.

The sound of revolving gears felt like home to Solís.

Scara shoved the door open and hurriedly waved Solís to follow. He charged up the steps and through the door. She scurried quickly, slamming the door closed behind her. With a swift maneuver of the tiles on this side of the door, she reengaged the lock and exhaled a deep sigh of relief.

Her reprieve was short-lived.

A loud, purring engine accompanied by a resonating war chant echoed into the tower.

Scara raced to the nearest window.

"They're here," she said, her panic shifting to fury. The threads beneath her flesh turned black and recoiled with rage as she watched the Marzans approach her home. "We have to keep moving. We need to get to the observation room."

They raced up the stone stairs.

This part of the castle was not covered in silk fibers and the moonstone beneath their feet was polished to shiny perfection.

It wasn't until they reached the top room of the tower that Solís's gaze shifted upward from his moving feet. They were surrounded by windows with a clear, panoramic view of this part of the moon. Drip-dried stone sediment formed a barrier around them, but somehow, he had a clear view through.

"How is that possible?" he asked without removing the regulator.

"Moon dust—like our flowers, threads, and stones—has magical properties. The Termes manipulated the dust to create a one-way shield. We can see out, but no one can see in."

Solís nodded, impressed.

"Still," Scara continued, "there are extra levels of protection I need to engage, hence the rush."

The pincers at her chin clicked together as she maneuvered around the circular room of windows. A long black rope hung from the center of the ceiling. She yanked it hard, unfurling countless magnetic moon threads outside the tower between them and the mound façade. They dangled loosely, evenly spaced and writhing with power.

"If the Marzans get too close, they will sense this magnetic field and retreat," Scara explained.

Solís had little invested in this fight. Only Emmeline and his fellow Solarpunks on Quintessence mattered to him.

"Come watch," Scara said, waving him over.

Though the view was now fractured by the hanging threads, it was a small obstruction. He could see everything: three long rows of hellions stationed along a dotted line that ran as far as he could see—a marking to delineate the arctic axis, he supposed. There were thousands of winged monsters at the ready. They had red petals glued over their noses and mouths, and their moon-disced eyes had turned black as they glared toward the red rock ship lowering itself toward them.

"What are the petals for?" Solís asked.

"Those petals are from venenum impedios blossoms. They protect us from the devil's poison," Scara replied.

The haunting war hymn echoed all around. As the notes ebbed and flowed, so did the agitated threads beneath the flesh of the hellions.

The alien ship landed with a resonating thud, kicking up moon dust and creating a barrier of silver grit between them and the hellions. Luna stood in the front line, fangs bared and wings spread—Solís could feel her fury from where he stood.

As the dust settled, a Marzan stepped onto the top deck of their ship. The moment Solís saw the intruder, he recognized it as a Devil of Delusion—these monsters had interactions and a social hierarchy beyond that of which he knew of them in Quintessence. It was curious and strange, a true shock to Solís, as he had wholeheartedly believed they lived and breathed to torment the Solarpunks and steal fire from the sun.

As it turned out, they tortured each other, too.

"We come in peace," the head devil shouted from a safe spot atop his ship.

Solís's eyes widened in shock. He removed his regulator and asked, "We can hear them from here?"

"Moon acoustics carry for miles, and the mound around us was built to amplify all noise on our otherwise silent terrain."

Solís nodded, returned the regulator to his mouth, and turned his attention back to the tense scene unraveling beyond.

"Helmer," Cèla responded to the Marzan king, seething as she stepped out of the line. "You never come in peace."

"You are right, but I hope you will hear me out. My daughter is a prisoner in the watery hellscape of Quintessence, and we seek your portals to retrieve her."

"The last time we bartered with you, you promised us peace and delivered warfare after we fulfilled our half of the deal. We will not make that same mistake again."

"That raid wasn't by my order," Helmer promised. "That act of treason was committed by a rebel militia—one that has plagued my flanks for years."

"They killed fifty-five Lunarian warriors."

"It was a travesty," Helmer agreed. "And though it took a while, my team finally found the rebel leader. As much as I'd like to punish him myself, I thought offering you that chance might garner some trust between us."

Cèla's gaze narrowed with intrigue as two Marzans pushed a third, chained Marzan onto the deck with Helmer.

"Here he is! And he is all yours if you want him."

"Nothing comes without a price," Cèla replied.

"All I ask is that you let us use a portal to save my daughter."

"And then what? You will leave Quintessence without causing further damage?"

"Do you truly care what we do to the Solarpunks on our visit?"

"No, actually. I don't. But I do care about your intentions regarding the source flame."

Helmer's bloodshot blue eyes gleamed with mischief. "All I care about is my daughter."

"Lies," Cèla challenged him.

"Let me prove it to you."

"Too much is on the line if you deceive us."

"You let my daughter use one of your portals, now help her return!"

"Are you blaming us for her capture? Need I remind you that the rebel standing beside you ruined that small treaty we created. We sent Deánira through the portal with the promise of peace, and days later, we were raided by your people."

"That's why I brought him here, to even the score. Kill him, torture him; I don't care! I just want my daughter back." Helmer took a deep breath to calm his agitation. "We don't want a war … "

"Neither do we, yet you continue to invade our space and steal our resources."

"As I said before, this time, we come in peace. We wish to form an alliance with you."

"An alliance?" Cèla scoffed, as did the thousands of warriors behind her. Their disapproval reverberated, rattling the tiny moon pebbles at their feet.

"You'll form one with the Solarpunks, the devils who have slaughtered countless moon beings, but not with us?"

"We have no alliance with those monsters," Cèla countered, though her confident expression wavered.

"Not yet, maybe," Helmer replied, "but it's coming."

"Not if I can help it."

"Division," Helmer mused. "I see."

"Against *you*, we are wholly united."

"It only takes a crack to crumble an empire."

Cèla raised her fist and the rows of warriors behind lunged with wings spread, fangs bared, and prepared to pounce. Long black threads buzzing with magnetic energy extended from their palms and were yielded like whips.

Helmer pushed the chained Marzan back into the ship.

"I came with a sacrifice, an offer of peace, and this is how you respond?"

Cèla unleashed a four-note whistle, to which a flock of Termes appeared in the sky. Their stone-chomping incisors clattered as they hovered overhead.

"Leave before we swarm your ship and tear it apart piece by piece," Cèla warned.

"Ah, the stone-eating termites. What a team you've got."

"Leave!"

Helmer's furious gaze scanned his enemy as he debated his next move. He took a step backward to appease Cèla, but his shifty eyes revealed he hadn't surrendered yet.

Cèla's fist remained in the air, prepared to drop at the first sign of aggression from Helmer.

Before either could make a first move, a blast erupted in the empty space between them, creating a plume of moon dust veiling the source of the intrusion.

Unsure if Helmer had caused the blast, Cèla lowered her fist, alerting her warriors to strike. Helmer did the same, sending forth a siege of Marzan fighters. As the opposing sides charged toward each other, the moon dust settled.

Standing in the middle of this budding battle was a single Solarpunk.

Sight of him startled both sides enough that their full-forced advance sputtered to a stop.

Solís pressed his hands against the window of the tower, a mixture of dismay and annoyance in his expression. He uttered a name.

"Louie."

Chapter 15

Louie's silver-blue eyes glimmered with waves of horror as he scanned the scene around him. His hope was to arrive secretly, covertly locate Emmeline, and bring her home. Instead, he had entered in the middle of a battle where everyone witnessed his arrival. He stood paralyzed in place, afraid to move, for monsters surrounded him on all sides.

"Louie?" a hellion shouted, stepping toward him.

"How do you know my name?" he replied, inhaling and exhaling deeply through his oxygen tank lungs—breathing on the moon was similar to breathing beneath the ocean.

"My name is Luna. I am friends with Emmeline." Though she spoke calmly, her tone was panicked; they didn't have long before the battle resumed. She asked, "Why are you here?"

"You know why," he barked. "Take me to her."

The shock of his arrival had subsided—the rows of Lunarians behind her had resumed their charge with threaded whips raised, and the Marzans' focus had shifted to Louie. Their bloodshot eyes were zeroed in on a prize much greater than an alliance with the Lunarians.

"Run to me!" Luna pled as she darted toward him.

Louie didn't budge.

Luna ran faster, moving in deep lunges toward him.

Terrified, Louie lifted the moonstone, which was wrapped in cloth, and repeated the incantation, but he only knew the words to activate the portal to the moon. He did not know the phrase to return to the sun.

"Take my hand! I can help you," the fast-approaching hellion shouted, but all Louie heard were lies to trick him. These were the monsters who held Emmeline prisoner; these were the creatures he needed to fight in order to save her.

"Did you imprison Solís, too?" Louie asked as the sounds of war resumed. Hellions on one side, devils on the other, all charging toward him.

"He's on his way to Emmeline," Luna answered, reaching for Louie, trying to make contact.

He leaned back, narrowly averting her grip. His brow furrowed at her reply. Before he could make demands to join Solís, a pair of claws snatched him by the shoulders.

Lifted into the air, feet dangling, Louie was seized by a devil. He glanced up—a chain of devils linked by their ankles hung from the top of the giant mooncraft. The devil directly above him let out a manic cackle and dug its sharp fingertips deeper into his flesh.

Louie howled in pain as he writhed and tried to break free. The devils swiftly recoiled their bodies, pulling Louie higher into the sky toward the ship deck.

Luna spread her wings and catapulted toward him. She flew with speed, but was stopped by an invisible barrier surrounding the mooncraft. She could get no closer.

"Look at me," Luna demanded, to which Louie shifted his panicked gaze. She mouthed, "Hide the stone."

Louie nodded and shoved the wrapped stone into a pocket on the inside of his pants.

"He is a low-level Solarpunk," Luna shouted at Helmer. "Capturing him gives you no leverage."

"Surely he can tell us something useful," Helmer replied with a devilish smirk.

"I'll never talk!" Louie roared.

"We'll see about that."

Louie was lugged onto the deck of the foreign red rock ship, immediately restrained, and then shuffled out of sight.

The Marzans retreated, having gained a far greater prize than an alliance with the Lunarians, and the Odonatas were left rushing a departing enemy.

Luna lowered herself back to the battlefield.

"What was that? Why did another Solarpunk show up here?" Cèla barked as she called her warriors to a halt.

93

Luna turned and looked toward the giant lunar rock mound Solís was concealed within.

"I don't know," Luna answered, "but Solís might."

"You've created more problems than you've solved."

"It will all be worth it in the end," Luna promised.

"Do you plan to save the punk who just got captured, too?"

"Yes," Luna replied, exasperated and painfully aware of the large task now added to her pile, "but first, I need to finish saving Emmeline."

"I don't know why you bother. She'll leave healed and nothing will change for us."

"Have a little faith."

"I lost my faith the day your brother was murdered."

"I miss him, too. I do this in his honor and for future generations—I do this to prevent that from ever happening again."

"You dishonor him," Cèla spat before storming off. Most of the warriors followed her to the nearest training crater to recap the short-lived battle. Odonata Arche departed for the inner world of the moon to consult the Monarchs, and Odonata Isone flew toward the far side to alert the rest of the Lunarians that it was safe to come out of hiding.

Luna turned her flight toward Solís. Glimmering wings pounding the weightless air, she rocketed to the mound he hid within. She knew the puzzle code to the door at the base of the mound, and after a quick reassortment of stone tiles, she entered the hidden space.

"Why is he here?" she shouted as she darted up the staircase. As she crossed the threshold into the observatory room, Solís greeted her with a shrug and a perplexed expression.

Luna ripped the regulator out of his mouth.

"Talk!" she demanded.

"It was probably some attempt to beat me at saving Emmeline. He's an idiot."

"How did he know how to get here?"

"He heard me use the incantation the first time I used the portal." Solís gasped for air. "He must've remembered it."

Luna handed back the regulator and Solís shoved it into his mouth. He held the air gauge up to Luna and tapped on the glass case. The dial was nearing the red empty line.

"Almost out of air, huh?" Luna commented. "Looks like your trip may be coming to an end."

"Get me some of those oxygen flowers," he said between breaths.

"I think it's better if you return home."

Solís checked the gauge again. "You promised to take me to Emmeline."

"I didn't foresee a Marzan attack upon our arrival."

"If you want my trust, help me stay a little longer."

Luna narrowed her silver gaze. "Fine. Now that we have the Marzan blood, Emmeline should be healed within the next full orbit."

Solís nodded.

"Coleo Scara," Luna said, speaking to the beetle guard. "Would you mind asking Antho Devorah to deliver a bundle of oxygeni blossoms to the laboratory?"

Scara nodded before departing toward the lunar garden.

"Follow me," Luna said to Solís before descending the long spiraling staircase.

As it was before, the stairs in the upperworld were sleek and smooth, but as soon as they crossed through the locked threshold, everything became covered in netted silk fibers.

Solís lifted his feet as best he could. Still, his gears were often snagged by the webs.

"I thought you were running out of air," Luna commented, annoyed as they stopped for Solís to untangle himself for the fifth time.

"I am," he mumbled through the regulator.

"Then pick up your feet!"

"Easier said than done."

"The flowers are getting delivered to the laboratory, not the Monarch fortress. If you run out of air before we get there, there's not much I can do to help you."

"I'm trying." Solís shook his foot free. "Let's go."

They exited the narrow stairway and traversed long corridors through multiple levels of the fortress. Solís did a better job lifting his feet and only found himself stuck twice more before reaching the exterior fortress doors. Upon exiting, Luna led him across a giant moon thread they had not walked previously. The magnetic threads Luna had attached to his ankles upon his arrival yanked toward the giant tightrope, adding a level of security for Solís.

They crossed three threads and four meteor platforms before Luna came to a stop.

"We're here."

Solís's golden eyes filled with bright anticipation—Emmeline was nearby.

They exited the large thread onto the platform of this meteor and Luna led him through a maze of rocky corridors. As the terrain flattened, a large structure with arching doorways appeared. It was carved into the meteor, top to bottom, and was filled with light.

Silhouettes of giant creatures sauntered back and forth in the open spaces.

"She's in there?" Solís asked through his mouthpiece.

Luna nodded.

A buzzing Lunarian with yellow and black ribbons tied to her wrists and neck appeared. She was small, flighty, and covered in silver pollen.

"You requested a bundle of oxygeni blossoms?" she asked.

"Yes, thank you, Antho Devorah," Luna replied.

Devorah sneezed, causing her to shake with a shiver, and the pollen latched to her dispelled with the blast. Solís covered his face, but he wasn't quick enough, and the silver grit got into his nose.

He sneezed as well.

"Sorry about that," Devorah offered. Her silver eyes held streaks of gold.

"Will it make me sick?" he asked through the regulator as he rubbed his eyes.

"It's oxygeni pollen. Should help you, actually."

Luna asked, "Is there a way to get the flowers' magic into his breathing tank?"

Devorah tilted her head in consideration. "If you crush the bundle and seal them in there, perhaps."

"Is that possible?" Luna asked Solís.

Solís shook his head and removed his mouthpiece. "It's airtight; the top doesn't screw off. We'd need a valve, hose, and gauge at the bare minimum."

"Then it looks like you'll be on a diet of flower petals until we get you home," Luna said, shoving the bouquet of blossoms into Solís's chest. He ripped five of the cerulean petals off one of the flowers and tossed them into his mouth. A few chomps of his teeth ground the petals to small flecks, and their potent magic filled him with oxygen. He could breathe again.

Solís inhaled deeply, enjoying the simple sensation he so often took for granted.

"Better?" Luna asked.

"Much. Thanks." Solís wrapped the long tube attached to the regulator around the empty tank on his back and then shoved the stems of the remaining flowers into the belt of his pants. "Can we see Emmeline now?"

"We can," Luna answered, then addressed the bee gardener. "Thanks again, Devorah."

"Yes, thank you," Solís added.

"My pleasure."

Devorah departed with a bumbling buzz.

Luna led Solís through the large archway, to which they emerged upon a bustling scene of Mantos and Coccinellies attending to various rooms of concealed patients.

"These other Lunarians … they look nothing like you," Solís said in shock.

"You've only seen Odonata warriors in Quintessence; we are the only ones who travel through those portals. The long lanky Lunarians are Mantos. They are scientists, designed in the image of a praying mantis."

"I have distant memories of dragonflies and bumblebees and butterflies from my time spent inside mortals on Earth, long before I was given this body. The humans called them bugs."

"Insects, yes. Lunéss chose these forms for us with anatomical and breathing modifications. She felt these designs would best suit our needs."

Solís observed the creatures bustling around the room, searching his memory for terminology he hadn't heard since leaving the mortal bodies his infant soul had grown within.

"Are the little round ones called ladybugs?"

"Coccinelli, yes—they are Lunarian medics and they are designed in the image of ladybugs."

"It's all very interesting," Solís said, dropping his judgment for a brief moment.

Luna smiled, enjoying this rare occurrence—Solís never lowered his defenses.

Solís continued, "And you use the source flame as protection against the Marzans?"

"That's one use. Our main use is to keep the earthlings alive. Without untraceable waves of heat from the moon, the humans would die the moment their side of Earth turned away from the sun. Heat from the moon keeps the nighttime temperatures livable."

"We have no issue with the mortals; we serve them, too," Solís said, deep in thought. "Why would Solédon pit us against you when our end goal is the same?"

"There are lots of theories, many revolving around Kólasi— He's always had it out for Gaia's beloved mortals."

"You think the god of chaos is in Solédon's ear, orchestrating our rivalries?"

"Seems possible. We suspect He is in Lunéss's ear, too."

"This is a lot to consider."

"The fact that you are considering it at all is a great start."
Solís huffed, his guard returning. "Where is Emmeline?"

"Follow me."

She led him through the chaotic medical room. Alcoves carved into the meteor held countless patients, all of whom were Lunarians. Solís peeked into every opening they passed.

"Why are they here?" he asked.

"Many have the same affliction as your sister—Marzan poisoning. Others are here due to routine work injuries."

"Do they need Marzan blood to heal also?"

"No, it latches to us differently. Instead of cementing to our insides, like it did to Emmeline, it seeps into our flesh as a vapor. It takes a lot of time, patience, and steam therapy for a Lunarian to heal from Marzan poison."

Luna stopped before reaching the last door along this stretch of hallway.

"Are you ready?"

Solís pushed past Luna, darting into the room where Emmeline lay.

Motionless, unconscious, his sister was comatose on a stone slab with black and silver cords threaded through her nose and out of her mouth. Her golden flesh lacked luster.

"Are you sure she's alive?" he asked.

"She is very much alive," Luna promised. She handed the vial of Marzan blood to one of the Mantos. "This team has been working hard on healing her, day in and day out. The ointment they make from this blood should be the last step in her recovery."

"Sit down," one of the Mantos instructed him as he sauntered by, long limbs swaying with each step.

Solís sat on a part of the rock wall that jutted out like a chair. Luna stood next to him.

"That is Manto Bogo. The other is Manto Maldi. They are two of the best scientists in Mōnalene."

"And what about the medics?"

"Coccinelli Marietta is the one greasing Emmeline's gears. Coccinelli Katica is monitoring her vitals and marble intake."

"How is she breathing?"

"Coccinelli Marietta has been crushing oxygeni flowers into her mouth."

Solís observed, unable to argue as Emmeline appeared to be in good hands.

"She is going to fight to stay once she learns what happened to Louie," Luna commented.

"That's why we aren't going to tell her," Solís replied.

"We have to … "

"What we *have* to do is get her home to Quintessence."

Luna responded with an outraged glare.

Solís added, "I will tell her once she is safe at home."

"She'll just beg me to bring her back."

"But you won't."

"I might."

"No, you won't," Solís insisted. "Not if you want me to help you ensure an alliance with my people."

"You want to leave Louie to die?"

"You are more than welcome to send a rescue team, but his recovery is at the bottom of my list of concerns," Solís said, sensing the harshness of his reply, then added, "When I return to Quintessence, I will consult with the heads of each faction and see if we have the resources or ability to aid in Louie's rescue. It's just not my top focus at the moment."

"Emmeline will hate you when she learns that you left without trying."

"My priority is delivering my sister home. I told Louie not to come here. It's not my duty to save him after he ignored my warnings."

Luna shook her head. "I don't think this will play out like you hope."

Emmeline fidgeted on the table—it was the first time she had moved since their arrival.

Solís jumped out of his chair to get a better view.

Manto Bogo was slowly unthreading the cords from her nose and mouth while Manto Maldi mixed the goopy Marzan blood into a jar of moon dust and turned it into a sparkling purple paste. With a scalpel, he carved out miniscule portions of the paste and spread it onto the insides of Emmeline's nostrils. Manto Bogo pulled the final thread from Emmeline's nose and she twitched again.

Manto Maldi finished spreading the paste into her nose and stepped back.

"It shouldn't take long to dissipate the poison," he said.

He was right.

In a matter of moments, Emmeline sneezed so hard her body shot upright and hard chunks of poison covered in purple paste rocketed across the room.

She sneezed three more times, clearing what was left of the poison out of her nose.

Emmeline inhaled dramatically, as if breathing for the first time in months, then opened her eyes.

Golden glow returned, Emmeline was fully awake.

Chapter 16

"I was in the darkness for so long," she expressed as the medics removed her restraints.

"You're back now," Luna assured her. "You are fully healed and won't be going back there."

"I am healed?"

"Yes. In addition to my curse, you also had Marzan poison in your nostrils."

"Marzan?" Emmeline asked.

"Devil of Delusion," Solís said, stepping into the conversation.

Emmeline's attention turned at the sound of his voice. Elated, eyes filled with oily tears, relief transformed her worried expression.

"Solís!" she exclaimed, trying not to hyperventilate with happiness. "How are you here?"

"You think I wouldn't come looking for you?"

"How did you know I was here?" She paused as all the crisscrossing information flooded her mind. "You let them finish their work?"

"I've seen a lot of things I hadn't expected to see upon arriving here. And though I was resistant to trust them, it seems I was right in doing so."

"I am so relieved," she expressed. "We have to relay their kindness to our people. The Solarpunks need to know that the Lunarians aren't monsters."

"Slow down," Solís said. "We need to get you back on your feet first."

"I'm healed," she insisted, jumping off the bed and landing with a wobble.

"You should take it slow," Luna confirmed.

"Can you send us back to Quintessence now?" Solís asked Luna.

"We should figure out a plan first."

"What do you mean?"

"To initiate our alliance."

"Like you said," Solís replied. "Emmeline should take it slow."

"We still need assurance that you will follow through on your end of this deal."

"You can trust me," Emmeline insisted. "I will spread the news far and wide. Visit me on my rooftop in a week and I'll have an update for you."

"Okay," Luna agreed, trusting Emmeline, but wary of Solís.

"Great, now take us back to Quintessence," Solís demanded.

"It can't be me," Luna revealed, eyeing Solís with warning.

"Why not?" Emmeline asked.

"My stone," Luna began, to which Solís's eyes widened with realization. "It's not in Quintessence anymore."

"Where is it?" Emmeline inquired.

Luna inhaled, holding it for a moment and gauging Solís's horrified expression that urged her to conceal the truth. She exhaled.

"It's on Deimos, a moon of Mars."

"How?"

Solís cut in, "It's a long story, one I can tell you once we're safely home." He looked to Luna. "Who will bring us home?"

"I'll request Odonata Arche for this mission. I'll also accompany you both with a new, curse-free portal stone, one you can keep close so I can travel back and forth again."

"No more moonstones," Solís objected.

"I wasn't talking to you. I was talking to Emmeline."

"Sounds like a perfect plan to me," Emmeline agreed.

Luna added, "You will spend the night here and we will leave in the morning."

"Why such a long wait?"

"You are not our only obligation. Odonata Arche, who I hope agrees to this mission, is likely swarmed with other tasks following the altercation with the Marzans. You will need to be patient," Luna said, her tone stern.

"We are grateful, and we can certainly be patient," Emmeline replied.

Luna nodded and then departed.

Emmeline and Solís waited in the laboratory while the Mantos and Coccinellies cleaned up the workspace. Neither spoke as they observed—they felt suddenly vulnerable without Luna there as their advocate.

"I wish Luna would hurry back," Solís said, squirming with discomfort in this foreign place.

"I knew you'd see her as an ally if you gave her a chance."

Solís shook his head. "I still see her as the enemy. She's just a little less threatening now."

"She saved my life, and you still don't trust her?"

"No."

"You're impossible."

Coccinelli Marietta reentered the room. "Your cots are ready," she said, then led them to a neighboring room to rest.

Luna returned the following morning with Odonata Arche. While he fidgeted, tapping his foot and swaying in place, Luna appeared revitalized and excited. She held a gleaming moonstone in her hands. She extended it to Emmeline, who recoiled at the offer.

"There's no curse attached to this one," Luna assured her. "It's clean."

Emmeline took the stone with her bare hands and felt no magic pull or overwhelming sensation. Reassured, she placed the stone into her pocket.

Luna continued, "You ought to take the rest of this salve also." She placed the glass jar of moon dust mixed with Marzan blood into a satchel. Then added a few Lunarian metal syringes. "What's in the jar should be enough to heal most of your people—you only need a small drop for each infection. But in case you need more Marzan blood, you can have these, too. The Formies made a few extra."

Luna thrust the satchel at Solís.

"That is so generous," Emmeline expressed. "Thank you."

Arche arrived and stood an entire head taller than Solís.

"Are you ready?" Arche asked, his voice raspy and meek. His large silver eyes were amplified by the magnified spectacles strapped to his head.

"We are," Solís answered.

"Take my hands," he instructed.

Emmeline immediately grabbed his left hand, while Solís hesitated before grabbing his right.

Arche's long silver fingers were cold and his palms were clammy. The armor-plated flesh on the back of his hand was smooth to the touch.

Luna placed her hand on Arche's shoulder.

Arche muttered the incantation under his breath, careful not to say it too loud, as he did not trust the Solarpunks, and the foursome swiftly entered the portal.

The moon was dark with a dusty silver glow; this portal was also dark, but the neon pastels of the cosmos illuminated this temporary space.

Emmeline squirmed with discomfort as they teleported—her newly healed insides lurched with a firm tug. She glanced at Solís, who had his eyes squeezed shut and wore a look of nausea as they crossed through the portal.

Though they moved with the speed of a blink, it was long enough to recognize and process the aching pull. It was long enough to notice her awe-inspiring surroundings. As Emmeline let the swirling colors soothe her discomfort, all of it was stripped away and replaced with the golden warmth of home.

The gilded glow arrived like a blast, and all four travelers had to close their eyes a moment to adjust to the sudden brightness.

Emmeline and Solís reopened theirs first, soon followed by Luna and Arche.

"It never gets easier," Luna said, blinking her wide silver eyes rapidly to help facilitate the transition.

The foursome remained under Arche's invisibility shield.

"Why are we over the Terrapunk city?" Solís asked, taking in the unexpected view of giant skyscrapers made of golden beams, gears, and springs.

"We scattered some portals across Quintessence so that we'd have the option to travel anywhere on the sun that we choose," Luna answered.

Arche squirmed uncomfortably—his distaste for her candor was apparent.

"I need to get back," Arche said.

"My tank is empty," Solís said, taking in their predicament. "I can't fly us anywhere until I refill it with helium."

"I can try to heat my heart," Emmeline offered. "I just don't know if I can carry your weight along with mine."

"No need," Luna cut in. "I will take you wherever you want to go before I depart. Arche, you can leave. I'll take it from here."

She grabbed Emmeline and Solís by their wrists, channeled her warrior rage, and as soon as her strength was engaged, Arche let go of the Solarpunks and departed through the portal.

Silver eyes coated in black, inner threads tangled with discord—Luna once again looked like the hellions Solís and Emmeline were trained to despise.

Solís scoffed and averted his gaze.

"Where would you like to go?" Luna asked.

"Let's try our house first."

"No," Solís objected. "The Pyro-Argo air base. I can refill my tank there."

"As you wish," Luna said before directing her flight toward the floating hangar base.

When they arrived, Luna lowered them carefully in a spot where no other Solarpunks were gathered.

The moment she let them go, they were no longer concealed within her invisibility shield.

"You can go home now," Solís stated.

"Are you sure?" Luna asked.

"Yes. Once my tank is refilled with helium, I can take us wherever we need to go."

"Don't worry," Emmeline said. "I am determined to shift the Solarpunks' perception of your people. If things go my way, we will be forming an official alliance soon."

"I'll check back in a week, like we agreed," Luna confirmed.

"Perfect!"

As Luna vanished through the portal, so did the faint scent of moon lilies.

Solís sniffed the air.

"She's gone," he confirmed.

"You need to be nicer to her. She's our ally."

"Not yet, she isn't."

Emmeline scoffed. "Are you even allowed to fill your tank when you aren't on duty? I thought the Aeropunks strictly regulated the helium."

"Things have changed a bit since you left. Avery filled us in on what you were working on with her, and we agreed to help. In addition to searching for you, we spent the last few weeks destroying our alliance with the Holloways in order to allow the Morrells to reclaim leadership. Things are still tense, but the Morrells now govern the Pilopunks and Argopunks, while the Holloways govern the gas spinners."

"How did this come about?"

"Avery and Remington dueled."

"To the death?"

"No, of course not. We live in evolved times. Whoever surrendered or depleted their helium heart first lost. It was a good battle, but Remington expended his helium faster than Avery and ended up losing."

"So, I missed the whole revolution?" Emmeline asked, grateful that Avery had succeeded but disappointed that she hadn't really helped at all.

"I personally don't think the Holloways are done fighting for total control of the Aeropunks, but for now, things are calm. And a perk of Avery winning is that we have freer access to helium. She has allowed us to fill our tanks at our discretion. She believes that those who sacrifice their lives to protect Quintessence should not be told when they can and can't fly — they should be allowed to fly into duty on a moment's notice."

"She is so smart," Emmeline stated, proud of her friend.

"In exchange, we keep the firestone bin heated at all times. Argopunks have unlimited access to activated firestones."

"That's a fair trade," Emmeline noted, futilely trying to silence the disappointment she felt for having missed all of this. "Well," she said, "you better fill up your tank so we can get going."

"I'm on it," Solís agreed before departing.

While he replenished his tank at the backside of the base, Emmeline went to the communal marble jar to test her ability to eat. The room was empty — no Pyropunks or Argopunks in sight. The tall glass jar was filled with marbles from all factions of Quintessence: clear glass, sea glass, obsidian rock, hardened clay. With countless colors and weights, Emmeline had plenty to choose from.

She stuck her hand into the jar and ran her fingers over the marbles. All smooth, but with different textures. She plucked a single glass marble out of the bunch. Its weight was light and felt like a safe place to start.

The glass marble rolled down her tongue and landed in her throat's holding pan with a clang, then continued its roll into her intricate system of chutes and gears. She had a few marbles nearing the end of their journey, so the addition of this new marble reinvigorated the speed with which her gears turned.

Emmeline waited a moment, wincing in anticipation, but she remained migraine free.

She ate another.

No pain.

Five marbles later, more than she had eaten in one sitting since acquiring the curse, and she was migraine free and feeling more energized than she had in a long time.

"Solís!" she exclaimed, excited to tell him the news, but as she turned the corner, she was greeted by a different Pyropunk.

"Little Dawes," he said, eyes alight with surprise. "You're alive!"

Emmeline furrowed her brow as she recalled his name. "Kiran?"

"You remembered," he said with a smile. "We've been looking for you. All of us. Everyone will be so happy to see that you're alive and seemingly healthy."

"I am better than I was before leaving," she confirmed.

"Can you still fly?" he asked.

"I haven't gotten the chance to try yet."

Kiran looked over his shoulder, then back to her. "There's no one around to watch besides me. Give it a go."

"I did just refuel," she said, more so to herself.

"I won't judge if it takes a few tries," he offered, his tone sincere. "And it's better than trying alone. I'll be here to catch you if you fall."

Emmeline eyed him with curiosity. She hardly knew him—they only had a brief encounter before she left for the moon, yet she believed the loyalty he offered was genuine.

His bright golden eyes glimmered with kindness.

"I believe in you," he offered.

The hope she had inspired in the Solarpunks before leaving still shone through him.

"Okay," she conceded. "I'll try."

"Excellent!"

As Emmeline began heating her heart, Kiran asked the question she had expected to hear first.

"So, where did you go? You were gone a while."

She hesitated, then replied, "It's best that you find out when everyone else does."

Kiran nodded and did not press the issue.

Emmeline's golden flesh began to glow red with the scorching hot fire of the sun. Her source flame heart heated to its highest temperature, and her tiny body began to lift toward the vaulted ceiling.

"You're doing it!" Kiran said.

"I wish I was wearing my wings. I can't fly or control my direction without them."

"The fact that you can still float means you'll be able to fly as soon as you have your wings."

He was right.

Emmeline grinned.

She could finish the work she had started before leaving.

"What is going on here?" Solís barked as he entered the room.

His abrupt entrance startled Emmeline, forcing her to lose her concentration and plummet out of the sky. A decent drop, one that would surely break a few bones, but Kiran leapt into action and caught her before she hit the ground.

She exhaled with relief.

"I told you I'd catch you," he said softly, his eyes twinkling and expression gentle.

"Thank you," she said before squirming out of his arms, then asked Solís, "Why'd you scare me like that?"

"You're supposed to be resting and healing!" he challenged.

"Kiran was here to make sure nothing bad happened."

"Why *are* you here?" Solís asked Kiran.

"Because I live here?" he said, sounding confused. "I'm not on shift until later tonight and I couldn't sleep. I heard commotion, so I came out to see what was going on."

Solís's scrutinizing gaze shifted between Kiran and Emmeline a few times before he responded.

"I suppose this is better than the pirate."

"Huh?" Kiran said.

Emmeline gasped, mortified by her brother's comment. Then a surge of guilt coursed through her—her thoughts were on flying instead of seeing Louie, her family, or her friends again.

"I need to see everyone," Emmeline said to Solís. "We need to get going."

"My tank is refilled. Let's go."

"Can I come?" Kiran asked.

"What for?" Solís countered.

"I can't sleep. And maybe I can help."

"We don't need your help."

"How can you be so sure?"

"Oh, just let him come," Emmeline interjected, her patience waning. She wanted to see her loved ones again. Louie most of all.

"Fine," Solís said. "Emmeline—climb on my back."

Emmeline obliged, securely wrapping her arms around her brother's neck.

Solís took off.

Kiran followed close behind.

They flew through the warm air of Quintessence, moving at such great speeds their trek appeared as rocketing orbs of fire to anyone watching. They made a quick pit stop at the Daweses family mansion and were greeted by empty rooms and darkness. No one was home.

"Not even Mom?" Emmeline asked as she exited the gilded great room.

"She's been in Hydra a lot lately with Dad," Solís replied, then looked to Kiran. "I thought Helix would be here. Wasn't he supposed to be bedridden as he healed?"

"He was," Kiran replied, his expression forlorn. "I have a guess where he might be."

"And where is that?"

"Where he gets his locomo in Terra."

Solís growled. "We don't have time for this. I'll have to look for him later."

As the trio exited the kitchen onto the attached deck, Cyrus came flying toward them. His eyes filled with oily tears at the sight of Emmeline.

"Emmie!" he shouted, cranking open the valve of his helium tank and pounding his wings to fly faster. He landed on the deck with a stumbling run and buried Emmeline in his arms. "I was so worried I'd never see you again."

"I missed you, too," she said, hugging him back and enjoying the comfort of his embrace. "I only left so I could heal."

Hands still on her shoulders, Cyrus leaned back.

"Are you healed?"

"I am," she answered.

"That's what matters most."

"Are Mom and Dad in Hydra?" Solís asked Cyrus.

"Yeah, I left to check on Helix."

"He isn't here," Solís informed him. "Kiran thinks he might be in Terra."

Cyrus threw his head back in aggravation and released a groan.

Solís added, "I'm reuniting Emmeline with Mom and Dad before I deal with Helix."

"Rightfully so," Cyrus agreed. "I'd like to see that reunion as well. All of Quintessence—Thermapunks, Hydropunks, Aeropunks, and most Terrapunks—will be thrilled by her return." Cyrus looked to Emmeline. "All the work you did to unite the factions has had a lasting effect, even in your absence."

"I was worried my absence would cause confusion and hope would be lost," she confessed.

"Nope. You showed them what was possible, and they never let go of that potential."

Emmeline smiled.

"Come with us to Hydra," Solís said to his brother. "We can deal with Helix after Emmeline is safe on Dad's ship."

"Sounds like a plan."

Cyrus joined them on their journey to Hydra. As soon as they lowered through the gate and reached Montgomery's ship, Cyrus's statement was proven correct. Every Nautipunk ship within eyesight halted and each crew member looked up at them in awe. The Thermapunks on Montgomery's ship hooted and hollered upon seeing Emmeline on Solís's back.

"What's the commotion?" Montgomery barked, nose deep into the map marked with all the locations they had already searched for his daughter.

Standing beside him was Avery, who grabbed the pair of binoculars hanging around Montgomery's neck to make sure what she was seeing was accurate.

"She's back," Avery said, her relief apparent.

"Who?" Montgomery asked, heart rate increasing.

"Look."

Avery lifted the binoculars to Montgomery's eyes.

"Emmeline," he said, his hope a hushed whisper. He snatched the binoculars and increased the magnification. "Is it true?"

He lowered the binoculars, squeezed his eyes shut momentarily, then looked through the magnified lenses again.

"It's her," he said, emotion shaking the words as they left his mouth. He lowered the binoculars and raised his arms. "My girl!" he shouted.

Montgomery darted toward the starboard gunwale. Cyrus, Kiran, Solís, and Emmeline slowed their flight and lowered toward him. As soon as they landed, Emmeline jumped off Solís's back and ran to her father.

He enveloped her in a hug filled with gratitude.

Emmeline absorbed his love, and a surge of thankfulness coursed through her as well. It wasn't until this moment, until feeling the extinguished grief of her father and his resulting joy, that she realized how closely she had toed the line of life and death. He held onto her with such fervor, such desperation, as if this hug was a gift he'd once thought he'd never get to experience again.

Emmeline cried. She felt terrible for making him suffer in this way.

"I'm sorry," she offered.

"I'm so happy to have you back," he replied. "I was beginning to worry I'd lost you forever."

"I came back as soon as I could. I'm sorry I left without explanation and caused you to worry, but once I explain everything, you'll understand."

Montgomery kissed the top of Emmeline's head. "You're home now. That's all that matters."

Melora burst out of her cabin, golden eyes ablaze with panic.

"Where is she?" she shouted, pushing through the crowd of Thermapunks to get to her daughter.

"Hey, Mom," Emmeline said.

"You are alive!" She grabbed Emmeline by the wrist, yanked her out of Montgomery's embrace, and pulled her close. For the first time since she was a child, she felt comfort in her mother's arms. "So much time had passed with no sign of your whereabouts," she said, holding back tears and choking on her words. "I feared you might be dead."

"I'm sorry that I worried you. It will all make sense soon, I promise."

Melora released a long-held grunt of frustration and let Emmeline go—expressing emotion was not her strong suit.

"Where were you? Why did you tell no one of your whereabouts before leaving?" Melora inquired.

Montgomery cut in, "Give her a minute. She just got back."

"Avery! Gemma!" Emmeline exclaimed as her friends pushed through the bodies of the Thermapunk crew to get to her.

They shared a group hug before Emmeline noticed a member of their crew was missing.

"Where is Clementine?"

"She's a slave to the sea," Gemma answered.

Avery leaned in and whispered, "Are you healed?"

"I am."

Gemma's silver eyes lit up. "Can I be healed, too?"

"Yes. I will help you and Clementine heal. I just need to figure out the logistics."

Emmeline looked past her friends, searching for the one face she wished to see most.

"Where is Louie?" she asked.

"He left through the portal to find you," Avery answered.

"The moonstone portal?"

"Yes. I told him not to go, but he wouldn't listen."

Fear and fury intertwined, Emmeline charged Solís.

"You were there! Where is he?" she asked her brother.

"Who?"

"You know who," Emmeline replied, tone seething.

"It's complicated. We should go somewhere to talk … "

"Where is he?" she repeated, her anger growing. "Tell me!"

Solís hesitated before answering.

"Louie is on Deimos."

Chapter 17

Deimos

Louie was strapped to a giant red rock on the lower deck of the ship. Hands and ankles bound, he was rendered immobile.

The normal buzzing hum of the mooncraft flying through space ceased without warning, and the ship landed with a resounding thud.

Louie gulped.

He was a prisoner on a foreign moon.

Far from the sun and the ocean that he called home, Louie prepared for the worst. The moonstone was tucked away in an interior pocket of his cargo pants. It was his one chance for rescue—he had to keep it hidden.

"Oh, fire boy!" a slimy, croaking voice taunted.

Louie could not determine the source or from where they approached. The room he was imprisoned in had countless doors and staircases surrounding the rock he was strapped to.

"I have no fire," he replied.

"Even better. Fire is a foe."

Louie furrowed his brow, perplexed by their statement.

"Fire gives life to whichever poor mortals you were tasked to serve."

"There are no mortals on Mars," they answered, stepping into view. The shadows blocked the details of their face, but Louie could now see the outline of their body. "Lunéss betrayed us in our creation—She gave us bodies that need cold in a galaxy tormented by heat."

"I'm sorry to hear of your suffering."

"You aren't," they spat, stepping closer.

Louie held his breath, unsure what this monster had planned for him. The other side of captivity felt strange—normally, *he* wrangled monsters into cages, not the other way around.

"What do you want from me?" Louie asked. "Why did you bring me here?"

"To learn, to study, to strategize. Despite our long history, we know little about the Solarpunks. How are you made? How do you fight? What are your strengths and weaknesses? To free ourselves from the fire, we need to fully understand the enemy who stands in our way."

Louie did not like these implications. "You can never be free of fire. The sun is a permanent fixture in this galaxy."

The devil stepped into the dim light—it was the king. His bloodshot eyes looked drier than usual and he wore a wretched expression of disgust for Louie.

"Seems you don't know all that much about us either," King Helmer said with a sneer.

"Tell me, then," Louie bartered.

"What's the point? You will never leave this place."

Louie silenced the tidal wave growing in his heart. Thinking quick, he flipped the narrative.

"If I'll never leave here, then what's the harm in telling me?"

The devil grinned. "Imagine dying with the knowledge that could have saved your people and your home. What a terrible dishonor."

"One I am sure you will bestow upon me."

"Perhaps. For now, my only concern is transporting you."

"Where?"

"To a place where they'll never find you," King Helmer replied. He placed his fingers into his mouth, produced an earsplitting whistle, and then shouted, "Guards!"

Four giant devils entered the room.

They uncoiled the chain-link rope holding Louie to the red boulder, and then forced him to his feet. King Helmer knotted a blindfold over his eyes. Wrists and ankles still bound, Louie couldn't run or fight back. And even if he could, where would he go?

His fate was at their mercy.

The four guards lifted him and carried him out of the mooncraft cellar.

Louie couldn't see where they were taking him, but he sensed they were traveling downward.

Darkness, then blinding light accompanied by the chattering metal teeth of what sounded like a horde of devils watching his transport.

When the noise ceased, so did the light, and darkness resumed.

Louie tried to count the turns, but without his own two feet on the ground, it was difficult to determine which way they carried him. And after ten turns, all of which he made guesses on the direction, Louie stopped trying. He'd have to find another way out of this nightmare.

When they finally placed him back onto his feet, it felt like a few hours had passed.

"Are we at my final destination?" Louie asked.

"Don't talk," one of the guards quipped in reply.

They pushed him up against a wall, fastened the chains on his ankles and wrists to anchors, and then removed his blindfold. The room was small, circular, and damp. It reeked of mold and blood. The walls and floors were made of solid red stone, and though he did not know the stone's density, its cold temperature, solid texture, and the lack of sound in the room made him suspect it was impenetrable. In fact, it felt as if this room was a stone coffin carved into the center of the moon. Louie cringed; this suffocating prison was his new home.

"I am Balor. This is Anwir," the guard stated, pointing to himself and the guard beside him. They were massive—bulging muscles with chainmail armor under a thin layer of flesh, blue eyes bloodshot with hollow fury, and blood-red hair shaved close to their scalps. They were covered in scars, many of which looked intentional. At the napes of their necks they wore a scarred branding of two interlinked circles.

Balor continued, "You'll be seeing a lot of us."

Louie scanned the coffin-like room.

"No windows?" he asked.

The guards laughed. "Windows to what? All that exists beyond these walls is more stone."

"Where do I sleep?"

Balor waved his arm at the knee-high boulders that lined the room, which were lumpy, curved, and not very wide.

"Take your pick," he answered.

Louie sighed. "Why am I chained to the wall if the door to this room locks?"

"We don't know what powers you have yet. Keeping you bound by Marzan chains ensures there's no trickery."

Louie fell to his knees.

"This is it, huh?" he said. "This is how it ends."

"For you, it appears so," Balor replied. He placed five red rock marbles beside Louie and then followed Anwir out of the room, locking the door behind him. The dim glow from the corridor was blocked and only a miniscule amount of light filtered through a barred rectangular door window. The room was a giant shadow, and in the darkness, Louie noticed that the glow came from the red rock.

There was no fire here, only the natural light that emanated from the terrain.

They left him alone in this room for days.

Louie didn't know how many—there was no outside light to indicate time—but based on his body's pull to slumber, he had been chained to this wall for at least four days.

They rolled five red rock marbles to him at sporadic intervals. Was it morning? Was it night? The time that passed between meals was inconsistent and did not help Louie gauge the days lost.

Quiet, isolated, doomed—Louie regretted using the moonstone portal. He had only been on the Moon of Fixation for a few minutes before getting swept off into a far worse situation. He never even saw Emmeline.

Louie felt like an idiot.

He touched the pocket where the moonstone hid.

Would the incantation he used previously work here? He did not suspect so.

He whispered the words anyway.

"Ad lunam lu. Accipe me."

To his surprise, his body lurched forward, yanking on the chains that kept him bound. He was not whisked away, his constraints to the red rock wall stopped him, but it was clear that the moment the chains were removed, escape was possible.

"It could work," he said in a hushed voice, hope restored.

He began picking at the skin beneath his wrist chains, attempting to make himself a fraction smaller so he could wriggle his hands free. But the chains were shackled too tight— no amount of flesh carving would make his hands or feet small enough to fit through.

Another day, or maybe two, passed.

They rolled five red rock marbles to him beneath the door.

"I need grease, too, you know," he said after his next delivery of marbles.

"What's grease?" a guard asked through the small window of Louie's door.

"Oily liquid to lubricate my gears."

The guard huffed. "We don't have that here, but I'll see what I can do. We need you in working order for your interrogation."

"Interrogation? I've been here for days! Shouldn't that have happened by now?"

The guard laughed. "Time is an illusion."

"Time exists," Louie argued, "it's just harder to keep track of in here."

"I'd stop trying to count the days if I were you. You'll only torture yourself."

The guard left the outside of Louie's door.

Alone again.

He whispered, "Ad lunam lu. Accipe me."

His body lurched, but he remained in this prison. The chain-link restraints kept him bound.

The portal would not work until he was set free from these chains.

Another delivery of marbles.
And then another.
How much time had passed?
He touched the pocket where the stone hid.
No one was coming for him.
He festered in solitude, alone with his deteriorating thoughts. The spiral he traveled hit depths he never knew existed. Dark, cold spaces in his mind—spots so ominous and deep, he lost sight of reality. There was no use climbing out of this negative headspace, for what waited above was far worse—he was a prisoner in enemy territory.
And no one was coming to rescue him.
Face pressed against the floor, staring at one of the few cracks in the foundation, Louie spiraled.
He fell deeper and deeper into regretful despair, losing count of the days as he disassociated from his current situation.
He chose depression over hope.
He chose surrender.
Curled into a fetal position, Louie detached himself from his mind.
Red rock marbles collected all around him.
Emptied and hollow, he lay motionless, waiting for death.

Another delivery of marbles.
They rolled and hit him in the face.
When he opened his eyes, he saw his mother's face. Long lost to the sea, she greeted him with a smile.
"Is it over?" he asked, lips cracked and bleeding. "Am I dead yet?"
Sub Anne Marie shook her head.
Louie's dry eyes struggled to produce tears, but his body convulsed with sobs.

"If I am seeing you, I must be dead, too," he tried to rationalize.

She smiled gently at him, her expression filled with love.

He held tight to the vision of his deceased mother.

It was the only comfort he had.

"He stopped pulling against the chains," said Balor, lead Marzan guard.

"Did he say anything during those attempts?" King Helmer asked, peering through the small window of the Solarpunk's door.

"Nothing coherent."

"How long has he been in this state of surrender?"

"One full rotation around Mars," Balor answered.

"He has only been with us for four days," King Helmer said with glee. "His mental deterioration is happening quicker than I expected."

"He is so disassociated, I don't think he even felt it when we greased his gears."

"Good. We need him wholly broken."

"Are you sure? He will neither show nor tell us his secrets in this state."

"Yes. Let him fester like this for a few more days. Then, when we gift him sunlight and hope, he will cower with gratitude and oblige my every request."

"Only if he's still functioning by then. He has stopped eating."

"Force the marbles down this throat," Helmer instructed. "Also, strip him of his clothes and put him into a uniform. When he reawakens, he needs to feel as disconnected from his former self as possible."

"Understood. I will submit a request for a uniform. That will take a day or two."

"Call me when he is ready."

King Helmer departed and Balor went back to his station—a desk at the center of a large circular room lined with prison doors. Warden to all the prisoners of Deimos, Balor took his seat and crossed the wires that would connect him to the Spinner. He snapped his fingers, sending an electric current through the wires. A slight buzz and noticeable tremor shook the room as his message was sent.

Louie felt the ground quake. He opened his silver-blue eyes for the first time in hours and saw the tiny foundation crack under his cheek extend ever so slightly.

A miniscule fracture in an indestructible space.

There was no escape from this place.

Chapter 18

"Psst," a voice hissed.

Louie stirred—this voice was different from the ones chattering inside his mind.

"Wake up," the voice said.

"Mom?" Louie asked, opening his eyes to an empty room. He groaned, irritated that the figments of his imagination had interrupted his surrender.

"I'm under an invisibility shield," the voice explained.

He propped himself onto his elbow, brow furrowed with annoyance. He rubbed his eyes with his free hand. Vision still fuzzy from slumber, the red room appeared before him in a haze.

"Show yourself," he demanded in a low and tired voice.

A swift swoosh and the face of a hellion appeared. No body, no limbs, just a head.

Instinctively, Louie recoiled—the hellions had brought nothing but torment and despair. But as the shadows of his blurry vision subsided, the hellion's face became clear.

It—she—was beautiful: wide eyes bright with a silver glow, long eyelashes that fluttered gently with each blink, soft flesh with a silver sheen encasing her exquisite bone structure. Black cords revolved beneath, not in knots, but in fluid order. Louie had never seen a hellion so lovely.

"Who are you?"

"My name is Luna. We've already met. I am a friend of Emmeline."

The mention of Emmeline snapped Louie back to his senses. He scrambled upright, desperately shaking the melancholic fog from his mind.

"Is she okay?" he asked.

"She is healed. She is home."

"She's back in Quintessence?"

Luna nodded, eyes darting toward the door every few moments to watch for the guards.

"When?" Louie asked.

"The timing of your arrival in Mōnalene was tragic on a few levels. Primarily because it landed you here. But also because Emmeline finished healing right after the Marzans captured you. If you had waited a day, you would have been reunited on the sun."

"Instead, I'm in an inescapable prison run by Devils of Delusion." Louie sighed. "It gives me some relief to know she is alive and well, though."

"Don't lose hope," Luna advised. "Where is my moonstone?"

Louie tapped the side of his leg. "It belongs to you?"

"Yes."

"So, *you* cursed Emmeline?" he asked as he handed the wrapped stone to Luna.

"Inadvertently. I also helped her heal."

"It's hard to see you as anything other than a monster."

"You'll come around," Luna said, her tone patient with a hint of fatigue. "Right now, we need to hide the stone. When I arrived, they were talking about changing you into a uniform. If they find the stone, I won't be able to return and bring you home."

"Take me home now," Louie pled.

"I can't teleport back with you until you are free from those chains. They coated those chains with a special property that prevents portal transportation."

"Can't you cut them?"

"Not without clippers made of lunar metal. This visit was to assess your situation. I will return with a plan to get you home."

"I've been here for weeks," Louie griped.

"It's only been a few days. Three or four, if I'm recalling correctly."

"Really?" Louie's eyes filled with dread. "You have to get me out of here."

"I will, but first, we need to hide the moonstone."

"Where?"

Luna's head bobbed to the small window in his prison door. After a careful scan and deeming they were safe from being caught, she examined the room.

"Not many options, huh?" she noted. Her hand appeared from beneath her shield. As she walked the circumference of the room, her fingers ran along the row of red boulders lining the wall. "Maybe I can find a nook between these rocks. Do you think this room is your forever cage? Or will they move you again?"

"They implied that this would be where I spent the rest of my days, but who knows," Louie said. "I wish it was easier to die."

"Remove thoughts like that from your head. I will get you out of here," she promised.

"Why, though? Why are you even bothering?"

"I am trying to build goodwill between the sun and my moon."

"I hold no sway among the Solarpunks. I am not important; my vote doesn't matter."

"You matter to Emmeline."

"Maybe. But her family would likely argue that it's better I stay here. They see me as a threat to her future."

"Well, I don't agree. And Emmeline won't be able to focus on anything else until she knows you are safe."

"Is that why you're helping me? So that Emmeline can focus on the alliance?"

"It's not the only reason," Luna said with a huff. "I'm also helping you because it is the right thing to do."

As Luna traced the boulders with her hand, looking for a space to hide the stone, Louie rustled with discomfort.

"Does she know I'm here?"

"I'm not sure. Solís promised to tell her once they were home, but I'm not sure how reliable his promises are."

"Not very if they don't serve his wants and needs."

"Good news is that we don't need either of them to get you out of here. I have a new portal stone in Quintessence now, so I can bring you directly home when that day arrives. I just need to return with a tool to cut your chains." Her hand found a nook between two boulders large enough for their needs. "This will work," she said as she hid the stone.

Metal against rock thudded outside his door. The loud footsteps gave Louie a shiver.

"They will kill me."

"Not yet, they won't," Luna assured him in a low voice. "They want information. Give them scraps. Nothing of importance, just enough to keep you alive for a second round."

"A second round?"

Luna disappeared beneath her invisibility shield.

She whispered, "I'll get you out of here before that happens."

The doorknob rattled as they inserted the key.

"Time to go," Balor announced as he opened the door to Louie's prison.

"First, you need to strip and put on this uniform," Anwir added, throwing a pair of beige pants at Louie.

"Why do I need to change?"

"You need to match all the other prisoners."

"No shirt?" he asked.

"We need full access to your back," Anwir answered, wearing a grin as he cracked the chain-link whip in his grip.

Still chained to the wall, Louie quickly changed out of his clothes and into the pants they had given him. The moment his bare chest was exposed, the guards snickered.

"Only one set of scars?" Balor asked, pointing at claw marks on both of his collarbones.

"I got them saving the girl I love," Louie answered, his defiance rising.

"You're a blank canvas," Anwir stated, unable to mask his glee. "This will be fun."

Balor laughed and added, "You'll be adding quite a few more scars to your collection."

"Also, for her," Louie said under his breath.

The guards linked the chains around his wrists to the metal belts they wore, then disconnected the chains attached to the wall.

"Ad lunam lu. Accipe me," he whispered, so low it was incoherent to the guards. His stomach lurched, but the chains kept him bound.

"Stop rambling," Balor demanded.

Louie sobbed, collapsing between them. The chains on his wrists that were connected to their waistbands kept his arms elevated, but the rest of his body dragged on the ground. Balor and Anwir were massive in size and had no trouble lugging Louie's body weight.

His zinc ankle and knee gears scraped against the rocks, creating an awful screeching sound. The contact shaved away at his gears, corroding them with each step the guards took.

Louie looked over his shoulder.

The figment of his mother stood in the doorway of his cell and mouthed the word *survive*.

Chapter 19

Hydra, Quintessence

"The moon that orbits Mars?" Emmeline asked her brother.

"Yes, Deimos. It's where the Devils of Delusion reside."

"We have to help him!"

"I plan to, but the timing has to be right, or we could make the situation worse." Solís wore an expression of grave empathy. "Be patient. I won't let you down."

He kissed the top of her head, then darted down a series of golden ladders to the main deck.

Emmeline paced the top deck of her father's ship, glaring at the devil's cage.

Marzans, she recalled, having heard Luna say their proper name.

Emmeline knew nothing about Mars or Deimos except its placement within their galaxy. She knew nothing about the beings there except the horrible things she had witnessed through their most recently acquired prisoner. Dreadful, manipulative, poisonous—Louie had been captured by the most wretched of creatures.

As she marched the deck, stewing in her thoughts, a notion crossed her mind that she could not silence—what if the Marzans were as misunderstood as the Lunarians?

She shook her head.

Luna despised them, too.

But what if?

She glared at the captured devil in her faraway cage. The monstrous creature wailed a horrendous cry of sorrow. Its voice resonated so loudly, it caused all of Quintessence to tremor.

Emmeline covered her ears, halting her stride and crouching. All of Hydra stuttered to a stop as the sea quaked and the terrain pipes above rattled. How far did this cry travel? Who else heard her woeful torment?

As the brash sound faded into a soft echo, all the punks in Hydra cautiously returned to their tasks. Emmeline stood, glaring at the monster.

Luna wouldn't return for a few more days and none of the punks had extensive knowledge about the Marzans.

This devil was the only one who might give her insight regarding Louie's safety.

"Why are they waiting to kill that thing?"

Emmeline turned around to find Kiran.

"Now that I'm back, I'm sure it'll be exterminated soon," she answered him, rotating back to face the monster. "The timing of its demise depends on if we have enough of its blood to heal all the infected punks."

Kiran leaned against the railing next to Emmeline. His body beside hers, her mind flashed to memories of when she and Louie stood like this. Her heart swelled with heated pressure.

"I miss him terribly," she said.

Kiran jolted and took a small step away from Emmeline, giving her space.

"Who?"

"Oh, right. You wouldn't know him," Emmeline said, holding back the tears she wished to cry. "His name is Louie. He's a Nautipunk, and apparently, he's a prisoner on Deimos."

"Deimos?"

"One of two moons that serve Mars."

"*Mars*?" Kiran asked, his expression bewildered. "How did he end up there?"

Emmeline faced Kiran, taking him in for a moment before speaking. He squirmed as she scrutinized him.

"I feel like I can trust you," she finally said.

"You can."

"Helix never told you what happened to me?" she asked before saying more.

"No. He just mentioned that you were sick, but always followed it by saying that he was grateful that your illness came with blessings. Unlike his addiction."

"What blessings?" she asked.

"The ability to fly."

"Oh, right," she responded, feeling silly. "I'm so caught up in the new problems I face that I sometimes forget all that I went through to get here."

"You are healed and can still fly," he added. "Seems like an incredible blessing."

Emmeline nodded. Kiran's spirit lifted hers, and she found herself feeling immense gratitude. His openness calmed her tortured mind.

"Thank you," she offered.

"For what?"

"For listening. For saying that. My mind has been so dark; I need to stay in the light."

"Stick with me, then. I live in the light," he said with a smile.

Emmeline exhaled with relief.

He went on, "So tell me more about the devil's blood. Or where you went when we were all searching for you."

Emmeline paused. He'd learn the truth at some point, but perhaps if she told him now, he would offer some good advice on how to tell her parents.

"You'll need to have an open mind," she warned.

"I'm ready."

"The hellions aren't monsters."

"They're not?" he asked, his tone cautious.

"No. They don't come here to steal the source flame for themselves. They need it to keep their mortals alive."

"What does this have to do with your sickness or where you went?"

"I touched a moonstone. It was deep beneath the sea. When I made contact, it cursed me. I couldn't eat marbles without pain, so I stopped eating completely. Subsequently, I shrank in size. Then I became light enough to fly with fire. Problem was, the curse ran rampant in my body, and it would have eventually killed me. A Lunarian, which you know as a hellion, saved me. She took me to her moon and cleansed me of the curse."

"How did she know how to heal you?"

"Because the curse came from her moonstone."

"So, she caused all your suffering and then offered the remedy?"

"She didn't curse me intentionally. And the Lunarian scientists needed to learn how to heal me—it had never been done before. Her people hate Solarpunks. She risked everything to save me."

"While I'm happy she did all of that … why?" he asked gently.

"She wants to build an alliance between the Solarpunks and Lunarians."

"An alliance … to what end?"

"Wouldn't it be nice to have one less monster to fight?"

Kiran leaned back, visibly perplexed by her simple and logical reply.

"I suppose it would be," he answered.

"My issue now, and I hope you might have some helpful insight … how do I tell my parents? How do I get them to agree to work with the Lunarians?"

Kiran tilted his head. "That's a tough one. Your parents have lived numerous centuries with a deep hatred for moon monsters. That's a lot of deep coding to rewire." Kiran paused in thought. "But you might have the element of modernization working on your side. You've already crushed all perceived normalcies when you took to the sky. Maybe this won't be much harder than that."

"They did accept that change with relative ease," Emmeline said.

"Just maybe leave out the part about the hellion *giving* you the curse. If they know that she inadvertently hurt you, it might be harder for them to trust her."

"Good point," Emmeline said, taking mental notes.

The Marzan screeched again. Its piercing howl ricocheted off the tall ceiling of Hydra and caused a storm of waves.

Both Emmeline and Kiran crouched beside the gunwale, letting the short wall block some of the noise, and covered their ears to muffle the rest. They faced each other as they waited for it to subside. Emmeline held Kiran's gaze and mimicked his slow and methodical breaths. Within seconds, her panic was soothed.

The screech tapered back to the monster's usual soft whimper and the bustle of Hydra resumed.

"I wish they'd kill it already," Kiran said, then revealed, "We can hear it above Hydra, too."

"I was wondering how far its cries reached."

"It's awful. All the gears rattle. The Tinkerpunks are constantly fixing loose screws and bolts due to this monster. They ought to kill it before it ruins everything we've worked so hard to build and maintain."

"I'll mention it to my father," Emmeline said.

"Mention what to me?"

Emmeline and Kiran whipped around to find Montgomery approaching. His shaggy, golden-brown hair was held back by a pair of ocular goggles strapped to his head.

"Hey, Dad," Emmeline greeted.

"Were you two discussing that impetuous monster?" he asked. "Trust me, I know. We will put it out of its misery soon."

"Yeah, we were just talking about the devil and how we worry its screams might destroy Quintessence from the inside out."

"The Horrigans have a crew specifically tasked to repair all the damage the screams cause."

"I'm surprised they're willing to help," Emmeline noted.

"The devil's poison seeped up through the ventilation tube at the rove and then wafted across the terrain. There are quite a few Terrapunks who need the blood remedy, too."

"Ah, there's always self-fulfilling motivation with them."

"You aren't wrong," Montgomery agreed. He turned to Kiran. "Would you mind giving me and my daughter a moment to talk?"

"Of course," Kiran agreed, taking his cue to leave.

Once they were alone, Montgomery looked at Emmeline with deep care in his golden eyes.

"I figured this would be easier without your mother here," he said. "Tell me everything."

"You need to have an open mind," she cautioned.

"I will try my best."

"Remember that sea stone that I thought was a monster egg?" Montgomery nodded, and she continued, "Well, it was a stone from the Moon of Fixation. When I touched it without a glove, I suffered its curse. Eating became agonizing. I became dependent on the false comfort the stone provided. What's interesting, though, is that the curse came with strange blessings as well."

"Flying isn't worth your health," Montgomery argued.

"It's more than that. It opened my mind to greater possibilities." Emmeline paused a moment, collecting her confidence. "Do you know who helped me heal?"

"No! That's what I'm waiting to hear."

"A hellion."

"Impossible."

"Her name is Luna, and the creatures we call hellions are actually called Lunarians. We could end the bloodshed and build a friendship with them."

He shook his head, visibly jarred by this news. "Why would she help you?"

"One, because we became friends. And two, because she hoped to show the Solarpunks the altruistic side of her people. She wants to build an alliance."

"Why? To gain access to the source flame? They can't have fire."

"They need fire to keep their mortals alive."

Montgomery shook his head again—this went against centuries of teachings. "No. The mortals get heat from us."

"During the day, yes. But at night, the Lunarians reflect small morsels of the source flame onto Earth, keeping the night warm enough for the mortals to survive. Without that heat in the cold of night, the earthlings would perish."

"She lied to you," Montgomery insisted.

"You should meet her. You can see for yourself that she is good."

"I don't want to befriend any monsters."

"Aren't you grateful that I am alive?"

"Of course, I am."

"Well, I am only alive because of her."

"You also were only sick because of her."

"You are missing the point, and I don't have time to waste. I need Luna to take Gemma and Clementine to Mōnalene so she can heal them, too. It would be a show of good faith to at least start talks of an alliance before she does more for us without receiving anything in return."

"I owe her nothing."

"My life is worth nothing to you?"

"Of course, it is. But you can't expect accolades or rewards when you fix a problem you caused."

"She is good. If you'd give her a chance, you'd see that for yourself."

"I have to protect you. There will be no further fraternization with the hellions."

"You said you'd have an open mind."

"A monster fixing its monstrous deeds after the act is not proof of altruism."

"But a monster feeling remorse and attempting to do better is."

"Where's the proof of her remorse?"

"If you met her, you'd sense it for yourself. Her choice to save me was not selfish; it was selfless. Her wish is to end the bloodshed."

"She is one of many monsters we hunt. Eliminating hellions from the list doesn't end our fight."

"But it gives us one less enemy."

"Have you considered the ramifications of such an alliance? If we make one with them, word will get out, and then all of the moon monsters will want an alliance."

"Possibly, but we can draw a firm boundary. The Lunarians are different. You need to trust me. You need to meet her."

"It's a hard no. I'm sorry."

Montgomery pulled Emmeline into a hug—one she did not reciprocate—and kissed the top of her head.

"I need *you* to trust *me*," he said. "I've been alive far longer than you. I've seen the brutal cruelness and the calculated kindness of the hellions countless times before today. They have no honor."

Though Emmeline could not argue against her father's firsthand experiences, her experiences were valid, too.

It would take time to change his mind.

Her eyes darted back to the Marzan in its cage and her priorities realigned.

Nothing truly mattered until Louie was safe.

She needed to speak to the devil.

Chapter 20

"I heard you helped my brothers get close to the devil," Emmeline said to Gemma.

"I did," Gemma replied. "I covered their suits in clay so the poison couldn't reach them."

"I need you to do that for me."

"Why?"

"I want to interrogate the monster. Maybe it can give us some insight into the type of torture Louie is experiencing."

"You really want that kind of information? You can't help him from here. Knowing his suffering will only torment you further."

"Or maybe it'll say something that will give me a clue on how to help him."

Gemma sighed. "I'll help you, of course. I'm just tired and cold."

"I'll give you a new batch of activated firestones."

"I want to heal."

Emmeline had been so hyper-focused on Louie that she wasn't seeing Gemma clearly. Her small friend stood before her, arms wrapped around her own body and fidgeting from a bad case of the shivers. Her silver skeletal legs showed beneath her tattered dress. They rattled as she trembled.

"I'm sorry," Emmeline said, her tone distraught. "Your suffering is my fault. I will beg Luna to take you back to Mōnalene with her when she visits. She should return in the next day or two."

"You have to beg her to help me?" Gemma's silver eyes shimmered with hurt.

"She wants to help you, but she also wants to secure an alliance. I'm not sure how many favors she'll perform before getting some kind of confirmation that an alliance is in the works."

"And you need her help to save Louie," Gemma said, realizing her place on the list.

"I don't know how else to bring him home."

"I understand." Gemma took a deep breath, swallowing her pride. "It makes sense. I am safe here. He is not safe there."

Emmeline nodded. "You and Clementine will get the help you need. I promise."

"Let's focus on this new mission. Is it just you and me doing this interrogation?"

"I want Avery and Kiran to come, too. I need witnesses, extra minds to process whatever the devil says."

"Avery and I outside the cage, you and Kiran inside?" Gemma asked to confirm.

"Yes."

Gemma began scraping her fingers against her palms, preparing enough clay to cover two suits.

Emmeline found Kiran huddled with her brothers near the captain's wheel.

"What are you lot conspiring?" she asked as she approached.

Kiran turned to face her, whereas Solís and Cyrus only lifted their gazes momentarily before resuming their conversation.

"Figuring out a plan to help Helix," Kiran answered.

"Do you know where he is?" Emmeline asked.

Cyrus replied, "I flew alongside one of the Revopunks, and after some coaxing, she told me that she saw him strung out near the scrapyard."

"I'd offer to help, but I need to interrogate the devil."

"Why?" Solís asked, attention shifted. "Why would you put yourself back in harm's way?"

"It might give me some information that could help us save Louie."

"You just got home! Revel in the feeling of safety for a change."

"Louie needs me."

Solís groaned. "I can't keep saving you from yourself."

"I never needed your help! Luna would've brought me home."

"Well, if you're here to ask for help, you won't get any from me."

"I'm here to ask Kiran, not you."

Solís grunted and turned away.

Emmeline addressed Kiran, "Will you help me? I need a second set of eyes and ears in the cage."

"Is it safe?" he asked, his hesitance apparent.

"No," Solís replied, his gaze still fixed on the map laid out between him and Cyrus.

Emmeline's expression tightened with frustration.

"No," she confirmed. "Not totally safe, but Gemma will cover us in clay to block out the poison. This method has worked before."

Cyrus stepped in, "It has worked *once* before. You'll be the second round of test dummies."

Emmeline's pretty golden eyes widened, pleading silently with Kiran to join.

His golden gaze matched hers, softening the longer he looked into her eyes.

"Fine," he conceded. "But you're responsible for nursing me back to health if it goes awry."

"Deal."

"So, you're just abandoning *our* mission?" Solís asked.

"Oh, right. Sorry," Kiran offered.

"Just go. We'll recruit someone else to help. Just make sure you protect her while you're in that cage."

"I will," he promised.

Emmeline grabbed Kiran by the wrist and pulled him away from her brothers. As they departed, she heard Cyrus quip, "He's a goner."

Followed by Solís repeating the same infuriating remark he made before. "Better than the pirate, though."

Emmeline charged forward, ignoring their commentary.

All of this was for Louie.

She would save him.

After grabbing two diving suits and helmets from the utility cabin, she and Kiran went to the top deck where Avery and Gemma waited.

The balloon was inflated with helium and ready to fly. Avery stood near the knobs and pedals, ready to pilot the vessel. Also waiting for them inside the basket was Gemma, who had four buckets of clay at her skeletal feet.

"Suit up," Avery commanded. "I'd like to get this over with."

As Avery soared the balloon toward the detention center, Emmeline and Kiran got dressed. They slid feetfirst through the neck of their suits, then sealed their suits by bolting their helmets to the rubber collar.

The monsters below roared and growled as the balloon passed overhead. The disharmony created a terrifying refrain — a song Emmeline wished to never hear again.

As she slathered the clay all over her suit, she tried to ignore the chilling noise from below.

"We're here," Avery announced, cranking the hand lever that pumped the wings to a stop. The metal dragon wings attached to the basket creaked as they retracted. Avery dropped an anchor, which landed in the water beside the cage holding the Ogre of Irritability. Droplets from the splash hit the monster and he howled in protest.

"Such a baby," Avery commented under her breath as she tightened the anchor line. "We're secure," she informed her friends.

"Ready to go?" Emmeline asked Kiran.

"As ready as I'll ever be." He grabbed the iron prodder that Montgomery had left in the basket for them and channeled his source flame heart. Through the thick, fireproof gloves of his suit, the heat extended into the pole and the pointed tips of the prodder blazed red.

They shimmied down two ropes slung over the side of the basket.

When they reached the top of the cage, they paused. The bars were greased with petroleum and set ablaze. With care, they dropped their ropes between the flaming bars and continued their descent.

The devil hissed as they entered its space.

Emmeline examined the monster closer—it was a female. Blood-red hair drenched with petroleum draped her face. She stared at Emmeline through her wet locks, no mercy in her blue gaze.

"Are you here about the boy?" the Marzan asked, her tone taunting.

Emmeline had reached the bottom of her rope. She let go and landed in a crouch.

"How do you know about him?" Emmeline asked.

"All this time I've been a prisoner here and you've learned nothing useful," she replied with a cackle. "Same can't be said for your friend, though. My people will uncover every secret he holds."

"What's your name?" Emmeline asked.

"Ha!" The Marzan stood, her intrigue piqued. "You aren't like the others."

"What's your name?" Emmeline repeated.

"Deánira."

"I'm Emmeline."

"I know."

"How could you possibly know my name?"

Deánira tapped the side of her head, then pushed her hair behind her ear.

"I listen," she replied.

Emmeline looked around, unsure how or when this creature heard her name mentioned. Her eyes landed on her father's boat, which hovered a few miles away.

"Do you have heightened hearing?" Emmeline asked.

"One might say that."

"Tell me about Louie. What do they want from him?"

"Secrets," Deánira answered.

"He doesn't have any."

"What he knows is more valuable than you realize."

"Explain," Emmeline demanded.

"Why should I?"

Kiran stepped closer and shoved the searing hot prodder toward Deánira, to which she recoiled.

"I don't wish to hurt you," Emmeline explained, "but if you don't talk, I will have no other choice."

Deánira narrowed her gaze. "You've already hurt me."

Emmeline examined the Marzan from afar, recalling the memory she had of this creature before leaving. Deánira was frailer and thinner now, and her bright red flesh had faded to a dull pink. She was ill; she was dying. What the Solarpunks were doing to her was just as evil as what the Marzans were likely doing to Louie.

"Let's work together," Emmeline offered. "Help me get Louie home, and I'll see to it that you are returned to your moon with no further injuries."

"I don't trust you," Deánira hissed.

"I can see why you wouldn't," Emmeline replied, her patience thinning, "but this is your only option."

"I'd rather die here than help you."

Emmeline clenched her teeth together, struggling to contain her fury.

"You have to conform," she demanded, fists shaking.

"Never," Deánira replied.

Emmeline snatched the prodder out of Kiran's grip and lunged at Deánira. The pronged tips of the prodder stopped right below Deánira's left eye, and the searing hot points gently touched her cheek.

Pressed against the ground of her cage, Deánira had nowhere to retreat. She squealed in agony as the prodder blistered her flesh.

"Talk!" Emmeline screamed.

"You cannot resurrect the dead!"

"What does that mean?" Emmeline demanded, her heart pounding at the implication.

"Louie won't survive whatever torture they have planned for him. My people know that I'm here and that your lot is killing me slowly. They will exact revenge upon that boy. They will do it in my honor."

"I will set you free if you work with me!" Emmeline tried again, removing the prodder from where it touched Deánira's face and handing it back to Kiran. "A life for a life; yours for Louie's. It's a fair trade."

"It's too late for that."

"Why?"

"I'm already dead," Deánira said, then held the spot of her blood extraction and explained, "I'll never recover from the Lunarian poison. The trade wouldn't be fair."

Emmeline looked to Kiran, who shrugged.

"Tell me your demands, then," Emmeline offered. "In exchange for Louie's safe return, I will honor your last wishes."

"You realize your bartering for a ghost, right? Louie has been there long enough; surely, they've begun interrogating him by now. Whoever returns, I can promise you it won't be Louie. It might look like him, but it won't be the boy you once knew."

"I'm willing to take that risk."

Deánira considered this offer, then said, "Return in a day and I'll have my demands prepared."

Emmeline exhaled deeply, relief coursing through her.

A scream came from above.

Emmeline and Kiran turned to find Avery holding Gemma, who was sobbing against her shoulder. Avery caught Emmeline's eye and pointed toward the ocean below the devil's cage.

A body floated in the water.

Emmeline gasped and stumbled backward.

Rusted over and dead.

The moonstone curse had killed Clementine.

Chapter 21

Deimos

"Speak!"

Another lash of the chain-link whip ripped across Louie's bare back.

Louie trembled where he knelt—wrists bound and chained to the top of a post and head bowed between his arms.

"I know nothing," he said between sobs.

"Answer our questions, or you will die chained to that post," Balor threatened.

"I wish that were so." Louie sniffled. "It'll take a lot more than that whip to kill me."

"Then tell us how so we can put you out of your misery."

Louie shook his head. "You'll use that information against my people."

"Possibly, but what does it matter to you? You'll be dead, too."

"I'll suffer for an eternity before I sell out my kind to you."

Balor walked in slow circles around Louie.

"They will die regardless," he informed Louie. "You have the power to make it painless."

"They will fight back. You cannot defeat the sun."

Balor smirked. "But we will."

Louie lifted his head. "Defeat the sun?" he asked.

"Darkness will consume this galaxy, and for the first time since our conception, the Marzans will live in peace."

"You're delusional," Louie argued.

"Am I? You don't know the extent of our powers."

"Then why haven't you done it by now?"

"We weren't able to get past your defenses until recently."

Louie's breathing intensified as he thought of the Marzan prisoner in Hydra. "How did she get into Quintessence?"

"First," Balor bartered, "tell me about Solédon. I know you know His secrets."

"I already told you. I know nothing about Solédon outside of what's in His holy doctrine."

Balor raised the whip and landed it on Louie's back.

Louie tensed as the metal sliced his flesh.

"Tell me!" Balor demanded, whip raised to strike again.

"Be more specific," Louie said, his voice a hoarse whisper.

"Does He visit Quintessence? Does He guard its source flame?"

"I've never seen Him," Louie answered.

"Have you heard others talk of His presence there?"

"No."

Balor paced in silence for a moment, then asked, "Do *you* think He visits in disguise?"

Louie shook his head. "The gods don't care about any of us."

"You didn't answer my question."

"The truth is that I don't know," Louie stated, bracing for impact, but he received no lashing in response to his lack of knowledge this time.

"And He is the one who pitted you against the moons?"

"As stated in the holy doctrine, written by Solédon Himself, we were created to protect the source flame from all moon creatures. We were tasked to protect the flame with our lives." Louie sighed. "The only way you will get to the source flame is by killing every Solarpunk on Quintessence."

"And since you won't tell us how to kill them, we will have to practice methods on you."

"All so you can take the source flame?" Louie asked.

"Not to take—we don't want fire. We intend to extinguish the source flame."

"That would kill everyone."

"Not us, though. Once everyone else is gone, this entire galaxy will belong to us. It's a shame you won't get to warn your loved ones of their imminent demise."

Louie writhed in his chains, livening up for the first time since entering this torture chamber.

"Oh," Balor said with a laugh. "Now you want to fight?"

He followed his question with a hard swing of the whip. It cracked as it slashed Louie's back, forcing him back into submission.

"You'll never get close to the source flame," Louie said, spitting out blood.

"We already have."

Balor left the room, leaving Louie alone with his fresh wounds.

King Helmer stood by the door, watching the interrogation.

"He knows nothing of value," Balor said as he shut the door behind him.

"Nothing about Solédon?" King Helmer asked.

"He has no concrete knowledge about whether Solédon visits or guards the sun in disguise. He doesn't seem to think so, but his response was uncertain."

"It is our only remaining obstacle. We can defeat the Solarpunks, but we cannot defeat a god."

"Has Deánira sent any news? Has she suspected any presence of a god?"

"I spoke to her yesterday. Our coded messages are short, but she felt no signs of omnipresent beings from her cage." King Helmer halted, his bloodshot eyes filling with rageful tears. "She will die in that cage."

"Is she doing worse?"

"Much worse. The Lunarian poison is corroding her chainmail armor."

"I'm so sorry," Balor expressed.

"We will be victorious," King Helmer insisted, restraining his anguish.

Balor traced the scar on the back of his neck and said, "So long as we keep you safe."

"You haven't failed me yet."

The distant echo of a bereaved cry reverberated overhead.

"My daughter," King Helmer said, more to himself than to Balor. "She needs me."

He ran up the red rock stairs, moving at full speed as he navigated the maze of narrow corridors. Their entire society existed underground, and though he was the King of Black Holes, he traveled as all Marzans did—on foot. Traveling at mortal speeds tested his patience, but it was safer this way. Even with his expertise, opening and traveling through a black hole within Deimos was too risky.

His queen awaited at the top level, closest to the surface of Deimos.

"Did you capture the cry?" he asked.

"Yes," Daeva replied. Her long blood-red hair was knotted into braids atop her head and adorned with crimson crystals. Her eyes held great sorrow. "We are losing her."

King Helmer charged into the vaulted underground cathedral. Its tall ceilings captured all sounds. As he opened the sliding stone door, Deánira's voice rang clear. Relief relaxed his shoulders—he hadn't missed her call.

He sat cross-legged in the middle of the room and deciphered the message.

"The boy is important to the Solarpunks," King Helmer mumbled to himself as he translated the message—each note had a corresponding number that represented a letter. King Helmer continued, "I am here. Let me finish them."

Helmer looked up at his wife, pure dread in his eyes.

"She hasn't mastered the darkness yet," he said.

"Do you have a better plan?" Daeva asked. "We tried to get the Lunarians to let us use their portals again, to no avail. Deánira might be the closest we will ever get to the source flame. This may be our only chance."

"She will kill herself in the process."

"She's halfway to death already. Let her finish her mission. Let her die with honor."

"This was never part of her mission." Helmer cupped his face in his hands. "But I understand. This might be the only way."

147

"Call to her," Daeva encouraged, extending a hand and helping Helmer to his feet. "Let her know that she has our blessing."

She kissed his hand, then let him go.

Helmer climbed the stairs along the side of the cathedral and exited onto the surface of Deimos. The top half of Mars protruded above the horizon. Red dust swirled in tiny twisters, coming and going at the will of the solar winds. A true hellscape—one Helmer worked hard to remedy.

"I tried to save you. I hope you know," Helmer said to himself, mapping out his message. "The Lunarians wouldn't let us use the portal stones. I interrogated the Solarpunk boy, but he could not tell us how to breach the outer defenses of Quintessence. He said he only knew about the sea. I am so sorry. I will keep trying."

Helmer took a deep breath and released a multi-toned bellow. Carried within the notes of his deafening cry was his message for Deánira.

Moments later, he received a reply.

Coded in a wretched but determined echo, she said, "I won't last long enough for you to save me. I love you. Let me finish them."

Furious and defeated, King Helmer swallowed his pride and sent a reply coded in a bellowing roar.

"You have my blessing."

Chapter 22

Hydra, Quintessence

"Stop!" Emmeline begged of Deánira, who had entered a fit of hysterics. Her deafening cries forced Emmeline and Kiran to their knees. The sea shook, the cage trembled, and a small trickle of magma dripped from both of their ears.

Kiran shook with his hands over his ears.

"Hand me the prodder," Emmeline shouted to him.

He did as she asked, and with a single jab, Emmeline silenced the screaming devil.

Deánira's melodic screeches turned into a whimper as she clutched her new wound.

Emmeline dropped the prodder and pressed her face to the floor bars, staring at her lifeless friend floating below.

Gears rusted to a halt, Clementine's body was stiff as steel. She remained rigid and unmoving as a crew of Nautipunks fished her out of the sea.

Emmeline cringed. Clementine's death and retrieval were eerily similar to Ruthanne's—they both suffered painful rigor mortis; both of their lives were halted prematurely.

Crippling guilt clutched Emmeline's heart—this was her fault. She glanced up at Gemma, who still sobbed in Avery's embrace. More determined than ever, Emmeline had to get Gemma to Mōnalene to heal.

"Killed by a lunar curse, huh?" Deánira asked, though she seemed to already know that she was correct. "Those Lunarians are the true devils."

"You know nothing," Emmeline seethed.

Deánira smirked. "You've befriended the wrong monster."

Emmeline's eyes widened with shocked outrage. How did the devil know? And what if she was right?

She had to trust her intuition.

"We don't have time for your games," she replied, then turned to Kiran. "Let's get out of here."

"I'll have a list of last requests ready by tomorrow," Deánira called after them as they climbed their ropes.

Emmeline ignored her—she was beginning to think that the devil would be of no help at all.

Back in the basket of the helium balloon, Emmeline went straight to Gemma.

"I will see Luna tomorrow. She will help you."

"I can feel the cold taking over. I fear that one day, it will freeze my gears, making me rigid in death, just like Clementine and Ruthanne."

"I won't let that happen," Emmeline promised. "You have access to as many firestones as you need until I can secure you a trip to Mōnalene."

"I've been cold for so long," Gemma said, defeat in her voice. "I can't remember the feeling of natural warmth."

"Things will get better. I promise."

"They didn't for Ruthanne or Clementine."

"I won't fail you, too."

Gemma's expression tightened and her eyes held deep compassion. "Don't beat yourself up. If it happens to me, I won't blame you. You didn't know what that stone was either. It's just bad luck."

Emmeline pulled Gemma into a hug and whispered, "I won't let it take you, too."

She let go of her friend and prepared to face the grave reality of Clementine's fate. Avery lowered the basket onto the landing deck of Montgomery's ship, and while she secured the aircraft with buckled belts, Emmeline, Gemma, and Kiran raced to join the crew of Thermapunks circled around Clementine's body.

"The corrosion reached her vital organs," said Edwin Doyle, a Thermadoc who served as both a welder and a mechanic on Montgomery's ship.

"I warned her that the solar salt within the sea would eventually kill her," Montgomery said. "While it's less harsh on zinc and other ferrous metals, it viciously deteriorates precious metals."

Edwin nodded. "The rust ate a hole through her golden heart and the flame within was snuffed."

"Snuffed by water or air?" Montgomery asked.

Edwin leaned in closer to Clementine's lifeless body and rapidly switched between the lenses attached to his bifocals. "The sea extinguished her flame."

"Better the sea than the air," Avery said, joining the group from above. She hovered over the crowd, pounding her copper wings against the salty sky.

"Why's that?" Edwin asked.

"There are all sorts of gases mixed in with the oxygen we breathe. If even a small fraction of hydrogen had entered the crack of her heart, she'd have exploded."

"It ends in death for her either way."

"But who would she have hurt in the process?" Avery asked.

"Fair point."

Emmeline pushed through the large bodies of the crew and knelt beside Clementine. She lifted her friend's hand and held it in hers, oily tears greasing her rose-gold cheeks.

The sight of her grief hushed the crowd, and many dispersed to give her space.

"I never had a chance to see her since coming home."

"This is not your fault," Montgomery said.

"But it is. I took that cursed stone out of the sea."

"You had no clue what it was capable of."

"And you warned Clementine," Gemma added. "She touched the stone knowing full well that it would hurt her."

Emmeline nodded—she was right. Clementine knew the risks.

"Her parents will be so upset," Emmeline said.

"Sadly, they gave up on her weeks ago," Melora informed her.

Emmeline sighed. "Let's take her body home. She deserves a proper Thermapunk farewell."

Avery prepared the balloon for departure.

Montgomery, Melora, Emmeline, and Gemma rode in the basket with Avery while Kiran, Solís, and Cyrus flew alongside it. Clementine's rigid body lay on the basket ground, making the ride home uncomfortable for everyone.

They traveled in silence.

After exiting the gates of Hydra, Avery steered the balloon toward Clementine's home. A few clicks east of the Dawes family mansion sat the Monroe manor. Cecelia and Ambrose Monroe were the Thermapunk nobles in charge of the Steamery and parents to Clementine and her younger siblings, Corisandra and Cordell, all of whom were expected to take on responsibility at the Steamery.

Cecelia sat on the front balcony, tinkering with a set of small pipes. She looked up, saw Montgomery and Melora, and dropped the gadgets in her hands. They landed on the golden tiles with a clang.

"Has the day arrived?" Cecelia shouted to them. "Have I lost my dear child to the sea?"

"I am so sorry," Melora responded, her tone sincere.

Cecelia fell to her knees and cradled her face in her hands. Ambrose came running out of the house, joining his bereaved wife.

"What happened?" he asked her.

Cecelia waved her hand toward the Daweses. Upon seeing them, Ambrose's face turned a furious shade of red.

"Is she dead?"

Montgomery nodded. "We tried to warn her that the sea salt would corrode her golden gears, but she persisted. She kept diving without the suit."

"Why, though? This desire of hers came out of nowhere."

"She was ill," Melora stepped in, preventing anyone in the basket from revealing Emmeline's role in Clementine's demise.

"Just like your daughter and the rest of the *Superpunks*," he scathed, emphasizing his distaste. "Although, *she* seems better now. Tell me, girl," he addressed Emmeline. "Why not share your secret remedy with your friends? Seems you got them into this mess—Clementine started acting strange after seeing you at your Soul Day celebration. How many are dead while you still live?"

"An illness no one could have predicted or prevented hit Hydra. This is no one's fault," Montgomery said in defense of his daughter.

Emmeline slowly retreated to the back of the basket, hoping to hide behind her parents, but as she stepped backward, she tripped over Clementine's body and landed on the ground next to her deceased friend. Clementine's lifeless golden gaze stared in her direction, adding to the grief Emmeline felt.

"I'm sorry I didn't get you help faster," she said, averting her eyes from Clementine's dead stare.

"Where is her body?" Cecelia asked through her snivels.

"We are here to deliver her to you. May we dock?"

"Yes, of course." Cecelia turned to Ambrose. "Let me handle this. Keep Corisandra and Cordell inside. They shouldn't see their sister like this."

As Avery moved the balloon closer to the Monroe manor, Emmeline stood up and leaned over the backside of the basket.

"Get me out of here," she pled in a whisper to Kiran and her brothers, who still flew alongside the balloon.

"Hop on," Solís offered, gliding closer to the basket where Emmeline could safely climb onto his back.

"Thanks," she said as she wrapped her arms around his neck.

The foursome flew off, doing a quick lap around the Monroe manor before redirecting toward the Dawes mansion.

They soared high above Terra in the airspace known as Fyree. This strip of Quintessence, which had full circumferential coverage of Quintessence, was designated strictly for the Thermapunks.

Kiran and Cyrus flew in spiral rotations, racing each other and practicing their flight speed—a critical Pyropunk technique while battling moon monsters in the upper levels of Gaslion.

Solís reached their floating home first and stopped at Emmeline's bedroom balcony.

153

"Can you bring me to the roof instead?" she asked.

"Don't you want to rest?"

"Yes, but I'd prefer to watch Clementine's farewell from a better vantage point."

"As you wish," Solís replied, pounding his wings against the warm sky and rocketing upward. With a few rotations of his shoulder blade gears, which flapped his giant titanium wings, they reached the roof.

He lowered Emmeline gently, making sure she was secure before letting go of her wrist.

"I'm sorry I didn't tell you about Louie sooner," he offered. "I just wanted to get you home."

"I get it. I just keep imagining how terribly he is suffering right now." Oily tears shimmered over her golden irises. "And it's my fault he's there."

"Arguably, it's mine," Solís corrected her. "Sure, he went to rescue you, but he only knew the incantation because he overheard me saying it. I warned him not to go, I swear, but he didn't listen."

"It all comes back to me. I am at the root of everyone's woes," Emmeline said, shoulders slouched. "I created such a mess."

"You've also gone above and beyond to fix your mistakes. Keep going," Solís encouraged her. "I need to go help Helix now. Please be safe up here."

"I will."

Solís did a backflip off the edge of the roof and disappeared.

Emmeline sat with her thoughts, allowing her many emotions to process. Guilt, grief, determination, hope—she would not give up.

Utterly exhausted, Emmeline rested her tired body against the smooth golden roof shingles and closed her eyes.

When she opened them again, the sky had turned dark. The nocturnal glow of night swirled all around, illuminating her tired eyes with pinks, purples, and greens.

Kiran sat beside her. He fiddled with his fingers as he watched the colorful sky ebb and flow.

"What are you doing here?" Emmeline asked, still groggy.

"Oh good, you're finally awake," he replied.

"How long was I asleep?"

"A few hours. After I finished helping your brothers bring Helix home, I came up here to keep an eye on you."

"Is Helix okay?" Emmeline asked, sitting upright and rubbing her eyes.

"Not really. Your brothers strapped him to his bed so he can't escape again. He needs to detox fully before his healing can begin."

"I need to be a better sister to him."

"Don't take on any more right now. Your brothers have it under control."

Emmeline nodded. "Did I miss the funeral?"

"Nope. I was planning to wake you when it began."

"Thanks," she said, her awakened senses returning. "Where is Gemma?" she asked. Emmeline needed her close by, as she wasn't sure the exact day Luna would return.

"She is napping in your room."

"Can you wake her and bring her up here? I want her with me during the memorial proceedings."

"Of course, but first, are you okay?"

"I'm as okay as I can be."

"I'm here for you if you need to talk," Kiran said, his eyes gleaming with genuine kindness.

This forced Emmeline to pause, and a sudden surge of guilt entered her heart.

"I appreciate that," she said, "but I need to make something clear: this is nothing more than friendship."

"I respect that ... but why?"

"I was with Louie before he left, and I will be with him again upon his return."

"I understand. I would never intentionally cause more problems or stress for you." He smiled and extended his hand. "Friends it is."

Emmeline smirked at the formality, but took his hand and shook. She hoped his concession was genuine.

"When do you think the ceremony will start?" Emmeline asked.

"Any minute now."

"You should go and get Gemma."

"Aye aye, Captain."

Wings spread wide, Kiran dove off the roof.

The moment he was out of sight, the dark horizon was set ablaze.

The funeral had commenced.

Emmeline clamped her hands together, seeking comfort within herself. When Kiran returned, Gemma took a seat next to Emmeline.

"I'm glad you're here," Emmeline said to her.

Gemma unfurled Emmeline's hands and interlaced her fingers into Emmeline's right hand. She squeezed it gently and said, "You need to be surrounded by people who understand. And no one understands better than me."

Emmeline was grateful to have Gemma as her friend.

The night sky lit up with reds, oranges, and yellows as the ceremonial caravan traversed Fyree. Pulled forward by four Pyropunks, a sled engulfed with flames held Clementine's body. Her parents were pulled on a chariot to the right of her body, and her younger siblings were escorted to the left.

Everyone in the procession sang the ritual hymn of death and rebirth. The chorus was repeated through the duration of the ceremony, and as they passed overhead, Emmeline and Kiran joined in.

"Death becomes us
in the end.
No bells, no whistles, just hollowness.
I beg:
Lift this spirit, regift this soul.
Rebuild what was lost into something whole.

May the gods see worthy this love of mine;
forever grateful, forever entwined.
I'll see you soon.
In that, I trust.
Together again
when death becomes us."

The song echoed across Fyree, and likely into Gaslion above and Terra below. The traveling hymnal was vibrant with life and effervescent sorrow—their energy was all-consuming. Corisandra and Cordell, Clementine's younger siblings, sang the song loud and proud with tears streaming from their eyes. The hope that their sister might return to them in a different form rang plainly in their desperate expressions. Clementine's parents displayed less hope. Cecelia wept and sang in a whisper while Ambrose mumbled the song, fists clenched and expression tight with anger.

Emmeline kept her focus on the sled carrying Clementine, praying their lyrics of rebirth might reach the gods and this unlikely favor would be granted.

She and Kiran sang the chorus four times before the procession moved too far away to hear. Rounding the circumference of this inner world within the sun, their voices faded and the fire flickered low. The dark glow of night resumed.

"That's a beautiful song," Gemma said.

"Do you have one similar for Terrapunk funerals?" Emmeline asked.

Gemma shook her head. "We don't get a song or celebration. Our parts are harvested and repurposed. We die with the hopes that our discarded bodies are used to build something useful."

"There is no moment to honor the life lost?" Kiran asked.

"The nobles get a ceremony, though I've never seen one," Gemma answered. "The rest of us are recycled without fanfare. I just hope my parts serve a greater good after I'm gone. It's a high hope—most common Terrapunk parts end up being wasted on gizmos and gadgets."

"You won't have to worry about that for a long time," Emmeline assured her.

The scent of moon lily wafted through the air.

Emmeline's eyes widened.

"Kiran," Emmeline said, "would you mind letting me and Gemma hang out alone for a bit?"

"Oh, yeah. Sure. I need to get back to the base anyway to check my schedule for next week. It was nice hanging out with you both," he said before departing.

"Why did you send him away?" Gemma asked.

"It's time for you to heal."

Chapter 23

"You can show yourself," Emmeline said to the empty sky.

A moment of silence lingered.

Nothing happened.

"Who are you talking to?" Gemma asked cautiously.

"Luna," Emmeline said to the sky. "I know you're there. It's safe to come out. Gemma is a friend."

"I only came to make sure you were still alive," Luna revealed in a low voice, still veiled within her shield.

"Why would you think otherwise?" Emmeline asked.

"I felt the pull of death."

Emmeline's fire heart surged with grief. "You must have felt Clementine. The moonstone curse took her from us earlier today."

"I am sorry to hear that."

"I was hoping you'd visit soon—that's why I have Gemma here with me. She also touched your moonstone and I don't want her to suffer the same fate."

Luna popped her head out from under her shield. Her large circular eyes shimmered silver and her long black hair held glimmering specks of stardust. Though she was in a state of tranquility, the black veins around her eyes hadn't fully faded from her last spell of rage.

"You want me to bring her back to Mōnalene with me and heal her?" Luna asked, voice stern but eyes filled with compassion.

"Yes, please."

Luna sighed. "I cannot do that until an alliance is agreed upon."

"Please," Emmeline begged, grabbing Gemma's hand. "I don't know how much time she has left. I don't want to lose her, too."

"If I heal her, I have no leverage. I have sacrificed too much to risk this alliance falling through."

"I am not leverage," Gemma chimed in, her voice meek. "Emmeline is the only one who cares if I live or die."

"Others care," Emmeline objected in defense of her friend, dropping Gemma's hand and turning to face her.

Gemma shot her a disapproving look. "You know that isn't true. They certainly wouldn't risk their lives to save me."

Emmeline could not argue this statement.

Luna asked, "Her health and survival will not sway those in charge to work with us?"

"I fear not," Emmeline answered. "Gemma is right. And if saving my life wasn't enough, hers won't make any difference." Emmeline's expression was creased with disappointment.

"Have you spoken to those in charge? Did your survival really mean nothing to them?"

"It means everything to them, but they still blame you for it happening in the first place. I asked them to speak with you. I said they'd see things differently if they gave you a chance."

"I will gladly take that meeting," Luna said, her energy lifted. "When can we arrange it?"

"My parents are a bit preoccupied with the return of my brother Helix, but that should settle in a few days."

"I'll return in two days. That gives me time to help Louie."

Emmeline perked up. "Louie? Have you seen him since he was taken?"

"Yes, and it isn't good."

"Why didn't you bring him back with you?"

"I couldn't. I had no way to cut through the Marzan chains. I have the Formies building a special pair of sheers for me."

"Bring me with you," Emmeline pled. "Let me help."

"No."

"Please!"

"You aren't prepared and I'm leaving now." Luna's kind eyes shifted back to Gemma. She hesitated a moment before adding, "I will bring your friend Gemma with me and deliver her to the medical ward for healing."

"You will?" Emmeline asked, elated.

"Yes, but I need to leave for Deimos immediately after, so you can't come. You aren't prepared for this type of travel."

"I will get ready."

"There isn't enough time. You will only delay Louie's rescue."

"Fine, I'll stay," Emmeline said in surrender.

"Plus, you have work to do here. You need to secure our alliance."

"I will keep trying."

Luna's head snapped to the north.

"Do you hear that?" Luna asked.

"Hear what?"

"That's a Marzan war cry," she said.

"It's probably coming from the captured Marzan in Hydra. She screams all the time."

"No. It came from above. I've heard it a million times at home, but never here." Luna's wide silver eyes were filled with dread. "We are running out of time. We have to align now before it's too late."

"What do you think they have planned?"

"I'm not sure," Luna said, then her expression lit up. "But maybe Louie does. He's been there for a while now; maybe he's overheard something."

"I really want to go with you," Emmeline expressed.

"Absolutely not," Solís said, crawling through the window and onto the roof.

"Why are you always lurking about?" Emmeline asked, annoyed.

"I'll go with you," Solís said to Luna. "It's my fault he's there. I should help save him."

"Have you grown a heart?" Luna asked, her tone sarcastic.

"Nah, still have the same one as before. Just looking to get better use out of it."

Emmeline's expression shifted with disbelief. "Who are you?"

"You act like I am incapable of kindness."

"You are, but not for Louie."

"I'm evolving," he stated plainly, then looked to Luna. "When are we going?"

"You aren't coming."

"If you can hear the devils from here, it's best not to waste time squabbling." Solís tapped the tank on his back. "It's filled with oxygen. I'm ready to go."

Luna rolled her eyes. "If you're ready to leave immediately, I suppose an extra set of hands wouldn't hurt."

"Let's go," he replied.

Luna extended her hand to Gemma, silver-sheened flesh shimmering in the nocturnal glow of Quintessence. Nails filed to a point, her long skinny fingers waved Gemma forward.

"Ready to heal?" she asked the frail Tinkerpunk.

Gemma took a deep breath, then placed her hand into Luna's.

"As ready as I'll ever be," Gemma answered.

Solís took Luna's other hand.

"Ad lunam lu," Luna muttered. The pendant hanging around her neck began to glow. "Accipe me."

The trio vanished.

Emmeline was alone again, her faith placed in Luna and Solís to heal her friend and save her love.

Chapter 24

Mōnalene

They landed on the arctic axis of the moon—one of six spots Luna had placed moonstones connected to her.

Gemma gasped as the air left her lungs.

Solís let her take a large inhale from his regulator while Luna reached into one of the many satchels attached to her waistband. She pulled out a blue blossom from an oxygeni flower.

"Chew and swallow," she said to Gemma, handing her the bud.

Gemma did as instructed, and within a moment, oxygen filled her lungs.

"Thank you," she said, savoring each breath.

"When you feel the effects starting to wear off, let me know and I will give you another."

Gemma nodded.

"Where to now?" Solís asked, his words muffled through the regulator clamped between his teeth.

"We need to drop her off with the Mantos, then visit the Formies for the clippers they're making. I can't free Louie without them."

"I kept my anklets," Solís said, pointing at the thin chains Luna had wrapped around his ankles the last time he was on Mōnalene.

"Were you hoping to see me again?" she asked, teasing him.

"I just thought I should save them, in case."

Luna smirked. "I see. Well, you'll need them. We'll be navigating the Weaver's web again."

"A web?" Gemma asked.

"The inner world of Mōnalene is a network of magnetic threads." Luna lifted her hand and pulled two small threads from her fingertip. She then knelt and wrapped them around Gemma's skeletal ankles. She had to wrap them multiple times to keep them tight. "There is no gravity anywhere on Mōnalene. These magnetic threads will keep you grounded."

Luna led them to a nearby rock formation that hid a pathway to the inner world of the moon.

At the end of the trail, they reached a ledge facing the intricate web of threads.

Creatures of all shapes and sizes traversed the cords and bustled about in an organized and structured society. Some looked like Luna; others looked nothing like her outside of their wide silver eyes and the black cords rotating beneath their semi-translucent silver flesh.

"Wow," Gemma said, her silver eyes bright with wonder.

"See," Luna stated, a kind smile on her face. "We aren't so monstrous after all."

Solís huffed. "Let's keep moving."

Luna glared at him, but said no more.

They traversed the maze of cords, following Luna's lead, and eventually reached the laboratory where Gemma would stay for healing.

"Another one?" Manto Maldi asked Luna upon their entry.

"Yes, should be the last for now."

"Has her healing been authorized by the Monarchs?"

"Lepido Dione gave me free range to do what was necessary to secure an alliance with Quintessence. Healing this Solarpunk is one of those necessary steps."

Manto Maldi's gaze narrowed, but he did not object. Instead, he helped Gemma onto the operating table. His gentle and meticulous nature calmed Gemma's shaking fists.

"Don't be afraid," he said to her, taking her hand and unfurling her fingers. Clumps of sand fell from her palms as they opened.

"Will it hurt?" she asked.

"It shouldn't. But if it does, just tell us. We have ways to numb the pain."

Gemma released a long-held breath.

"Can we leave her in your care?" Luna asked him.

"She is safe with us."

"Thank you. I will be back soon to check on her progress."

Manto Maldi returned his attention to Gemma and resumed his line of questions.

Luna led Solís out of the laboratory and back toward the surface of the moon.

As Solís matched her furious pace, he mumbled through his regulator, "You know that Gemma holds no sway in your alliance with my people, right?"

"I know that."

"Then why did you lie? And why are you helping her?"

"Because it's the right thing to do."

Her candid answer silenced Solís.

They hurried along the giant cords, crisscrossing from thread to thread until they reached the exit Luna desired.

"This leads directly to Macrotermes Mountain," she informed him. "Hopefully, they've finished building my shears."

She began her ascent up a stone ladder carved into the wall. Solís gave her space, then followed.

When she reached the end, she unlatched the door overhead and crawled through. Luna extended her hand to Solís. He accepted the offer and she yanked him upward. A quick tug and he flew through the opening, landing on his feet beside her.

Eyes wide with shock, he said, "Geez, you're strong."

Luna smirked. "Better not mess with me."

"I'm learning quickly," he replied with a laugh.

Luna made her way toward a group of builders.

"Formi Antton," she said in greeting. "How goes the build?"

"Oh, it's been done since yesterday," he replied, his high-pitched voice carried an occasional squeak. "Cèla was supposed to tell you."

"I was away. I only just returned. May I see the shears?"

"Cèla told me not to give them to you until she had a chance to talk to you," Antton said, his voice quivering.

"You know that's not how this works," Luna said, remaining calm.

Antton leaned in closer. "She said she'd tie my antennae together if I gave them to you without her approval."

Luna placed a gentle hand on the side of his circular face. "She just wanted to scare you. She won't do that."

"How can you be so sure?"

"Because I know her well. She is fierce, but she isn't cruel. Especially not to someone undeserving. You have done nothing wrong. Now, give me the shears."

Antton released a heavy breath before turning away. He returned a moment later with a pair of clippers made of the strongest lunar metal. The razor-sharp edges gleamed in the faint light of the mountain.

"Here you go," he said, offering them to her.

"Thank you. They are the perfect size," she said as she secured them to her waistband. With a rope through the finger inserts and another around the blades, the shears were safe for transport.

"Will you tell me now why you need those clippers?" Antton asked.

"So you can report back to Cèla? I think not," Luna answered. "Thank you again for your help."

"You serve the Monarchs, as do I," he replied with a bow of his head.

Luna nodded, grabbed Solís's wrist, and led him toward an exterior exit of the hollowed-out mountain. They zigzagged through a few tight bends of tall rock walls, and when they reached the end, Luna turned a rock knob that unlatched a hidden door. She stepped outside, yanking Solís with her, and then closed the door behind her.

"Our veil blocks satellites and telescopes from seeing us, but the earthlings sometimes send little robots here to explore their moon," she explained to Solís. "We have to keep the surface looking as bare as possible."

"I don't remember learning that during my time spent inside mortal minds. When did they start doing that?" Solís asked through his breathing regulator.

"Decades ago. They've sent actual humans here, too. But more frequently, it's the little rovers."

"Have they ever seen anything they shouldn't?"

"We've had to destroy a few robots because they got too close to the warrior training grounds, or because they caught sight of one of us. With enough lunar dust clogging the gears, the robots' demise looks natural."

"I don't have much experience with the mortals," Solís said, still clenching the regulator between his teeth. "I've only seen their world through the eyes of the mortals my soul grew within. But that was long ago when my soul was infantile and in development. My memories from that time are select and hazy."

"Those memories are blurry for me also. What remains vivid in my mind is their impermanence and fragility—the mortals need us."

Solís nodded. "That's what I remember most, too."

"And right now, I have a creeping suspicion that they need us more than ever. The Marzans are up to something nefarious. We have to uncover their plans."

"Better get moving then. Louie is our best shot."

Luna spread her enormous dragonfly wings. Their iridescent film shimmered an array of pastels in the cosmic light of the moon. She extended her hand to Solís.

"Take my hand," she instructed.

With less hesitation than he had shown in the past, Solís grabbed her hand and held it tight.

Luna closed her eyes and sent a surge of power through her body and into Solís's. An icy-cold tingle ran across his flesh—a fast-moving prickle that covered every inch of him.

"What was that?" he asked when the sensation stopped.

"Invisibility," she answered. "Now, we can enter Deimos safely."

She muttered an incantation, her voice low and the words inaudible, and with a lurch, they were transported.

The space between here and there was a silent void with cosmic colors swirling around them at dizzying speeds. It was a space of brevity; they exited the tunnel almost as quickly as they had entered.

They landed in Louie's prison cell—a circular room made of thick red rock.

Louie was sprawled out across the floor, wrists chained to the wall and body writhing in discomfort.

While Luna assessed their surroundings, Solís doubled over with a heave.

"Shh," Luna whispered. "They can't see us, but they can still hear us."

Solís heaved again, covering his mouth and trying to settle the nauseous feeling the portal left him with.

Louie screamed.

The noise he made was high-pitched and frantic, and it sounded like his throat was stripped raw as the scream left his mouth.

Louie cried, "Mom!"

"She isn't here!" a guard said from outside his door. "Be quiet!"

A smoking pellet was tossed into the room through the bars of the door window, filling the small space with a suffocating fog. The thick vapor held a sedative component, which quickly gripped Luna.

"We have to get out of here," she said in a choking whisper.

"What's wrong?" Solís asked, still breathing through his regulator.

"Don't breathe in the smoke," she said, her eyes closing. She fell to her knees. "And don't let go of my hand."

"Why not?" Solís asked, kneeling beside her.

Her huge, beautiful silver eyes shimmered beneath her fluttering lashes.

"If you let go, they'll be able to see you," she answered before succumbing to the smoke and closing her eyes. She fell into Solís, who caught her before she hit the ground. With a careful shift of positions, he sat on the floor and held Luna in his lap.

Solís kept a firm grip on Luna's hand while checking his oxygen gauge with his free hand. His tank was half full.

His gaze moved to Louie, whose writhing body was now limp.

The only one in the room still conscious, Solís had no choice but to wait out the effects of the sleeping gas.

He dropped the oxygen gauge and used his free hand to trace the outline of Luna's face. She was beautiful, undeniably, and though a deep-rooted part of himself struggled to let go of his learned hatred, the other part was eager to push through. Seeing her like this—vulnerable and in need of his protection— something inside of him awakened. He would guard her, he would shelter her, and there was nothing that could stop him from doing so.

In slumber, her sharp facial features softened. Her heart was good—he knew that now—and he would not let anything happen to her while she relied on his protection.

Time was impossible to track in this room—no light, no windows, no noise besides the occasional sound of guards switching shifts. Solís glanced at Louie, whose limp body was covered in fresh wounds, and understood how someone might lose their sanity here.

The only way to measure time was by monitoring his turning gears. As he felt his gears beginning to slow, he determined half a day must have passed. He reached into the satchel attached to his waistband and grabbed five marbles. Breath held, he removed his mouthpiece and popped the marbles into his mouth. He clamped the regulator back between his teeth before letting the marbles roll into his holding pan.

His gears picked up speed, turning faster as new marbles entered the intricate machine that gave him life.

Solís checked Luna's pulse again. It was faint, but there—she was alive, just lost deep within a forced sleep.

There were no signs that she'd wake up anytime soon. He looked at his oxygen gauge again—only a quarter tank left.

Solís examined Louie from afar, wondering how he breathed without a tank. Surely, his oxygen reserve had depleted by now.

His answer came as two guards barreled through the prison door.

Solís held Luna close, remaining as still and quiet as possible beneath their shield of invisibility.

The Marzan guards wore face masks to avoid suffering the same fate as Louie.

"He's been out almost a full day," one of the guards said. "How many gas pellets did you toss in here?"

"Three," the other replied.

"That's too many! He's due for another interrogation tonight. Keep the door open to air this room out." As he gave these orders, he knelt beside Louie's unconscious body. He placed his giant hand over Louie's mouth and scanned for something unseen.

"No wonder he's been out for so long. The bubble is so thin it's practically gone. We need to reapply," he finally said.

"Feed him first," the other guard said.

"Right. Good call."

The kneeling guard tossed a few crudely carved red rock marbles into Louie's mouth. The guard who was still standing took a sheer sheet of film out of his knapsack, tried to uncrumple it the best he could, then handed it to the guard kneeling beside Louie. He outlined Louie's nose and mouth with the film, pressing the edges into Louie's zinc-hued flesh until they stuck. Before sealing the last corner, the guard retrieved a small cylinder tank from his tool belt and placed a skinny hose beneath the film. With a few pumps of the tank's trigger, the film around the bottom half of Louie's face began to expand like a balloon until it was stretched so wide the film became invisible.

The guard sealed the last bit of film to Louie's face before returning to his feet.

"That should hold for a day or two. The fresh oxygen should also speed up his recovery." He shook his head. "Three pellets?"

170

"I wanted to make sure it was enough to penetrate the film."

"Let's just hope he wakes up before his scheduled interrogation with King Helmer."

As the guards left, leaving the door open to air out the room, Luna's eyes shot open.

Breathing heavy, heart racing, her eyes scanned the room as she lay in Solís's lap.

"You are safe," he whispered to her, placing his hand on her cheek.

The fear sent her body into fight mode. Her silver eyes turned black, her teeth sharpened to fangs, and black veins appeared around her eyes. The cords within her body tangled into knots, forcing her to battle the rage growing inside of her.

"You are safe," Solís repeated, his warm hand gently caressing the side of her face.

She stared up at him, focusing on his kind, golden eyes.

"I am not a monster," she said, shaking as she struggled to calm her adrenaline.

"I know," he answered genuinely.

Luna closed her eyes and focused on finding her serenity. It took a moment for the knotted cords to untangle and the veins around her eyes to dissipate.

When she reopened her eyes, the darkness was replaced by brilliant silver luminosity. The glow was captivating and Solís could not look away. An enchanted smile crept across his face.

"What are you smiling about?" she asked as she regained her bearings.

"You."

"Me?"

"I see you clearly now."

Luna furrowed her brow. "I'm not sure what that means, but we need to get out of here. How's your tank?"

"Almost empty."

Luna turned her attention to Louie. "Any sign of life from him?"

As the question left her lips, Louie began to stir.

Luna stood, still holding Solís's hand, and moved closer to Louie.

"Louie, it's us," she whispered. "Luna and Solís. You need to be quiet or they'll gas us again."

Louie whimpered as both his consciousness and his pain returned.

"We are going to die," he said, teeth chattering and body trembling.

"No, we aren't," Luna corrected him. She lowered the shield from her face so Louie could see her. "I have the tools to set you free this time. We are going to get you out of here."

Louie stared up at her intensely. His silver-blue eyes were bloodshot and glimmered with desperation. "It doesn't matter where we go," he said, voice raspy from the torture and malnutrition. "Nowhere is safe."

"They conditioned you to believe that."

"It's the truth!" Louie said, the volume of his voice rising.

"Shh," Luna urged while untying the sheers from her belt. "We can talk after you're free." Connection broken from Solís, the invisibility shield lowered. Luna handed the sheers to Solís and said, "We have to work quickly."

Solís nodded and began weakening the chain links holding Louie captive.

"It will end in death," Louie said.

Luna knelt beside him and cradled him against her chest. The young Nautipunk was a shell of himself, utterly dismantled and broken.

"Everyone is going to die," he said.

"It's okay. You are safe now. And once we are out of this place, you can tell us everything you know and we will stop the Marzans' plans."

"They've already begun," Louie said, unable to contain his sorrow any longer. He broke into tears and convulsed in Luna's embrace.

She glanced up at Solís, who managed to cut through the first constraint.

Three left to go.

"We will stop them," Luna promised.

"You can't," Louie sniveled.

Solís cut through the second constraint.

"You will feel better as soon as we get you out of here," Luna encouraged. "This place has stripped you of all hope."

"This place opened my eyes to reality," Louie countered.

Solís cut through the third constraint; one more to go.

"Reality awaits you in Quintessence," Luna said.

Solís cut through the fourth and final chain.

Luna waved at him to rejoin them. He raced to her side and clasped her hand.

"Time to go," she said, eager to leave before the Marzans came back around to check on Louie.

"Where are we going?" Louie asked, writhing within Luna's grip.

"Back to Quintessence."

"It isn't safe there!"

"You aren't thinking clearly," Luna said, fighting to keep Louie connected to her. Solís shifted his body to face hers, and together, they sandwiched Louie between them.

"Let me go! I'm safer here!" Louie insisted.

"Stop fighting us," Solís demanded.

"They are going to extinguish the sun!"

"Wha—" Solís began, but his question never got a chance to leave his lips.

Luna had activated the portal and they were wrenched out of the Marzan prison at lightspeed.

Chapter 25

Mōnalene

They shot through the portal and landed on the moon with a stumble.

"Sorry," Luna apologized. "It was a hasty exit."

"Why did you bring us here instead of Quintessence?" Solís asked through his regulator while checking the gauge of his oxygen tank.

"We need to hear what Louie is trying to tell us."

"I need a flower, then. I'm almost out of air."

Luna handed Solís an oxygeni blossom, then crouched beside Louie, who was shaking where he knelt. "Tell us everything. You are safe now."

"Where am I?" he asked.

"Mōnalene. Moon of the hellions," Solís answered.

"Lunarians," Luna corrected him.

"I know that, but he doesn't," Solís quipped.

"You've been here before," Luna said to Louie.

"Briefly," Solís chimed in.

Louie looked around, taking in the gray dust and silver glow of this place.

"I remember," he finally said.

"Tell us what you overheard the Marzans say."

"They plan to extinguish the source flame," Louie said. His body still trembled from the trauma he had endured.

"Impossible," Solís replied.

"That would kill every living being in this galaxy," Luna added.

"They know that," Louie said. "It's what they want."

"They would die, too."

"Based on what they were saying, it seems like they'd thrive without the sun."

Luna took a pause to consider this, then finally said, "Fire is their greatest foe."

Solís stepped in, "As much as it might be their foe, it also gives them life. They must realize that."

Louie shook his head. "They were adamant that they would thrive without the sun."

"Extinguishing the source flame is an impossible task," Solís added. "They will never succeed."

"They said the plan was already in motion," Louie revealed.

"How?" Solís asked.

"They didn't specify, but I think it has something to do with the Marzan prisoner in Hydra."

Solís pulled Luna aside.

"We have to go back to Quintessence. I have to warn my father."

"I will take you back," she promised.

"This is your chance to show the leaders of Quintessence the value of an alliance with the Lunarians."

"How so?"

"You know how to fight the Marzans, right?" he asked her, his expression grave.

Luna nodded.

"Teach us," he implored her.

"We've fought them for centuries. We know their weaknesses and have possession of the only tools known to defeat them." She pointed to the magnetic threads still knotted around Solís's ankles.

"These threads are a weapon?"

"They are a lot of things, a weapon being one of them. I'm still surprised you didn't cut them off as soon as you got home."

Solís shrugged. "I kind of like how they look."

Luna smirked, sensing that he was fonder of this place, and possibly her, than he was willing to admit. She kept these thoughts to herself. "We need to come up with a plan."

"An alliance between your people and mine is imperative," Solís said without hesitation.

"You've really had a full change of heart."

"With these new developments, it just makes sense."

"You do realize this alliance is not temporary. It needs to endure long after we help you defeat the Marzans. It has to serve both of us, not just you."

"That is how alliances work, isn't it?" Solís said, his sarcasm and impatience potent. "We will hammer out the details. Let's get you in front of my parents. We have to explain all of this to them."

They returned to Louie, who was a shell of his former self, and together, they teleported back to Quintessence. Emerging in the sky above the billowing mauve sails of Montgomery's flying ship, the trio had a moment to assess their surroundings beneath a shield of invisibility before rejoining the bustle.

Solís kept his attention on his family below.

Luna zeroed in on the Marzan in her distant cage.

"Something isn't right," Luna stated.

"What do you mean?" Solís asked, Louie's limp body slung over his shoulder.

"I feel a pull," she said, her words vague. "I feel the tug of obsolescence."

"What does that mean?" Solís repeated, his patience thinning.

Luna's silver eyes began shifting to black as her rage heightened.

"I think I figured out their plan," she stated, gaze glued on the imprisoned Marzan.

"What is it?"

"Let me confirm my suspicions first."

With a speedy swoop, Luna lowered Solís and Louie to the ship below, dropping them off before racing toward the Marzan's cage.

Her invisibility shield disengaged the moment she let go of Solís.

Solís shouted at her, trying to warn her, but Luna was engulfed by her fury. Vision tunneled and sounds muffled beneath the ringing of her rage, Luna was unreachable.

Her dragonfly wings thrashed with such speed the iridescent film formed a colorful aura around Luna's dark silhouette. She was a terror to behold, and every Solarpunk in Hydra stopped what they were doing to watch in horror as a monster they feared tore freely across their skies.

"Shoot 'er down!" Red Fang Ralph called to his crew, who hurried across the top deck to man their cannons. "Aye, Monty boy!" he shouted up at Montgomery's ship, which floated above his. "You seein' this?"

Montgomery was already leaning against the port gunwale, golden eyes reddening with anger as his fire heart sweltered.

"I see," he replied through gritted teeth.

"Yer want 'er dead? Or captured to keelhaul?" Ralph's silver-blue eyes lit up with excitement. "Haven't done a proper dragging in months. Me vote is fer the keelhaul!"

"Leave her be for now," Montgomery said, his grave stillness alarming. "I want to see what she does."

"Arrrghh." Ralph groaned, took a swig of his grog, then spoke to his crew. "Hold off until I give the order!"

"Dad," Solís said, out of breath after searching the whole boat for him. "Don't strike. She's here to save us."

"That hellion?" Montgomery spat in question. "Don't tell me you've bought their lies, too."

"Just watch."

"I thought you were more grounded than your sister," Montgomery said with a click of his tongue. "I do plan to observe before striking, but that monster will not survive the day."

"You will change your mind," Solís said, his confidence unwavering. "If I can be swayed, so can you."

They stood next to each other in silence. Solís prayed that Luna was correct and that whatever happened next was enough to change his father's opinion of her.

Emmeline joined them, standing next to Solís.

"Thank you for bringing Louie back," she said in a low voice. "He's resting in my cabin now."

"You're welcome," Solís replied. "How is he doing?"

"Not good."

"They thoroughly broke him. It will take him a while to recover."

"I know." Emmeline held back tears. "It's all my fault."

"Do not carry his burden. He made the decision to use the portal."

"For *me* … he only did it to help *me*."

"I told him I had it under control."

Emmeline shook her head, frustrated by all the chaos she had caused. "I will stay by his side as he heals. I won't let this ruin him."

"That's the right thing to do, but don't let it ruin you, too," Solís cautiously advised. "You've been looking skinnier since Clementine died. Are you eating?"

"I am. I just forget sometimes."

"Don't let the grief consume you."

"I'm trying to focus on what I *can* fix. Louie is home and alive. I have to help him."

"He might push you away, he might fight you—if he doesn't want your help, don't force it."

"You're so negative."

"I'm realistic. I've seen Pyropunk soldiers traumatized by war. It's never an easy fix."

"I won't give up on him."

"Nor should you. Just don't lose yourself while helping him find himself."

Emmeline sighed, eyes on the scene unraveling around them, and changed the topic. "We have to protect Luna."

"Now more than ever."

"You agree?" Emmeline asked, shocked by her brother's change of heart.

"She is the key to our survival. She is the only one who can teach us how to defeat the Marzans."

"What did you learn during the rescue mission?"

"That the Marzans plan to extinguish the sun," Solís spoke louder, hoping his father was listening to their conversation.

"How?" Emmeline asked, eyes wide with fright.

"Not sure, but I think we are about to find out. When we arrived here, Luna's face shifted with rage, turning her back into monster form, and she sped off toward the Marzan cage. She said she figured out their plan."

Montgomery's stern stance shifted and his furious energy softened ever so slightly.

No longer needing to barter with Deánira for Louie's safety, Emmeline dropped her quest to negotiate with the Marzan and trusted Luna to do whatever was necessary.

Solís and Emmeline resumed their silence, watching with hope as Luna reached the Marzan's cage.

Chapter 26

A tiny black hole swirled at the center of the Marzan's cage.

"Not on my watch," Luna said through bared fangs.

Arms extended through the bars of the cage, Luna activated her magnetism. The Marzan was yanked away from her black hole creation and secured in Luna's grip.

"No!" the Marzan screeched.

The monsters in the neighboring cages howled, roared, and wailed—a mixture of rage and excitement as they watched their fellow moon beings clash.

"Did you really think it would be that easy?" Luna asked the Marzan in a low and menacing voice.

"You should be on *our* side," the Marzan pled, "not the Solarpunks. They are our common enemy!"

"No, *you* are the enemy. The Lunarians have no desire to extinguish the sun."

"Do you not serve Lunéss?"

"Of course, we do," Luna spat.

"Then you should be on our side. We only serve Her purpose."

"Lies!"

Luna strengthened her magnetism, constraining the Marzan further.

"Please, stop. Lunéss wants to turn the lights off in this galaxy."

"Sounds more like something Kólasi would request."

The Marzan smirked, then asked, "What do you know about Kólasi?"

"Chaos, destruction, death—His existence thrives on mayhem."

"Soon, Kólasi will become the one true god."

Luna pulled tighter, constricting the chains beneath the Marzan's flesh. Gooey blood trickled from her ears.

"Are you working with *Him*?" Luna asked, fanged teeth bared.

"I never said that."

"Answer me!" Luna demanded, the black veins around her eyes bulging.

"Never."

Infuriated, Luna increased the magnetism radiating off of her body. With a single pull, she constricted the Marzan's interior chains, forcing them to slice through her insides.

The Marzan crumpled to a heap on the floor of her cage.

Dead.

The attentive audience of caged monsters surrounding the lifeless Marzan erupted in a frenzy. Clawing at their own faces, ripping out their hair, slamming their foreheads against the bars of their prisons—they were broken and feral, no longer resembling her refined and respectable allies from the Lunarlight Coalition. Their time imprisoned in Hydra had morphed them into savages.

Though she wished to save them, she wondered if their damage was too deep, too irreversible.

Luna flew a few paces away from the detention center, unaware of the giant thermal balloon draped in golden chains floating toward her.

"Turn and face me," Montgomery said, announcing his arrival to Luna.

Startled, Luna turned before calming her adrenaline and returning to her docile state. She was in full rage mode, and the sight of her made Montgomery recoil in disgust.

"Seize her!" he shouted, giving the Thermapunk crew on his nearby airship authority to strike.

"Wait," Luna pled, but hooked ropes were already being lobbed in her direction.

She flew higher to avoid capture, all while futilely trying to reverse her rage.

The monsters rampaged within their cages at the arrival of Montgomery. The air thickened the hot breath of their roaring protest—their visceral hatred for him was almost tangible.

Aboard Montgomery's anchored airship, Emmeline and Solís sprung into action.

"Stop!" Emmeline pled, snatching a hooked rope out of the nearest Thermapunk's hands while Solís tackled the Thermapunks preparing to fire rockets.

"Is no one paying attention?" Luna shouted at them. "That devil was crafting a black hole within her cage!"

Avery flew Montgomery's golden balloon closer to the cage, which still sizzled with petroleum fire. Between the bars, he saw what Luna spoke of: a thimble-sized black hole rotated at the center of the cage.

Visibly repulsed by his lack of options, Montgomery lifted a hand to halt the ensuing attack.

"How do we get rid of it?" he asked her.

"You can't."

"We have no defense against black holes."

"No one does."

"Then what use are you to me?" he asked harshly.

"I just stopped the Marzan before this small black hole became one large enough for other Marzans to travel through."

"They travel through black holes?" Montgomery asked, his anger turning into horrified curiosity.

"Yes!"

"And you know how to kill them?"

"Clearly."

Montgomery nodded, his golden gaze darting between Luna and the lifeless Marzan in its cage.

He continued, "You *want* to help us?"

"Yes! I've been trying to prove I'm not a monster for weeks now."

"Look at you!" Montgomery countered. "Fanged and soulless—your eyes are black voids."

"I am not your enemy," Luna insisted, refocusing on calming her adrenaline. "I risked great divide among my people to heal your daughter, I risked my life to save Louie, I brought Gemma to Mōnalene to heal, I just saved all of you from this Marzan's black hole—what more do I need to do to prove I can be trusted?"

"Solédon instructed us not to trust any moon monsters," Montgomery said, his confusion apparent. "It is written in His holy doctrine."

"Either you have a false doctrine or Solédon has teamed up with Kólasi because a rivalry between the sun and our moon was never part of the greater plan."

"How would *you* know the greater plan?"

"Because I've heard the greater plan, spoken directly from Lunéss's mouth."

"You've spoken to Her?" Montgomery asked, face slack with disbelief.

"I have. She visited Mōnalene when I was a young girl. She addressed the entire nation of Lunarians. And when someone asked Her to make our acquisition of fire easier, She promised us that the Solarpunks were given orders by Solédon to coexist harmoniously with the Lunarians. When that same person expressed our difficulties, Lunéss swore that She would speak to Solédon." Luna looked defeated, her appearance returning to its natural state. "It's been over a decade since that promise was made."

"Well, I can assure you that Solédon has not teamed up with Kólasi. I also struggle to believe that the doctrine we possess is a fraud. We've had it in our possession since our creation."

"All I know is that we're supposed to exist in harmony. And with the looming threat of the Marzans trying to extinguish the sun, the time to align is now."

"I overheard my children saying something about that," Montgomery said. "Tell me more."

Luna's teeth were no longer fanged and her eyes had resumed their normal shade of alluring silver. The cords beneath her flesh had untangled and the black veins around her eyes were still visible, but rapidly fading.

She explained, "The Marzans are the only moon beings in this galaxy who find discomfort living in the constant presence of the sun—fire is one of their fatal foes. It appears their plan is to swallow and extinguish the sun through one of their black holes."

"Can they create black holes remotely?"

"I think they'd need to be here, but I'm not sure. What's worse is that I think they might have Kólasi on their side."

Avery, who listened in silence near the balloon's pedal controls, gasped at this news. "What? How?" she asked.

"Before I killed the Marzan, she said that Kólasi would become the one true god. I assume that means He plans to take over, or destroy, all of the planets, suns, moons, and stars belonging to the other gods until all that's left are entities under His control."

"The gods would never allow it," Montgomery said.

"Do they even know what He's doing?" Luna countered.

"As far as I know," Avery stepped in, "we've never heard from Solédon directly."

"And I was a child the last time we heard from Lunéss. Before that, it had been centuries since She visited. The universe is massive; who knows how many galaxies the gods oversee."

"So, it's up to us to save this sun from destruction," Montgomery stated with grave determination.

"It appears so."

Montgomery looked to Luna, his golden eyes ablaze with intense uncertainty.

"You are willing to help?" he asked.

"We are, but you cannot shut us out from the fire after we defeat the Marzans. We use the flame to keep our mortals on Earth alive; we use the flame to protect ourselves from the Marzans. We have no nefarious use for fire."

Montgomery nodded. "I am open to this discussion. I cannot fathom allowing unrestrained access to the source flame, but perhaps a rationed delivery of fire would be a fair trade."

"I think the Monarchs of Mōnalene would be happy with that deal."

Luna extended her hand to Montgomery. Her slick and shimmering silver flesh was lustrous in the dim, flickering light of Hydra.

Montgomery hesitated. Luna no longer looked like the monsters he loathed. In her current docile state, her beauty, kindness, and sincerity radiated.

"If you betray us, I will kill you myself," Montgomery warned.

Luna lowered her hand. "And I return that sentiment if you renege on your half of the deal after we take care of the Marzans for you."

"Let's come to an agreement on terms before we make promises we cannot keep," Montgomery suggested. "How much fire do you need to keep your mortals alive? How much do you need for your personal defenses?"

"How do you measure fire?" Luna asked, unsure how to answer.

"It's not the size of the flame that matters; it's the intensity. How much heat does it hold? How much power will it provide?" Montgomery explained. "Joules measure heat."

Luna cupped her hands together and asked, "If I was holding an orb of fire that fit perfectly into my hands, how many joules would that be?"

Montgomery silently assessed the size of her cupped hands.

"Impossible to say for certain without measuring the intensity of the fire orb, but if it held the average amount of power, my guess would be around one thousand joules."

"We use about twenty fire orbs during each rotation around Earth. Twenty thousand joules per day is the bare minimum to keep the Earthlings alive. Thirty would make it easier."

"I'll allow fifty thousand joules per day to keep the mortals alive," Montgomery said. Luna's silver eyes widened. He asked, "And how about for your defenses?"

"I'm not as involved in that department anymore."

185

"I'll match the fifty, but not on a daily basis. Fifty thousand joules per day for the mortals. Fifty thousand joules per month for your personal defenses. Do you think your leaders will accept this agreement?"

"I hope so. It's very generous."

"I hope so, too, because that's the highest I'll go. We don't have time to barter—I offered high because I need them to accept. We need to prepare our defenses against the Marzan devils immediately."

"This alliance includes safety from your militia, correct?"

"Yes."

"My soldiers will not need to fear capture and imprisonment while they're here?"

"Of course, not. We need your help."

"And after we've succeeded in saving the sun?"

"If we're successful and you've proven your trustworthiness, the alliance will stand."

"Excellent. I will return and relay your offer. If it is accepted, I will return with an army of Odonata warriors."

"As you've stated, the time to align is now. The Solarpunks aren't the only ones who will perish if the Marzans swallow our sun."

"I am aware."

Montgomery nodded and instructed Avery to redirect their golden balloon back to his hovering airship.

Montgomery wore a battling look of distrust and hope as they sailed away from the detention center, leaving the caged monsters behind. Their horrifying and inescapable howls echoed across Hydra. Montgomery clenched his teeth in annoyance, hoping his departure would soon silence the beasts.

Halfway back to his anchored airship, they crossed paths with Solís and Emmeline. They flew toward the detention center using the wings strapped to their backs—Solís using helium and titanium wings, Emmeline using her heated weightlessness and golden wings.

"You've gotten your wish," Montgomery shouted at them with a growl. "An alliance with the hellions is in the works."

"You won't regret it," Emmeline assured him. "She is the key to saving us."

"At the cost of a million and a half joules each month," Montgomery grumbled.

"Better than death."

Solís added, "The sun creates infinite joules. A few million won't dent our power production in the slightest."

Montgomery eyed his son with perplexed disbelief. "You have transformed," he stated plainly. "I suppose I should be happy that you two are now working together rather than arguing all the time."

"It hasn't been easy," Solís said, "but I have to admit that I was wrong about everything. Luna isn't a monster. Emmeline was right all along."

"Time will tell."

"Trust me, it's easier to let go of our old hatreds than it is to harbor them," Solís advised. "The sooner you accept this new reality, the easier moving forward will become."

Montgomery groaned. "I've done enough for one day. I will revisit all of this after a full night of sleep." Montgomery turned to Avery wearing a weary expression. "Please take me home."

"Of course," Avery replied, shifting the gears and pedals that controlled the giant dragon wings attached to the sides of the basket. She placed her lips around a small pipe that snaked up the ropes and blew helium into the base of the balloon.

As they lifted higher into the sky, Avery leaned over the side of the basket, made eye contact with Emmeline, and mouthed, *I'll fill you in later.*

The gilded balloon draped in golden chains drifted upward toward the faraway gates of Hydra.

"Things are moving in the right direction," Solís stated.

Emmeline nodded, clearly still bothered by everything else that weighed on her. "We are far from the finish line, though."

"There is no such thing as a finish line," Solís said. "Life is ever moving; there will always be new trials to navigate."

"I just want the chaos I caused to finally end. I want everyone I love to be okay."

"The chaos you caused is the only reason we might survive this attack. If you hadn't befriended Luna, we would have had to fight the Marzans on our own."

"Maybe. Or maybe we would have found a way to survive with fewer Solarpunks dying or suffering in the process."

Solís sighed. "Louie will be okay. He just needs time."

"I don't want to talk about it," Emmeline said, pounding her golden wings against the salty air and rocketing toward the detention center.

Solís followed.

The closer they got, the louder the monsters became. A symphony of horror; a chorale of abhorrence. Their hatred knew no limits.

Luna hovered, waiting patiently for them.

"They are so loud," Solís said, his expression twisted with discomfort.

"They are hurting," Luna replied.

"Would it be safe to set them free?" Emmeline asked.

Luna shook her head. "I don't think so. They bear little resemblance to their unshackled counterparts in space. They are stuck in states of rage."

"Like your rage face?" Emmeline asked.

"Yes. If I was trapped in that state of mind for too long, I'm not sure I'd be able to recover either."

"Are these monsters docile moon beings like the Lunarians?"

"Not all, but most of them are. We work closely together in an organization called the Lunarlight Coalition. These are my allies, my friends." Luna's silver eyes held deep remorse. "At least they used to be."

"Things are rapidly changing," Solís promised, stepping into the conversation. "We might not be able to save these particular moon beings, but the day is soon coming that no celestial creature will ever suffer again at the hands of their neighbors. We just need to save the sun first."

Luna's grave expression bent with a tilted smile. "You're like a whole new person."

"I have you to thank for that," Solís stated candidly.

"Ahem." Emmeline forced a fake cough.

"And you, too," Solís added. "I see everything differently now."

"I like this new and improved Solís," Luna said, her smile widening.

"I like you, too."

Emmeline's bewilderment had reached its limits and she blurted out, "What is *this*? What is happening here?"

"Just some long overdue growth," Solís replied.

"No, no. I meant between the two of you."

"An unlikely friendship born from the ashes of foolish hatred," Solís answered, his golden eyes glimmering.

"Looks like more than friendship to me," Emmeline countered, teasing them playfully.

"We have work to do," Luna said, ending their banter, though her silver eyes still held an enchanted sparkle. "Is the moonstone I gave you safe?"

"Yes," Emmeline answered.

"Good. If anything changes between now and my return, use the stone to travel to Mōnalene and alert me. You know the phrase to get to the moon." She expelled a black cord from her fingertip and handed it to Emmeline. "This cord is a part of me; therefore, it is connected to the stone you have here in Hydra. Wrap it around your wrist or ankle as Solís has done. This will help you return to Quintessence from the moon. The phrase to travel from the moon to the sun is *Ad solem quin. Accipe me.*"

"Thank you," Emmeline expressed, wrapping the cord around her wrist. "Will you check on Gemma's recovery while you're there?"

"Of course. There's a lot riding on the success of our teamwork. I have to get going." With that, Luna clutched the amulet hanging around her neck and whispered, "Ad lunam lu. Accipe me."

The scent of moon lily lingered a moment before disappearing with Luna.

It was time to prepare the rest of the Solarpunk factions for war.

Chapter 27

"Get away from me," Louie shouted at Emmeline.

"I want to help you," she expressed, sitting next to where he lay and trying not to cry.

"There's no point!" He turned over in his cot to face away from her. He winced in agony as the fresh wounds on his back were irritated by his sudden movement. The pain was so intense he needed to take a few deep breaths before he spoke again. "We are all going to die."

"We plan to fight back."

"I'm done fighting."

"You can't give up now," Emmeline pled. "There's so much to live for."

"Like what?"

"Like us! Isn't our love worth fighting for?"

"I almost died for our love, needlessly, I might add. I was there for days before Luna came." He paused; the venom in his words thickened. "And *you* never came at all."

"They wouldn't let me!" Emmeline countered. "I begged Luna to bring me with her."

"Clearly, you didn't try very hard to convince her."

"I did! And when she left me here, I took it upon myself to find other ways to help you. I tried to make a deal with the devil to save you!"

He glanced over his shoulder at her, then stated plainly, "They cannot be bargained with."

"I risked my life trying to barter with that monster."

"Let's not compare our efforts to save each other. You won't like the result."

Emmeline's heart contracted. She took a deep breath to regulate her emotions, then said, "I'm not trying to compare my efforts to yours, I'm just trying to say that I tried." She paused. "And that I love you."

"Don't lie to me."

The tears she was holding back finally fell. "I'm not lying."

"Go away."

"Please look at me," Emmeline pled. She placed her hand on his shoulder, to which he winced.

"Stop hurting me!"

Emmeline quickly retracted her hand.

"I'm sorry," she offered.

"Go away!"

She stood and took a step backward toward the door.

"I will keep trying," she promised.

"I wish you wouldn't."

"But I will. I won't let this break us."

"You're too late. I'm already broken."

"I will fix you."

"You can't fix what you broke and expect things to just be the same."

Emmeline inhaled deeply, holding tight to all the guilt she felt.

"You're right," she said. "This is my fault. Which is why I'm so desperate to right my wrongs."

"You have plenty of victims to choose from," he said, his anger deflating. "Go save someone else."

Unable to hold back her emotions any longer, Emmeline darted out of the room to find privacy elsewhere. Blinded by her tears and dizzy from the rejection, she did not see Kiran in her path until she walked headfirst into him.

"Oh, I'm sorry," she offered, avoiding his concerned gaze.

"I tried to get your attention, but you didn't seem to hear me. Are you okay?"

"No," she answered. The honesty dismantled any strength she had left. She collapsed into Kiran's chest and began to sob.

He wrapped his arms around her and gently guided her toward a more private place to talk.

"What happened?" he asked.

"Louie," she said between sniffles. "He hates me."

"I have a hard time believing that."

"He does! He won't even look at me when I visit him."

"He's just hurting," Kiran tried to rationalize.

"He's hurting me, too," she confessed.

"Then maybe you both need some space."

"If I give him space, I'm afraid I'll lose him. Or that he'll think I'm not trying. His suffering is my fault; I have to fix it. I need to prove my remorse; I need to prove my love."

"You don't need to prove anything," Kiran corrected her. "The fact that you think you do is worrying."

"He's injured because of me. I can't just turn my back on him."

"Creating space is not the same as abandoning someone. He knows you want to help and be there for him. When he's ready, he'll come around."

Emmeline wiped the tears off her cheeks.

"Maybe you're right," she said. "Maybe I'm making it worse by smothering him."

"Take a deep breath," he encouraged her. "Everything will be okay."

"Thank you. I feel a little better."

"Good," he replied with a smile.

"I need a task. Something to distract me and make me feel useful."

"Want to have lunch before I leave to check on Helix?"

"I'm not hungry, but I'll go with you to see Helix." Emmeline stood tall and regained her composure. She then added, "I've never tried flying home from Hydra before."

"It's a long flight. I wouldn't risk it. You can ride on my back, or we can see if Avery can take us."

Emmeline shook her head. "Avery took my father home. She isn't here."

"Then on my back it is." Kiran knelt on one knee. "Climb aboard."

As Emmeline wrapped her arms around Kiran's neck, an angry shout halted her.

"What is *this*?"

Emmeline turned to find Louie limping toward them.

"Avery isn't here, so Kiran is giving me a ride home," she answered, voice shaking.

"Kiran?" Louie asked, tone venomous. "How quickly I was replaced."

"It's not like that," Emmeline swore, letting go of Kiran's neck.

Louie's silver-blue eyes were bloodshot with manic sorrow.

"You almost had me believing that you cared," Louie spat. "That you tried to help while I was being tortured on Deimos. Meanwhile, you found a new boyfriend." He let out a frenzied laugh. "I am such a fool."

"Stop! You're misinterpreting everything. Kiran is only helping me get to Helix."

"She's telling the truth," Kiran said, hoping to help diffuse Louie's panicked jealousy.

"Don't speak to me," Louie growled at Kiran, then returned his gaze to Emmeline. "I almost died for you."

"Let me help you. I want to be by your side while you heal."

"Looks like you'd rather be with *him*."

"No," Emmeline swore. "*You* keep pushing me away, so I decided to visit Helix and give you a little space. You are healing from severe trauma. I understand why your nerves are on edge, but I am simply trying to get home."

"Everything I've endured, everything I've lost, all ties back to you," Louie said, jaw muscles bulging as he clenched his teeth. "All you do is cause me pain."

"I still love you," Emmeline said, the tears returning to her eyes.

"Your lies only hurt me more."

"I'm not lying," she swore, then repeated, "I love you."

Louie shook his head, furious tears brimming in his pretty eyes.

"I don't love you," he said, voice shaking. "Not anymore."

"You don't mean that," Emmeline said, her cheeks streaked with tears.

"I do," Louie spat. His fists were clenched. "Unlike you, I'm not a liar."

He turned and limped away; his wounds bled through the white shirt he wore.

Emmeline trembled where she stood.

"Are you okay?" Kiran asked cautiously. He placed his hand on her shoulder, which she immediately swatted away.

"Don't touch me," she barked. "What if he turns around?"

"He's acting irrationally."

"It doesn't matter. I'm not trying to fuel his anger or worsen his pain. I've hurt him enough already."

"He is in the wrong here, not you," Kiran stated. "How he treated you just now was out of line. He owes you an apology."

"He owes me nothing."

Kiran shook his head. "I hope you start to see this situation clearly soon. Otherwise, your misguided repentance will consume you."

"You're not helping matters."

"This is *not* my fault."

Emmeline inhaled deeply, trying to organize her irrational thoughts. When she exhaled, her heightened emotions calmed and she reminded herself of Louie's current reality.

"He is in a state of severe trauma," Emmeline rationalized. "He didn't mean what he said."

"No matter the state he is in … you don't deserve to be treated that way."

"I don't want to talk about it anymore. Please take me to see Helix."

Kiran bent to one knee so Emmeline could latch on. After taking a thorough scan of her surroundings to ensure Louie was not watching, she climbed onto Kiran's back. He twisted the knob at the top of his tank, which was situated between himself and Emmeline. As the helium released, they lifted into the air.

He rotated his shoulder gears and his giant titanium wings spread wide. They flew through the thick, salty air of Hydra toward the giant gate above. As they approached, the gate began to open, and Montgomery's thermal balloon lowered into Hydra.

"You weren't gone long," Emmeline shouted to her father while simultaneously giving Avery a wave.

"I had a vision of the Marzans filtering an army through that black hole." He shuddered slightly. "I need to figure out how to close it."

"Let me know if there's any way I can help," Emmeline offered.

"Me, too," Kiran chimed in.

"I will," Montgomery said. "Cyrus and Solís will assist me with my first assessment of the black hole. I will keep you posted." Montgomery waved his hand, instructing Avery to lower them.

Kiran flew through the many crisscrossing bars of the gate before they closed. They soared through Terra and continued upward into Lower Gaslion, leaving the rows of massive Terra gears and Tinker Markets behind. The air here was tepid, and as they crossed into Fyree, it got even warmer.

Kiran was strong and Emmeline felt secure on his back. The safety she felt with him allowed her to use this trip to decompress from the altercation with Louie. Though she knew Louie was only projecting his own hurt onto her, it didn't lessen the sting of his words. She tried to empathize with his suffering, tried to understand his perspective, and ultimately settled on believing that he meant none of what he said. She had to believe this—the alternative was too devastating.

"We're here," Kiran announced as he landed on the lower deck attached to the basement.

Emmeline was home.

This golden mansion used to feel like a prison, but at this moment, it felt like a sanctuary. Hydra was home to her broken heart; it no longer gave her comfort.

She let go of Kiran's neck and dropped to the golden tiles.

"Have you seen Helix recently?" she asked Kiran as she led him inside.

"Last time I saw him he was really sick. Your brothers strapped him to his bed because he kept sneaking out to get more locomo. Helix fought the constraints, thrashing about like a maniac. It was hard to watch."

Emmeline sighed. "Hopefully, this time in confinement has helped him heal."

They made their way up the stairs, and when they arrived at his closed bedroom door, Emmeline took a brief pause before knocking.

"Helix, it's me," she announced. "I'm here with Kiran. Can we come in?"

"Emmeline!" Helix responded through the door. "Yes, yes. Come in."

She opened the door, afraid of the sight that might greet her. To her relief, it wasn't as bad as Kiran had described.

Though Helix was still confined to his bed by straps, he rested calmly in a state of peaceful surrender. A smile stretched across his tired face, temporarily camouflaging the hollowness beneath his cheeks.

"I was worried we might've lost you," he said as Emmeline hurried to his side. She took his right hand with both of hers and held it to her heart.

"I left to heal," she told him while scanning her older brother's deteriorating appearance. His golden-hued flesh was pale, his face was gaunt, and the circles under his eyes were dark gray.

"Did it work?" he asked her.

"Yes, I no longer suffer from the moonstone curse. I can eat without getting migraines again."

"Then why do you still look so skinny?"

"The migraines are gone," she said defensively. "That was the main issue."

"But are you eating again?"

"Yes!"

"Okay, good," Helix said before entering a coughing fit. Wet and rattling, each cough sounded painful.

197

"And what of your healing?" she asked him.

"I'm better today than I was yesterday."

Kiran chimed in, "And way better than he was a week ago."

"It's true," Helix confirmed.

Emmeline lowered Helix's hand, still holding it tight.

"How could you let it get this bad?" she asked.

"I didn't really have much control over it. The dust is addicting and I spiraled."

"Did Solís and Cyrus make any progress with stopping the Terrapunks from making and distributing locomo?" Emmeline asked.

"No," Kiran answered.

"They'll never stop," Helix added. "It's one of their few leverages against us. Even if they only lure in a few weak links from each group, it's still a victory in their eyes. They weaken us from the inside."

"But you're better now. They didn't win," Emmeline countered.

"I suppose so."

"We need you to help in our fight against the Marzans."

"The what?"

"The Devils of Delusion. They are the moon monsters who serve Mars."

"I really did miss a lot, huh?"

"They intend to swallow the source flame through a black hole, extinguishing it and leaving the rest of us for dead in its absence."

"How will we stop them?" Helix asked. "Are they easy to defeat?"

"No, not at all. They have the ability to breathe a crippling poison that infects anyone within range. They have chainmail armor beneath their flesh, making their skin nearly impenetrable. Their screams are powerful enough to move the ocean and shake the foundations of Quintessence. Oh, and don't forget … they can make black holes."

"What's this poison they breathe? I'm a pretty decent chemist. Perhaps I can make an antidote or something for a counterattack."

"We don't know what the poison is exactly, but you could probably get some small samples to test. Though they've started healing the infected Nautipunks and Terrapunks with the ointment Luna gave us, there are still many waiting for treatment."

Helix considered this for a moment. "I think I could really help."

His golden eyes lit up with intention and determination—a spark of life no one had seen from Helix in years.

"You should try," Emmeline encouraged him. "Any help is good help."

"Can you unstrap me?" Helix asked.

Emmeline looked to Kiran, who wore an uncertain expression.

Helix added, "I'm doing much better. I don't want to get high; I want to help you fight the Marzans."

"I'm inclined to set you free," Emmeline said, "but I don't want to be the reason you relapse."

"I won't relapse. I promise."

"You said that the first time," Kiran warned.

"I think it's best we make this decision as a family," Emmeline said. "And with the guidance of the Thermadoc."

Helix groaned. "Fine."

"Can I get you anything in the meantime before we leave?" Emmeline asked.

Helix hesitated, then answered, "There's this flower ... I don't know how it gets here, but sometimes when I wake up, I find it resting against my cheek. It calms me, eases my breathing, makes recovery more bearable."

"What does it look like?" Emmeline asked, her curiosity piqued.

"I've never seen anything like it before. Its pale pink petals twist at their ends and its black stem is covered with spiraling green tendrils."

"What does it smell like?"

Helix thought for a moment. "Stardust, but with a hint of floral honey."

Emmeline smiled.

"Luna has been helping you, too."

Chapter 28

Deimos

Golden light beamed through a tiny pinhole hovering above King Helmer's open palm.

"I found her black hole," he announced. "I found my dear Deánira's dying creation."

"It's so small," Queen Daeva noted. "We can't fit an army through that."

"No, we can't. Not until we make it bigger," Helmer agreed, then repositioned his hand and lowered his ear to the golden beam of light. "In the meantime, we can listen and observe."

"What are they saying?" Daeva asked.

"They are trying to close the black hole," he answered. "But they have no idea how."

"Make it louder," Daeva requested.

Helmer raised his hand and sent a surge of energy through his arm. Everything he could see and hear through the tiny black hole projected onto the nearest red rock wall.

The image was grainy from the swirl of stars and dust stirring within the black hole, and the audio was muffled by the gurgling churn, but they were able to witness what was happening on the other side.

Three Solarpunks, each with golden-brown hair, stood directly in front of the tiny black hole. Their expressions held a mix of frustration, concern, and fury. Two of them wore titanium wings and were dressed in sleek, aerodynamic suits. The third was older and wore a tweed vest over a white dress shirt. Gadgets decorated his outfit, scaling up his arms and around his waist. He lowered his goggles, closed his left eye, and flipped through an assortment of magnified lenses that lowered over his right eye. His golden iris shifted sizes with each lens.

"Do you see anything?" one of the young men standing beside him asked. The cords wrapped around his ankles were the only thing differentiating his attire from the other young Solarpunk.

"Nothing but darkness," he replied. He then lifted his finger and pressed it to the tiny hole.

The Marzans' projection was temporarily blocked. Above Helmer's open palm, they could see the Solarpunk's fatty golden flesh pushing into the black hole. If he wanted to, Helmer could touch the flesh and inject it with poison, but now was not the time to strike. Instead, they waited for the Solarpunk to remove his finger so they could continue observing.

When he finally did, the projected image returned to the wall.

"It's cold," the older Solarpunk informed the others.

"Do you think we could plug the hole?" asked the younger Solarpunk wearing ankle cords.

"That wouldn't be a permanent fix."

"Perhaps we could stitch it shut?"

"Do you know how to stitch air?"

"No, but the Holloways might."

The older Solarpunk considered this for a moment before responding, "I suppose it's worth a try. In the meantime, let's set this cage back on fire. If they try to get through, not only will they be imprisoned by titanium bars, but also by flames."

"What are we going to do with the body?" the young Solarpunk without ankle cords asked, pointing at Deánira's corpse. "It's been laying here a while and it's starting to smell."

The older Solarpunk wore a look of pure disgust, then returned his gaze to his younger counterparts. "Incinerate it."

"No!" Daeva cried. "Not with fire. That is the greatest dishonor!"

"There is nothing we can do," Helmer replied. Though his voice was calm, his expression contorted with anger.

"I can't watch," she said between sobs.

"Then look away."

"You want to see this?" she asked, confused.

202

"I *need* to see this," he replied. "It will sharpen my motivation."

His voice was emotionless—witnessing the desecration of his daughter's deceased body was a means to strengthen his contempt.

Daeva did not challenge him, she simply left in a fit of tears.

Bloodshot eyes vacant of all emotion except fury, Helmer zeroed his attention onto the projection.

The Solarpunk wearing ankle cords bent and reached his hand toward Deánira.

"Don't touch her, Solís," the other Solarpunk warned. "She's dead, but she might still be poisonous."

Solís retracted his hand. "We need to move her before we burn her, or we risk burning all the monsters in the cages beneath hers, too."

The other Solarpunk shouted up to the older Solarpunk, who was climbing a rope ladder out of the cage. "Dad, can you drop two suits once you get back to the ship?"

"Sure thing, Cyrus."

A few moments passed before two diving suits dropped from the sky. Solís and Cyrus clambered into their protective gear sans helmets, and then resumed their mission. Hands gloved, they lifted Deánira by her armpits and dragged her to the side of the cage where the petroleum flames were dwindling. Behind her crumpled body was wide open sky with no neighboring cages in reach.

"Ready?" Cyrus asked.

Solís tilted his head and cracked his neck.

"Ready," he replied.

No longer needing to touch the Marzan, they unlaced their suits and let them fall to the floor.

They both closed their eyes and heated their hearts to scorching temperatures. When they reached their maximum heat, their golden-hued flesh glowed red. Solís opened his eyes first; his golden irises were now bright crimson.

Eyes open, hearts heated to their maximum capacity, they both were prepared to expel their full force upon the lifeless Marzan.

They lifted their wrists, which had metal bracelets with spouts clamped into their flesh, and aimed.

"On the count of three," Cyrus said. "One, two, three."

They opened fire.

Gushing streams of magma shot from their wrists. The liquid fire was so hot it took mere seconds to incinerate Deánira. Her flesh and organs were cremated, leaving only her skeleton and chainmail behind. Solís and Cyrus lowered their arms.

"She's gone," Cyrus confirmed.

Solís stepped toward the pile of bones and chains covered in ashes.

"We should save the chains," he said. "They could be useful."

"What about the bones?"

"Souvenirs?" Solís said with a devilish smirk. "Perhaps we should decorate our ships with its bones as a warning to any Marzans foolish enough to come here."

Cyrus shrugged. "I hope I never see another Marzan again."

They collected Deánira's chains and bones, and then flew out of view.

Having seen and heard enough, Helmer lowered his hand and removed the projection from the wall. He carefully walked to the wall of black holes and added this one to his ever-growing collection. It was much smaller than the others, but had quickly become the most important gateway in his possession.

He thought of the final words he heard the ruthless Solarpunks say.

"You'll be seeing me soon," Helmer promised.

Chapter 29

Solís barged into Helix's room.

"I heard talking in here, wasn't expecting you two," he said to Emmeline and Kiran, then looked at Helix. "You look better."

"Unstrap me, please," Helix begged.

"The last time I let you out, you ran back to Terra and scored a large baggie of locomo. I'm not making that mistake again."

"I'm better this time. You just said it yourself."

"I said you *look* better. As for your mental state, I have no clue."

Helix groaned.

Solís looked to Emmeline and asked, "Is the moonstone in your room?"

"No, it's in my pocket," she answered, tapping the side of her cargo pants.

"I need it."

"Why?"

"I spent hours assessing the black hole with Dad, Cyrus, and a whole team of Thermapunk specialists. We cannot figure out how to get rid of it. I'm hoping Luna might have some advice."

Emmeline reached into her pocket, retrieved the stone, and handed it to Solís.

"Sounds to me like you just want a reason to see Luna again," she teased.

"Wrong," Solís quipped. "I'm trying to save the sun."

"If Luna knew how to close the black hole, I think she would've told us before she left."

"I have a theory that the gas spinners might be able to stitch it shut, and while Dad and Cyrus speak to the Holloways, I'm going to consult with Luna. Assuming they can even do it, we need to make sure it's a permanent solution."

Emmeline's brow raised at the mention of the Holloways.

"I haven't seen them since I returned."

"Since losing the duel, they're more reclusive than ever."

"When are Dad and Cyrus meeting with them?" Emmeline asked Solís.

"Today, I think."

"I'm going with them."

Helix squirmed within his restraints.

"You're all just going to leave me here?" he asked.

"Mom should be home soon," Solís said.

"I'll stay with you until she gets here," Kiran offered.

Helix huffed. "Fine. Maybe *she* will let me out."

"Come with me," Solís said to Emmeline, who followed him out of Helix's room.

After closing the door, Solís gave Emmeline a grave look.

"Be careful," he said. "You weren't here for the duel between the Holloways and Morrells, but it was brutal, and the Holloways blamed you for sparking that revolution."

"I didn't start it!"

"No, but you helped fuel it."

"I missed everything! And I'm still getting blamed?"

"While the duel took place, many of the Pilopunks and Argopunks gathered around and shouted your name."

"But I wasn't even there."

"While you were away, Cyrus and I stepped in on your behalf to support the revolution, and we sort of built up their role in your absence. While Remington fought Avery, many shouted profanities at him in your honor."

"Won't they be mad to learn it was a lie? And that the Holloways had nothing to do with it?"

"We didn't know where you were; the revolting Aeropunks knew it was just our suspicions. Plus, they wanted freedom from the Holloways long before you vanished. They would have accepted any story that furthered their mission. The timing of your disappearance just happened to work perfectly."

"But it left the Holloways with a greater hatred for me."

"Correct. Sorry about that. Just be careful if you go to that meeting."

"Thanks for the heads up." Emmeline then added, "Make sure to leave the moonstone here so you can get back."

Solís handed it back to her. "You hang onto it."

Emmeline held the stone in her hands as Solís said the incantation.

"Ad lunam lu. Accipe me."

Solís vanished.

Emmeline tucked the stone into a pocket near her left knee gears before departing. When she entered the kitchen, her mother was at the counter fixing a plate of marbles.

"You're back," Emmeline said in greeting.

Melora briefly glanced over her shoulder with an eyebrow raised, then returned to her work.

"I'm fixing a plate for Helix. Would you like something to eat?"

"I have a pocket full of clay marbles," Emmeline replied, tapping her right pocket, "but thank you."

"Did you see Helix? How is he doing?"

"He looks great to me. He has ideas on how he can help us defeat the Marzans, too."

"Interesting."

"My vote is to unconfine him, but I also didn't see him at his worst, so you'd know better."

Melora nodded. "I appreciate your input. I will consider it as I assess Helix's progress and consult your father. I've been too soft and forgiving with Helix. Every time I believe what he tells me, he makes me look like a fool. I can't trust myself with him."

Melora's vulnerability forced Emmeline to halt—she hardly ever saw this side of her mother, nor did her mother ever so willingly share this side of herself with Emmeline.

"You love him. You want to trust him. There's nothing wrong with that," Emmeline offered.

"It is a weakness, particularly since my softness continuously leads to him harming himself again."

"I'm no expert, but I think this time might be different. He seems really eager to help."

"Having a positive purpose is something he was missing prior. Perhaps this time *will* be different."

"I have faith in him," Emmeline offered.

Melora looked over her shoulder again and gave Emmeline a weak smile. The emotional battle she'd been waging over the past few months read plainly in her expression.

Emmeline added, "I'm going to join Dad and Cyrus at their meeting with the Holloways."

"You better hurry along then," Melora stated. "I crossed paths with them in the sky on my way home."

"Can I ask Regis to fly me there?"

"Of course. I'll let him know he's reassigned to you for the day."

As Melora opened the kitchen window and called for Regis's attention, Emmeline darted out the door onto the kitchen balcony and around the corner to where the family thermal balloons were docked.

Regis was there, too, nodding his head as Melora finished speaking to him through the window.

"Be careful," she said to both Emmeline and Regis.

"We will be," Emmeline promised.

Regis adjusted his wedged garrison cap.

"Where to?" he asked, copper eyes glowing a pinkish orange.

"Into Upper Gaslion. I need to join my father's meeting with the Holloways."

"As you wish," Regis said, opening the door to the nearest thermal balloon basket. After Emmeline stepped inside, he untied the rope from the cleat, closed the little door behind him, and latched it before heading to the control panel. He twisted two knobs that extended a pair of metal wings sheathed with a golden cloth. As they unfolded and extended, he blew helium into a tube that ran up into the balloon. His right foot found the pedal that pumped the wings, and as he rotated it, they lifted into the sky. The helium gave them lift and the wings gave them direction.

"If you'd like a bit more speed, feel free to add fire to the pan. I believe Avery taught you how to man one of these aircrafts."

"She did," Emmeline confirmed. She lifted her hands, cupping them to the base of the pan, and then heated her heart. Her entire body glowed red as her temperature increased, and once the pan sweltered bright crimson, she lowered her hands and the balloon moved upward faster.

It wasn't long before they crossed the invisible border between Fyree and Upper Gaslion. The only telling sign was the slight drop in temperature. Upper Gaslion was cooler and the clouds slightly bluer among the swirling reds, oranges, and yellows of the solar shield.

It also wasn't long before the thermal balloon was caught within the whirlwind of hidden gas spinners circling them like sharks.

"Show yourself!" Emmeline demanded.

"You aren't welcome here," a raspy voice responded from within the windstorm.

Emmeline recognized it as Remington.

"Don't be sour," she spat. "I heard you lost the duel fair and square."

The speed at which he and his fellow gas spinners circled the balloon increased.

"I heard you inspired them to rise against us," he said with a snarl.

"No. For that, the credit is all yours. Your family's arrogant absence inspired them to take back control."

Two hands grabbed the side of the basket and Remington's face appeared as he abruptly stopped circling the balloon. His copper eyes were filled with rage.

"I will take back what is mine," he said.

"You don't *own* the Pilopunks or Argopunks. They are individuals who own themselves."

"They belong to me," he repeated.

"That type of thinking is what made them revolt," Emmeline stated calmly. "Now, let go of my aircraft, and tell your cronies to stop circling us and let us pass."

"As I said before … you are not welcome here."

"Your conceited outlook on the world will kill us all. If you took a moment to ask *why* I was here, you'd learn that we need to work together."

"Work together on what?"

"Saving Quintessence. Saving the sun."

Remington's gaze narrowed. "From what?"

"The black hole in Hydra."

All the gas spinners stopped at once, eliminating the whirlwind and revealing eight winged Aeropunks with mouths agape.

"How did a black hole form in Hydra?" Remington asked.

"A Marzan imprisoned there created it. She is dead now, but we have to find a way to close the hole before it enlarges."

"How could you let something like that happen?" Remington accosted Emmeline.

"Let's focus on solutions rather than blame."

"We have no experience with black holes. How can we possibly help?"

"You are master manipulators of air and gas. We were hoping there might be some way to sew the hole shut."

"You want us to stitch air?" he asked, wearing an incredulous expression.

"If you think it might be possible, yes."

"That is not within our skill set."

"Do you think it's something you might be able to learn?" she asked, her patience depleting.

Remington paused in thought. "Perhaps. Our price is full control of all Aeropunks."

Emmeline laughed. "You will do it to save the sun."

"I demand compensation."

Emmeline shook her head and added, "You will do it because it is the right thing to do."

"I'll need to see this threat for myself."

"Honestly, your opinion is insignificant. My father and brother are speaking to your parents now. They will understand the risk and do the right thing."

"Is that why they are here?"

"Yes, I was hoping to join the meeting, but you got in my way. I imagine it's nearly done by now."

"Most likely."

"Well, now you know what's going on, too." Her golden eyes gleamed with sincere concern. "Hopefully your family is more sensible than you."

"They'll want to understand the threat, too."

"It's life or death." Emmeline turned to Regis. "Let's go home."

He nodded, cranked the lever that flapped the mechanical wings, and turned the balloon around. Emmeline rescinded heat from the pan as Regis sucked small amounts of helium out of the balloon through a skinny pipe.

The gas spinners hovered where they were. Everyone looked scared except for Remington.

Emmeline prayed to Solédon, hoping Remington's selfishness did not impede their plan.

Chapter 30

Mōnalene

Solís landed near a mountainous rock formation.

Where was Luna?

He quickly inserted the regulator into his mouth and began breathing the oxygen in his tank.

A quick scan of the dusty, silver terrain revealed no signs of life.

Solís turned to face the jagged rock wall. He knew life swarmed beneath his feet, he just needed to find the door.

He traced his hand along the wall, feeling for nooks, handles, knobs, or covert openings. As his fingers traced the sharp edges of the rock, a voice greeted him from behind.

"I wasn't expecting to see you again so soon."

Solís turned and saw Luna gliding toward him. Her wings were spread wide and her pretty silver eyes glowed with the reflection of the stars above.

"Do you think a black hole can be sewn shut?" he asked, wasting no time.

"Sewn? It's air, dark matter, and gravity. There's nothing tangible to stitch."

She landed in front of him, her talons touching the ground so gently she dispersed no dust.

"We have a group among the Solarpunks who are master manipulators of air and gas," Solís explained.

"I suppose they could try, but they better be careful not to accidentally make the hole bigger."

"How does that happen?"

"A single tear at the edge of the hole could cause it to stretch."

"I see," Solís noted. "I'll make sure to warn them."

"They need to be very careful," Luna warned.

"Do you think it could work?"

"I highly doubt it, but if they are cautious, I suppose it's worth a try."

"Do you have any suggestions on how to close it? We couldn't think of anything else besides sewing it shut," Solís said. "That was our only idea."

"I know little more about black holes than you. That's a Marzan specialty," Luna confessed. "Speaking of them, I have to get going. I'm on task to do a bit of spying."

"On the Marzans?"

"Yes. My moonstone is still hidden in Louie's old prison."

Solís looked around; she had no backup.

"Are you going alone?" he asked.

"Yes. It's safer that way."

"No, it's not. Let me join you."

"You are a liability."

"I kept you safe last time!" Solís objected. "When the gas knocked you out, remember? And without me, you would've had a much harder time cutting Louie free."

"Neither of those things will be concerns this time," she argued.

"But what new obstacles will you encounter? It's always better to have help."

Luna narrowed her shimmering eyes at him, internally debating his logic.

"I suppose I don't know what I'll encounter this time," she finally said. "Fine, you can come. Just promise to follow my lead."

"I promise." Solís extended his arm and wiggled his fingers, signaling Luna to take his hand. The golden gears at his finger joints spun faster as he beckoned her toward him.

"I remember when you were repulsed by the idea of touching me," Luna said as she took his hand.

"Oh, how times have changed," Solís said with a smile.

"Ad Deimos lu. Accipe me."

They lurched back into the portal and left Mōnalene behind.

Solís clutched his stomach with his free hand and fought off the sudden bout of nausea as best he could. They only spent a few seconds in the dizzying tunnel, but the swirling colors, monotonous, low-humming buzz, and stench of burnt stardust were enough to make Solís sick.

When they landed in Louie's old prison at the center of Deimos, Solís was in too much of a stupor to notice the new inmate.

Luna grabbed his bicep and yanked him back toward the wall. She carefully reached between the boulders lining the wall to retrieve her moonstone.

Solís heaved.

"Shh," Luna expressed in a whisper, keeping them concealed within her shield of invisibility.

Solís recentered himself with closed eyes, and when he opened them, he saw a Behemoth of Fatigue sitting against the opposite wall, picking at its fangs with its stone fingernails.

"That's a Behemoth of Fatigue," Solís said in a hushed voice.

"No," Luna corrected him. "That's an Unar of Umbriel. They serve the Uranians of Uranus. That one there is a soldier. You can tell by the symbol carved into his chest."

A diamond with two lines slashed through was inscribed into his muddy flesh. He blinked his clay-covered eyelids slowly and tilted his head until the bones within cracked. His movements were just as slow as the monsters the Behemoths of Fatigue captured in Hydra.

"Are the Unars part of your moon alliance?" Solís asked.

Luna nodded.

Solís added, "Maybe we can recruit them to help fight the Marzans."

Luna shook her head.

"Be quiet," she hissed.

The massive Unar snapped his gaze to where they were hiding beneath the shield. His cavernous black eyes gleamed with feverish intrigue as he shifted to all fours and lunged as far as his ankle chains allowed.

Luna and Solís climbed onto the red boulders lining the wall and pressed their bodies as flat as they could. The Unar sniffed the air in a frenzy, moving quicker than Solís had ever seen a Behemoth move.

Still pressed against the wall, Luna tugged Solís along as she tiptoed atop the boulders toward the door.

The Unar swiped his long arm at the space Luna and Solís had just vacated, then growled.

"I can smell you," the Unar said between snarls. He sniffed the air again and followed the scent. His head turned toward where Luna and Solís crept along the wall. "Moon lily and solar gold. Impossible."

He swiped his arms at them again.

Solís narrowly dodged his reach as they scurried faster.

"Show yourself!" the Unar roared.

The prison door swung open.

Balor barged through with an electrified prodder aimed at the Unar, who stood to his full height in retaliation against the Marzan guard.

"Stand down, Oberion," Balor demanded before shoving the prodder into Oberion's gut.

Oberion doubled over in pain as he howled.

"What were you shouting about?" Balor asked.

Oberion hesitated, then lied, "I just felt like shouting."

"You are infuriating. Why can't you sit in here quietly?" Balor demanded.

Oberion ignored him and spat. "I will kill you one day."

Balor laughed. "This galaxy will be obliterated long before you get the chance."

As Balor took another step into the prison cell, threatening to shock Oberion a second time, Luna and Solís slipped out of the door unnoticed.

Luna kept the invisibility shield engaged as they hurried away from the prison cell.

There were no other guards in the circular room of prison doors, and once Luna was certain the coast was clear, she exhaled deeply.

"He could have killed us," she said.

"Who? The Unar or the Marzan guard."

"Either," Luna confessed, "but I was referring to the Unar; Oberion."

"I thought you said they were in an alliance with you?"

"With me, yes. Not with you. No one hates Solarpunks more than the Unars. He would've killed us both before we got a chance to explain."

"Hmph. Seems I *am* a liability this time," Solís noted.

"Let's just keep moving."

"Are you going to hide your stone someplace else?"

"Depends. I am hoping we get all the information we need on this trip and never have to come back."

"I think you should leave it here in case we need to strike first. If you can send three people through the portal, I imagine you could send an army through."

Luna considered this. "If I leave it, I need to pick a good spot for an army to enter."

"We'll scope out the options as we keep moving forward." Solís paused. "What is our mission, exactly?"

"To learn if they have Kólasi on their side, and if so, how much of a presence He has."

"So, we will just eavesdrop?"

"Ideally, we will find King Helmer and follow him around for the day."

The door to Oberion's prison slammed shut and Balor reentered the circular room. He took his seat at the desk in the center of the room and fussed with the many wires protruding from three tiered red rock slabs. He bent and twisted specific wires together, sending a private message via electric frequency. After coiling a final set of wires, the room trembled ever so slightly.

"What was that?" Solís asked in a whisper.

"I don't know," Luna replied, holding her moonstone against her chest with one hand and Solís's hand with the other.

A thin fissure snaked across the rock floor, splintering and spreading beneath Luna and Solís's feet.

"Something isn't right. We need to leave," Luna said.

"But we didn't get the information we came for."

The ground near Balor split open, retracting on wheeled springs and revealing a circular cavity beneath.

The sound of rock scraping against rock sent a chill down Solís's golden spine. When it finally stopped and the door was fully open, an eerie silence blanketed the room. Balor made no noise as he stood near the edge of the hole, and the subtle murmuring of the surrounding prisoners ceased.

It was as if everyone was holding their breath, aware of what came next, except Luna and Solís.

"You're right," Solís whispered. "Something is off."

Before Luna could reply, motion stirred within the darkness. One by one, eight enormous legs lifted and perched along the edge of the hole; they covered the vast circumference with ease.

The creature within was massive.

Eight glowing red eyes emerged over the edge of the void.

Luna became rigid with fear.

"What is *that*?" Solís asked.

"A Weaver," she answered through hollow breaths. "I think the Marzans call theirs a Spinner. Every moon has one. When they aren't dormant, fabricating vessels for life, they are executioners."

"Why did the guard summon it?"

"I don't know," Luna answered between shallow breaths.

The Spinner emerged farther out of its lair.

"Why have you called for me?" the monstrous spider asked, its voice a low hiss.

"I apologize, beloved Spinner, I did not wish to disturb you, but there has been a breach only you can remedy."

"A breach of what kind?"

"A prisoner informed me that they smelled lunar lilies and solar gold."

"How many?"

"Maybe two? No more than five."

"You could have handled this yourself," the Spinner hissed.

"They are under a Lunarian shield."

The Spinner grunted. "I see."

Its eight red eyes shifted slowly, scanning the room for things unseen. The tiny hairs on its legs tremored, taking in the aromas filtering through this enclosed space.

"Say the incantation," Solís urged Luna, who stood paralyzed with fear.

The Spinner's eyes landed on them, seemingly peering through their shield of invisibility.

Solís squeezed Luna's hand as hard as he could, hoping to snap her out of her trance.

Fangs bared, the Spinner slowly rotated its body.

Solís removed the regulator from his mouth and spoke loudly.

"Ad lunam lu," he said as the backside spinneret aimed directly at them. "Accipe me!"

They vanished as a long web of sticky silk thread hit the wall where they previously stood.

Chapter 31

"I knew you shouldn't have come," Luna barked as they landed in Mōnalene.

"Excuse me?" Solís retorted, becoming quite skilled at speaking with the regulator in his mouth. "I'm the only reason we got out of there in time!"

"We wouldn't have needed to escape if I had gone alone. I could have talked to Oberion. He never would have snitched if he hadn't caught your scent."

"I only went to help."

"I didn't need your help," Luna said with a groan.

Solís paused, his defenses lifting. "So, we're back to being enemies again? That easily?"

"No," Luna scoffed. "Of course not. But I'm allowed to feel frustrated right now."

"Well, stop blaming me. It's not my fault."

"It just would have gone differently if you hadn't tagged along." She lifted her moonstone. "And now we don't have a stone on Deimos."

An echoing war cry reverberated across the stars. The ominous sound was an alarm—they weren't free from the Marzans yet.

"They are coming," Luna stated. "You should go home."

"Can I do anything to help?" he countered.

"You can't even breathe here ... how exactly do you think you'll help?"

Solís lifted his arms into the sky, clenched his fingers into fists, and tilted them back. The wristlets connected to his veins engaged and two streams of magma shot forward into the sky. He showered the sky with liquid fire just long enough to remind Luna of his power. The fiery droplets rained over a barren patch of moon in the distance. Once his point was proven, he tilted his fists forward, closing the valves, and the streams of magma ceased.

"Fire is the Marzans' greatest foe, correct?"

Luna crossed her arms over her chest, struggling to admit she was wrong.

Solís went on, "That's one of many ways I can fight with fire."

"Fine. You can stay. But don't do anything unless I give you some sort of signal to engage. We've fought the Marzans for a long time; we know their methods. There's no use provoking them when you're the only Thermapunk here with that power."

"Should I go home and return with a crew?"

Luna paused in thought, then asked, "How long would it take for you to gather and prepare your crew? When would you return?"

"Depends. How many should I bring?"

"However many it would take to defeat the Marzan Spinner."

"Do you think they're bringing that creature with them?"

"It's possible. They've already summoned her out of her lair."

"I know nothing about these arachnids," Solís confessed. "Are they dimidivinus like us? Are their bodies plush or armor-plated?"

"I can only speak for the Lunarian Weaver. Dimidivinus, yes—so I assume the Marzan Spinner is also semi-immortal."

"Does *your* Weaver have any weaknesses?" Solís asked, words muffled through the regulator.

"Surely, she must … I just don't know what they are. The arachnids have been here long before any of us."

"Well, maybe while I'm recruiting a crew, you can ask her."

"Wish I could, but she does not speak to us," Luna said. "None of the arachnids comingle with the beings they serve."

"Why not?"

"They prefer silent isolation. They only emerge for situations of grave peril."

"That's why the Spinner seemed so agitated about being summoned to locate us," Solís realized.

"Correct. But now that she has surfaced, she may want to finish the job."

"I'll come back with as big of a crew as I can rally with such short notice."

Luna extended her pointer finger and expelled a long silver thread. She coiled it into a small loop, then handed it to Solís.

"Hopefully this is enough. Give every recruit a piece and teach them the incantation to return to Quintessence."

"Why do they need your thread?"

"The moonstone on Quintessence is connected to me. The incantation will only take them home if they have a piece of me with them—it's like having a moonstone. They need a way to retreat if the battle here turns deadly."

Solís nodded. "Thank you."

He quickly glanced at the magnetic cords wrapped around his ankle—his connection to the moonstone back on Quintessence—and then recited the incantation.

"Ad solem quin. Accipe me."

Solís lurched backward and vanished.

As he disappeared, a caravan of Odonata warriors approached. They lunged and flew at terrifying speeds.

Luna stood tall, prepared to stand her ground.

"What happened on your mission?" Cèla demanded as her furious dash skidded to a stop directly in front of Luna. Face contorted with rage, the veins around Cèla's black eyes pulsated violently.

"They caught my scent and summoned their Spinner."

The Odonatas crowded behind Cèla gasped.

Cèla took a step back. "Their arachnid? They woke her?"

"Yes, and I'm sure you heard their approaching war cry. They are on their way here."

"Do you think they are bringing their arachnid with them?"

"Possibly," Luna replied. "We need to wake the Weaver."

"Arche," Cèla barked.

Odonata Arche stepped forward, adjusting his magnified spectacles.

Cèla continued, "Gather a small crew and inform the Monarchs. Only Lepido Dione can wake the Weaver."

Arche nodded, selected ten Odonatas to join him, and then departed.

"Isone," Cèla said, turning her attention to another lead Odonata. "Guide all civilian Lunarians into hiding. I have a feeling this encounter will be more eventful than the last."

Isone, a damselfly among dragonflies, spread her petite wings and rose into the air with unrivaled confidence. She selected seven of her subordinates with a finger point, then waved her hand for them to follow. She flew toward Termes Mountain, and the seven selected Odonatas lifted into the sky and followed her lead.

"Is there anything else I need to know?" Cèla asked Luna.

Luna wanted to lie, but knew it served her people to tell the truth.

"An Unar of Umbriel named Oberion was imprisoned in the cell where my moonstone was left."

"They are an ally," Cèla noted. "Did he help you?"

"No, he is the reason they learned I was there. He caught my scent first."

"And he snitched?" Cèla asked, her outrage growing.

"Not at first, but eventually."

"That's very unlike the Unars. They are fiercely loyal."

"Yes, well, I had Solís with me. Oberion smelled solar gold and felt betrayed, I assume."

"You were supposed to go alone," Cèla said, her tone filled with ridicule.

"I was going to, but then Solís showed up to ask about the black hole in Quintessence, and when I told him where I was headed, he insisted it wasn't safe to go alone," Luna rambled, aware that she was in the wrong. "In fairness, he saved me last time. I thought having a second set of hands would be helpful."

"Instead, he ruined your mission." Cèla spat on the ground. "Your judgment is askew."

"My judgment is just fine. Thanks to me, we have powerful allies."

"They have yet to prove their allegiance."

"You will see proof of it soon," Luna said, deciding to reveal no more.

Red smoke slowly crept into the silver glow emanating across the horizon. Crimson light shadowed the barren moonscape, arriving so gradually that Luna and Cèla did not notice the change until they heard the whirring red rock spacecraft hovering above.

It was larger than the vessel they had arrived with during their last visit, and Luna's gut wobbled with dread. She had a terrible feeling the Spinner was on board.

As the Marzan spacecraft lowered closer to Mōnalene, thousands of Odonata warriors filtered out of the craters and mountains to form rows of defense.

Luna and Cèla lifted into the sky to get an overhead view.

"If they brought their Spinner, it won't matter how prepared we are," Cèla noted.

"The Weaver will assist us," Luna assured her, fully confident in the Weaver's capabilities, but also hoping Solís followed through on his promise.

A door slid open on the top balcony of the spacecraft and King Helmer emerged.

"Where are your beloved Solarpunks?" he shouted. "I thought we'd find them here with you."

"What do you want?" Cèla demanded.

"Since you won't align with us, it appears we need to carry on without you."

"Carry on then. Be gone!"

"No, no," Helmer said, the wicked smile on his face growing bigger. "You misunderstand. Your only option was to align with us. You chose to align with the Solarpunks instead. Now, your only option is death."

"You realize we have an arachnid, too, right?" Cèla said, confidence unwavering.

"Ah, I see you were warned. No matter; yours is nowhere in sight. Our arachnid has the advantage of time."

Helmer yanked a lever on the wall and the belly of the spacecraft opened. A giant spider fell from the sky, landing on the dusty terrain of Mōnalene with a quaking thud. It slowly straightened its legs from the ball it was curled into.

"Attack!" Cèla instructed, urging her warriors to act while the arachnid was still dazed.

Spears, daggers, and axes made of Lunarian metal were lobbed at the Spinner, lodging into her hairy black exoskeleton.

As she unraveled her legs, one by one, and took her full form, all the weapons wedged into her body looked miniscule in comparison. She was massive, and she was angry.

Their defenses were not working; their weapons were useless against her.

The Spinner bared her fangs and released a bone-quivering growl. As the noise echoed, the force dislodged the weapons and sent them hurling back at the front row of defense.

It happened so fast, only a few lifted their shields in time. The rest were impaled by their own weapons.

Many injured, some killed, the front row of Odonata warriors was decimated.

"Take to the sky," Cèla commanded, to which all the warriors spread their wings and took flight. They rose to great heights, not stopping until they were well above the Spinner.

Though it was the smart move, it was also a sign of weakness—they were forced to abandon their original plan and reevaluate their defenses.

The Marzan ship rocked with boisterous cheering.

Luna shot a quick glance upward to find that each window revealed a viewing party. They planned to let the Spinner annihilate the Lunarians and never get their hands dirty.

Enraged, Luna's silver eyes turned black.

"Fight us yourselves, you cowards!" she shouted, flying higher.

King Helmer stood atop his mooncraft, still smiling as if failure was unfathomable.

"Where are your fire friends?" he asked, taunting her. "Or is it a one-sided alliance? You help them, but they don't help you?"

"You will not win," Luna seethed.

"But we will. We have Kólasi on our side."

Chapter 32

Quintessence

Solís traveled through the portal and materialized next to Emmeline in the open sky of Fyree.

He dropped the regulator from his mouth and shouted, "Catch me!"

As he fell, Emmeline, Cyrus, and Kiran dove into action, seizing Solís by his arms and legs and keeping him air bound.

"Why can't you fly?" Cyrus asked, his voice a harsh whisper.

"My tank is filled with oxygen," Solís answered, adrenaline calming as he took in the scene before him. Hundreds of thermal balloons hovered in the sky alongside hundreds of Aeropunks floating on various contraptions. His parents floated in their thermal balloon above the congregation and were joined by the Holloways.

"You got here just in time for the start of the meeting," Emmeline informed Solís.

"We are facing an imminent threat," Montgomery shouted into his megaphone. His voice echoed across the sky and downward into Terra, where all the Terrapunks, except the Revos, congregated.

Montgomery continued, "The devils, also known as the Marzans of Deimos, can create black holes. If they get close enough to the source flame, they could swallow it whole, extinguishing the sun forever."

A collective gasp came from every Aeropunk, Thermapunk, and Terrapunk.

"Can the Pyro-Argo fighters stop them?" Cecelia Monroe asked from her golden chariot.

"Not on their own," Montgomery answered. "The unity we experienced at the hands of the Superpunks is needed now more than ever. We must band together if we wish to survive the forthcoming attack."

Upon mention of the Superpunks, tears filled Cecelia's eyes—her daughter's legacy lived on.

"What do you need from us?" Torsten Horrigan shouted up into the sky through his own megaphone. It took a moment for the echo of his voice to reach them in Fyree.

"Collect every magnetic alloy you can mine. The Marzans have a layer of chainmail armor between their bones and flesh—we can fight them with magnetism."

"And what of us?" Reuben Holloway asked Montgomery.

"Help us find a way to close the black hole."

Reuben nodded. "We will do our best."

"That's all any of us can do. Let us pray." Montgomery lifted his arms into the sky. "Solédon! Despite Your absence, we serve You devoutly. We've asked for little throughout the years, but need You now. Hear our prayer."

"Ascent!" the group said in unison.

"Grant us protection. Deliver us peace. Hear our prayer."

"Ascent!"

Solís still hung from the sky by the strength of Cyrus, Kiran, and Emmeline.

"If you can't fly, how did you even get up here?" Kiran asked, holding Solís's legs.

"And why is your tank filled with oxygen?" Cyrus added.

"I'll explain later," Solís said. "Do they really think Solédon will hear these prayers?"

"We've never prayed as a united front before," a voice answered from above.

Solís looked up to find Helix unshackled from his bed and smiling.

"You're free," Solís exclaimed.

"Shh," Emmeline hushed him.

"We don't have time to waste," Solís urged. "I need you all to go to Mōnalene with me."

"Why?" Emmeline asked.

"They are being attacked."

"When?"

"Probably right now!"

"You want us to go there and help them fight?" Kiran asked.

"Yes," Solís replied. "All we need to do is rain fire upon the Marzans."

"It sounds dangerous," Cyrus commented.

"Would you rather the battle take place here?" Solís retorted, his anger growing. "If we can stop them on Mōnalene, perhaps we will never see war on Quintessence."

Emmeline added, "Plus, we are in an alliance with the Lunarians. It is our duty to help them."

"We'll need more than the five of us," Cyrus noted.

"We can rally a crew of Pyropunks," Solís said.

Emmeline scanned the sky, looking for Avery among the Aeropunks floating between thermal balloons.

She caught the pinkish-orange gleam of her copper gaze near where a fleet of Argopunks hovered in prayer.

When Avery finally sensed Emmeline's stare, she opened her eyes and furrowed her brow.

Emmeline jerked her head, indicating that Avery join her and her brothers.

Avery made her way through the crowd, moving slowly so as to not distract from the prayer.

"What's going on?" she asked in a whisper.

"We are gathering a crew to go to Mōnalene. We'd like you, and whichever Argopunks you trust most, to join."

"I need more details," Avery said.

"The Lunarians are being attacked by Marzans and we need to help them with fire. Not only because we are aligned with them, but also because it might prevent the war from coming here."

Avery nodded her head. "Okay, but do we have a way to leave if the battle gets too deadly?"

"Yes," Solís chimed in. "The same way we get there through the portal, we can also leave."

"It will also be a great way to see what we're up against in case the battle does come to Quintessence one day," Cyrus added.

"Great," Solís said. "Avery, gather at least ten Argopunks and meet us at the base in five minutes."

Avery nodded and flew off.

Cyrus and Kiran carried Solís to the base while Emmeline and Helix detoured to recruit more Pyropunks.

They circled the congregation of Thermapunks and Aeropunks, who were deep in prayer, pleading with Solédon to save them. Emmeline worried their requests fell on deaf ears— Solédon hadn't answered a prayer in years.

She and Helix tapped the shoulder of Felicity Sinclair, a top Pyropunk fighter, who helped them recruit another ten Pyropunks.

At the Pyro-Argo base, Solís began doling out orders.

"Every Pyropunk needs to fill an empty tank with oxygen. It's how we will breathe on Mōnalene."

"How will we fly?" Brion Foster, one of the recruited Pyropunks, asked.

"We will forgo flying for breathing on this mission."

Solís began passing tanks from the storage closet to Kiran, who then placed them next to Helix. Helix worked on filling the tanks while Cyrus got the harnesses ready.

"Do you think I can check on Gemma while we're there?" Emmeline asked Solís, who placed the final tank next to Kiran.

"No," he answered. "We will be entering a war and we need every ounce of firepower."

"After the battle, I meant."

"Stay focused," Solís urged her as he moved on to his next task—giving each member of his crew a piece of Luna's silver thread.

Emmeline nodded, temporarily silencing her desire to save at least one of the people she had accidentally hurt. Distractions now would only present greater risk to their mission, and she refused to be the cause of more suffering.

Solís cut the coiled thread into pieces and then wrapped them around each of his crewmembers' fingers.

"These rings are your only connection to home," he informed them. "We will leave the moonstone here at the base, and when you say the incantation, you will be brought here. Do not lose your ring. If you do, the incantation won't work."

"What's the phrase?" Cyrus asked.

"Ad solem quin. Accipe me."

As the crew of Pyropunks repeated the incantation to themselves repeatedly, making sure they had it thoroughly memorized, a sweeping breeze ripped through the base.

Avery and a crew of fifteen Argopunks flew into the wide hangar bay. Beside her were the lead Argopunks: Jessamine Davenport and her cousin Willie Morrell.

"Reporting for duty," Avery announced.

"As are we," a raspy voice hidden within a swirling blur of black commented.

"No," Emmeline said, but it was too late. Raven and Remington were standing beside Avery, expressions alight with fury.

"You need us," Raven said, her conviction booming.

Emmeline turned to Solís and whispered, "We can't teach them the incantation. They will misuse it in the future."

"We said Argopunks," Solís said to Avery. "Not gas spinners."

"They were eavesdropping in a whirl of invisibility as I was recruiting Argopunks," she explained with a shrug.

Solís grumbled, then wrapped Luna's thread around the thumb of each Argopunk and quietly told them the incantation.

"You are trouble," Cyrus said to the Holloway siblings.

"We can help," Remington insisted. "We want to see the monsters for ourselves."

"We are only attacking the Marzans," Emmeline reminded them. "The Lunarians are on our side."

"A monster is a monster," Raven commented.

"You cannot join if that is your stance."

Raven rolled her eyes, then asked, "How will we be able to tell the monsters apart?"

"The Marzans are red."

"Should be easy enough."

Solís had finished giving each of the Argopunks a thread.

"What about us?" Remington asked.

"I'm all out," Solís said with a shrug.

"What's the ring for?"

"It's the only way to get back to Quintessence. Either don't come, or stay close to someone with a ring while we're there."

Remington narrowed his gaze. "You did that on purpose."

"I'm not saying you can't come, just be careful not to get left behind." Solís then slapped one of the tanks filled with oxygen. "Strap up if you still wish to fight."

"I don't need a tank to fly," Remington snapped.

"You're right, but you will need it to breathe."

"They're filled with oxygen," Cyrus explained to Remington.

"Have you forgotten that Aeropunks are made of gas? We can store oxygen in our lungs before departing."

"You're accompanying us to exhale explosive gas, not oxygen," Cyrus reminded him.

"I am aware."

Solís cut in, "Can you conjure and hold flammable gas within your lungs while also maintaining an oxygen reserve? If so, fine, just don't bother us for air if your reserves run dry."

Remington snatched two tanks and angrily shoved one of them at his sister.

Solís secretly placed the moonstone on a counter near the back wall of the communal space and had all the Aeropunks and Thermapunks line up with hands on each other's shoulders. Once everyone was connected, he took his spot at the front of the group with Emmeline. Cyrus linked to Solís and Helix linked to Emmeline.

"Everyone ready?" Solís shouted, to which he received no objection.

He mumbled the incantation beneath his breath, loud enough that only his siblings heard the words.

"Ad lunam lu. Accipe me."

The caravan of Solarpunk fighters was ripped through the portal and sent to Mōnalene.

A collective grumble accompanied their quick trip—nausea, joint pain, dizziness—no one was immune to the forceful tug and pull of the portal.

Emmeline blinked three times before landing on the dusty terrain of the moon.

Silver dust lifted and scattered, veiling not only their arrival but also their view of the scene around them.

"Activate your tanks," Solís commanded as the sounds of monstrous roars shook the ground.

All the Solarpunks opened the valves of their oxygen tanks and placed their regulators into their mouths.

Emmeline nudged Solís and pointed up—Luna hovered overhead, Cèla beside her.

"I can't see anything!" Avery griped from behind Helix.

"It doesn't sound good," Cyrus noted as a resounded thud echoed across the moon.

The dust began to settle and the sight of two colossal arachnids came into view.

The battle between them was so fierce, so violent, the Solarpunks took a step backward in unintended unison.

"You want us to fight *that*?" Remington shouted from the back of the group.

"We are just here to assist," Solís reminded them. "Fire and gas will help the Lunarians win."

The red rock spacecraft on the opposite side of the battle buzzed with cheering Marzans.

King Helmer stepped onto the top deck and bellowed, "The wrath of Kólasi knows no bounds!"

He unscrewed the lid of a glass jar, and hundreds of tiny gold flies dispersed across the battlefield.

First contact between a golden fly and Odonata Arche revealed the nature of this new threat.

Arche was mid-swing of his poison-tipped javelin when the golden fly rocketed into his ear and rendered him immobile.

"No!" Cèla shouted, watching from above.

A moment of paralysis passed before an internal jolt shoved Arche from within. His body lurched forward, and when his eyes opened, they were foggy white orbs.

Possessed by the distant grip of Kólasi, Arche was no longer himself.

Arche turned, his movements meticulous and slow, before lifting his poison-tipped javelin and releasing a horrifying shriek as he charged his nearest Odonata comrade.

Chapter 33

"What are *those*?" Solís shouted up at Luna while pointing at the golden flies attacking the Lunarians.

Luna's face was still contorted with warrior rage. Upon seeing Solís and Emmeline, she lowered, fury softening as she saw the large crew of Solarpunks Solís had recruited to help.

"You came through," she said, more so to herself.

"Of course, I did."

"What is the meaning of this?" Cèla demanded, lowering to join.

"Would you like their help or not?" Luna barked.

Cèla challenged her no more.

Solís asked, "What are those golden flies Helmer unleashed? And how do we defeat them?"

"Helmer mentioned the wrath of Kólasi before releasing them. It's new to us, too."

Odonata warriors were being turned into white-eyed zombies at a rapid pace.

"Where do you need us most?" Emmeline asked, aware that their time was dwindling.

Luna glanced over her shoulder—the arachnids still battled, and Helmer and his fleet of Marzans were thoroughly enjoying the assault of flies on the Lunarians.

"Do you think they saw your arrival?" Luna asked.

"I don't think so," Emmeline answered. "We are pretty far from the mooncraft."

"And there's a lot happening between us and them," Solís added.

Luna nodded, then extended her hands and threw an invisibility shield over the entire Solarpunk crew.

"Stay near me and you will remain concealed," she explained.

"Who will you attack first?" Cèla asked, unable to see them but intrigued by the notion of unlimited fire as a defense.

"I think we should start by scorching the golden flies, then turn our fire upon Helmer," Luna replied.

Cèla nodded. "The Spinner will leave when Helmer retreats. Can I help in any way?"

"Help our fallen warriors after we clear the flies."

Mission accepted, Cèla tore toward the active assault, hovering high above until the Solarpunks cleared the mayhem.

The Spinner broke free from the Weaver's stronghold and shot another web into the fray. A giant silk thread shot across the battlefield, tangling twenty Odonata warriors and making them easier prey for the flies.

"Hold," Luna said, unwilling to enter the battle and risk the lives of the Solarpunks until the Weaver regained control over the Spinner.

"They are goliaths," Emmeline said as she watched the giant spiders' ferocious battle.

"They are the only thing standing in each other's way. We'd be easily annihilated if our own arachnid was not here to protect us."

"So, while they cancel each other out," Solís commented, "we weaken the Marzans as much as possible."

"Exactly," Luna confirmed.

The Weaver wrapped its two front legs around the Spinner's back legs and dug its fangs into its exoskeleton.

The Spinner roared in protest.

"Ready?" Luna asked the crew of Solarpunks now that the arachnids were focused on one another again.

They mumbled their collective preparedness.

"Let's go," Solís said.

As Luna led them toward the heart of the battle, Solís and Cyrus prepped their crew.

"Start heating up now," Solís instructed. "Have a surplus of fire at the ready."

"Unlatch your lava wristlets," Cyrus added. "We might need to hit them with something stronger than flames."

"What kind of gas will you need from us?" Avery asked.

"Chlorotriflouride, for sure," Cyrus answered.

"We need to incinerate these flies," Solís added.

The Argopunks prepared gaseous concoctions in their gut, focusing primarily on chlorotriflouride.

They marched toward the battlefield, preparing as quietly as possible. The closer they got, the more horrors they saw. These golden flies had turned the Odonata warriors against one another, and under Kólasi's control, they fought each other with brutal force.

"We have to hurry," Luna urged.

As they crossed into the outer edges of the battle, each Thermapunk shifted within the group to pair with an Aeropunk.

Emmeline stood beside Avery.

"Let's begin," Emmeline said, target focused on a golden fly zipping toward a healthy Lunarian fighting off an infected Lunarian.

Emmeline formed a fireball in her palm while Avery removed her regulator, cupped her hands to the sides of her mouth, and prepared to unleash chlorotriflouride.

Beneath Luna's umbrella of invisibility, they inched closer.

"Now," Emmeline directed.

Avery blew her lethal gas toward the golden fly, and Emmeline rocketed her fireball forward with the jab of her arm.

The fly flew through the scorching blaze, completely unfazed.

"It didn't work," Emmeline griped, looking around to find that every duo faced the same dilemma.

"I have an idea," Avery said while rolling the cuffs of her blouse. She quickly massaged each of her fingers until small holes opened at the tips. "Get a fireball ready."

Emmeline heated her heart and formed another fiery orb.

Avery's copper irises lightened to pale pinkish orange as she channeled the gas within her veins.

"Liquid nitrogen?" Emmeline asked, catching onto Avery's plan.

"Yes. I think we need to weaken the fly's golden armor for the fire to work."

"It's worth a try."

Avery lifted her hands, which had lost their copper hue and were now stark white and filled with liquid nitrogen.

"Three, two, one," Avery counted before sending a stream of freezing gas at the fly. It was so cold it had the power to burn. The fly froze midair, Emmeline blasted it with her fireball, and the fly disappeared with a small poof of crystallized ash.

"It worked!" Emmeline exclaimed in as low of a voice as her excitement allowed.

"I was worried they might be immortal," Avery noted. "They are creatures of Kólasi's design, after all."

"Liquid nitrogen and a fireball," Emmeline said over her shoulder to Helix, who then passed the information along to Solís. As the winning combination spread through the group, they moved swiftly through the battle, vaporizing the flies with greater speed.

Odonata Isone fought Odonata Arche when a golden fly barreled toward her. It was centimeters from her face when Kiran and Raven froze and incinerated it.

"How?" Isone asked with a gasp, still blocking Arche's attempts to kill her.

Luna led the crew of Solarpunks quietly past them.

Cèla lowered from overhead to help Isone constrain Arche.

Luna glanced up at Helmer, who wore a look of confusion — he was catching on to their progress, noticing that more than half of the golden flies were now gone.

He leaned against the railing of the mooncraft balcony, pure rage in his expression.

"How?" he bellowed. "Troops, prepare to deploy!"

Luna shouted, "We have to shower them with fire before he sends his fighters to the ground. The surviving Odonatas can't save the infected while also battling Marzans."

Fifty more golden flies incinerated, and the threat of Kólasi was temporarily vanquished.

The arachnids still battled each other, the Weaver doing a superb job keeping the Spinner occupied.

Beneath their shield of invisibility, Luna and the Solarpunks made their way to the base of the Marzan spacecraft.

"We need to spread out," Cyrus stated.

"I only have the shield set to a certain radius," Luna said. "If I lift the shield to adjust, you'll be seen."

"Maybe they *should* see us," Emmeline said through her regulator. "Maybe it's time we showed them our strength." She took a deep breath from her tank. "They will not destroy the sun, not without a fight."

"I agree," Solís said.

"As do I," Cyrus added.

The crew of Thermapunks and Aeropunks murmured in agreement.

"Alright then," Luna conceded. "Are you ready?"

Cyrus glanced over his shoulder. "Thermas—when the shield drops, spread out around the base of the aircraft. Since we can't fly, we will send fireballs and lava upward at the ship." Cyrus paused to breathe through his regulator. "Aeros—lift into the sky to attack from above. I think chlorotriflouride will work, but maintain ready access to liquid nitrogen as well." He turned back to Luna. "We are ready."

She nodded and raised her arms. "Let them feel your wrath."

Luna lowered her arms and the shield dropped. The Thermapunks raced to their places underneath the mooncraft while the Aeropunks rocketed into the sky. The lack of gravity sent them soaring. Many had to reverse the direction of their wings to correct how far they overshot their target.

"What is this?" King Helmer shouted from his balcony where he had full view of the forthcoming attack.

"This is your end," Remington replied from where he hovered, then shot a massive blast of liquid nitrogen at the Marzan king.

A nearby Marzan guard tossed his body in front of his king, catching the blast instead. The gaseous liquid covered his right arm, freezing it stiff.

"It burns!" the Marzan guard cried.

"Shield the king!" another Marzan guard shouted.

King Helmer was ushered into the mooncraft by two of his guards while the rest of his army shifted their focus from ground offense to sky defense. As they scrambled along the sides of the ship, racing to reach the cannons, the Thermapunks shot fireballs into the sky. As they collided with the spacecraft, the Aeropunks sent gusts of chlorotriflouride to the points of impact, creating massive explosions.

The Marzans in line with the blasts fell from great heights, plummeting to the moon below and creating heaping plumes of silver dust with each landing.

Helmer appeared again behind a window near the balcony. Beads of sweat dripped down his face, traveling along the creased lines of his fury.

"Spinner!" he bellowed, his voice resonating with a ferocious boom.

The Marzan arachnid turned to the call, but was thwarted by the Lunarian arachnid.

"Foray!" Cyrus shouted, aiming his fireball directly at the window Helmer hid behind.

The team of Thermpunks followed suit and lobbed their freshly crafted fireballs at the Marzan ship. They collided with the perfectly timed expulsion of gas from the Aeropunks. Enormous blasts erupted, causing great damage to the ship.

Cyrus's fireball connected with Raven's gas, and Helmer's balcony was engulfed by flames.

"Did we get him?" Cyrus asked.

"He was there a moment ago," Helix stated. "I didn't see if he retreated inside."

The Marzan ship creaked as it lifted higher into the atmosphere.

"They're retreating!" Luna exclaimed.

"Prepare another round," Cyrus instructed his crew.

In the few seconds it took for them to craft new fireballs, the Marzan Spinner used all its might to launch itself away from the Weaver and toward the slowly departing mooncraft.

"Aim at the spider," Cyrus instructed. "Foray!"

A swarm of fireballs rocketed toward the fleeing arachnid. As it latched to the bottom of the ship, the explosions connected with the spider and severed its back two legs. A shrieking wail of agony emanated from the arachnid as the mooncraft picked up speed and zoomed off.

The giant hairy spider legs fell to the silver terrain of Mōnalene. Their loud landing indicated Lunarian victory.

Those unaffected by the golden flies cheered while constraining their unlucky zombie-like counterparts.

The Monarchs appeared across the horizon. The purple outlines within their giant orange butterfly wings shimmered in the moonlight as they flew toward the field of victory.

Lepido Dione met with Cèla in the sky while Lepido Elir circled above, assessing the fresh war scene. Lifeless Lunarians lay scattered among the surviving warriors still battling those who were infected.

"This is a peculiar vision of victory," Dione said to Cèla, disturbed by the sight of her white-eyed Odonatas. "What happened to them?"

"A curse from Kólasi," Cèla answered. "He is working with the Marzans. He gifted them with golden flies that infest the mind and put the victim under Kólasi's control."

Dione's stern expression shifted with anger. "You're sure this is Kólasi's doing?"

"Positive. Helmer said so himself before releasing the flies."

The Weaver limped toward where the queen hovered beside Cèla.

"May I return to my chambers?" the arachnid asked, fresh wounds covering her entire body.

"Of course. Thank you for your valiant service," Dione replied.

The Weaver scurried away with a stagger, disappearing behind a jagged formation of moon rocks.

Dione glanced directly beneath her for the first time and her silver eyes widened with shock.

A large crew of Solarpunks stared up at her, their golden and copper eyes alight with a mix of awe and apprehension.

"Solarpunks?" she asked Cèla.

"It pains me to admit this, but we would not have secured a victory without them."

Dione's eyes located Luna within the group, then smiled.

"It appears all your hard work has resulted in a true alliance," Dione said to Luna.

"For which I am thankful," Luna replied. "But our fight isn't over yet."

"From what I've just learned, it seems it has only just begun," Dione agreed.

Solís removed his regulator from his mouth and stepped forward.

"We will win this war together," he said.

"With Kólasi helping the Marzans, the only other option is to die together," Dione replied, her comment grave.

Solís nodded. "The sun will not perish under our protection."

Chapter 34

Dione rose higher, wings carrying her with regal authority.

"Those who are not infected," the Lunarian queen instructed, "please bring the infected to the vault. They will be quarantined there until we figure out how to heal them."

The Odonatas wasted no time heeding her command. They dragged their poisoned brethren toward the vault located on the dark side of the moon.

Arche was in Isone's possession. Stripped of his weapons and wrists bound together by Isone's inner threads, his white eyes smoldered with panic as she hauled him by his feet. He clawed at the ground, but to no avail. He would be a prisoner until he was cured.

Emmeline turned to Luna.

"Can I see Gemma?" she asked through her regulator.

Luna's victorious energy lowered. "Last I saw her, she wasn't doing well."

"The remedy that worked for me isn't working for her?" Emmeline asked, her gut contracting with dread as she took a deep inhale from her tank.

"It's not holding. The curse leeched deep inside of her. It's a miracle we got you here when we did. Otherwise, you might be facing the same setback."

"I was infected longer than her, though."

Luna shrugged. "Her fight isn't over yet. The Mantos and Coccinellies are working hard to heal her."

"Please let me see her," Emmeline begged.

Luna glanced at Solís for guidance; they both understood Emmeline's fragility when it came to the health of her friends.

"I'll go with you," Solís offered, then turned to Cyrus. "You know the incantation. Lead everyone else home."

"Will do," Cyrus said. "I'll update the leaders of Quintessence about Kólasi's involvement."

242

"We have a long and brutal fight ahead of us, brother."

Cyrus nodded, his expression solemn.

"Before we go," Helix cut in, "let me grab some samples from the fallen Marzans. Maybe I can concoct some sort of potion to use against them."

"Go for it," Cyrus encouraged, waving his arm forward.

Helix advanced toward the lifeless Marzan bodies smashed against the ground of Mōnalene.

Equipped with his chemist toolbelt overtop of his Pyropunk suit, he had vials, scalpels, test tubes, corks, crucible tongs, a scoopula, a pipet, tweezers, and four syringes. The first body he stepped close to was mangled beyond recognition—charred flesh from the explosions and limbs bent in unnatural directions. He lightly kicked the body, and the delicate layer of burnt flesh still covering the Marzan disintegrated, revealing the Marzan's chainmail armor beneath. Completely dried up from the fire, Helix had little to sample from this body.

He moved to the next.

Careful and deliberate in his choices, Helix moved slowly while the small team of Solarpunks waited to go home.

"Hurry up!" Felicity shouted while checking her oxygen level gauge.

The next Marzan body he came to had less damage from the fire. Helix knelt beside it and used his tweezers to poke the wet flesh. It was damp and soft; liquid and moisture still existed within this body.

Another body lay only a few paces away. Helix hurried to it to compare. Also free from excessive mutilation from the explosions, either would give him sufficient samples to experiment with.

"We have a few punks low on oxygen," Cyrus called out to him. "Get your samples and let's go."

Helix needed time; he needed space to think. He could not rush the sample collection process and potentially ruin the data. The crew of Solarpunks was growing antsy, fidgeting restlessly where they waited for him.

His only option was to bring the bodies with him.

He grabbed the ankle of one and the wrist of the other and lugged them back to the group.

"What are you doing?" Cyrus asked.

"They're coming with us. I don't know which parts of them I'll need, so I'll just bring all of them."

"They'll take our spots on the trip back," Solís chimed in with a smirk. Emmeline wore a look of repulsion.

"They reek of sulfur," Raven complained as Helix squeezed in beside her.

"Ready to go!" Helix declared.

The Solarpunks connected by placing their hands on each other's shoulders, each still wearing Luna's threads on their finger.

"Everyone linked?" Cyrus asked.

"All good on my end," Avery shouted from the opposite side of the group.

"Looks good in the middle," Kiran confirmed.

The Solarpunks mumbled in agreement, adding no declarations of dissent.

Cyrus whispered the incantation, and the entire crew of Solarpunks vanished with a blink.

"How's your oxygen?" Luna asked Emmeline and Solís.

"Low," Emmeline replied.

"Same," Solís confirmed.

Luna reached into one of the many mini satchels latched to her belt and retrieved two oxygeni blossoms.

"Antho Devorah upgraded my clearance level at the garden. I am now allowed to pick and carry these blossoms at my discretion," Luna said as she handed the blossoms to Emmeline and Solís.

Solís removed his regulator, placed the flower into his mouth, and chewed. Emmeline followed his lead.

It only took a few chews for the flower's capacities to engage. Cold liquid lathered their throats, turning into oxygen as it seeped into their lungs.

Emmeline exhaled dramatically.

"Wow," she exclaimed. "That's powerful stuff!"

"Should last long enough to allow a quick visit with Gemma," Luna said.

Experiencing the magic of moon flowers reminded her of the flowers that had helped Helix.

"Thank you for helping Helix," Emmeline said.

Luna smiled. "Happy to."

Solís's brow furrowed, but before he could ask what they were talking about, Luna had darted ahead.

"What was that?" he asked his sister.

"She left healing flowers for Helix while he was recovering," Emmeline answered before chasing after Luna.

Solís smiled to himself as he caught up.

Luna led them around the field of Lunarians battling their infected brethren. The white-eyed Lunarians fought with all their might against those who attempted to constrain them. In many cases, it required two Lunarians for every one of the infected to get them restrained.

"I hope you can heal them," Emmeline offered as they took the long route around the struggle.

"I hope so, too," Luna said.

"If there are any remnants of the flies left inside their heads, be sure to save a few samples for us to study as well," Solís requested. "Perhaps we can help."

Luna nodded. "The flies are the creation of a god ... we will need all the help we can get."

They reached one of the many massive moon rock mountains. Luna ducked around the corner of a jagged rock wall and disappeared. Solís and Emmeline followed.

A long, narrow path led them to the center of Mōnalene.

"You have your moon threads, right?" Luna asked as they reached the ledge. Countless corded webs crisscrossed the vast openness before them.

"I've got mine," Solís said, pointing at his ankle.

"Is this enough?" Emmeline asked, holding up her pointer finger, which had a small thread coiled around it.

Luna shook her head and extracted a long cord from her fingertip. The thread turned wiry as it left Luna's body and hit the outside air.

"Wrap this around one of your ankles," she instructed. "Inside the meteor structures you can fly if you wish, but out here you need to stay grounded to the cords with magnetism."

Emmeline took the wired thread and twisted its ends to secure it in place.

"Great, now we can run," Luna said before darting forward. She leapt onto the nearest cord, her body floating momentarily until the magnetism within her reconnected her to the cord. She leapt again, her body soaring but never straying too far off course. Her wings stayed secured against her back at all times.

"Do not use your wings unless you want to splatter against one of the interior walls," Solís warned Emmeline before racing after Luna. He kept both feet on the ground and darted forward with furious speed.

Emmeline placed her foot without Luna's thread over the ledge and onto the massive cord. It immediately lifted upward—the lack of gravity within the center of Mōnalene was powerful.

She retracted her foot and placed the other onto the cord. The magnetism from Luna's thread kept Emmeline's foot grounded. She shifted her body forward and felt a massive pull—the space around her tried to lift her upward, but Luna's thread kept her from floating away. Afraid to lift her secured foot off the cord, she dragged it as her free foot stepped forward.

Luna and Solís had already reached the nearest meteor platform.

"You're hobbling like a peg-legged Nautipunk," Solís teased her.

"The pull is strong," Luna added, "but you can walk more freely than that."

"It feels like I'll get yanked into the sky if I lift this foot!" Emmeline replied.

"Unless you propel forward with massive force, you won't. The threads on your ankle will prevent that from happening."

"You do need to move faster, though," Solís encouraged her. "We only have so much air left to breathe."

He was right, and she needed time with Gemma.

Emmeline took a deep breath and found her courage.

She pushed forward with her unbound foot and lifted upward. She pushed her magnetized foot forward and returned to the cord.

It wasn't graceful like Luna's leaps, or controlled like Solís's dart, but it worked. She was moving faster now.

Adrenaline racing, fear morphing into excitement, Emmeline's fire heart sweltered.

Upon joining them on the meteor platform, her wide smile counteracted the panic in her eyes.

"That was a rush," she proclaimed.

Solís snickered.

"Two more cords to go," Luna informed them, then carried onward.

The world within Mōnalene held a hazy silver glow. There were innumerable levels of cords canvassing the open space between the meteors. Lunarians of all kinds leapt, ran, and swung from them as they went about their daily business.

Emmeline observed in awe as she followed Luna and Solís. The silver radiance was almost hypnotizing and she had to shake her head a few times to keep her bearings.

"We're here," Luna announced, shaking Emmeline from her lucid daze.

They stood on a platform attached to a giant meteor.

"This is the laboratory," Luna explained.

"It looks like a giant rock," Emmeline replied, adrenaline still racing.

Luna smiled. "Well, it is a giant rock. All of our establishments reside within meteors."

She led them inside.

Small coves carved into the meteor served as rooms for patients. Silver sheets hung from the ceiling to create privacy for the occupied beds, but many were sheetless and vacant.

Luna led them through an archway into an area where a circular hallway surrounded a room in the middle. Light poured through the giant windows. Beyond them were lanky shadows huddled together, accompanied by smaller circular shadows pacing back and forth.

"We're here," Luna stated before walking through the door.

At the center of the room was Gemma, lying unconscious on a moon rock table. Braided black cords ran up her nose and came out of her mouth.

"Is she alive?" Emmeline asked, her fear apparent.

"She is," one of the lanky bug-eyed scientists replied. "She's not healing as well as you did, though."

"Do you remember Manto Maldi?" Luna asked.

"I remember everyone's faces, but not their names."

"He helped heal you, along with Manto Bogo, Coccinelli Marietta, and Coccinelli Katica."

"Thank you all," Emmeline offered, embarrassed that she had little memory of them.

With her head slightly bowed, she shuffled to Gemma's side and grabbed her friend's cold, limp hand.

"Why aren't the threads working?" Emmeline asked.

"They are," Manto Bogo answered. "They're just not working as efficiently. The curse seems to have seeped deeper into her."

"So, you'll just need to use more threads then," Emmeline stated.

"Possibly ... but it's also possible that we won't be able to extract all of the curse. If it has soaked into her tissue, nerves, or bloodstream, this method of healing won't work."

"Then we figure out a new method."

"It's not that simple ... "

"It has to be," Emmeline insisted. "She has to survive."

Gemma stirred where she lay.

Emmeline's bright eyes glimmered with tears.

"Gemma," she whispered. "Can you hear me?"

Gemma nodded her head ever so slightly.

"You have to stay strong," Emmeline encouraged.

"It's so dark and cold," Gemma said, her voice a hoarse whisper.

"I've been in that room. It's awful, I know. Just look for the light."

"It comes and goes."

"This will pass," Emmeline promised.

"I will never feel warmth again."

"Please," Emmeline begged, "don't lose hope."

Gemma coughed, and her frail, skeletal body tremored violently.

"Step back," Coccinelli Katica insisted as she pushed Emmeline aside.

Emmeline stepped backward, her spirit deflated. It was her fault Gemma was in this predicament.

Emmeline turned to Luna and pled, "I need to stay here with her."

"You don't have enough oxygen."

"Give me more of those flowers."

Luna shook her head. "You need to go home."

"Why?"

"The Mantos and Coccinellies have this under control. You are needed on the sun."

"For what? All I offer is chaos. I am of no use to anyone! I need to fix what I broke before I can do any good elsewhere."

"It's time to leave," Solís said, taking Emmeline by the hand.

She snatched her hand out of his. "I cannot leave her!"

"You have to. We can come back to check on her soon," Solís promised.

"What if she dies before then? I introduced her to that cursed moonstone. This is my fault. The least I can do is stay by her side."

"You have no knowledge to offer here. No skills to contribute to her survival," Solís said, his words harsh. "Whereas on Quintessence, you can help us prepare for battle against the Marzans. You can inspire legions of Solarpunks to rise to the occasion."

"No one should trust a word I say," she said, her desperation to help Gemma morphing into self-loathing.

"Stop," Solís demanded. "You're acting pathetic."

"I'm speaking the truth."

"Take my hand."

"I want to stay here," Emmeline stated, her tone low and serious.

"Take my hand," he repeated, returning her furious glare. "Now."

"I will not give you any more oxygeni flowers," Luna added, backing up Solís.

Emmeline shot her a look of betrayal.

"You're supposed to be *my* friend," Emmeline said.

"In this case, Solís is right, and I need to side with him. Your presence among your people is imperative to the war effort. You are an inspiration, even if you don't feel like one."

"Pull it together," Solís said, his tone stern. "You are a Dawes. Act like one."

Fighting with him was pointless; she was outnumbered and had no means to survive on Mōnalene without Luna's help.

Emmeline calmly walked out of the laboratory door, stood in the hall, and glared at her older brother, holding his gaze as she said the words to take herself home.

"Ad solem quin. Accipe me."

Emmeline vanished.

Solís darted after her, grabbing at the air where she previously stood.

"She is so insolent," Solís said with a grumble.

"Coming from the most insolent individual I have ever met," Luna retorted with a laugh. She joined Solís in the hallway.

"Had the *pleasure* to meet," Solís jokingly corrected her.

"Wonder where she learned such insolence from?"

"My father," Solís answered candidly. "It's where we all learned it from."

"I thought your father is one of the leaders of Quintessence."

"He is, but he broke a lot of rules when he took to the seas of Hydra. Thermapunks weren't allowed there for centuries, but when the Nautipunks continually failed to stop the moon monsters—err, moon beings—from stealing the source flame, my father took it upon himself to intervene. My brothers and I took a similarly uncharted path when we formed the Pyro-Argo Militia. Something like that had never been done before."

"And Emmeline was the first to rally all the Solarpunk factions together," Luna noted.

Solís nodded. "Insolence is in our blood."

"Seems your insolence often serves the greater good of your people."

"On the grander scale, yes. It's the little day-to-day interactions that can become bothersome."

"Oh, I am aware," Luna said with a snicker. "I've been on your bothered side."

Solís grinned. "Infuriating, but endearing, I've been told."

"Somehow, you pull it off."

Solís side-glanced at the open doorway—the Mantos and Coccinellies had their backs to them and were focused intently on Gemma.

He looked back at Luna and took a step closer to her. His golden gaze smoldered as it met hers.

She narrowed her own gaze with curiosity, but stood her ground.

He took another step closer, his fire heart racing with forbidden desire. His nose touched her brow, and he tilted his head until their foreheads touched.

Neither said a word.

Adrenaline spiking, her silver eyes lifted to look at him.

"There's something about you," Solís said. "I have never felt this way for anyone."

"What do you feel?" Luna asked, her voice soft.

"Desire and devotion," Solís confessed. "Do you feel it, too?"

"I do."

He lowered himself slightly to kiss her.

Silver and gold.

The moon and the sun.

A predictable pairing on paper, yet forbidden in practicality.

Cursed by eons of conflict, now bound by a simple kiss, their impossible desires swirled with violent potency.

Luna pulled away first.

"How could this ever work?" she asked.

"I don't know," Solís admitted. "But I want it to."

"We will be shunned from our homes."

"I don't care. I only want you."

Luna shook her head and stepped back. "You should care."

"I don't!"

He grabbed her hands and pulled her back to him. The energy between their bodies radiated.

Aware of the danger, he kissed her again.

This love could start a war.

Chapter 35

Quintessence

Emmeline reappeared at the Pyro-Argo base.

She landed in a crouch near the shelf where the moonstone sat.

"How was your friend?" Kiran asked.

Emmeline stood and brushed the moon dust off her cargo pants.

"She's not doing well."

"I'm sorry," Kiran offered.

"It's not your fault. It's mine."

"I know. I just meant I'm sorry she's sick at all."

"So am I," Emmeline said. "Has anything noteworthy happened while we were gone?"

Kiran hesitated, then said, "The black hole has gotten bigger."

"What are they doing about it?" Emmeline asked, panicked.

"Praying," Kiran answered, wearing an unenthused expression.

"Solédon is a last resort—He can't be counted on," she said. "Where are Raven and Remington?"

"They joined the other gas spinners in Hydra. Stitching the hole closed hasn't worked yet."

"We need to join them."

Emmeline ripped the empty oxygen tank off her back and placed it beside the others. She charged toward the hangar base opening, then looked over her shoulder.

"Are you coming?" she asked.

"Oh, me too? Yeah, I'll join. I don't have a shift until tomorrow morning."

Kiran grabbed Emmeline's empty tank and brought it to the gas pump.

"Where are Cyrus and Helix?" she asked as Kiran turned the lever from oxygen to helium and filled the cylinder.

"I don't know where Cyrus went. Helix turned one of the war rooms here at the base into his personal laboratory. He locked himself in there with the Marzan bodies as soon as we got back."

"I'll be right back," she said, then tore down the hall.

She knocked on the only door that was closed.

"I'm working!" Helix shouted.

"Open up," Emmeline replied.

The sound of clinking and clanging was accompanied by shuffling feet.

The door cracked open.

"What?" Helix asked, peering through.

"Why are you acting sketchy?"

"I can't open the door all the way, or the fumes I'm bathing the bodies in will leak out."

"Are *you* okay?" she asked.

"I'm better than ever," he swore.

"These fumes aren't going to trigger a relapse?"

"No, no," he insisted. "The chemicals possess completely different compounds than locomo."

"Okay," she said. "Please tell me if you feel any kind of pull back to the addiction. I will help you."

"Yeah, I will." He scanned her skinny arms and collarbones—the only parts of her body not covered by her clothes. "I need you to do the same."

"What do you mean?"

"You're smaller than you were before you left. You say you're healed, but you look worse."

"I am healed. I am no longer cursed; the marble-induced migraines are gone."

"Then why are you still losing weight?"

"I'm stressed."

"That's not a good reason to starve yourself."

Furious about the accusation, Emmeline reached into her pocket, retrieved eight clay marbles, and ate them all in one shot.

They made a cacophony of ringing clangs as they ricocheted down her throat and into the holding pan. After eight thudding clinks, she asked, "Happy now?"

"That proves nothing. Just because your addiction is different from mine doesn't mean it's not as serious."

"What addiction?" she asked, exasperated.

"Your obsession with being small."

"I don't care about being small. I care about being in control," she said.

"And when you can't control the world unraveling around you, you revert to controlling the only thing you *can* control: yourself, your body."

"What's wrong with that?"

"You're making yourself sick."

"I am not," she objected. "Stop trying to deflect your issues onto me."

"I'm just trying to help," he offered, expression sincere.

"I think I liked you better when you were high," she spat, her words cutting.

Emmeline grabbed the doorknob and pulled the door shut. She clenched her fists and released an utterly enraged growl. Her brother's implications were infuriating.

"What's wrong?" Kiran asked as Emmeline stormed back into the community space.

"I need a break from everything."

"There is a lot going on," he empathized.

"And I feel like most of it lands on me."

"No one expects you to solve it all. Without you, we probably would have been attacked and taken over without warning. The alliance you built with the Lunarians is what will likely save us."

"They don't know how to close the black hole either."

"At least we aren't fighting the Marzans alone."

Emmeline's anger was subsiding. She exhaled deeply.

"Let's get going," she said and then walked to the edge of the hangar bay platform.

Her heart heated to sweltering temperatures and her golden-hued flesh glowed red. Once hot enough, her body lifted. She spread her golden wings and pounded them against the sky. Kiran followed, fueled by helium and propelled forward by titanium wings.

They stayed in Fyree, never lifting or lowering into Gaslion. They passed the Dawes home—which stood alone and separated from the other noble homes of Fyree. A few minutes later, they reached the rows of giant golden mansions belonging to the other noble Thermapunks. Each manor floated in the sky via heat sourced through golden tethers. Emmeline glanced over at Kiran, realizing she knew little about him.

"Which one belongs to your family?" she shouted through the rushing wind.

"None of them."

"Where did you grow up?"

"In the ranks."

Emmeline nodded—the ranks was a section of Fyree where the majority of Thermapunks resided, all of whom were not considered noble. It was modest but respectable living. The homes were small but functional, made of pinchbeck, not gold. These Thermapunks often served as workers at the Steamery, as crewmates aboard Montgomery's ship in Hydra, or as fighters in the Pyro-Argo militia.

"We'd be nothing without the hard workers from the ranks," Emmeline offered, the wind tossing her long golden braids.

Kiran tightened his expression, visibly uncomfortable.

She added, "It's nothing to be ashamed of."

"I'm not ashamed. I'm proud of where I come from. I just don't like being defined by where I grew up; I don't appreciate the division between social classes."

"I don't like it either," Emmeline agreed.

"I know. That's why I like you so much."

Kiran immediately blushed, realizing what he had admitted after the words had already left his mouth.

"It's fine," Emmeline said.

"I appreciate our friendship," Kiran blubbered.

"I do, too." Emmeline offered him a kind smile.

"I know you're still processing the whole Louie thing," Kiran added. "I didn't mean to imply anything or make you uncomfortable."

"Louie," Emmeline said with a grumble. "I don't even know where to begin. Kindness hasn't worked. Giving him space hasn't worked. He blames me for his suffering, but won't let me help him heal. I feel terrible guilt. He loved me, and I ruined him."

"I don't know the answer, but I do know that *you* didn't ruin him. You didn't force him to travel with the moonstone. You didn't torture him on Deimos. At some point, he needs to do a little self-reflection and take some accountability."

"I don't see that happening anytime soon."

"Maybe not. He needs to heal himself first."

"That could take years," Emmeline said, her worry apparent. "I heard he's already neglecting his healing by participating in missions again."

"I hope you don't plan to wait for him."

"Of course, I will wait."

Kiran shook his head. "Don't let someone else's shackles constrain you, too."

"He would never forgive me if I didn't wait."

"That's his problem, not yours. If he is your person, you'll find each other again when the time is right, and there will be no animosity for what happened while you lived separate lives. He's the one pushing you away, after all. He'll have to live with the consequences of that choice."

"I never thought about it that way."

"Well, you ought to. You deserve happiness also."

Emmeline was tired. "Thank you."

They reached the Thermapunk prayer group still stationed in the sky.

"Have they been praying this whole time?" she asked Kiran.

"I think so. Punks come and go, but the core group hasn't stopped since they began."

Ambrose and Cecelia Monroe—Clementine's parents—led the prayer group.

Emmeline and Kiran lifted and flew over the crowd, suspended on contraptions manned by Pilopunks.

"Solédon," Ambrose bellowed from his helium balloon. "Hear our prayers!"

"Ascent," the rest of the prayer group said in unison.

"Save us from the wrath of the Marzans," Ambrose pled. "Cloak Deimos in fire. Let Your mercy for us, Your devoted subjects, rain upon them with fatal finality. Hear our prayers!"

"Ascent!" the prayer group declared.

Ambrose continued, asking for more action from Solédon, always followed by the group's upheaval of the prayer from Ambrose's mouth into the heavens.

"I hope their prayers work," Emmeline said as they flew beyond the group. "Kólasi will be impossible to beat without Him."

"Yeah, I hope He hears them, too," Kiran agreed.

They reached the gates of Hydra and tilted their bodies forward to descend.

Speed increased, they rocketed through the titanium bars of the gates and flew into the massive underground world of Hydra. The ocean below spat mist and foam with each crashing wave. In the distance was a solitary rove, and even further was Dawes Detention Center for Demons. Though it was far and hardly visible at this distance, the commotion around the cages was noticeable. All attention was on the black hole—nothing else in Hydra took precedence.

As Emmeline and Kiran got closer to the detention center, it became apparent that every Nautipunk ship in Hydra was congregated there.

The vacant Marzan cage had new, raging flames dancing along its bars, and the black hole within was bigger than before.

What once was the size of a pinhole was now the size of a head. It had also shifted to the left, closer to the wall of the cage.

"It's larger, but has it also moved?"

"I think you're right," Kiran agreed. "It's rolling toward freedom."

"They can't attack us until the hole is outside of the cage," Emmeline said, this realization profound. "We still have time."

Their conversation garnered the attention of the crew below.

"Not much," Edwin Doyle shouted up to them from where he stitched a wound on Reservoir Robert's wrist. "At the rate it's moving, it'll be beyond the confines of the cage within a day or two."

The shutters of the captain's quarters window slammed open and Montgomery's head popped out.

"Were you fighting on the moon, too?" Montgomery asked Emmeline.

"Who told you?"

"Cyrus filled me in."

"Yeah, I was there, too. Did he tell you about Kólasi?"

"He did," Montgomery replied, his expression grave. He left the window and exited his captain's quarters, followed by Red Fang Ralph, who carried a stack of folded parchments, Cyrus, Avery, and Louie, who still walked with a serious limp.

"Good meeting, aye," Ralph guffawed. "A plan is afoot. I'll station me archers. Have 'em ready ter ambush the black hole."

"Make sure they understand that they can only use arrowheads made of Lunarian metal."

"As soon as ye get it ter me, I'll have me cutler sharpen the tips."

"That's where you come in," Montgomery said to Emmeline. "We need Luna to deliver Lunarian metal to us so we can reinforce all of our artillery."

"I can do that," she said.

"Fantastic," he replied before curtly changing course and charging toward his crew of Thermapunks gathered around the cannons. Red Fang Ralph and Cyrus followed.

Louie glared up at Emmeline and Kiran. His eyes were bloodshot and the wounds from his lashings on Deimos snaked up his neck from beneath the popped collar of his shirt.

"Him, again?" he sneered.

"Oh, stop it," Avery said in defense of Emmeline. "You're acting like a child."

"You've rejected my attempts to fix things between us," Emmeline reminded him. "I've tried … what else am I supposed to do?"

"You're right, actually," he said, voice laced with venom. "It's better if you do nothing. We all know the chaos your attempts to help cause."

"That's not fair," Emmeline said, but Louie had already snagged the rope ladder draped over the gunwale and retreated from the conversation.

Emmeline wore an expression of pure defeat.

"He'll come around," Avery said as she lifted into the sky. "And if he doesn't, that's his problem, not yours."

Kiran nodded. "Exactly what I've been saying."

"It's just easier said than done," Emmeline griped.

"I'm sure, but to our collective misfortune, we have much bigger issues to focus on."

"A fatal distraction, if you will," Kiran said, trying to make a joke.

Neither was amused.

"How is Gemma?" Avery asked.

"Not good," Emmeline answered. "The methods they used on me aren't working as well for her."

"I see." Though this news upset Avery, keeping Emmeline's spirit invigorated was her priority. "Gemma is strong," Avery reminded Emmeline. "Her will is unrivaled. Don't count her out yet."

"I'm not. I just want her to be okay."

"We all do."

"I need to get some Lunarian metal from Luna," Emmeline said, trying to redirect her focus.

"Looks like you won't need to make any trips to relay that request," Avery said, pointing upward at the gates of Hydra.

Solís and Luna flew high in the sky above. Solís, an image of golden regality. Luna, a fluid swirl of black and silver. She did not wear her shield of invisibility; she flew freely and fully exposed. The flickering light of the source flame radiated upward through the crashing waves and sporadically illuminated her iridescent wings. Pastel rainbow bursts decorated her flight toward Montgomery's hovering ship.

As they got closer, their faces came into view.

Solís wore a smile Emmeline had never seen on him before— blissful glee. Luna's expression matched until her attention shifted to the cage beyond the ship. Dark veins appeared around her eyes, and as her silver irises turned black, she shouted, "Watch out!"

Emmeline snapped her attention to the empty prison.

A blood-red Marzan hand had reached through the black hole.

Chapter 36

Luna twisted her body midair, aiming feetfirst at the black hole. Rocketing at a furious speed, she entered the cage through the open gate at the top and used her talons to slice the Marzan's fingers clean off.

A distant howl accompanied the dactylectomy, and the fingerless Marzan hand retracted back into the hole.

"The black hole has grown in size," she noted with a scowl while lifting and exiting the burning cage. "Has it moved also?"

"It moves closer to exiting the cage every hour," Ramsay Bowler, a Thermapunk guard stationed atop the cage, replied. Flames danced around his ankles. He wore a look of repulsed confusion as he spoke to Luna—it wasn't long ago that he saw her as a monster.

Luna ignored his very apparent internal battle.

"Have they made any other attempts to exit yet?" she asked.

"No," he replied. "That was the first time any part of them exited the black hole."

She nodded, then looked up to where Emmeline, Solís, and Avery watched from the side of the ship. Around them was the rest of the Thermapunk crew, including Montgomery, who looked on in horror.

"We are running out of time," she shouted to them.

"I was on my way to ask for Lunarian metal to reinforce our weaponry when you arrived in Hydra," Emmeline answered.

"I can get you the metal, but it won't be enough."

Montgomery lifted his gold-plated bullhorn and spoke into it.

"We have other preparations as well," he began, his voice amplified and echoing across Hydra.

"Shh!" Luna urged. "Do not announce your plans so loudly. They can eavesdrop through the hole."

Montgomery lowered his bullhorn, clearly frustrated.

"We ought to organize our plans; make sure they're aligned," he shouted.

"Yes, of course. But I should stay here to guard the black hole."

"You can guard it from the safety of my ship," Montgomery said. "They can't do much until they nudge the hole out of the cage. Plus, we can discuss our plans more quietly here."

"Be wary," Luna warned. "One of the Marzans' strengths is their hearing. I suspect they could hear a whisper near that gate in the sky."

"Well then, if that's the case, they already know our plans and we ought to convene immediately to restrategize."

Luna took a deep breath. As her adrenaline calmed, the veins around her eyes retracted and silver streaks inked her black eyes.

She left the Thermapunk standing guard and lifted higher into the sky.

"We need to work fast," Luna declared as she reached Montgomery's ship. Her talons scraped the planked steel deck upon landing. "Can we convene above Hydra to strategize?" she asked Montgomery.

"Yes," he answered, then turned to his crew. "Until further notice, the plan we've discussed stands. Anyone assigned to guard the black hole, please disembark. Red Fang Ralph will house you on his boat until I return."

The majority of the Thermapunk crew exited the ship via rope ladders, along with any Nautipunks on board.

Avery prepped for departure. Once the tanks were full, she manned the wheel and pulled the various levers attached to the pipes snaking into the ship's four balloons. Helium released upward, lifting the massive ship higher into the sky. Montgomery climbed the tallest mast, which extended higher than the balloons, and when they reached the giant gate in the sky, he inserted his master key. Four twists and the doors opened. As the creaking and clicking gears churned and the coiled springs retracted, Montgomery descended the mast to rejoin the small group.

Just his family, Kiran, Avery, Luna, and four Thermapunks from his crew remained.

He doubled over, hands on his knees, exhausted from the climb.

"I can lock the gate once we cross through," Cyrus offered.

Montgomery handed him the master key without responding.

Avery lifted the ship upward past the gate's threshold.

Cyrus spread his titanium wings and leapt off the side of the ship, locking the gate behind them. Once Cyrus was safely back on board, Emmeline crafted a flame in the palm of her hand and heated the pipe connected to the propellers. The heated air moved the blades faster and rocketed the ship forward. As they blazed through the sky, Luna stood exposed near the bow, taking in the freedom of her new standing within Quintessence.

Though every Solarpunk was now aware of their alliance with the Lunarians, it did not stop passersby—Thermas and Aeros—from looking on in shock.

The wind whipped Luna's long black hair and the golden glow of Quintessence shimmered in her silver eyes. She was radiant, confident, and serene—a vision of pure intimidation to anyone unsure of their own standing.

They reached the prayer group in Fyree, still led by Ambrose and Cecelia Monroe. Melora sat with them on their chariot, actively engaged in the group prayer.

"Let's stop here for a moment," Montgomery instructed Avery and Emmeline, who slowed the ship's speed.

"Ascent," the group chanted, finishing this section of prayer.

"Darling!" Montgomery shouted, catching Melora's attention.

Her eyes opened and her serenity was replaced with repulsion upon seeing Luna.

"You brought it *here*?" she asked.

"She is our ally," he said, attempting to stifle his embarrassment.

"I understand, but I thought you'd restrict their presence to Hydra."

Solís stepped into the conversation. "Your intolerance will instigate our demise."

"I'm not intolerant, just shocked," she said.

"She's here to save us. Show a little gratitude."

Melora huffed. "I still have faith that Solédon will save us." She then glared at Montgomery. "Why have you interrupted our prayer?"

"To let you know that war will be upon us soon. Possibly within the day."

"Why so soon?" Ambrose asked.

"The black hole continues to roll toward freedom."

"Why haven't you built a new cage in the direction it's moving?" Melora asked, her tone harsh, as if this solution were obvious.

"It's not a bad idea," Cyrus said, revealing they hadn't thought of this prior.

"No, it's not," Montgomery agreed. "But it would only be a temporary solution, and without additional posts secured to the obsidian source flame shield, we could only build the cage out so far."

"Buy us time," Melora said, her energy softer. "As much as you can. We think our prayers are growing strong enough to reach the gods."

"We will discuss this option. Thank you," Montgomery said. "Still, everyone must make any necessary preparations. Whether it's tomorrow or in a few days, war is coming."

Everyone in the prayer group nodded, their expressions a mixture of terror and determination.

"Onward to the Pyro-Argo base," Montgomery instructed Avery.

The ship lurched forward, using both helium and heat for propulsion.

Restless and ready for battle, the small crew disembarked from the ship and onto the hangar bay with haste, eager to lay out a victorious plan. They charged past the off-duty punks hanging out in the common area and reconvened in the war room at the back of the base.

"Building out the cages isn't a bad idea," Cyrus reiterated as they congregated around a large table.

"It will only delay the inevitable," Montgomery stated.

"But it would give us more time to prepare."

"It would split our resources," Montgomery argued. "It would take more than half our Thermapunk crew to solder a cage that fast. We need everyone focused on the forthcoming battle, not caught up in trying to delay the inevitable."

"Plus," Solís added, "would they really be able to finish the cage in time?"

"Fine," Cyrus conceded. "Onto the next idea."

Luna stood beside Solís, her energy calm as she listened to them squabble.

"Magnetism," Montgomery stated, his attention on Luna. "We have the Terrapunks mining for magnetic minerals. Not only will we be armed with this power in Hydra, but so will the Nautipunks in the water and the Terrapunks hiding in the pipes above.

Luna nodded, then asked, "You spoke of this plan while you were in Hydra?"

"We did."

"Then we must hope that the Marzans do not have consistent surveillance listening through the black hole. Or that there was enough noise around your conversations to block their ability to hear."

"The crew is always loud," Emmeline said. "And when the Nautipunks are docked below, there's an extra level of noise."

"Then perhaps they did not hear."

"Do you think it's a good plan?" Montgomery asked.

"Yes," Luna replied. "It's a great plan if the battle happens in Hydra."

"What do you mean? Where else would it happen?"

"I think we ought to strike first. A black hole works two ways—just as they can enter Hydra through it, we can go to them from our side."

A tense moment of silence lingered among the group.

"Are you sure it wouldn't be a bloodbath?" Montgomery finally asked.

"They don't know how to kill you—Louie is proof of that. And we will formulate a secure plan before making an attempt. If it works, you'll never have to see war at home."

"I would rather the battle happen elsewhere," Montgomery said, his thoughts spinning.

"How do you suggest we go about this?" Solís asked Luna.

"With fire. Send a swirling inferno through the hole, then enter through the camouflage of the blaze."

"Do you know what awaits us on the other side?" Emmeline asked.

"I don't, but I can assure you that they aren't expecting you to strike first. Solarpunks have never once taken their fight against the moons beyond the sun. You leaving your home base would catch them off guard."

"It's not a bad idea," Solís said.

"I think it's a great idea," Cyrus reaffirmed. "We should stop them there to prevent the war from happening here."

"I like it also," Montgomery agreed, "but we should still make preparations in case we fail and they bring the battle to us."

Cyrus suggested, "We can keep the rotating crew of Thermapunks fueled and prepared to guard the black hole opening. If there are any signs that the Marzans are attempting to cross through, they unleash a relentless stream of fire."

"That will force them to exit as a unit rather than filtering through one by one," Luna said. "This is good, so long as they don't try to fit one of their ships through. Magnetism won't work on their aircraft."

"The hole isn't big enough for a ship," Solís said.

"Not yet, it isn't," Emmeline warned, then asked, "What about the Lunarian metal? Are we still planning to reinforce our weapons?"

"You ought to," Luna advised. "Even with all of these preparations, anything could happen, and only Lunarian metal is strong enough to cut through the Marzans' chainmail armor."

"We don't have much time," Solís said.

"I'll leave and retrieve some now."

"Will you bring reinforcements upon your return?" Montgomery asked. "Other Lunarians to help us fight?"

"I'll bring whoever is able. Many of our best fighters were infected by Kólasi's flies. Bring my moonstone back to Hydra with you. We will want to enter there." She grabbed the amulet hanging around her neck and scanned the Solarpunks' faces around the table. "Is there anything else I should know before departing?"

"No," Montgomery answered.

"Just hurry back," Solís added.

Luna nodded, gave Solís a small smile, whispered the incantation, and disappeared.

Montgomery side-eyed Solís, but chose not to ask questions. Instead, he doled out instructions.

"Cyrus and Kiran, I need you to check on the magnet harvest in Terra. Whatever they've collected thus far, retrieve it and bring it to Hydra. We need to arm our crew and the Nautipunks."

"Sure thing," Cyrus said.

"Be back in time for our attack on the black hole. We will strike tonight."

Cyrus and Kiran exited the room.

"Solís and Avery," Montgomery continued. "I need you to prepare the Pyropunks and Argopunks for battle. Our gravest threat is no longer near the solar shield, it is within Hydra. We will be traveling through the black hole tonight to fight our enemy."

"How many soldiers do we need for this mission?"

"One hundred of each," Montgomery answered. "Our militia isn't large; we never needed it to be, but we cannot risk the entire fleet on this mission. My hope is that the element of surprise makes our small force seem much larger. Plus, the Lunarians will add to our numbers."

They nodded.

"Avery," he continued, "do the tanks on my ship have enough helium for a return trip to Hydra?"

"Yes, just make sure to dock once you reach the detention center. I'll refill them once I'm back from gathering the Argopunks."

"Great."

Solís and Avery departed.

Only Emmeline was left.

Montgomery looked at her with concern.

"You should've returned to your normal size by now," he said.

"I don't think my gears will grow back. I think this is my new normal size."

"Have you been eating?"

"Yes," Emmeline replied with a groan.

"You can't blame me for worrying."

"I know. But I'm fine."

"Are you sure?"

"I'm as fine as I can be considering all that is going on."

"I know how close you were to Louie—"

"Stop," she demanded, then lowered her voice. "Please."

"Losing friends to death is devastating, but losing them while they're still living is a different kind of grief. Sometimes more agonizing, I'd argue."

"I'm very aware."

"And Gemma is not healed yet?" Montgomery asked.

"No."

Montgomery sighed. "You are dealing with a lot. Please do not neglect yourself while grieving the well-being of those you love."

"I'm trying my best."

A solar quake rattled the base where it hovered.

Emmeline clutched the table for stability while Montgomery leaned against the wall.

The tremors stopped.

"What was that?" Emmeline asked.

"Solar quakes only happen when the source flame is disrupted," Montgomery answered. "It's a warning—I haven't felt one of those in decades."

"We need to go back," Emmeline insisted.

They boarded the ship and steered it to Hydra, unsure what new horror would greet them upon their return.

Chapter 37

Hydra

The sunquake stopped.

Louie crawled out from under the stacked crates he had taken shelter beneath.

A thick spider thread extended from the black hole down into the ocean, narrowly missing Red Fang Ralph's boat where it pierced the sea. As the crew reemerged and bustled about in a frenzy, Louie paused to breathe. The trauma of his imprisonment on Deimos had not yet faded, and every inclination of danger put his nerves on edge. He leaned against the gunwale, pressing all of his weight into the deteriorating railing.

Another deep breath.

Louie felt no relief.

The world was crumbling around him and he had no strength left to fight.

"Ain't no time fer lollygagging," Red Fang Ralph declared upon seeing him hunched over the gunwale. "We need ter sever the kraken's thread!"

Louie nodded.

"I need me grog!" Ralph shouted, flailing his arms about as he zigzagged across the main deck, shouting orders as he searched for his blood-infused ale.

Waves from the quake still thrashed violently against the side of the ship.

Louie took a moment, unsure what the point of fighting was. He felt the Marzans' cruelty, he saw their vicious determination—no matter how long the Solarpunks held them off, they would come back relentlessly until they claimed victory.

Doom was inevitable.

Pippin Picklefish stumbled toward him, just as drunk as he'd been on all the other crews he was barred from joining again.

"I know that look," he stammered.

"Excuse me?" Louie replied.

"The look o' hopelessness." Pippin hiccupped. "I know the cure."

"And what is that?"

Pippin reached into his vest and retrieved a flask from a hidden pocket. He extended it to Louie while swaying ever so slightly in place.

"Take a swig."

"What is it?" Louie asked.

"Hope."

Louie raised a brow. "You mean whiskey?"

"Some call it that."

"That will only worsen my despair."

"Not if ye keep drinking it." Pippin shook the flask at Louie. "The trick is: don't stop."

"Sounds like a trap."

"I'd rather be trapped like this than forced ter face reality without its warm embrace." Pippin shivered, then took a swig. "It dulls the pain."

Louie snatched the flask from Pippin and took a long guzzle. When he lowered the drink, he scowled with disgust.

"Tastes awful."

"But it feels so nice," Pippin replied with a loopy smile.

Louie took another swig.

"Tastes like poison," he said with a grimace.

"Technically, it is," Pippin revealed. "But it be a pleasant poison, and we all got ta die sometime, aye?"

"How much do I need to feel better?"

"Keep the flask," Pippin said, his eyes glazed. He opened his vest and revealed four more flasks secured to the inner lining. "I've got more fer meself."

"Thanks," Louie said, unsure that this was a wise choice, but he was tired of living in constant agony.

"Aye, aye," Pippin mumbled as he stumbled away.

Louie took another smaller sip, cringing the whole time. He swallowed with a shudder. This was a terrible plan to feel better, but he was at his breaking point and nothing else he had tried had worked.

"Are ye goin' ter help or not?" Red Fang Ralph shouted at him from the crow's nest where he oversaw his crew's attempts to saw through the thread.

Louie climbed onto the gunwale. As he tried to locate his balance, the effects of the whiskey kicked in. A warm and fuzzy sensation embraced his mind in a tight hug and his surroundings swayed disharmoniously with the rhythm of the ship.

He lurched forward, dangling dangerously over the ship's ledge. Barely maintaining his balance and about to fall overboard, a giant wave tilted the ship in the opposite direction and threw Louie onto the main deck.

His very sore body hit the hard ground with force, but the shield of alcohol prevented him from feeling additional pain.

Louie took another swig.

The exaggerated sway of the ship kept him glued to the ground.

Lying flat with his arms and legs spread wide, Louie surrendered to his incapacitation. The longer he stayed still, the more amplified the motion of rocking became. It lulled him to surrender, as did the narrowing scope of his vision.

He lifted the flask to his lips and let the whiskey dribble into his mouth.

It didn't taste as awful anymore.

Pippin was right—this was a pleasant poisoning. If he was going to die, he'd rather go out in this state of mind.

Overhead was the sight of Nautipunks scaling the detention center cages and swinging from rope pulleys while cutting at the alien thread. Louie watched, amused, as the scene played out in a blur.

"It's too sticky," shouted one of his Nautipunk crewmates.

"N' thick," said another.

"Our saws be getting stuck in the goo."

"Douse it with water," Red Fang Ralph bellowed at them.

"That only makes the goo thicker n' stickier!"

"Argh!"

Another sip from his flask and the facial features of those he observed melted, leaving fuzzy blobs with blank faces. Blurs of blue bobbed up and down a long white line, swinging and yelling and making no progress. The scene spun in circles over Louie's face, a dizzying sight in his state of inebriation.

Streaks of gold joined the fray, entering with a frenzied flash. The blues and golds swirled together, and Louie's watery heart beat faster. A sense of calm lined with sorrow overtook him as he watched the colors bleed into each other.

Blue and gold.

Tears leaked from his eyes. He didn't notice he was crying until the briny droplets rolled down his cheeks and into his mouth. The salt paired perfectly with the lingering taste of poison.

A blast of red and orange illuminated the world, and when those colors faded, the white line was gone and the blues and golds had separated. A muffled cheer rang all around as Louie lifted the flask to his lips.

The final drops of whiskey landed on his tongue, accompanied by a familiar voice.

"Blimey! Who gave ye grog? It don't suit ye," the voice said before snatching the flask from his grip.

Louie mumbled belligerently, no idea what he was arguing about, when his ankles were seized and his body was dragged across the deck. Everything began to darken. He mumbled louder in protest as the world went black.

"Will he be okay?" a pretty voice asked.

"He oughta be alright," said the voice from before—Louie now recognized it as belonging to Red Fang Ralph. "He's been blacked out fer hours."

Louie kept his eyes shut.

He did not wish to face the day.

Ralph continued, "I got ter get ter the rove. He might wake in a fit."

A male voice replied, "We can keep an eye on him a little longer, but we'll need to return to Fyree soon. My brother sent a carrier saying he's made progress on some kind of potion."

"Aye, well, do what ye have to. Louie will be fine with or without yer company."

The door opened and closed.

Louie wished the others would leave, too.

"He's spiraling out of control," said the pretty voice. "He needs help. He needs better support."

"Sadly, the timing is terrible. He's unraveling when he needs to be strong. Our focus must remain on the forthcoming war, not his mental health."

"I just feel so terrible."

"Let's head back to Fyree. He needs to rest and we need to talk to Helix."

"I can't leave him like this."

"He doesn't seem any more awake than he did an hour ago."

Louie groaned, annoyed by their chatter.

He slowly opened his eyes.

A vision of gold sat at the end of the bed he was tucked into. Within the blur was the face of the girl he loved most. Seeing her sent daggers through his heart.

He closed his eyes.

"I cannot face you," he said.

"Me?" Emmeline asked. "Why not? I only want to help."

"This is mortifying," he said, feeling utterly pathetic in his current state.

"There's nothing to be embarrassed about," she insisted. "You are trying to deal with your trauma alone. Let us help."

Louie shook his head. "I have to do it alone."

"We don't have time for this," Solís, who sat beside Emmeline, declared. He stood and walked toward the door. "Let's go."

Louie opened his eyes a slit and watched them through interlaced eyelashes.

"He needs us," Emmeline asserted.

"Are your ears clogged? He just said he wants to be alone. We have much bigger matters to attend to."

"Fine, you go. I'll stay with him," Emmeline stated with obstinance.

"Please go," Louie chimed in, his voice desperate.

A moment of silence lingered between them.

Solís broke it. "You should respect his wishes."

Oily tears welled in Emmeline's eyes and her expression contorted with deep hurt. She stood terrifyingly still as she stared at Louie, radiating her hurt onto him.

"I don't know how much more of this I can take," she said as the tears fell.

"Set yourself free of me," Louie said, his self-loathing at an all-time high. "I am not worth the heartache."

"But you are," Emmeline pled, emotion overcoming her. "You are worth the fight."

"I am hollow," he sniveled. "You deserve someone who is whole."

"He's right," Solís said, his tone soft and cautious.

Emmeline huffed. "This is temporary. You will be whole again."

"And what if I'm not? What if this has changed me forever?"

"Then we deal with it day by day."

Louie shook his head. "I am not dragging you into my healing, not when the damage is this bad. I don't know how long it will take and I'll only make you sad." He took a deep breath, then confessed, "You can't love me like this."

"But I do."

"Then stop. I am not the same person I was before getting captured by the Marzans."

Emmeline groaned. "Fine. If this is what you want, then I'll go. Just remember that I tried."

She turned and stormed out of the room.

"You're a glutton for misery, huh?" Solís asked Louie.

"I don't know what I am anymore."

"You will lose her if you don't let her in," he warned.

"That's probably for the best," Louie replied.

"If this is how you behave when times are hard, then yeah, maybe you're right."

Solís turned to leave.

"Your fight is futile," Louie added before Solís reached the door.

"What do you mean?"

"Fighting the Marzans," he explained. "There is no point. I've seen how ruthless they are. You won't be able to stop them."

"So, you suggest that we lay down and die?"

"I suggest we all make peace with our fate."

"That's a coward's move," Solís spat.

"A wise man accepts what he cannot change," Louie countered.

"Your time on Deimos really did damage you. The Louie I knew was infuriating, but never a coward."

"It's true. I am changed."

"You aren't changed—you are defeated," Solís corrected him before leaving the cabin and slamming the door closed.

Alone again.

A sense of relief washed over Louie.

When the world ended, so would his suffering.

Chapter 38

The long spider thread hung from the black hole, its severed end still sizzling from where the Pyropunks disconnected its attachment to the black obsidian shield around the source flame.

A crew of divers, both Nautipunk and Thermapunk, emerged from the sea—they had retrieved the bottom half of the thread for dissection and examination.

"Had to burn it off the shield," Bram Wilkinson, a Thermapunk crew member and excellent diver, told Montgomery as he reached the top rung of the rope ladder and dropped his end of the giant thread onto the deck. "It was latched on securely."

"But it seems the salt water took away some of the adhesive quality to the outer parts of the thread," added another Thermapunk diver as he climbed over the gunwale.

The crew made their way back onto the boat, each carrying a part of the thread. By the time they were all back on board, the thread was a piled mountain between them and Montgomery.

"Slice off a few chunks that can be studied," Montgomery instructed. "Burn the rest."

As his crew got to work, Luna reappeared unexpectedly. She landed directly in Montgomery's path, startling him so much he jumped.

"You have my moonstone?" she asked.

"Yes," he said, clutching his heart. "It's in my pocket."

Luna swung a large satchel off her shoulder and dropped it to the floor. It landed with a thunderous thud. She then lifted a four-piped metal chime off her belt and into the air. A small shake, and the air around them was filled with the sound of bells.

"Five thousand pocket-sized cubes of Lunarian metal," Luna informed him in a soft voice, letting the piercing chimes drown her words from any eavesdropping Marzans. "You can use your fire to shape them however you wish."

"Thank you," Montgomery said while waving over his nearest Thermapunk crew member. Bram Wilkinson approached, still wringing out his long golden locks from the dive he just helped complete.

"Yes, sir?" he asked.

Montgomery lifted the heavy satchel, shocked by the weight. He side-eyed Luna with disbelief as he struggled to hand it to Bram.

"This is heavy!"

"Well, it's a lot of metal," Luna answered.

"You carried it with such ease."

"I have Lunarian strength."

Montgomery shook his head and waved a second member of his crew over. Ramsay Bowler trotted over. Head of the fire brigade tasked to guard the black hole, Ramsay was not dripping in salt water.

Montgomery reached outward and brushed his fingers against the chimes Luna still held outright. Ringing music filled the air.

"Bring this bag of moon metal to the bilge," Montgomery instructed them. "Use the furnace to melt it, and then reshape it into arrowheads, spear tips, bullets, and cannonballs."

Ramsay and Bram nodded, then used their combined strength to lift the heavy satchel and carry it to the bilge.

"Where is Solís?" Luna asked Montgomery, her large silver eyes scanning the bustling ship deck.

"I thought you were better friends with Emmeline."

"I am friends with both of them."

"I don't know where he is," Montgomery said. He struck the chimes once more, then asked, "Where is the crew of fighters you were going to bring back to help us?"

"They are ready. I wanted to make sure they'd arrive in Hydra and not above before I brought them here."

"Go get them. We are ready to strike."

Luna touched the amulet around her neck, whispered the incantation, and disappeared.

"Where'd she go?" Solís shouted as he ran toward his father from the opposite side of the enormous ship.

Montgomery sighed, looking around for some way to make enough noise to drown out their conversation. He grabbed a bronze-rod broom that was leaning against the nearest mast and began whacking it against the steel mast.

"Home to get her fighters," he answered Solís, his words masked within the noise. "The force of that spider thread moved the black hole closer to freedom. We need to strike immediately."

"Avery and I have our soldiers lined up on the top deck. I was going to go check on Helix—he sent a carrier saying he discovered something."

"There's no time. I need you here. As soon as Luna returns, we will strike. Say no more."

Montgomery dropped the broom and the noise ceased.

"We need to find a better way to drown out our conversations here," Solís commented.

"I have a small task force working on it. They're building a marble music machine adorned with giant megaphones. It's almost complete."

"Sooner than later, hopefully."

As the words left his mouth, the magical sound of fabric-wrapped silver marbles rhythmically hitting xylophone keys filled the air. The bustling of Hydra ceased and silence honored the enchanting melody now echoing through the sky.

"I thought it would be noise," Solís commented to his father in a whisper. "But it's music."

"That's why it took them some time to build the machine. If we had to add more noise to our lives, I wanted to make sure it was beautiful. Something that would add joy, not stress."

Montgomery smiled and closed his eyes, appreciating the captivating song. The engineers chose the perfect pattern of notes to capture the feeling of hope during wartime. The melody was haunting, yet inspiring, and the collective motivation to survive these trying times lifted.

"I think this is just what we needed," Montgomery said, delighted by the new addition to his ship. "Not only so we can speak freely, but to unite and encourage our resolve. Music holds great power and influence; this will be our war cry."

"And after we are victorious, it will become our triumphant war song," Solís added.

"Indeed."

The sound of a thousand dragonfly wings pounding the salty air joined the jangling marble melody.

Montgomery and Solís looked up—a large army of Lunarians swarmed above them.

"It's time," Montgomery revealed.

The marble music continued to play as he led their allies toward the top deck.

Every Thermapunk and Nautipunk aboard watched the procession with mouths agape. It wasn't long ago that the sight of one Lunarian would cause panic. Now, a full army graced their home and they were expected to show tolerance.

The energy was tense—trust was not fully formed—but the Solarpunks behaved themselves, placing their trust in the Dawes family, who swore these moon creatures were allies.

On the top deck near the bow, one hundred Pyropunks and one hundred Argopunks stood in two straight lines, winged and ready for battle.

Avery and Emmeline stood at the front, facing the soldiers.

When the sight of three hundred rage-fueled Lunarian warriors arrived, Avery's body tensed. Inner threads tangled, dark veins framing their black eyes, fangs bared—their allies looked like the monsters she was trained to hate.

The marble music still echoed loudly across Hydra.

"It is time to strike," Montgomery announced, joining Avery and Emmeline at the front of the lineup.

Luna held her Odonata warriors at the back of the Solarpunk militia, awaiting further instruction on the plan.

"Lunarians," Montgomery instructed, "the order for entry is Pyropunks, Lunarians, then Argopunks. Fire and magnetism are needed most. Avery and Emmeline will create a gaseous explosion to camouflage our arrival. Pyropunks will walk through the fire and immediately cast new streams of fire within. Once the fire around the black hole simmers, Lunarians and Argopunks will join. Is the plan clear?"

"Yes, sir," shouted every member of the Pyro-Argo militia in attendance.

Montgomery glanced upward at Luna.

"The plan is clear," she said. "We are ready."

She raised her arm, flicked her wrist, and a threaded whip sizzling with magnetism extended from her palm. As she draped its excess length over her shoulder, the Odonata warriors behind her grumbled with anticipation. They were a fearsome bunch; their lust for battle was far stronger than that of the Solarpunks.

"Remember," Montgomery warned them all, "no talking once you are at the detention center. Let's begin."

Avery and Emmeline lifted into the sky. Though Montgomery's ship hovered near the detention center, there was still a short flight to the burning cage containing the black hole.

Emmeline glowed bright red as the fire within her fueled her flight. Still as small as ever, heat was all she needed to gain lift. The Pyropunks, on the other hand, wore two tanks—one with helium for flying and another with oxygen to help them breathe on the other side of the black hole. The Argopunks wore oxygen tanks as well for precaution. They could store oxygen in their lungs and manipulate the air around them, morphing an unbreathable space into something survivable, but since no one knew what awaited them on the other side, it was best that they wore oxygen tanks as well.

Emmeline and Avery, who wore a fireproof Argopunk suit, reached the cage with the black hole first. The gate on the roof of the cage was open with two Thermapunks standing guard.

Emmeline pointed to the side gate of the cage and motioned for one of the guards to unlock it. He nodded, then scaled down the side of the cage and opened a second entryway.

Emmeline and Avery entered from above while the Pyropunks, Argopunks, and Lunarians lined up at the side door, which directly faced the ever-growing black hole. They stood on opposite sides of the swirling portal, preparing to send a massive blaze through.

Solís and Cyrus stood at the front of the line, crouched in deep lunges and ready to sprint. Their golden gazes were laser-focused on the black hole.

Avery closed her eyes and mustered a manicured breath from the depths of her gaseous gut. Chlorotrifluoride—the most flammable gas in existence—expelled from her mouth. She blew it all around the black hole, then inward. As the gas crept over the threshold of the hole, Emmeline lifted the giant fireballs that had formed in the palms of her hands and lobbed them into the black hole. A massive explosion erupted on the other side. For a moment, the space between here and there was illuminated, revealing a scene of destruction and mayhem.

"Now!" Montgomery shouted, to which Cyrus and Solís darted into action.

They catapulted into the flames and through the black hole. Their small army of Pyropunks followed their lead, disappearing into the portal behind them.

"Lessen the flames," Montgomery shouted to Emmeline, who lowered her hands. He then commanded, "Lunarians, go!"

Luna led her fleet of Odonata warriors into the black hole at full speed. Fangs bared, cords tangled, they zipped past in a fuzzy blur of darkness before vanishing into the battle.

War raged beyond the black hole, yet Hydra was silent.

"I wish I could hear what is going on," Emmeline said, her anxiety rising.

"Have faith," Montgomery encouraged. He looked to the last leg of their offense—the Argopunks. "Now!" he instructed, waving his arm and motioning them forward.

Remington stood among the Argopunks, no longer looking like his entitled former self, but a soldier desperate to survive. A fire burned within him, one that Emmeline recognized burned within her, too. No sacrifice was too great if it meant saving the sun.

The crew of Argopunks charged through the black hole.

There was no one else to send, no additional reinforcements to help secure their victory.

If this surprise attack did not defeat the Marzans, war upon the sun was inevitable.

Emmeline's heart raced.

She looked down through the bars of the cage and found Red Fang Ralph's ship floating below. While the crew buzzed about in a flurry, Louie stood in the basket of the tallest crow's nest, staring up at Emmeline.

Solís had told her of his conversation with Louie after she left, how Louie lost all hope and believed their fight against the Marzans was futile. He told her that Louie had given up, that he had surrendered before the fight had begun.

Disappointment coursed through her as the boy she once adored appeared unrecognizable. The love remained, but it was tarnished.

She was determined to prove him wrong.

They would survive, no matter the sacrifices required, and when a new day of peace emerged, they would determine what to do with the scattered pieces of their broken love.

Chapter 39

Deimos

Fire danced along the inner walls of the Marzan cathedral, unable to latch onto the red rock, but incinerating everything else in its path.

Marzans screeched in horror as they were burned alive. Others tried to escape the attack, flailing about as flames engulfed their suits of armor.

While the Thermapunks and Argopunks remained grounded, the Lunarians hovered above, magnetically lassoing any Marzan trying to flee and tossing them back into the fire.

Solís removed his breathing regulator.

"Where is your king?" Solís bellowed to the massive crowd of Marzan soldiers.

He received no answer, only the continuation of bloodcurdling screams.

Hundreds of Marzans had been gathered in this large room when they entered through the black hole. Now, they trampled over each other in an attempt to reach the singular exit.

"Give us your king and we will douse the flames," Solís bartered, speaking through his regulator this time. His voice was muffled, but clear.

"You've already killed half of us," a Marzan writhing on the floor by Solís's feet croaked. He was charred from the initial blast and had small flames crawling up his suit.

"I'll spare those who remain if you lead me to Helmer," Solís promised.

"Never! Our sacrifice saves the masses."

Solís pressed his bare foot against the Marzan's neck. His body glowed red as he channeled the source flame and sent the heat into his foot.

The Marzan squealed in agony.

"Tell me where he is!" Solís demanded.

The Marzan flesh beneath his foot began to melt.

"Never!" The Marzan coughed, then gagged as tears of pain leaked from his bloodshot blue eyes.

"Then everyone in this room will die," Solís concluded, pressing his foot harder into the Marzan's neck.

"We die so the others can live."

"Wrong. I will murder every Marzan in my hunt for Helmer. You could have saved them and yourself, but you won't talk."

"Deimos is a death maze. You'll never find my king."

Solís had heard enough. The heat from his foot burned through the Marzan's neck, leaving him decapitated. The only thing connecting his head to his lifeless body was the chainmail under his first layer of flesh.

Solís removed his regulator and shouted.

"Kill them all!"

With no opposition to stop them, the mission was a slaughter. King Helmer sent no reinforcements to save the soldiers in the cathedral.

Each Lunarian nose-dived and seized the nearest living Marzan, wrapping them in tight hugs and using their magnetism to assassinate. Strong magnetic tugs ripped the Marzans' interior chainmail armor through their flesh, slicing apart their insides in the process.

The Argopunks lifted into the sky and rocketed toward any Marzans left standing. Using the wristlets connected to their veins, they rained liquid nitrogen over them. The fluid was so cold it burned, and the Marzans in its path froze mid-motion, becoming giant red statues still living within their frozen paralysis.

Remington swooped downward to get a closer look at his work.

The Marzan he froze fidgeted within its constraints, bloodshot eyes darting all around, searching for a way out.

"It lives," he shouted to the fleet of Argopunks above. He then burped up a glass marble and spat it at the Marzan.

Upon contact, the Marzan splintered into a million frozen shards.

The Argopunks above did the same, shooting marbles at their victims, and the clinking chime of shattering Marzans echoed through the great cathedral.

There was no need for fire, not at this moment. Solís and Cyrus stood near the black hole with their fellow Pyropunks, observing their swift victory.

The screaming and shouting lessened as more and more Marzans were killed, and slowly, the only sounds echoing off the high ceilings were the pounding of the Argopunks' titanium wings, the buzzing flutter of the Odonatas' dragonfly wings, and the gurgling surge of the swirling black hole.

"That felt too easy," Cyrus noted.

"I agree," Kiran said from where he stood behind them.

"A victory is a victory," Solís stated as he scanned the Marzan bodies scattered all over the room. "If we killed one hundred Marzans today, maybe two hundred, that's two hundred fewer Marzans to attack us later."

The Argopunks lowered themselves back to the ground and walked toward the black hole to join the Pyropunks.

"Their king is a coward," Remington spat. "He allowed this slaughter instead of fighting back."

"All he had to do was show himself, and most of this bloodshed could have been prevented," Solís agreed.

"He knows his time is running short." Remington looked possessed as he looked toward the door; the deep-seated fire of hatred burned in his orange-pink gaze.

"Indeed, it is, but it won't run short today," Solís countered.

"Why not? We are already here," Remington argued.

Solís shook his head. "This massacre will be message enough."

"Or revitalized motivation," Cyrus theorized. "It might further spark his rage."

"Good. Let him try to attack us at home. They were easy to kill."

Solís motioned his arms toward the black hole, allowing the Argopunks to exit first. The Lunarians followed second. Though everyone moved with intention, it took a few minutes to filter through the hole. The Pyropunks stood at the ready with their lava wristlets raised and engaged in case a second fleet of Marzans arrived before they made their exit.

Their golden-hued flesh glowed bright with fire, illuminating their golden bones and gears beneath.

"Don't linger too long," Luna's voice said from where she flew above. It shook Solís from his concentrated war stance.

She was the last of the Lunarians left on this side of the black hole. The monstrous way her face contorted with rage during an adrenaline spike no longer fazed him. He only saw the woman he had grown to adore.

Solís smiled up at her, grateful to have her on his side.

"I'll be right behind you," he promised.

Luna nodded, unable to shake the grave expression she wore.

"I feel like we are missing an opportunity to stop them forever," Cyrus said, his face aglow from the heat radiating throughout his body.

"There's no telling what horrors we'd find on the other side of that door," Solís warned. "Or if we'd be able to find our way back to this room. We don't know where we are; we don't know the layout of this place."

"I understand, but I still feel like we could do more."

"How about a firebomb?" Kiran suggested.

Solís and Cyrus glanced over their shoulders—they were used to having Helix as their third brain during strategy talks.

"And let it detonate this room?" Cyrus asked to confirm.

"Yeah. Demolish it as completely as we can. At the least, it should delay them from striking back."

Solís nodded. "It's a good idea." He then tapped his waistband, looking for the tools necessary. "I don't have a nitro stone on me," he revealed.

"Neither do I," Cyrus added.

"I have a stash of black powder pebbles," Kiran revealed, patting a full satchel attached to his belt.

"Where'd you get those?" Cyrus asked. "I've been working on the Terrapunks for over a year now, trying to find some kind of trade deal that includes those pebbles."

"I'm best friends with Helix, remember? While he bartered for locomo dust, I found merchants willing to give me black powder pebbles."

"For firestones?" Solís asked.

Kiran nodded. "Lower-level Terrapunks are easier to bargain with."

"It's an illegal acquisition without approval from the Horrigans," Cyrus said.

Kiran shrugged, then added, "They are a low explosive, but I think I have enough to make a serious dent in their moon."

"Worth a try," Solís said. "Pile them by the doorframe. If the structural build within this moon is anything like what we are used to, destroying the framework will cause the most damage."

Kiran leapt over lifeless Marzan bodies as he quickly made his way to the opposite side of the room. He untied the pouch from his belt and left it open on the ground.

Beyond the door was darkness.

The corridor was long and unlit.

Kiran took one step past the threshold and listened. The distant sound of enraged growls echoed down the hall. He stood there a moment longer and the noise grew louder.

"They're coming!" he shouted before turning and darting back toward Solís and Cyrus, who were still in their fighting stances.

"Don't stop running," Solís ordered. "Exit through the hole!"

Kiran did as he said, launching his body through the hole at full speed.

He was gone.

Only Solís and Cyrus remained.

The stomping feet and angry cries of Marzans echoed louder through the doorway.

"Who's taking the shot?" Cyrus asked.

"I am. Go," Solís demanded.

"Don't miss."

Solís's expression shifted with insult, but his concentration never left the little pouch of black powder pebbles sitting in the faraway doorframe.

"Just go!" Solís shouted at his older brother.

Cyrus crawled through the hole, vanishing from sight.

The Marzan shouts were louder than ever as they stampeded toward the room.

Solís took a step closer to the black hole and farther from his target. Though this made his shot harder, it facilitated his escape.

He extended his arm outward and used the rectangular sight on the back of his wristlet to aim. With a simple downward flick of his fist, the wristlet activated. The miniscule dams lifted and the needles inserted into his veins sucked in the lava and spat it out in a single shot. A little bullet of liquid fire shot through the air, arching perfectly toward the pouch of ammunition. Solís scrambled backward, pausing to make sure his shot hit the target.

As the glowing projectile got closer, a swirling buzz of gold materialized before him, consuming the lava bullet. Debris caught in the whirlwind slapped Solís repeatedly as the tornado grew in size. He shielded his eyes to get a better look.

A thousand golden flies swarmed in a tight circle. Beyond them, illuminated by their gilded glow, were a thousand pairs of angry eyes running toward him.

Out of the mouth of the tornado rose a faceless man, his silhouette outlined with gold. Misty shadows of darkness rotated around him, hugging tight to his body but traveling in erratic patterns with violent speed.

<<I am dark matter. I am death,>> the deity bellowed from a place far beyond this realm of existence. <<I am the King of Darkness.>>

"You don't belong here," Solís countered through this breathing regulator, suppressing his fear.

The dark deity tilted His head downward. No eyes, no mouth, no face—just darkness. Though His expression went unseen, the wicked energy from His shadowed smirk hit Solís like a punch in the gut.

<<*I have taken this moon from Lunéss.*>>

"You will not extinguish the sun, and neither will the Marzans."

<<*If you wish to stop me, you must defeat me.*>>

"If You wish to stop *me*, go ahead and kill me," Solís shouted, lifting his arm and shooting a second lava bullet at the bag of black powder pebbles across the room.

His fire made contact with the bag and the detonation threw Solís's body backward through the black hole.

In a blink, he was back in Hydra.

He rolled onto the caged floor of the prison, ripping the breathing regulator from his mouth. A deafening ring filled his head. Stunned by the blast, terrified by his final sight before returning home, Solís frantically patted himself to make sure he was still alive. His grave stare remained fixated on the black hole, waiting for Kólasi to follow him through.

Nothing emerged through the swirling darkness.

The moment he shifted his gaze from the black hole to his changed surroundings, the world began to spin. Everything was silent, all he could hear was the deafening hum from after the blast, but the smell of salt water and petroleum still slicked to the cage graced his senses. Solís stumbled back onto his feet.

Adrenaline racing, he looked around, trying to assimilate to the safety of his surroundings. His father, Cyrus, and Emmeline stood in the cage with him, saying words he could not hear through the ringing in his ears.

Luna hovered above, staying a safe distance from the flames. She wore a look of similar concern.

"He's coming," Solís said, unaware he was shouting.

"Who?" Emmeline asked.

Solís could read her lips.

"Kólasi."

Chapter 40

Everyone took a step back from the black hole.

"Kólasi?" Montgomery asked. "The god of chaos?"

"Are you sure?" Cyrus asked.

Solís was still deafened from the blast, so he watched their lips as they spoke.

"He called Himself dark matter and death. Said He was the King of Darkness."

"You *saw* Him?" Emmeline asked in disbelief.

Solís nodded.

"Why didn't He kill you?"

Solís shrugged. "I told him to; I said He'd have to kill me to stop me from blowing up that room." Solís paused. "He did nothing. He let me do it."

"Maybe He let you live so you'd come back and tell us?" Cyrus theorized.

"Why, though?" Emmeline asked.

"To instill fear and hopelessness. To lower our resolve to fight back. How will we ever beat the Marzans when they have a primordial god on their side?"

"We've fought them a few times now, knowing they had Kólasi on their side," Emmeline countered.

"Then why let him live?"

The ringing in Solís's ears lessened and the echoing chimes of the melodic marble machine became audible. It still played an enchanting song that muffled the private conversations within Hydra, preventing the Marzans from eavesdropping.

Solís spoke again.

"I don't think *He* could kill me.

"What do you mean?" Luna asked, stepping closer to him to examine the injuries on his face. Small pieces of shrapnel from the bomb were lodged in his flesh. With a tender touch, she began coaxing them out of his skin.

"When I told Him to kill me, His shadow emanated this strange energy, one of rage and defeat. I think that's why He has the Marzans doing His dirty work for Him—He can't do it Himself."

"It adds up," Cyrus said.

"Let's not make dangerous assumptions," Montgomery advised. "Thinking we are safe from His full wrath is unwise."

"He said He stole Deimos from Lunéss," Solís added.

"We're still trying to reach Her through prayer," Luna said as she extracted a sharp red rock from above his eyebrow.

"And Melora is leading a prayer group to Solédon above," Montgomery said, then sighed. "Let's continue this discussion back on the ship. Helix is waiting for us there. He says he made some kind of discovery."

Willie Morrell, one of the lead Argopunk fighters, stepped forward. "I will lead this small group of Argos and Pyros back to the base and debrief the others."

"Yes," Montgomery agreed. "Prepare the full fleet."

The Argopunk and Pyropunk soldiers departed.

As the rest of the group headed to Montgomery's ship, Solís and Luna lingered a moment. They stared into each other's eyes, and without saying a word, they knew how the other was feeling—relief and gratitude that neither had died in battle. Unafraid of who saw, Solís grabbed Luna's hand and lifted into the sky with her. A quick look at the levels on his gauge showed he still had half a tank of helium left to fly with.

Many of the Odonatas saw their display of affection and watched their tandem flight with scrutinizing stares. Solís did not notice, but Luna did—she squirmed internally, terrified of the backlash she'd face during their debriefing.

As soon as they landed on Montgomery's ship, Luna gave Solís's hand a quick squeeze of appreciation before letting go.

"I have to take my warriors back to Mōnalene," Luna said. "We need to regroup before the next attack."

"Hurry back," Solís said, then whispered. "I want to kiss you."

"Better that you didn't," she warned, then glanced up at the Odonatas, who fervently watched their every move.

"Slow and steady," he agreed. "It will be a hard pairing for both sides to accept, but with time, they will."

"I hope so."

Luna lifted into the sky.

"Wait!" Emmeline shouted. "Please check on Gemma."

"I will," Luna promised.

"Bring her home if she's ready."

"I'll see if they made any progress with her healing."

Emmeline nodded, hoping she'd see her friend again soon.

The Lunarians disappeared and Emmeline joined the huddle surrounding Helix.

"Most importantly, it has to land in their eyes," Helix said.

"What does?" Emmeline asked.

"The solution I created."

"What's it made of?"

"I just explained all of this," Helix said with a groan.

"Well, explain it again!"

Helix huffed. "The Marzans have a unique genetic makeup. Besides their flesh being super sensitive to heat and having a bonus layer of chainmail, there's an element of glass within their flesh. Upon further research, I learned that their eyes are completely made of glass." Helix smirked. "To stop them, we will blind them."

"With the solution?"

"Yes. Molten sodium hydroxide dissolves glass. Thermapunks provide the fire, Terrapunks provide the mineral."

"Have the Horrigans agreed to this plan?" Montgomery asked his son.

"No, but my dealers in the black market have. That's how I got the small sample of sodium hydroxide for my tests."

"They're accepting firestones as payment?" Cyrus asked.

Helix nodded.

"We have to involve the Horrigans," Montgomery insisted.

"The Horrigans will have a higher price," Helix warned.

"Maybe, but they can also thwart this project if they learn they've been excluded from the process."

"I have a crew of Digipunks mining for the materials already. Involving the Horrigans will slow them down."

"Dad," Emmeline interjected. "We don't have time to follow every usual protocol. Just let them work."

"Fine."

"What about the flies?" Emmeline asked. "They are the bigger threat."

"Well, we know how to kill them: liquid nitrogen plus fire."

"How do they attack?" Montgomery asked.

"They entered through the ears," Cyrus said, recalling the horrifying scene they had witnessed on Mōnalene.

Avery added, "They definitely infected the brains of their victims. I imagine they could enter through the nose or mouth and achieve the same effect."

"Blimey!" Ralph exclaimed, then took a swig from his flask.

"Diving helmets," Emmeline suggested.

"That could work," Avery said.

"But we don't have enough for everyone," Emmeline finished.

Montgomery jumped in, "I'll assign a team of welders to start making new ones."

"Better get to it," Solís said. "They could come through the black hole at any time."

Montgomery left, leaving Red Fang Ralph, Emmeline, Solís, Cyrus, Helix, Avery, and Kiran behind.

Emmeline found herself scanning the ship, silently searching for Louie.

Red Fang Ralph, Avery, and Kiran noticed.

"Who ye be lookin' for, lass?" Ralph asked.

"Louie."

Ralph grunted. "Ye won't find him here. He's been drowning in the bottle at the gin mill on Smuggler's Rove."

Emmeline groaned.

"Speakin' o' which," he continued, "I'm outta grog."

Red Fang Ralph stumbled to the hogshead where his blood-infused liquor was stored.

"Sometimes it's healthier to walk away," Kiran suggested to Emmeline.

"I'm trying," Emmeline grumbled. "It's hard to stop caring."

Solís was listening in. "Are you talking about Louie?" he asked.

"Yeah," Avery answered.

"He thinks the Marzans will defeat us. Once we are victorious, his true healing will begin."

"Or he will stay as he is," Kiran countered.

"Maybe," Solís replied. "But after this war is won, he won't be able to blame the threat of death for his pathetic behavior. He will either stand up and heal, or he will wallow. Either way, it is his choice." Solís looked at Emmeline, who was as thin as she had been prior to her own healing. "You've done all you can to help him, to the detriment of your own health. No more hurting yourself to help him. It's time to let go and allow his fate to unfold organically."

"I know, I know," Emmeline said. "And what's the deal with you and Luna?"

"I'm curious also," Cyrus chimed in.

"I've never met a woman as brave and fierce as her," Solís admitted. "She is inspiring."

"Inspiration? That's it? I suspect you're feeling more than that," Emmeline coaxed.

"Time will tell," Solís answered, refusing to divulge any more. Solís turned his attention to the black hole in an attempt to ignore his siblings.

"Good luck," Cyrus said, shaking his head. "It doesn't bother me personally, but the memory of hellions is still fresh in the minds of our people. I doubt our fellow Solarpunks will accept a noble Thermapunk partnered romantically with a moon monster."

"Similarly," Emmeline added, "I doubt the Lunarians will appreciate her being with you."

"None of that matters right now," Solís barked. "Look!"

Everyone turned their attention to the black hole.

It still existed within the burning cage, but circling within the obscurity was an ever-growing golden swirl. It grew larger with each passing second, slowly recoloring the darkness.

"What is it?" Emmeline asked.

"I don't know, but something is coming," Solís said, his voice low. He looked to Avery. "Quick—refill our helium tanks."

Emmeline engaged her source flame heart, heating her body as Avery helped her brothers and Kiran. She was ready to fly before them, so she lifted into the air and took off. She made a quick stop at the wheel of the boat to grab her father's megaphone, then flew onward.

A radiant beam of gold shined like a beacon through the black hole.

Every Nautipunk on this side of Hydra felt its glow.

Emmeline kept her sights on the impending threat—would the Marzans come through, or perhaps Kólasi?

The golden light combusted into a thousand little orbs.

It was the golden flies—Kólasi's horrifying, mind-stealing insects. This swarm was ten times the size of the one they had faced on Mōnalene.

"Cover your faces!" she shouted into the megaphone. "Ears, mouths, noses—don't let the flies enter your body!"

She called this warning repeatedly, first over her father's ship, then over Ralph's.

The flies swarmed where the bodies were—on the ships and roves. They hadn't yet detected Emmeline.

Solís, Cyrus, Helix, Kiran, and Avery joined her in the sky.

"Dad is handing out helmets, but there won't be enough," Cyrus told her.

Emmeline lifted the megaphone. "Scarves, jackets, empty marble satchels—whatever you can find! Wrap it around your heads!"

"We're off to seal the gate," Solís told Emmeline.

"How?"

"The sails from Father's ship. He's going to meet us there."

"Be careful."

"You're coming with us," Solís stated.

"No, I'm helping here."

"Everyone heard your warning. There's not much else you can do."

"She could help me and Avery," Helix suggested.

Solís shot him a nasty glare.

"What are you doing?" Emmeline asked.

"Catching and burning the golden flies," Helix replied with a devious smirk. He held up a long pole connected to an old fishing net. The netting was placed inside an extra-large marble satchel that was also fastened to the pole to prevent the tiny flies from escaping. "We can freeze and burn in bulk. It was easy to make and there are plenty of materials to make more."

"She's going home," Solís objected.

"No!" Emmeline countered. "I'll stay and catch flies."

"Hurry and make your net," Helix encouraged her.

Solís shoved Helix before departing for the faraway gate in the sky.

"Be careful," Cyrus said to Emmeline.

"I will be," she promised.

Kiran added, "I'll come and help you after we seal the gate."

Cyrus and Kiran departed.

Hundreds of thousands of golden flies swarmed the world below.

"I can't freeze them all on my own," Avery griped. "There are too many."

"Didn't Raven and Remington stay behind?" Helix asked. "I don't think they left with the Argopunks."

The sound of an explosion rocked Hydra. A moment later, a massive cannonball soared directly past where Emmeline, Helix, and Avery hovered.

"Hey, watch it!" Helix shouted down.

"Argh, sorry, mate!" Red Fang Ralph shouted back. "Just tryn'ta kill these nasty buggers."

Ralph repositioned his cannon and aimed at another teeming cloud of gold.

A second blast filled the sky.

There were too many flies for the trio to eliminate on their own.

"We need to restrategize," Helix said. "We won't have enough liquid nitrogen to freeze them in mass quantities. But if we split up and focus on filling our nets, we can freeze and burn what we've caught in one shot. Here, take my flycatcher," Helix offered to Emmeline. "I'll make another and come back with Raven and Remington."

"Hurry," Avery said.

Helix handed his catcher to Emmeline, then pinched his titanium wings together and flew toward Montgomery's airship.

"Are you sure these nets will work?" Emmeline asked Avery.

"No," she answered bluntly. "We don't know the full capabilities of the flies, but if their only power over us is their ability to burrow into our minds, then at the least we can contain them or slow them down." Avery removed the scarf from around her neck and handed it to Emmeline. "Put your goggles on and tie this around your ears."

Emmeline latched the megaphone to her waistband, pulled down the goggles she wore like a headband, and wrapped Avery's white scarf around her head.

Avery continued, "I think the key is speed. The faster you move, the less likely the flies will escape the satchel."

Emmeline nodded.

Avery's brave but kind expression held deep worry. "Once you have a full net, find me and I'll freeze them so you can burn them. Good luck."

"I'll see you soon," Emmeline assured her.

Avery threw a handful of glass marbles into her mouth before darting toward Dawes Detention Center.

Emmeline headed toward Smuggler's Rove. She reached into the satchel of assorted marbles tied to her waistband, realizing she hadn't refueled in hours. Two clay, four sea glass, and one golden marble—she popped them into her mouth and lowered her position in the sky. The pole she held was long. If she used it right, she shouldn't need to get too close to the flies to catch them.

Hovering above a cluster of golden flies circling the rove's market, Emmeline swung her net and caught half the swarm in a single swoop. She immediately flew higher to flee the scene, traveling as fast as she could. The flies in her net fought their new constraints violently.

Emmeline needed to slow down and lower herself so she could catch more, but she did not want to risk losing the flies already in her net.

She flew in a giant circle high above the heart of the battle, twisting her wrists and forcing the net to spin in figure eights. She slowed down to see if this motion kept the flies in place, and when none escaped at her slower speed, she silently rejoiced before nose-diving back into battle.

The Hydropunks with garments tied around their heads ran aimlessly about the rove—they had nowhere to flee, nowhere to escape. The rove was surrounded by water.

Emmeline wondered ...

She flew lower toward a crowd of Hydropunks huddled between two tall structures. They held baskets over their heads. She paused her flight, never ceasing the spinning motion of her net.

"Have you tried escaping into the sea?" she asked them.

"We tried," a man replied from underneath his basket. "That's what the Hydros near the coasts did at the start. But I had to go home to get my family and the infected punks are hunting us. If we leave this hiding place, they pin us down, expose our faces, and let the flies take us."

"Getting underwater might be the only way for you to survive," Emmeline countered. "Let me guide you from above."

Emmeline lifted higher into the sky to get a better view.

The rove was a giant maze of tall structures. The bulk of the flies attacking this area of Hydra were currently preoccupied on the opposite side of the rove.

The Hydropunk man cautiously lifted the basket just enough for him to peer up at Emmeline for direction.

She waved him forward.

The crew of nine Hydropunks hiding with him, all varying in ages, followed.

Emmeline flew the course they needed to walk. When she flew to the right, they turned right. If she stopped, they stopped.

The flies were spreading across the rove now, as were more infected Hydropunks.

They were running out of time.

An infected woman nearby aggressively searched for the uninfected, ripping open doors and kicking over street barrels. She was getting closer to where the Hydropunk family awaited further instruction from Emmeline.

Emmeline held out her free hand, motioning for them to stay put as she mapped out an alternate route. Upon finding one, she had the family backtrack two turns, then run down a back alleyway that led toward the water.

A swarm of flies raced along the coast, threatening to intersect with the Hydropunk family before they could reach the ocean.

"Keep running straight," she called down to the family. "The ocean is directly in front of you."

Emmeline dove closer to the action, positioning herself on the coast. Straight ahead, she saw where the collision would happen. Net raised and spinning, she flew full speed toward the golden flies. As she passed the road the family raced down, the golden flies were upon her. She snagged a large portion of them in her net, flew upward in a somersault, and then tore downward again to capture the rest.

A few straggling flies remained free, but the path was clear enough for the family to pass through without issue.

"Thank you!" the man said as he raced down the pier and dove into the sea. His entire family followed, diving gracefully behind him.

They would live.

Emmeline lifted higher into the sky, proud of this small success, when a familiar voice shouted up at her.

"Watch out!"

She looked down to find Louie standing on the roof of the gin mill.

Before she could see what he was warning her about, a body much bigger than hers slammed into her and a pair of cold hands wrapped around her neck.

She held tight to the pole of her net, still twisting her wrists and refusing to lose her fluttering prisoners.

"Drop it," her captor seethed.

Emmeline looked up to see Remington.

His eyes were orbs of pure white and his expression was distorted with fury.

He was infected.

Chapter 41

"Let me go!" Emmeline demanded.

Remington tightened his grip around her neck.

His copper-hued fingers pressed into her glowing golden flesh. The heat did not bother him. His mind was a vacant vessel now controlled by Kólasi—he could not feel pain.

Emmeline increased the heat, burning as hot as possible.

The stench of Remington's burning flesh assaulted her senses, but his grip did not loosen.

A rotating lasso hurtled past them.

Emmeline couldn't move her head, but was able to glance down and see Louie collecting the excess rope to try again. He swung the lasso over his head and made a second attempt to land it around Remington.

Another miss.

Louie cursed loudly, his words incoherent. He stumbled back toward the market and began climbing the slanted establishments.

"Drop the net!" Remington demanded, his voice low and menacing.

Though her air was running thin, Emmeline managed to hold on and clamp the fabric of the net together between her feet. She could not see her positioning and hoped there were no small gaps where the flies could escape.

Remington shook her violently and unleashed a savage scream.

Louie scaled the large, unevenly stacked container boxes. Each step was wobbly and unbalanced. When he reached the roof, he knelt for a second, swaying in place. The world spun around him. He stood, regaining his balance, and swung the lasso overhead a third time, circling it repeatedly to build speed.

This toss hit his target.

The looped rope wrapped around Remington's neck, and Louie yanked him and Emmeline out of the sky. Remington fought back, but he was no match for Louie's drunken rage. When they hit the ground, Louie's fury zeroed in on Remington.

"What's wrong with you?" Louie shouted, followed by a swift kick to Remington's gut.

Remington roared, not from pain, but in protest.

"He's infected," Emmeline said, massaging the area of her neck where Remington previously held her in a chokehold.

"By what?"

"Kólasi's flies."

"Flies?" Louie hiccupped.

"Yeah, have you not noticed all of the chaos?" she asked, to which Louie furrowed his brow and looked around, confused.

"All the little bugs?" he asked.

Emmeline chose not to address his drunken obliviousness and instead explained, "They fly into their victims' heads and take over. It's mind control; the infected become soldiers for Kólasi."

"Oh, that's bad."

"No kidding."

"What's the cure?"

"We don't know yet."

"I know how to fix *him*," Louie grumbled. With great strength, he dragged Remington's thrashing body toward the ocean.

"Don't kill him! The Lunarians are researching a cure!"

"Sometimes the cure is death," Louie spat in reply.

The water deepened with each step.

Lost in a drunken trance, Louie ignored his thrashing prisoner as his thoughts spiraled around Emmeline.

The torture he had endured on Deimos still haunted him, and he struggled to differentiate reality from his nightmares. Was Emmeline to blame for his time spent on Deimos? Or was it his own fault? He had punished her for his suffering and pushed her away, but what if his anger was misplaced? And if he was wrong, could she ever forgive him? Did he deserve her forgiveness? His hopeless self-loathing was merciless, and the only reprieve he found hid deep within the bottle.

His desire to disappear only separated them further—he knew this, but found no other way to cope.

She deserved better.

And what he could not give to her in love, he could offer in protection.

The water was up to his chest now.

Startled by how far he had walked, he looked over his shoulder at Remington, who splashed in protest.

Louie scowled. It wasn't really Remington anymore—it was an imposter, a body snatcher; his prisoner was some alternate form of Kólasi.

Battle raged above.

Golden swarms flew in captivating patterns as they meticulously dove and attacked Nautipunk ships. Fire-laced cannonballs and tidal wave water blasts exploded in retaliation, but it wasn't enough to stop the flies.

The water rose to Louie's chin, then the bridge of his nose. He took one last look at the chaos imploding all around him before submerging.

"Nooo—" Remington shouted as Louie yanked him downward. His loud objection was stifled into a gurgle as his head went underwater.

Louie swam deeper, towing Remington by the rope around his neck. Sporadic blasts of light from the source flame illuminated the way.

He stopped at a depth where Remington could not easily return to the surface if he managed to escape. Remington flailed about, making furious attempts to swim back to the surface.

Louie was strong, and within the sea, he was even stronger. No amount of resistance from Remington could move Louie from where he had anchored himself. He waited patiently, ignoring the pounding headache forming as his body began to sober.

As dimidivinus mortals, this could take a while.

Louie's thoughts returned to Emmeline—he hoped she was okay, that she had managed to hide or join her family near Hydra's gates. The longer he waited for Remington to die, the greater his worry became that Emmeline might have new aggressors above that she needed help fighting off.

Louie tugged the rope.

Remington's ever-weakening fight to swim toward the surface slowed even more. He was losing his strength; he was losing this battle. Though he could store oxygen in his lungs and breathe where there was no air, the fly inside Remington's head hadn't thought to do that before its submersion. He also had no protective gear to protect him from the corrosive salt water.

Every time Remington opened his mouth instinctually to breathe, more water seeped into his body. Solar salt water coated his copper bones and gears—the interior corrosion could kill him before the lack of air.

Louie watched and waited, wondering whether suffocation or deterioration would prevail.

The obsidian rock around the source flame shifted and additional beams of light were sent in his direction. Fractured by the moving currents, dulled by the dark sea water, these momentary flashes highlighted the slow murder of Remington Holloway.

It was cruel, it was callous—but it wasn't Remington.

It was Kólasi.

Louie felt no remorse.

Remington stopped flailing; he no longer fought Louie's constraints.

Relieved, Louie pulled on the rope and tugged Remington's body toward him to ensure the golden fly within had perished before returning to the surface.

In the darkness surrounding Louie, countless pairs of watching eyes emerged—hundreds of refugee Hydropunks waded in the water, watching his battle against one of Kólasi's victims.

As Remington's limp body floated into Louie's arms, Louie addressed the crowd observing him.

"This was a smart place to seek refuge," he said, his words loud, but muffled by the water. "Stay here as long as your oxygen reserves allow. It is not safe above."

Head throbbing as his hangover kicked in, Louie squeezed his eyes shut until the searing pain passed. When he opened them again, Remington's head twitched. The rest of his body remained limp—only his head moved. The small spasm quickly turned to a full tremor and then suddenly stopped. The moment Remington was still again, the golden fly that had nested within his head shot out of his ear and rocketed toward the surface of the sea.

"No!" Louie shouted. He looked down at Remington, prepared to drop his body to its demise, but something stopped him. Louie placed two fingers to Remington's sternum—the marbles within still churned.

He had to stop the fly, but he needed to save Remington, too.

Louie hooked his left arm under Remington's chin and hurtled after the fly.

Right arm outstretched, fingers spread wide, he chased the golden fly.

Louie was at an advantage in the water. He propelled upward, gaining speed and lessening the distance between him and his target. Remington's weight slowed him down, but not enough. While in the water, Louie was still faster than the fly.

They were almost at the surface.

Louie released a guttural growl as he kicked his feet even faster. He would catch this winged terror.

As his fingers breached the surface, Louie curled his fingers and snatched the fly in his grip.

"Call an Aerodoc!" he shouted, mind still groggy from all the gin he drank prior to this unexpected mission. "He can be saved."

He towed Remington through the shallow water and onto the shore.

"I caught one," Louie said as he dragged Remington's limp body to where Emmeline hid and regained her energy between two large piles of wooden crates.

"A fly?" she asked.

Louie nodded and shook his clenched fist.

"Don't let it go," she warned, still clutching her knotted net.

"It's not going anywhere."

Louie saw an empty bottle among a pile of trash. He dropped Remington onto the sand to retrieve it. Using his teeth, he pulled the cork, forced the fly into the bottle, then shoved the cork back into place.

Emmeline looked down at Remington. "He needs a medic." She then glanced up at her father's airship floating high above the rove. "I'm too weak to fly."

In unison, Louie and Emmeline turned their heads toward the unruly mayhem of the rove. Those infected by the flies fought brutally against those still trying to flee.

"We should hide out under there," Louie suggested, pointing toward the underside of a nearby pier.

They each grabbed one of Remington's arms and dragged him with them.

"Why aren't you with your family above?" Louie asked as he crouched beside Remington's body. Remington's unmoving body lay between them.

"I was trying to catch as many flies as I could. Trying to save as many punks as I could."

Louie massaged the nape of his neck where a migraine was forming and said, "You did good."

"I did?"

Louie nodded. "Hundreds of Hydropunks are hiding in the sea."

Emmeline exhaled dramatically. "I'm so happy to hear that."

"They'll need to come up at some point to refill their tanks, though," Louie continued. He paused in thought, then offered, "I can bring straws and tubes down to them. That way, they can breathe in the air and refill without having to emerge."

"That's a great idea. We need them to survive."

Louie looked down at Remington. Two fingers to his sternum revealed his marbles still churned, but his gears were waterlogged and moved dangerously slow.

"If he survives," Louie noted, "then we know how to save the other infected punks."

Emmeline rummaged through her satchel of marbles and snagged two made of glass. She gently pried Remington's lips and teeth open, dropped both marbles into his mouth, and then tilted his head upward slightly to help them roll down his throat and into his holding pan.

"Hopefully that buys us some time," she said.

Louie stared at her intently, gaze soft and expression kind.

"Other than the raging headache growing at the base of my skull, this feels like old times," he said.

Emmeline's eyes filled with oily tears. "Maybe we could make this feeling last."

"I wish it was that easy."

"Why can't it be?"

"It just isn't." Louie fidgeted where he knelt. The lingering buzz accompanying his fast-growing hangover was fading. "I need a drink."

"A drink?"

"It's the only thing that helps me silence the rotten thoughts in my head."

"Clearly, it *doesn't* help if you're having them now. Weren't you just at the gin mill?"

"The buzz is wearing off."

"Talk to me. Maybe that will help."

"It won't."

"Humor me. Tell me what's going on inside your head."

Louie hesitated. The expression he wore was tormented.

"I'm thinking about how much I hate myself," Louie finally confessed, his words choked.

"Why?" Emmeline asked, her tears falling.

"I hate what they did to me—I hate how it changed me: how I see the world, how I see the people I used to love, how I have no hope for the future. I hate how I treated you; I cringe every time I think about how I made you cry." Louie's chest rose and fell dramatically. "I don't deserve your kindness or patience, and I certainly don't deserve your love. I need solitude. I need to rediscover who I am."

"I understand," Emmeline said, wiping the tears off her face. "I won't stop you from doing that, nor will I stand in your way. But you cannot get better while actively making yourself sick. You want to heal, yet you choose poison as your antidote."

"It's the only medicine that works."

"No," Emmeline objected, her sorrow turning into anger. "It doesn't work; it only numbs your problems temporarily."

"What's wrong with a band-aid while I sort it all out?"

"Because you aren't sorting anything out while you're drunk! It's an easy escape, a convenient one, too. You can do better."

"I'm doing the best I can," he said, his lack of will pathetic.

She saw their situation clearly for the first time.

"The Louie I loved would have never chosen alcohol over me."

"I'm not choosing anything. I'm just trying to survive."

"No, you are making a very clear choice." Emmeline stood and took a step away from him. "You're right. I do deserve better."

"I know you do. I've been trying to tell you that."

Utterly frustrated, Emmeline battled her returning tears.

"I will miss you," she offered. "I hope you find yourself."

Louie nodded, saying nothing as she backed away from him.

They both understood that this was the end.

Energy restored, she engaged her source flame heart and heated it until she had enough lift to fly. Emmeline dropped a handful of marbles into the sand near Remington's head.

"Keep him alive," she said before flying away.

Louie watched her depart in detached silence.

This wasn't the first time he had watched her leave, but he suspected it would be the last.

Chapter 42

The flies still swarmed the boats and roves—anyone who wasn't underwater by now was likely gone.

Emmeline lifted higher into the sky to get a better view.

There were more golden flies than available bodies, and it was only a matter of time before the flies shifted their attack toward the only exit in Hydra.

Avery, Helix, and Raven flew in methodical patterns with their nets, catching as many flies as they could, but there were too many. They'd never catch them all.

Emmeline flew toward the gate in the sky.

Cyrus, Kiran, and Solís were hammering the final nails into the edges of the sail. The light that normally poured into Hydra was blocked and this layer of the world within the sun was blanketed in shadows.

"Edwin Doyle!" Emmeline shouted as she approached her father's airship.

The steady murmur of chaos greeted her arrival.

She soared in a circle around the ship, searching for the prestigious Thermadoc.

A loud moan echoed from the stern.

Emmeline flew to the sound of pain and found Edwin stitching a large gash down the side of her father's face.

"What happened?" she asked as she landed beside them, tightening the knot that sealed the bag of flies she still carried.

"Did you know those stupid flies have *teeth*?" Montgomery replied. "One was latched to the scarf tied around my head. When I noticed it there, I swatted it away, but it came back and bit my cheek! I tried to pry it off of me, but its bite was locked. I had to rip it off, flesh and all."

Emmeline winced. "That's going to leave a scar."

"Better than becoming a servant to the god of death and chaos."

"Fair point," Emmeline said, but before she could tell her father the news about Remington, her brothers and Kiran swooped onto the deck.

"The gate is fully sealed," Cyrus informed them.

"Excellent," Montgomery replied, squirming with discomfort as Edwin laced another stitch through his flesh. "Ramsay and Bram are in charge of a net-making crew. They're somewhere near the bow." Montgomery waved his arm in their general direction.

Kiran looked at Emmeline and asked, "How bad is it?"

"Really bad," she answered. "We need the Argopunks."

"For now, it's only us."

"Has anyone sent a message to them?" she asked.

"We sent a summons through the Stone Patrol standing guard at the gate," Solís answered.

Emmeline shook her head. "That will take too long. I'll leave and deliver the message myself."

Solís groaned. "I'll go with you."

"No, stay here and fight. Capture as many of the flies as you can. Avery and Raven can freeze your hauls until I return with more Aeropunks."

Solís nodded, then darted off toward the front of the boat. Cyrus and Kiran followed.

"I'll go to the base with you," Montgomery offered to Emmeline.

"No, you're injured and will slow me down." She turned to Edwin Doyle. "Before I go, I need your help."

"How can I assist?" Edwin asked, still tending to her father's wound.

"Louie might have figured out a way to free the punks who have been infected."

"Straight Leg Louie? I heard he lost his mind."

"He's just lost *within* his mind," Emmeline said.

"Well, what did he discover?" Edwin asked, intrigued.

"We aren't totally sure if it worked yet. We still need to see if a doctor can revive him."

"Who?"

"Remington Holloway. He was infected, tried to kill me—or get me infected—and Louie saved me. He wrangled Remington and dragged him into the sea to drown. The fly exited Remington on its own, probably as soon as it thought its host was dying."

"And you are sure he isn't dead?" Edwin asked.

"The marbles in his body still roll, and his gears still churn, just very slowly. Dangerously slow. If they don't resume normal speed, he will die."

"Where is he?"

"Under a pier on Smuggler's Rove," Emmeline answered.

"I'm not going down there," Edwin protested as he tightened the final stitch in Montgomery's cheek.

"You have to! His survival determines whether or not we found a way to help everyone else."

"I am the only doctor left in Hydra," Edwin replied.

"He's right," Montgomery cut in. "He's too valuable to send into the swarm."

"You do realize it's only a matter of time before the flies notice all of you up here, right?" Emmeline asked. "There are thousands still looking for bodies to invade."

"We will deal with that if it happens," Montgomery said. "If you return quickly with the Argopunks, perhaps the flies will never find us up here."

"And once the flies are cleared, we will have easier access to Remington," Edwin added. "Sounds like he might be the key to curing the others."

"You're right," Emmeline conceded, hoping Remington could survive the wait. "I'll get going." She placed her writhing bag of flies on the deck. "Keep an eye on them … if they can chew through your face, they can probably chew through that bag."

While Edwin double-bagged her knotted satchel, Montgomery grabbed the hammer Kiran had left on the crate next to him.

"Take this."

Emmeline took the hammer and then lifted into the sky.

Though the flies were far away, she flew slowly to avoid drawing attention to herself. When she reached the gate, she used the backside of the hammer to pry three of the nails loose. Metal scraped against metal—a horrible, shiver-inducing noise. She then chiseled through the adhesive used to seal the areas of tarp between the nails. The corner of the sail flapped over and a thin beam of sunlight gleamed through.

Emmeline snapped her attention downward to make sure the light and noise hadn't caught the attention of the flies.

To her relief and dismay, the flies appeared wholly focused on overtaking the crew tasked to catch them.

She needed to work fast.

Hands latched to the bars of the gate and wings pinned to her back, she squeezed through the small opening. Before flying off, she removed her long sleeve bolero and covered the opening to prevent light from shining through. Left in just a tank top and a pair of capris stitched with ribbon and lace, she took flight.

The air of Terra was light and fresh compared to Hydra, and the sound of surging waves was replaced by the clinking of the shifting cogwheels and the steady rumble of the Terra gears. The golden glow on this side of Quintessence set her nerves at ease—she was home. Now, she had to keep her home safe from the threat swarming below. She stayed in Terra as she flew toward the Pyro-Argo base, hovering high enough to soar over the large Terra gears and Tinker Markets, but never too high that she left this space and entered Lower Gaslion.

Her golden wings pounded the warm air with each flap. A vision of warning, a symbol of hope—her flight was observed by all the Terrapunks below.

Their large silver eyes glimmered brightly with the reflection of her fiery silhouette.

"War is upon us!" she shouted to them. "It has begun!"

Their fervent murmuring echoed into the sky.

"Take your stations," she instructed them. "Ready the magnets. Your time to fight is fast approaching."

None of them moved. They simply stared up at her with terror and confusion.

Her time was running out; she needed to get back to Hydra with the militia, but she remained—the Terrapunks were a crucial part of their defense.

Hovering above one of the larger Tinker markets, she shouted, "The Horrigans were supposed to tell you the plan."

"We gave all of the magnets we mined to your brothers," a Tinkerpunk standing on the roof of a repair shop yelled in reply. "We thought our job was done."

"No, we need you to help us fight!"

"Fight?" the Tinkerpunk asked.

"Our aggressors are Marzans from Deimos. Beneath their flesh is a layer of chainmail steel, making them highly vulnerable to magnetism. If they attack, we need all Terrapunks stationed in the nooks and crannies among the pipes separating Hydra from Terra. From there, you'll use as much magnetism as you can muster to help us fight the Marzans."

The Terrapunks whispered among themselves.

Emmeline flew in a large circle, anxiously waiting for some kind of response.

The Tinkerpunk on the repair shop roof finally shouted up in reply.

"You can count on us. We will spread the word as well."

"Thank you!" Emmeline said. "It could happen any day now. We are currently battling a swarm of mind-invading flies. They belong to Kólasi, so they are hard to kill. Hoping to stop them before they lift to the ceiling of Hydra. The gate is sealed, but it wouldn't take them long to find the crevices between the pipes."

"We can lather the gaps with clay," he suggested.

"Yes, but wait on my cue—we might be able to stop them before needing to make that mess. If things go awry, cover your faces however you can. These flies enter through the ears, nose, or mouth, then attack the brain. They also bite."

316

The crowd mumbled and heeded the warning.

"And what of the job your brother Helix gave us?" a different Terrapunk shouted out. Emmeline located the source—it was a skinny Digipunk miner covered in soot and sediment.

"You can give the materials to me," she suggested.

"Do you have the payment?" he asked.

"Not at the moment."

"No deal, then."

"The payment is worthless if we all die."

The Digipunk stared at her with mistrust.

"You know we are good for it," she added.

"I have many ways of causing mayhem for you if the payment never arrives."

"It will."

"Fine. I will drop the materials down the pipe connected to Smuggler's Rove. Don't let them sit there too long—moisture will alter the mineral."

"Understood."

Emmeline needed to move on with her mission.

She took a deep breath before flying upward into Lower Gaslion and then into Fyree. Her anxiety morphed into relief; she had managed to facilitate the delivery of Helix's minerals and inform the Terrapunks of their role in this fight—a huge component in the fight that everyone assumed the Horrigans had already handled. Without help from the Terrapunks, a Marzan attack in Hydra could turn into a slaughter.

The Pyro-Argo base came into view.

Emmeline lifted higher into the sky and landed on the open hangar platform.

The common area was filled with off-duty Argos and Pyros, most of whom had participated in the battle on Mōnalene and the preemptive strike on Deimos.

"Suit up!" she shouted.

Everyone in the room turned their attention to her.

"What's going on?" Pyropunk Felicity Sinclair asked, standing up from the couch she rested on.

"They sent Kólasi's flies through the black hole," Emmeline explained. "We need more hands in Hydra."

"The zombie flies?" Argopunk Jessamine Davenport asked with a shudder.

"Yes. We need liquid nitrogen."

Willie Morrell, cousin to Avery and leader of the Argopunks, stepped forward and shouted orders. "You heard her! Suit up. We have a battle to fight."

The Dawes brothers led the Pyropunks, and in their absence, Felicity took charge.

"Fill your tanks, Pyros," she instructed.

"Hurry," Emmeline urged. "The majority of the Hydropunks are infected and those who aren't are hiding under the sea. The flies will redirect their attention to the ceiling of Hydra soon."

The Pyropunks quickly filled their tanks with helium, suited up, and joined the Argopunks near the hangar base opening.

The entire fleet of twelve hundred punk soldiers stood ready for battle.

Willie and Felicity were at the head of the lines.

"All here?" Willie shouted to the Argopunks.

"Confirmed," Jessamine replied from the back of the line.

"All here?" Felicity asked the Pyropunks.

"Confirmed." Brion Foster, a new recruit, answered from the back of the line.

Willie and Felicity dove off the ledge in unison, plummeting into the open sky. Five seconds into their freefall, they opened their titanium wings and soared toward the gates of Hydra.

The Argopunks and Pyropunks behind them in line followed their lead. Each duo dove with timed precision, creating a synchronized flow of fighters tearing through the sky.

Jessamine and Brion jumped last, and Emmeline followed, her entry into the sky far less graceful.

They flew much faster than Emmeline, but she did her best to keep up.

When they reached the gate, they lowered their flight to conserve their energy and formed a circle around its perimeter.

Emmeline caught up and hovered above.

"That corner is unsealed," she explained, pointing to where she had exited through. "You can enter there."

Willie walked to the small opening, knelt beside it, and peered through. When he looked up, his expression was grave.

"There is a golden haze over the sea," he said.

"Those are the flies," Emmeline explained. "I know there are a lot, but we have to try."

"I can't fit through this small opening," Willie said, standing up. "Jessamine, you go first. Pry it open a little more once you're through."

Jessamine stepped onto the only bar of the gate without the sail beneath it. She pinched her wings together, hugged herself tightly, and stepped over the edge. Her body fell through the small opening, and the moment she was through, she opened her wings and caught herself in midair.

Emmeline grabbed the hammer off her belt and handed it through the hole.

"Use this to pry the nails out," she suggested.

Jessamine took the hammer, removed three more nails, and ripped the opening wider.

The large crew of Argopunks and Pyropunks jumped through the bars of the gate.

Emmeline watched them disappear into Hydra. Her energy was waning and she was struggling to maintain an elevated temperature. She reached into her marble satchel and grabbed a handful. Three glass, four clay, and one gold—she tossed them all into her mouth at once. They rolled down her tongue and into her throat one by one. As the first marble hit her holding pan and then spun into her inner geared mechanism, her energy boosted.

She relit the fire in her heart and levitated. Though the heat gave her lift, she coaxed her body downward by crawling through the bars of the gate. Once on the other side, she spread her wings and let go, adjusting her heat levels to manipulate her position in the sky.

While the rest of the Pyropunks and Argopunks had descended to Montgomery's ship to strategize a plan of attack, Jessamine still hovered by the gate.

"Figured we'd need to reseal it," she said, holding up the hammer.

"Yes," Emmeline replied, retrieving the nails she had collected during her departure, "and quickly. We can't give the flies easy access to the world above."

While Jessamine hammered in the nails, Emmeline followed and pressed the fabric of the sail firmly against what remained of the adhesive. A small amount of heat reactivated its stickiness.

As the final nail was set in place, the furious buzz of the flies below grew louder.

Emmeline and Jessamine looked down in unison.

The swarm was flying toward them.

"It's our time to shine," Jessamine said with a grin before diving down to join the rest of the militia hovering in the sky beneath Montgomery's ship. Emmeline stayed behind to check on her father.

Willie led the Argopunks, who gathered behind him in V formation.

Felicity had the Pyropunks form two rows of defense behind the Argopunks.

Willie shouted, "Charge!"

Felicity kept her fist up, indicating the Argopunks hold their line. Jessamine joined the back line of defense.

Like a squalling blizzard, the Argopunks showered the flies in liquid nitrogen. The gas effectively froze the top layer of flies.

Felicity dropped her fist. "Charge!"

The Pyropunks attacked them with fire, incinerating the frozen flies before they fell into the sea.

Both groups reformed their lines of defense above the thinned-out swarm and repeated the process: freeze and burn.

After three rounds, the swarm was half of its original size. The remaining flies were visibly agitated and exceedingly vicious.

"I got bit!" Brion shouted, shaking his wrist where a fly had its sharp incisors latched to his golden-hued flesh. He activated the flame in his heart, sending heat to his wrist, hoping to burn it off, but the fly did not let go.

"Return to the ship for treatment," Felicity instructed him.

The Dawes brothers, along with Kiran, Avery, and Raven, joined the others in the sky.

"Good work, Felicity," Cyrus said. "Now we just need to capture and kill the stragglers, starting with the ones in our nets."

Willie extended his hand and sent a blast of liquid nitrogen into each of the nets held by Cyrus, Solís, and Helix.

Avery and Raven had already frozen their captured flies, so Felicity stepped in with a burst of fire to finish the job.

A small cloud of disoriented but volatile flies still buzzed below.

"One more round," Willie commanded, to which a smaller crew of Argos and Pyros left to freeze and incinerate the remaining flies.

"We have a new problem," Emmeline declared, pointing at the detention center as this leg of the battle was resolved.

The black hole was no longer in the vacant cage ... it now hovered above the ocean, free from its fiery titanium confinements.

As one problem resolved, a new one emerged.

"It's only a matter of time before they come through," Felicity said.

"We need to heal the infected before the Marzans attack," Avery urged.

"The flies can be ejected if you bring their host close to death," Emmeline informed them.

"How did you discover this?" Solís asked.

"It was Louie's discovery. Remington got infected and tried to kill me. In turn, Louie tried to kill Remington. But he might have ended up saving him. We need to bring his body here so Edwin can tend to him."

At the mention of Remington's name, Raven began to cry. She had been quietly performing any task asked of her, but the emotion of losing her brother finally bubbled to the surface.

"I saw them take him," she sobbed. "I thought he was dead or lost forever."

"We might be able to save him along with everyone else who was taken by the flies," Emmeline responded.

An echoing roar filled Hydra, halting everyone in their tracks.

The steady rhythm of a menacing war chant filled the silence.

Emmeline returned her attention to the black hole below.

A long red arm with sharpened black fingernails reached through.

The worst of this war was yet to come.

Chapter 43

Emmeline reached into her pocket and squeezed the moonstone.

"The Marzans are here!" she declared, hoping the message would reach Luna.

"I think we got them all," Willie responded as he returned to the airship with his fellow Argopunks. The remaining flies had been exterminated.

"Felicity, Brion, and Kiran," Cyrus said, "head down there now and douse the black hole with fire. Their entry into Hydra will not be easy."

"Help me refill their tanks," Avery instructed her fellow Aeropunks, to which they all partnered with a Pyropunk and breathed helium into their tanks. Once every Pyropunk had a full tank, the trio assigned to the black hole lifted and took off. Their hearts blazed, preparing the fire they were about to unleash.

Cyrus continued doling out orders to the Pyropunks on the ship and the Argopunks hovering above.

"Solís and I will retrieve Remington," Cyrus continued. "If he can survive, perhaps the other infected punks can, too."

"The rest of you," Solís jumped in, "start tying up the infected Hydropunks, particularly the Nautipunks. In their current state, they are numbers for the Marzans and they will fight against us. We can't have that. Constrain them however possible."

The army of twelve hundred Pyropunks and Argopunks left the safety of Montgomery's airship and soared toward the chaos below.

Only Emmeline, Cyrus, Solís, Helix, Raven, and Avery remained in the huddle.

"Your minerals were delivered," Emmeline informed Helix.

"The sodium hydroxide?"

"Yes. Through the pipe on Smuggler's Rove."

"Too much exposure to water will ruin it!" Helix exclaimed before lifting into the sky and darting toward the rove.

Emmeline addressed the group.

"Our main focus is protecting the source flame," Emmeline reminded them. "That's what they came here for."

"She's right," Avery agreed.

"And only the Hydropunks can stop the Marzans if they enter the water," Emmeline added.

"We can help with that, too," a pretty voice announced from above.

Everyone looked up.

Luna had arrived.

"Where is your army?" Avery asked.

"They are ready," she replied. "I heard Emmeline through the moonstone and wanted to bring Gemma home first."

Emmeline perked up. "Gemma? Where is she?"

"I dropped her off near the main wheel. Your father was there and offered to find her a place to rest."

"Is she healed?"

Luna shook her head. "They exhausted all options. Both the curse and Marzan poison seeped too deep. They actually thought they lost her … she was comatose with no pulse for a full minute, but luckily, she woke up."

Emmeline darted away, leaving the group where they congregated.

The early sounds of war echoed all around her, but all she heard were the guilt-ridden thoughts echoing inside her head.

Montgomery was holding Gemma upright as he led her into a vacant cabin to rest.

"Gemma!" Emmeline shouted.

Montgomery halted and turned Gemma to face Emmeline.

Pretty face gaunt and silver gaze hollow, Gemma was smaller and appeared much sicker than when Emmeline last saw her. She wore many new scars and marks on the parts of her body still covered in flesh.

"What happened?" Emmeline asked.

"They did the best they could," Gemma replied. "Surviving wasn't in the cards for me."

"So, they just gave up?"

"No, I told them to stop and asked to go home."

"Is it because you almost died? Luna told me … "

Gemma nodded. "There was nothing more they could do for me."

"But what if the next attempt worked?"

Gemma shook her head. "I had enough of their poking and prodding. If I'm going to die, I want to do so at home, where I am comfortable and have friends, not in foreign territory."

Emmeline could no longer contain her emotions. She opened her arms and wrapped Gemma in a hug. Montgomery yanked his arm out of Emmeline's tight embrace and let her hold up Gemma.

"You ought to let her rest," he gently suggested.

"I will," Emmeline replied, then said to Gemma, "I am so sorry."

"I don't blame you. I never did." Gemma's voice was soft and filled with love. "You need to stop blaming yourself."

"I don't know how."

"Shift your perspective. Without your friendship with Luna, we'd be ill-prepared to fight the Marzans and they likely would have extinguished the source flame by now. Every casualty along the way played some part in the sun's survival."

Emmeline released a heavy sigh. "It's hard to see the bigger picture when you're suffering right in front of me."

"Try."

"I will."

Gemma nodded and smiled. "I'm just happy to be home."

"I'm happy you're home, too. Let's get you comfortable."

Emmeline led her into the cabin, helped her onto the cot, and draped a warm blanket over her friend.

"War is on our doorstep, but you'll be safe here," Emmeline promised.

"You'll stop them," Gemma said, her voice low, but full of confidence.

"That's the plan."

Montgomery stepped into the room and placed a bell on the nightstand. "If you need anything, ring this bell, and someone will check on you."

"Thank you," Gemma said.

Montgomery and Emmeline exited the room, closing the door behind them.

The calm hush before the start of battle had erupted into full chaos.

A full fleet of Lunarians had arrived in Hydra through the moonstone portal, far more than had fought in the previous battle. They circled Luna as she doled out orders, their massive dragonfly wings buzzing as they rotated around her. Emmeline could not hear what she said from where she stood on the airship.

Without warning, the Lunarians nose-dived in unison toward the detention center. Their cascading descent surrounded all sides of the airship, creating momentary darkness as they catapulted into battle. The loud darkness lasted long enough for everyone on board to pause and witness the foreign show of strength. Grateful, terrified, uneasy—the Thermapunks shared a mixture of emotions while engulfed by the Lunarian swarm. The sound of their descent was deafeningly steady and created a strange form of silence. Their whizzing plunge drowned out the frantic noise of uncertainty that accompanied the start of war, and to those who trusted the Lunarians, it was a loud, yet calming moment of peace.

When the last of the Lunarians passed, the whooshing buzz ceased and the clammer of chaos resumed.

"We can trust them, right?" Montgomery asked, his voice wary.

"Absolutely," Emmeline answered.

Luna led the massive army of Odonatas. As they got closer to the detention center, she instructed them to split up. Half of the group went to the right, the other half to the left. Once they fully surrounded the cages, she held her fist in the sky, alerting them to stop and wait for further instruction.

A trio of Pyropunks stood on top of the empty cage that used to contain the black hole. The cage was no longer set ablaze—the only fire left was that which the Pyropunks shot at the relocated black hole.

Luna recognized Kiran standing atop the cage.

"How can we help?" she asked him from above.

"Find Solís or Cyrus and tell them we need reinforcements," Kiran answered. "We are draining ourselves. We won't last much longer."

"I'll do you one better," she replied. "Cèla's group, descend! Everyone else, gather behind me."

Cèla led half of the army into the sea. Fifteen hundred Odonatas plummeted, each making a tiny splash as they disappeared beneath the water.

"We will keep them at bay with magnetic repulsion," Luna explained to Kiran. "While we hold them off, seek reinforcements. We will need fire from all sides if they break through."

"Okay, let us know when we can cease fire."

Luna addressed her warriors. "Repulsion on three! One … two … three!"

The Odonatas took a collective breath, extended their arms outward, and an invisible magnetic forcefield pressed against the black hole.

"You can relax," Luna told Kiran. The veins around her eyes were darker than usual and her body shook as the magnetic threads within her body blackened and tangled.

Kiran, Felicity, and Brion spread their titanium wings and departed to search for help.

A brief scan of the chaos revealed that the other Pyros and Argos were actively fighting and restraining the infected Hydropunks.

"I see Helix," Brion shouted to the others as they circled above Smuggler's Rove.

The trio dove toward the shore where Helix fought Pippin Picklefish.

Pippin's body was wasted, utterly blasted, but the golden fly nestled inside his brain gave direction to each wobbly step.

"He's so drunk the fly can't properly control him," Helix called out to the trio as they raced toward him to help. "But he's still got those alcohol muscles."

As the words left his mouth, Pippin stumbled forward, arms swinging wildly. His left fist connected with Helix's face and the force sent them both to their knees.

Helix was doubled over, unmoving as he recollected his whereabouts. Pippin staggered to his feet, but tripped continuously in his attempts.

"Grab him!" Kiran shouted.

The trio raced to where Pippin teetered between standing and falling. Brion tripped him and Kiran straddled Pippin's back the moment he hit the ground.

Helix returned to his feet, rubbing the side of his face, and tossed two ropes to them.

Kiran knotted Pippin's wrists together while Felicity bound Pippin's ankles.

"I need to get this satchel to my father's ship," Helix stated. "It's the sodium hydroxide I'll use to make the capsuled bullets."

He looked to the sky and saw Jessamine flying overhead.

Helix stuck his fingers in his mouth and released a loud whistle.

Jessamine halted her flight.

"What's wrong?" she called down.

"Can you deliver this satchel to the airship?"

Jessamine lowered. "Sure."

"Tell the Thermapunk crew to melt the contents down into a liquid and to keep it burning until I get there."

He tossed the bag up to Jessamine, who caught it and rocketed upward toward the faraway airship.

Brion and Kiran still had Pippin pinned to the ground.

"Where are you putting all the infected punks?" Felicity asked Helix.

"In the empty cage," he answered, pointing up at the cage where the Devil of Delusion, now known as a Marzan, had once resided.

"So close to the black hole?" Kiran asked.

"You should lock them in the bilge of Cuda Ray's man-o-war," a voice suggested.

Everyone turned their heads to find Louie trudging through the sand toward them.

"Where is Remington?" Helix asked.

Louie waved his arm at the sky. "Taken to safety."

Helix refocused on Louie's prior suggestion. "I thought Cuda Ray's ship was destroyed?"

"He stole a tugboat, lugged the remains of his ship out to Seadog Rove on the other side of Hydra, and rebuilt it there."

Helix considered this.

"If the infected break free of their constraints, it would be an easy escape," Helix argued.

Louie shook his head. "There are cages down there. Croctopus has his own secret detention center and I heard this new prison he built is bigger than the previous one."

"How many cellblocks?"

"It runs the length and width of his ship," Louie answered. "It might not hold every infected punk, but you could double or triple them up in each cage." Louie burped. "Having them all there will make it easier if we need to enact a quick termination. The rebuild is still covered in petroleum and highly explosive."

"Why would we need to kill them? I thought you freed Remington of the fly in his head," Felicity inquired.

"I did, but I can't say for sure that he survived. I had to bring him real close to death to get that thing to flee." Louie shrugged. "Blowing them up in that ship is just an option if it turns out they can't be saved."

"It's not a bad idea," Helix mumbled to himself, then asked Louie, "Where is Cuda Ray's ship?"

Louie pointed to the west.

A few miles offshore sat the man-o-war, anchored in place.

"Do you know if Cuda Ray was infected?"

"I have no clue."

"Brion," Helix said as he lifted Pippin by his bicep. "Help me carry him over to the ship. Kiran and Felicity, you fly with Louie."

"I'm not going with you," Louie objected.

"Yes, you are," Helix countered. "We might need extra hands if we have to constrain any Nautipunks on that ship."

"I have a migraine," Louie argued.

"Not my problem."

Helix and Brion lifted into the sky with Pippin in tow.

"Ready?" Kiran asked Louie, to which Louie looked at him for the first time.

"*You* aren't touching me," Louie spat.

"I can't carry you by myself," Felicity said.

"I'll swim."

Louie ran toward the ocean and dove into the water.

"Do you think he'll actually swim to the ship?" Felicity asked Kiran.

"Who cares. We don't need him."

The duo lifted into the sky and soared to the ship.

Below them, to their surprise, Louie kept his word. He was a fast swimmer, as were all Hydropunks, and his pace in the water matched theirs in the sky.

When they reached Cuda Ray's man-o-war, Louie scaled the metal ladder bolted to the side of the ship while Kiran and Felicity joined Helix and Brion in the sky. They hovered above a lively crew of Nautipunks. Cuda Ray stood at the front of the pack.

"I ain't surprised they got ole Picklefish." Cuda Ray guffawed. "Pippin was a scabby sea bass."

"We need your cages," Helix demanded.

"Get outter me skies!"

"You need to cooperate."

"I ain't got cages. Yer mistaken."

"Don't lie to them," Louie said as he climbed over the gunwale.

"Argh, I was hopin' ye of all punks were lost ter the flies."

"The sentiment is mutual," Louie countered with a smile.

"We don't have time for this," Helix argued.

"You can't bluff while I'm here," Louie said to Cuda Ray.

"Me cages are occupied."

"By who?" Helix demanded.

"Ye won't like it."

"I'm sure I won't, but you have no other choice but to let them all go so we can use your prisons for the infected. We need to keep them safe until we can heal them."

"Whattabout that cage in the sky? I been seein' yer lot bringin' 'em there."

"It's too close to the black hole," Helix answered. "No more squabbling. Lead us to the bilge."

Cuda Ray didn't move. The long scar across his face ran through the snarl he wore.

"You better heat up," Louie warned Helix from where he leaned against a mast, far from the confrontation.

Helix heeded the warning and activated his heart. The source flame within him sweltered, causing his golden-hued flesh to glow red. Kiran, Felicity, and Brion followed his lead and quickly matched Helix's temperature.

Free hand lifted, fire forming in his palm, the threat he presented silenced every Nautipunk aboard the ship.

Reflection of the flame flickered in Cuda Ray's icy blue gaze.

"No need fer dramatics," he said. Though his words were docile, the energy he radiated was volatile. "Follow me."

Cuda Ray limped toward an open hatch with stairs that led below the main deck.

"Stay lit," Helix advised his fellow Pyropunks, all of whom maintained the fire they held. Louie followed at the rear.

Three sets of stairs led them to the bottom of the ship.

Cuda Ray paused at a locked door with a giant wheeled knob.

"Ye can't hold what yer about ter discover against me," he said.

"I don't make promises with criminals," Helix replied.

"Yer one ter talk," Cuda Ray spat.

"I'm not a criminal."

"But yer a junkie. Only a matter of time before ya start stealin' ter get yer fix."

"Enough," Helix said, unwilling to explain himself or ask how he could possibly know this about him. "Open the door."

Cuda Ray unclipped the clasps locking the wheel in place. With a massive spin, the sound of moving gears within the door clicked and churned. He spun the wheel a second time, instigating the retraction of a large rod that crossed from the door into the doorframe. As it rescinded into the door, it made an awful noise—metal scraping against metal.

"Been meaning ter grease that," Cuda Ray commented casually as everyone else recoiled.

The door swung open.

Helix gasped at the sight—four long rows of stacked cages stretched before them. They piled up to the ceiling, and each row was four or five cages tall. The walls were slick with both fresh and dried petroleum, and the room reeked of gasoline and sulfur.

"I'm surprised you haven't self-detonated yet," Helix commented.

"When I rebuilt me ship after Ruthanne tore it apart, I added more vents." He glanced at Louie. "Also sealed shut the hatches hidden in the hull."

Helix remained in the doorframe, scanning the horrifying scene. Many of the cages were occupied by malnourished and decaying Solarpunks.

"Who are all these punks?" he asked.

"Just me collection."

Louie pushed past Helix. "The cages were empty when Ruthanne destroyed his ship."

"Aye, lad. They were. Now they ain't."

"It's only been a few months," Louie said, his disbelief rampant. "How do you have so many new prisoners?"

"They ain't new, just decided ter keep me enemies a little closer after the rebuild."

"I don't understand … "

"Listen," Cuda Ray cut him off. "If ye want me cages, fine. Put Pippin in one o' the empty ones. But ye can't release who I got here already. I'll bring 'em back ter Seadog Rove, lock 'em up how I had 'em before."

"I don't think so," Helix replied as he and Brion shoved Pippin into a vacant cage. "These punks are very sick and need medical attention."

"They're me prisoners! Prisoners don't get doctors."

"We will need to do a thorough investigation of each prisoner you have here. I suspect none of them deserve this fate."

"Who is *we*?" Cuda Ray barked. "There ain't no rulers in Hydra. No one can tell me what ter do!"

"My father governs Hydra and he has graced the lot of you with bountiful freedom. You are abusing his generosity."

"We didn't choose him … he gave himself that role."

"Because the lot of you couldn't be trusted to protect and preserve the source flame."

"Get out!" Cuda Ray shouted.

Helix raised his hands, which still glowed with the heat of the source flame. "We don't want a fight, but this," Helix said, waving his arm at the unethical detainment of punks, "is unacceptable."

Louie was livid. "I want to walk the rows and see who you have here."

"Ain't no one walkin' these rows," Cuda Ray seethed, stepping closer to Louie. He was only a few inches taller, but he stood so close that his long beard touched Louie's chin.

Louie stood strong.

"Who do you have here?" he demanded.

"I heard yer new home is at the bottom o' the bottle," Cuda Ray taunted.

"Who do you have here?" Louie repeated, his voice louder now.

"Yer liquid courage ain't impressive."

Louie leaned back and then threw a heavy punch. His fist made contact with Cuda Ray's right eye. A loud crack followed by a rush of blood—black octopus ink gushed from the fresh wound on his face.

Without hesitation, Cuda Ray seized Louie by the neck, lifted him off the ground, and slammed his body into the nearest stack of cages. They wobbled ominously upon impact.

"Yer a rotten scoundrel," Cuda Ray spat.

"At least I'm not evil," Louie replied, his words strained as he tried to breathe despite the firm grip around his neck. "You're the one who belongs in a cage."

Cuda Ray smirked. "Yet here I am, free. Wanna know why? 'Cause fortune favors those who know how ter steal it."

Louie spat in Cuda Ray's face, further angering the ruthless Nautipunk.

"That's enough!" Helix shouted, grabbing Cuda Ray's wrist with his heated hand.

"Ow!" Cuda Ray bellowed, dropping Louie.

Helix let go and Cuda Ray recoiled, cradling his scorched wrist.

"Little Louie is a big man now," Cuda Ray jeered. "But ye still can't fight yer own battles."

"Let's go," Helix said to Louie, to which Louie obliged.

Cuda Ray rambled on, "That's right! Go hide in a bottle o' rum." He cackled. "Straight Leg Louie ain't so straight no more. Time fer a new name."

"Ignore him," Helix urged Louie.

"I'm freeing every punk trapped in this hellish boat."

"And I'll help you."

Helix's promise to help calmed Louie down. As they joined Kiran, Felicity, and Brion at the door, a small voice among the cages called out.

"Louie?"

So frail and meek, it was almost inaudible between the sounds of their footsteps.

Louie paused.

"Did you hear that?" he asked Helix, who shook his head.

"Louie," the voice repeated, a little bit louder this time.

Louie's eyes widened as he looked at Helix, who acknowledged he heard the voice with a nod.

"I know that voice," Louie said as he faced the rows of cages. His expression held a mixture of horror, hope, and rage. He shot a murderous glare at Cuda Ray.

"Get out, I said!" Cuda Ray barked, raising a hand at Louie.

"If you touch me, I will kill you," Louie calmly replied, his energy so violent, Cuda Ray actually halted his advance.

The room was silent besides the slow and subtle movements within the cages.

"Louie," the voice repeated, this time shaking with deep sorrow.

"Mom," Louie gasped, the word hardly a whisper.

He raced down the long row of stacked cages, frantically looking inside each and every one, searching for a face he hadn't seen in years—a face he dreamed of so often, her absence in reality had become a living nightmare.

He found her halfway down the line in the third cage up. She was emaciated and unable to move.

Louie grabbed the cage bars and pressed his face into them. "Mom," he sobbed.

"My boy," she whispered. "I'm so sorry."

"Stop."

"I'm sorry I wasn't there for you all these years."

"I'm okay," he promised her, tears rolling down his cheeks. He reached for the lock on the door of the cage—it required a key.

His sorrow shifted to rage as he turned to find Cuda Ray.

"Let her out." His words came out as a low growl.

"No can do," Cuda Ray replied, then spat a loogie on the floor. "That one there be the biggest thorn in me side. I ain't lettin' her out just to let her run amuck on me again."

"Let her out!"

"No."

Fury carried Louie to Cuda Ray in record time. In a breath, he stood chest to chest with the infuriating pirate.

"Where are the keys?" Louie demanded.

"Ye ain't getting' yer way on this one, boy."

Louie's anger exploded.

With a strength he never felt prior, Louie grabbed Cuda Ray by the neck and squeezed so hard his neck gears and marble chute dented from the pressure.

Before anyone could intervene or offer an alternate solution, Louie ripped the knife from Cuda Ray's belt and stabbed him in the chest. He dragged the knife downward, splaying Cuda Ray wide open.

Cuda Ray fell to his knees.

"Ye can't kill me, boy," he barked, wobbling where he knelt and struggling to defend himself.

"I can do much worse."

Louie pushed the side of Cuda Ray's head, knocking him to the floor. He knelt beside him and plunged the knife into Cuda Ray's tanked lungs. Five punctures in each tank rendered them useless. He then seized Cuda Ray's ocean heart and yanked it from the safety of his zinc ribcage and placed it in his pocket.

The tanks could be patched, but punk hearts were irreplicable.

"You're my prisoner now," Louie seethed.

"The keys are yers if ye give me heart back," Cuda Ray croaked.

Louie shook his head. "I'll find another way."

The adrenaline coursing through him blurred his vision. Bodies stood around them, watching the assault in shock.

Louie looked up at the crowd around them, unfazed by their stunned expressions.

"He deserves worse," Louie stated as he stood.

No one argued.

"You don't need the keys to get them out," Helix offered. "We can melt the locks."

Louie nodded, grateful for the offer. He followed Helix to his mother's prison while Kiran, Brion, and Felicity spread out to free the others.

"There's a war going on out there," Helix reminded Louie.

"A war we won't win," Louie said. "If this is my last living moment, I want to spend it with my mom."

"Or maybe," Helix countered, "the unexpected return of your mother could serve as motivation to *win* this war. Surely a lifetime with her is better than a moment. That has to be worth fighting for."

Louie didn't reply.

There were a lot of things worth fighting for, but until now, none of them had the power to shake him free from the trauma he carried.

Everything felt different now.

Discovering that his mother had been alive all these years broke his heart, and though it felt like additional trauma, it was pain that held great hope. They could rebuild, they could reconnect, they could make up for all the lost years. He wanted to be a man his mother could be proud of, not a drunken, self-destructive fool. Her assumed death was a nightmare he had lived with the majority of his life, but now, she was back. Miraculously. Her survival was a gift, and he planned to treat it as such.

Elongating their renewed time together was certainly worth fighting for.

But Louie wasn't ready to admit that—not until he freed her from her cage.

Helix held the lock and heated his body to such great temperatures, the steel lock melted in his grip. He stepped back and cooled off while Louie helped his mother out of the cage. The last time he saw her, he was a small child. Now, he was a grown man and he was able to cradle her in his arms the same way she used to carry him.

"I'll do better," he said, more so to himself. "I will be better."

Helix walked beside them.

"Sub Anne Marie, a true legend," Helix stated. "My father will be delighted to hear that you're alive."

She was too weak to reply. She simply rested against Louie's chest, letting go of her fight to survive and surrendering to her newfound safety.

"All the cages are unlocked," Felicity announced as she joined them by the door. "But most are too weak to leave on their own."

Kiran jumped in, "Not sure we should spend the time carrying them all to safety right now."

"No," Helix agreed. "We need to help with the war beyond the confines of this ship."

"This is my ship now," Louie stated as he marched out of the prison room, still carrying his mother. The Pyropunks followed. "I'll have my crew attend to the prisoners and prepare the cages for the infected."

"Are you sure they will switch their allegiance to you?" Helix asked.

"I have Cuda Ray's heart. If you defeat a captain, you become the captain. It's been the way of the Nautipunks since the start." Louie paused. "And if they don't, they'll be fed to the flies."

"We don't need more aggressive zombies on our hands," Kiran said from the back of the group.

"They'll be locked away first."

"Prepare them for battle against the Marzans," Helix requested as they made their way up the final set of stairs. "Yours is the last Nautipunk crew standing. You can move ocean currents; you can fight underwater. If the Marzans enter the sea, you are our main line of defense."

"I understand. You can count on us."

They reemerged on the main deck to a crew wearing looks of confusion.

"Where's Cuda Ray?" a burly Nautipunk asked.

"I am your captain now," Louie answered.

The crew grumbled with dissonance.

"Show us proof!"

Louie carefully transferred his mother into Helix's arms, and then reached into his pocket and lifted Cuda Ray's heart into the air.

The crew gasped in collective shock—no one had ever come close to defeating Cuda Ray before.

Louie bellowed, "Fall in line or face the flies!"

The large crew of Nautipunks grumbled at the change of command, but respected the ways of the sea. Louie was in charge now, and they would follow his lead.

Louie observed their obedience with secure authority.

The tides were changing, not only on this ship, but also in his mind and heart. It was a bumpy road to get here, but he finally relocated his purpose.

"All is well here," he said to Helix.

"Let me bring your mother to my father's ship. Not only will she be safer there, but we also have a Thermadoc on board."

"No, I need her here with me."

"You need to focus on the war."

A loud roar echoed above—the Lunarians were struggling to keep the Marzans from exiting through the black hole.

Helix added, "If we don't defeat the Marzans, she'll never get to enjoy her freedom."

Louie nodded. "Keep her safe."

"She will be protected by fire."

This eased Louie's nerves—fire was the Marzans' greatest foe.

Helix lifted into the sky carrying his mother, the notorious Sub Anne Marie.

Louie watched as they flew away, determined to see her again.

But first, he had a war to win.

Chapter 44

"Let me help," Gemma begged Emmeline.

"Your plan is preposterous."

"It will work."

"It's suicide!" Emmeline argued.

"I'm going to die either way."

"You don't know that for certain."

Gemma caressed the newly formed crescent-shaped freckle on her wrist. "Yes, I do."

"No, you don't."

"We should do it now before they exit the black hole."

"I said no!"

"Fine, then I'll present my idea to your father. He'll let me do it," Gemma scoffed.

"No, he won't. There are other ways to survive this. We don't need to sacrifice anyone in the process."

Gemma coughed violently where she lay.

"You are unwell and aren't thinking clearly," Emmeline said, softening her tone. "Just rest. I will return and check on you soon."

Emmeline left the cabin and closed the door behind her. She leaned her body against the wall and took a moment to decompress from Gemma's outlandish plan.

A Thermapunk crew was boiling Helix's minerals in a glass gallipot near the bow.

There are other ways to stop the Marzans, Emmeline reinforced in thought.

Edwin Doyle darted past, running toward Solís and Cyrus, who were carefully lowering Remington onto the main deck.

Everything was working out as planned.

Emmeline looked over the side of the boat toward the detention center—the Lunarians continued to hold a solid defense against the Marzans.

Now was not the time for martyrs; it was imperative they stuck to the plan.

"Another surge," Luna called out to her fleet of Odonata warriors.

With a massive collective push, they sent a wave of repulsive magnetism at the black hole, creating a forcefield that kept the Marzans from crossing through.

Luna looked below—Solís and Cyrus had returned from delivering Remington to the airship and were now relocating the infected punks from the detention center cage to a pirate ship below. From that same ship, Helix departed, flying toward Montgomery's airship carrying a limp body, and Louie steered the massive ship covered in petroleum toward the detention center.

"Hold the force field," Luna shouted.

Every Odonata expelled deterrent magnetism.

Cèla stood beside Luna.

"Is this the only plan?" she asked. "Do the punks plan to help at all?"

"They are clearing the rove of infected punks so the Marzans don't have additional soldiers if they get through."

"And then what?"

"They will join us with fire."

"Do we have a plan to stop them?"

Before Luna could answer, Solís lifted into the sky, hovering just below the fleet of Lunarians.

"We have almost all of the infected punks wrangled," he announced. "How are you doing?"

"We can't hold this force field forever," Luna answered. "What's the plan?"

"My army is coming with fire and explosive gas. We will blast chlorotrifluoride into the black hole."

Luna scanned the world below.

The Pyropunks and Argopunks were scattered all over Hydra. One by one, they flew toward the black hole, preparing to help, but as they approached, a massive surge pulsated from the black hole and pushed the large group of Lunarians backward.

"What was that?" Odonata Isone asked.

"I don't know," Luna replied.

"What was what?" Solís asked.

"You didn't feel that?" Luna asked.

Solís shook his head.

The Lunarians quickly regained their stance in the sky and resumed their magnetic repulsion, but when a second surge of this invisible force emanated from the black hole, the massive fleet of Lunarians was knocked out of the sky. They free-fell into the ocean, bodies limp and unmoving.

Solís chased after Luna while the rest of the Pyropunks began blasting fire at the black hole. The Argopunks joined them, churning the formula for chlorotrifluoride in their guts.

The energetic surges continued with a low pulsating buzz, but they did not affect the Solarpunks. As the Argopunks lined up and prepared to add their gas to the flames, the tip of a vessel poked out of the black hole.

"Foray!" Willie shouted, initiating the release of the highly flammable gas, but the colossal explosions did not stop the vessel from progressing forward.

Inch by inch, a massive fireproof mooncraft exited the black hole.

The Pyros and Argos were forced back.

Cyrus shouted, "Prepare for combat!"

Solís lifted into the sky, soaking wet and carrying Luna, who was weak but no longer unconscious.

"The Lunarians are okay," Solís whispered to his brother. "They were stunned temporarily but are now hiding out within the sea with Cèla's fleet, prepared to fight underwater if the Marzans get that far."

"Excellent."

A moment of tense silence lingered among the Solarpunks, who stopped blasting fire and gas to conserve their energy. The massive mooncraft exited the black hole and entered their airspace.

"The sun has cast its final flame," King Helmer declared through a window near the top of the mooncraft. "Today is the day our galaxy stops revolving around fire."

"You'll kill everything!" Solís shouted.

"As our god decrees."

The window slammed shut.

"We need to get them out of their ship," Willie said, joining Solís and Cyrus where they hovered. Felicity followed.

As the foursome deliberated, Cuda Ray's man-o-war, now commanded by Louie, sailed into action with water cannons casting high-pressure streams of salt water at the ship. As he made contact, the corrosive water eroded the stone shell of the ship.

"It's working," Solís said in shock.

The mooncraft lifted higher into the sky to escape the attack.

"Gather above the mooncraft!" Cyrus directed his fellow fighters.

"Luna and I will join Louie on the ship," Solís said. "She needs solid ground to recuperate."

Cyrus nodded, and they parted ways.

While Cyrus and the Pyro-Argo fighters used all their strength to push the ship downward from above, Solís lowered himself and Luna to the man-o-war.

"Is this your ship now?" Solís asked Louie after gently placing Luna down on a crate to rest.

"Yep."

"How?"

Louie glared at him without replying, then refocused on the water cannon he had aimed at the mooncraft.

Solís tried again with a different question. "How'd you know salt water would work?"

"The red rock looked brittle. Figured it was worth a shot."

Saltwater mist and red rock dust rained down over them.

Louie continued, "Shouldn't be long before we've drilled a hole into their hull."

"Good to know they can't go directly to the source flame in that ship. I was worried they might be able to."

Louie hardly looked at Solís as he spoke.

"I know you don't like me," Solís said, "but it's good to see you acting like your old self again."

Louie nodded.

"What can I do to help?" Solís asked.

"Ready your fire. They'll start abandoning ship soon."

As predicted, the Marzans began evacuating their crumbling mooncraft.

Solís lifted into the sky, body blazing with heat and ready to fight, when the falling Marzans started blipping in and out of sight. They came and went so quickly, Solís couldn't keep tabs on any of them.

"What is happening?" he shouted.

Luna answered from below. "They are using their black hole magic to stay above water."

"They are using it to fly," Solís noted, "sort of. There is no continuous path for any of them."

Thousands of Marzans were now glitching across the sky, flying erratically as they regrouped.

A golden blur dashed through the sky.

Emmeline soared near the Terra pipes.

"Now is the time!" she shouted, hoping the Terrapunks were hiding there and could hear her.

The sound of feet clinking against the pipes answered her call.

"On my count," a hidden Terrapunk announced. "Three, two, one, drop!"

All at once, hundreds of Terrapunks attached to bungee cords fell from the sky. A mixture of Tinkies and Digis joined the fight. Their cords stretched for miles, allowing them to reach the lower plane where the Marzans raced in and out of their black holes.

The Terrapunks took a moment to observe before they struck.

Palms radiating magnetism, they caught the fast-moving Marzans by the chains in their bodies.

The Pyropunks and Argopunks lifted into the sky to join their offensive.

Each Marzan seized by a Terrapunk was either choked with flames by a Pyropunk or doused in liquid nitrogen by an Argopunk. Both options allotted the Terrapunks more time to use their magnetism to collapse their inner chains and shred the Marzans from the inside out.

It was a successful strategy, but slow-moving—the damage caused was not large enough or fast enough, and the Marzans were blipping through their black holes closer to the sea.

"If they enter the sea, it'll land on the Hydropunks and Lunarians to stop them," Cyrus shouted.

"Keep thinning their numbers," Solís replied. "The fewer Marzans that enter the sea, the better."

The Pyros and Argos continued to assist the Terrapunks as they caught and annihilated Marzans. They eliminated a fifth of their enemy's large task force before the Marzans started dipping below the sea's surface.

"Thanks for your help," Solís said to the Terrapunk he last assisted with his hand extended.

The small male Terrapunk wore an expression of shock— never had a noble Thermapunk spoken directly to him before, nor offered their hand in gratitude. He accepted Solís's outstretched hand, shaking it with a firm grip.

"There's a massive prayer group still gathered in Fyree," the Terrapunk informed him. "They've been there for days."

"It would be better if they were preparing to fight," Solís countered, letting go of the Terrapunk's hand.

"Maybe Solédon will answer."

"I'm not counting on that, and neither should anyone else." Solís tilted his wings and flew to Louie's ship.

While he raced downward, the Terrapunks flipped the levers on their belts and recoiled upward, disappearing among the ceiling pipes.

"Louie," Solís barked. "Enough with the water cannons. You and your crew need to dive."

"I have a squad suiting up," he replied, still fixated on destroying the entire Marzan mooncraft.

"You *all* need to dive. You're the only Nautipunk crew left standing; all the others are infected and locked in cages."

Louie cranked the spigot of his cannon, lessening and eventually stopping the flow of water.

"Alright," Louie shouted to the members of his crew on cannon duty. "You heard him. Seal your tanks and prepare to fight."

The crew of fifty locked their tanked lungs, preventing sea water from entering, and then dove off the side of the boat.

Louie waited until his entire crew was submerged, then turned to Solís.

"If I don't see this side of the sea again, tell my mom and Emmeline that I love them."

"You will tell them that yourself," Solís refuted.

Louie nodded, his expression grim. "I hope so."

He dove off the gunwale, hardly making a splash as he disappeared into the sea.

Solís and Luna were alone on the boat.

She walked toward him, her energy returning.

"Do you think the others have recuperated enough to fight?" Solís asked her.

"I'm feeling much stronger now," she answered. "They should be at full strength and able to stop them."

"They are our only hope."

Luna leaned in and rested her head against Solís's chest. The stardust in her long black ponytail glittered in the light of his golden glow. He wrapped his arms around her, cherishing every second of this fleeting bliss.

"I should join them and help," she finally said.

"I know it's selfish, but I'd rather you stay here with me." He paused. "I can't lose you."

"You'll only lose me if the Marzans succeed. We either see tomorrow, or we don't. In life or in death, we will be together," she replied.

He held her tighter.

"Let's hope it's in life," he said, then kissed the top of her head.

Luna held him a moment longer, then gently pulled herself out of his embrace.

He grabbed her face and kissed her. Luna lingered, doing everything in her power not to melt from his affection. She returned his kiss, but held on to her rage, letting the love mix with her furious adrenaline.

Solís pulled back, golden eyes beaming.

"I will come back," she promised.

"I'll be here when you do."

Luna stepped onto the ledge of the gunwale, preparing to enter the sea, when Emmeline, Avery, and Helix flew toward them. He carried a large glass beaker filled with sizzling liquid.

"Wait! We need you," Emmeline shouted, stopping Luna from jumping.

"I need to help my fellow warriors stop the Marzans from reaching the source flame," Luna said.

"We think there is another way," Emmeline replied.

"They're all connected to the king," Helix said. "That's my theory, at least."

"As in, their lives are connected to his?" Solís asked.

"Yes. If we kill him, we kill them all."

"What makes you think that?"

"It's something I saw while dissecting the Marzan bodies; I wish I had made the connection sooner. Both Marzan bodies had a permanent marking burned into their flesh—two circles linked, displayed vertically, and the top ring had a triangle etched into it."

"The gods use circles to symbolize their divinity," Luna said.

"Yes, but these markings were mutilations," Helix said. "They were made after birth, and I think triangles symbolize royalty, meaning the commoners are directly linked to the king in some way," Helix explained. He looked at Luna and said, "You know the most about them. Is any of this adding up?"

Luna contemplated quietly.

She stepped off the gunwale and paced as she spoke her thoughts aloud.

"King Helmer never fights. He has never once left the safety of his ship while invading Mōnalene. My brother got close to him once. He shot an arrow through King Helmer's left ankle." Luna gasped. "The Marzan I was fighting on the ground fell to his left knee when it happened. I never thought to question why. I killed him and moved on to the next."

"Maybe my theory is right," Helix said, his excitement growing.

"It's worth a try," Luna agreed. "We will need to board the mooncraft to get to King Helmer."

Helix was already lifting into the sky. "There is no time to waste!"

Luna, Solís, Avery, and Emmeline followed him.

The group flew through the enormous hole in the hull of the Marzan mooncraft.

"He will be in his chambers above," Luna said in a low voice.

With care, they flew through four levels of the damaged ship. When they reached their first ceiling, they found a nearby set of stairs that led to an adjacent door.

"Surely, he has guards," Avery said.

"He does. We aren't at the top yet," Luna replied.

They climbed another set of stairs.

The inside of the vessel was ice-cold, damp, and dark. Emmeline shivered as they made their way through another set of open doors and into a great room lined with room-length bench seating.

Everyone stopped to scan their surroundings—two Marzans stood on the far end guarding a door. Avery saw them first.

"Over there," she whispered, grabbing Emmeline by the wrist and pulling her down into a crouch. Helix, Solís, and Luna also lowered to their knees, and the group crawled between two rows of benches toward the guarded door.

"I'll take the guard on the right," Luna said, the black veins around her eyes darkening. "You and Helix take the one on the left."

Luna bared her sharpened teeth and lifted her hands. As her magnetism yanked the guard to her, Solís and Helix charged the second guard. Hands heated, Solís held him to the ground with fire. Helix yanked the pipette from his tool belt, retrieved some of the boiling-hot liquid from his beaker, and released two drops of the molten sodium hydroxide into the Marzan's eyes.

The Marzan howled in pain. Though it did not kill him, it blinded him, making it easier for Solís and Helix to hold his massive body down until Luna could use her magnetism on him.

Luna increased her power on the Marzan she fought and pulled his inner chains until they were on the outside.

The guard dropped dead.

She went over to the second guard to finish him off.

Emmeline and Avery worked on the intricate door lock.

"I wish Gemma was here," Emmeline said. "She'd have the tools and skills to crack this lock."

"She'll be with us on the next adventure," Avery replied, still turning the dial on the lock with her ear pressed to the door, listening for distinctive clicks.

As Luna diced the second guard, Avery finessed the lock.

"That's it," Avery said, pulling at the lock. The top and bottom disconnected, allowing them to remove the metal rod from the lock hatch.

A fully open door revealed another staircase.

"Move quietly," Emmeline cautioned. "King Helmer could be at the top."

"And more guards," Luna added.

Solís gently pushed past Luna, Avery, and Emmeline to take the lead.

As he reached the top, he paused to peer over the top step. Five Marzan guards formed a semi-circle around King Helmer, who stood near a one-sided window observing the chaos in Hydra.

"Five guards and the king," Solís informed the group. He looked to Emmeline. "Everyone needs to fight."

"I can fight," she said, aware she was the only one in the group without combat experience.

"Rely on your fire," Helix advised.

Solís and Luna stood, followed by Helix, Emmeline, and Avery.

Their arrival was revealed.

The Marzan guards stirred with fury, but did not leave their stations protecting their king.

"Your Highness," one of them whispered in a growl, alerting Helmer to the intrusion.

The king turned slowly, a wicked grin across his face.

"Surely, you realize the end is upon you," Helmer sneered. "There's nothing you can do to stop us now."

"You will die, too," Solís argued.

King Helmer shook his head. "Our allegiance to Kólasi will save us. After we eliminate the sun, He will rebuild this galaxy and tailor it to our survival needs."

"Why does He need you to do His dirty work for Him? Why can't He just smother the sun Himself?" Emmeline asked.

"The gods cannot destroy the belongings of other gods. They can influence, but They cannot do it Themselves."

"Do you really trust that the god of death and chaos will honor His promise to you?" Solís asked.

"I have complete faith in Him," Helmer countered, then jeered, "Have you asked all your questions? Are you ready to die now?"

The Marzan guards did not wait for a reply. They charged the uninvited Solarpunks.

The largest of the Marzans went for Solís, who was already blazing red and tossing defensive fireballs. It quickly turned into brutal hand-to-hand combat, in which they were equally matched.

Avery avoided physical combat and used the liquid nitrogen in her veins to slow her aggressor. It took a lot of flying sprints and dodging, but she managed to slowly cover the Marzan with the icy-hot gas.

Emmeline lobbed fireballs at the Marzan who charged her. The Marzans could not fly, so she leveraged this advantage and rained fire from above.

Luna made quick work of her Marzan guard using magnetism, then shifted her focus to help Emmeline.

Without losing all the liquid contents within his beaker, Helix thrust the glass container with enough force to launch a small batch of the sodium hydroxide at his attacker. The heated tonic covered the Marzan's face, getting in his eyes, and sent him to his knees howling in pain. Luna and Emmeline had taken down a second guard and now redirected to finish off Helix's.

Avery's guard was rock solid, frozen in place. A simple foot tap to the head, and he shattered.

Three guards gone.

Luna shredded Helix's blinded Marzan.

While everyone redirected their attention to help Solís constrain the largest and fiercest of the guards, Helix turned his attention to King Helmer, who had shuffled far away from the fight and was discreetly crafting a black hole.

"He's going to get away!" Helix shouted, fumbling with his beaker of molten liquid.

Caught in action, King Helmer worked faster. With a single thrust of his hand, the black hole tripled in size.

Luna and Solís immediately averted their attention from the fifth guard, who Avery had thoroughly constrained using liquid nitrogen, to the fleeing king.

They charged him, running full speed.

King Helmer noticed their approach, but instead of hurrying his escape, he clutched the black stone hanging from a chain around his neck and thrust his arm toward Luna and Solís.

A black hole ripped into existence, separating him from those who wished to kill him.

It formed so fast they couldn't change course.

Luna and Solís ran straight into the black hole.

Gone.

Swallowed by darkness.

"No!" Emmeline shouted from where she knelt beside the guard Avery was freezing.

"I've got this. Help Helix," Avery said.

Helmer was about to make his exit through the first black hole he had created.

Emmeline heated her heart, lifted into the air, and chucked a fireball at Helmer's head. It hit him in the ear, sending flames down and across his neck. The momentary pause in his attempt to flee was all Helix needed to get close enough to toss the full contents of his beaker into Helmer's face.

The molten tonic sizzled as it liquified Helmer's eyes.

Blinded and defeated, he bellowed in bereaved pain as he flailed his arms and searched for his black hole. Helix quickly bound his ankles, preparing him as an easy target for Avery.

Avery tapped the final guard between his frozen eyebrows and his entire body shattered. She stood and calmly walked toward where Helmer writhed in agony.

"This is the end," she said. "When I kill you, so will I kill your soldiers. They have not yet extinguished the source flame. Existence as we know it will survive."

Avery lifted both of her arms, flexed her hands upward, and blasted Helmer with the liquid nitrogen coursing through her veins.

The process was slow, but effective.

Helmer swung his fists wildly, making contact with no one.

He released a sun-shaking scream.

The mooncraft quaked violently, Emmeline and Helix crouched and covered their ears, but Avery stood strong.

Nitrogen blood leaked from her ears.

"Your daughter used to scream like that," Avery said, holding her stream of icy gas. "Annoying, but tolerable with practice."

Helmer held the long, formidable shriek until his lungs gave out.

As the gas frosted over Helmer's body, his mobility lessened. With great effort, he pushed through the debilitating effects of the gas and grabbed the black stone hanging around his neck.

"I beg for Your mercy," Helmer whimpered.

"Never," Avery replied.

<<He is not speaking to you.>>

A cold, gear-stopping breeze swept the room, paralyzing Avery, Emmeline, and Helix.

They couldn't move, they couldn't speak; they were alive, but incapacitated.

Sporadic gold sparks illuminated the massive shadow now darkening the space. The deep, wicked voice spoke again.

<<He is speaking to me.>>

Chapter 45

Louie and his fellow Hydropunks fought alongside the Lunarians beneath the sea.

The water cyclone he used to contain each Marzan he fought sputtered to a stop as he reassessed their current standing in this fight.

The Marzans still outnumbered them. The battle was lopsided, but the Marzans only fought back when directly attacked—their collective focus was on creating a black hole near the source flame.

"Do everything you can to keep them from finishing that hole!" Louie shouted, his voice muffled by the sea, but still loud. "Distract them, force them to fight you!"

Every member of his Nautipunk crew had a Marzan engaged in combat; it was the Hydropunks taking shelter within the water who needed to find the courage to join the fight.

"Every second matters," Louie urged. "Every dead Marzan helps slow their progress!"

Louie had already fought and weakened five Marzans, letting a Lunarian quickly finish them off in their weakened state. He plunged toward the swarm of red devils crafting the black hole and yanked his sixth opponent from the frenzied herd by his long black hair.

Fueled by fury, Louie pummeled the disoriented Marzan, furthering his confusion.

Once the Marzan realized that he had been stripped from his task at the black hole, he attempted to fight back, but Louie already had the upper hand—he was five punches ahead and far superior at moving swiftly in the water.

The Marzan tried to scream, tried to weaken Louie with his explosive soundwaves, but that particular skill set did not work underwater. His formidable shriek was stifled by the sea.

Louie swam in a circle overhead, twisting the long black hair and creating a new waterspout around his opponent. As the force of his cyclone grew, Louie searched for a receptive Lunarian.

Cèla was nearby, ripping the chains out of the Marzan she fought.

"Ready for another?" Louie shouted to her.

She snapped her head in his direction, expression contorted with rage. She dropped the remnant of her victim, letting the shredded pieces sink to the ocean floor, then grinned.

"Send them over!"

Louie channeled the force of his waterspout and ejected the captured Marzan in Cèla's direction. She grabbed him by the ankle as he soared overhead, pulling him into her magnetic field and tearing him apart.

Their work was far from done.

While Louie's cyclone continued to spin, he returned to the swarm and seized a seventh Marzan. This one was smaller; it was female. He lifted her by her hair and removed her from the swarm. She flailed violently in his grip, making him work hard to relocate her. Halfway to the cyclone, she stopped fighting him.

Louie looked over his shoulder and found her wailing in agony with her hands over her eyes. He stopped swimming and kicked one of her hands away from her face—her eyes had turned to goo in their sockets. Exposure to the water quickly washed the slime away, leaving her eyeless.

The swarm of Marzans working on the black hole had also stuttered to a stop. Their frenzied focus turned into chaotic panic.

Louie scanned the ocean and found that every Hydropunk and Lunarian was dealing with a newly blinded Marzan.

"What happened?" he shouted.

"Their eyes fell out," Cèla replied.

"It happened to all of them?" Louie asked. "At the same time?"

"Seems so."

"This is our chance to stop them for good," he exclaimed.

But as the words left his mouth, a dark shadow and paralyzing current swept the sea, locking everyone but the Marzans in place.

<<*Finish the job!*>> an ethereal voice bellowed beneath the sea.

Louie's heart contracted—he knew immediately that it belonged to Kólasi.

The Marzans swam blindly.

<<*Follow the warmth!*>>

Those already huddled around the growing black hole continued their work, holding on to each other's shoulder to prevent them from drifting away with the ocean current. But the Marzans near the back of the group had already been displaced. The tides had shifted their positions during the first few seconds of their blindness, and now, they were just as lost as those who were scattered across the sea fighting the Lunarians and Hydropunks.

While the Marzans struggled to relocate their whereabouts, the Solarpunks and Lunarians had a far worse predicament to solve.

Frozen in place, they could no longer swim, and their paralyzed bodies were sinking toward the obsidian ocean floor that shielded the source flame. These temperatures were too hot to survive; only the Thermapunks could get close to the source flame, and even they never stayed too long.

Louie could not move his extremities, but his insides still churned. Water was harder to manipulate without complimentary motion, but it was possible.

He channeled his ocean heart, and then with all his might, shifted the water flowing beneath him. It was a true challenge, but with time and consistency, he managed to create a current that lifted his sinking body. Once he secured the rhythm and the flow felt solid, he slowly expanded its reach. He caught Cèla, along with three other Lunarians and four Hydropunks, from sinking to the source flame. Their paralyzed bodies rose, and members of his crew began to notice.

They channeled their ocean hearts, mimicking Louie's actions and gradually saving themselves and the Lunarians around them with an upward current.

Though this saved them from a fiery death, it did not stop the Marzans.

The black hole was still growing and the sun was not yet saved.

Louie knew what he had to do, but it would risk the lives of everyone safely floating in his current.

The tide turned his rigid body to face Cèla.

They made eye contact.

Louie tilted his gaze downward at the Marzans, then swept his silver-blue irises in a diagonal swipe.

Cèla let her silver irises show through the darkness of her rage, and with them, she matched his motion.

The current turned her body away from Louie.

Cèla had given him her blessing.

This was the right move, the only move.

Louie stripped the current out from underneath himself and the others he had saved, and redirected it toward the Marzans.

He, Cèla, and the others immediately sank toward the source flame again. He felt their terror radiating through the water.

There was no time for fear.

Louie smacked the blind Marzans near the black hole with the strongest current he could muster.

They swayed with the tide, some losing their grip on their comrades' shoulders and getting swept away, but most held on tight.

Louie needed to hit them harder.

His paralyzed body rotated in circles as he sank, making it hard to aim, but he gathered his strength and ushered a stronger current in the direction of the Marzans.

This second wave dislodged half of them, tearing them away from the black hole.

It was a good dent, but not enough.

Louie couldn't move, but he could feel everything, and the warmth from the fast-approaching source flame was beginning to burn his toes.

Fight on and die, or take a reprieve and die.

Louie looped his current back to where he and the others fell to catch them before they reached the source flame shield. Exhausted, but determined, Louie lifted them away from the fire, saving them once again.

As he rotated in the current, he caught sight of the Marzans' progress—the black hole was much larger than before.

Even if he sent another riptide to barrel them down, it was likely too late; the hole was too big.

I'm sorry, he thought to himself, apologizing to everyone he felt he had let down.

Oily tears escaped from his eyes and mixed with the ocean water.

This was the end.

As Louie struggled to find peace in his surrender, the ocean illuminated with blinding light.

If this was Death, it came in peace, cradling each life with a gentle touch.

Chapter 46

Montgomery's airship sailed toward the detention center.

Besides Kólasi's massive shadow formation, it was the only moving thing in Hydra.

<<*Who dares to approach me?*>> He questioned.

The massive mauve sail billowed in the wind, carrying the ship forward.

When it reached the empty cage that used to house the black hole, an anchor dropped over the gunwale.

Gemma stepped out from behind the wheel, frail as ever.

<<*Who are you?*>> Kólasi asked. <<*And why aren't you under my paralysis spell?*>>

Gemma held up her wrist and revealed the crescent-shaped mark.

<<*You have protection from Lunéss?*>> He asked. <<*How?*>>

"I died on Her moon. She visited me in purgatory and granted me safe passage back to the living world so I could be with my loved ones before Incarna possessed my soul." Gemma's silver glare was murderous. "But You are trying to rob me of that."

<<*Give it a few more minutes and your loved ones will die with you.*>>

Gemma walked past all the paralyzed Solarpunks aboard the airship. They were frozen moments after hearing Kólasi's voice, and their postures and expressions reflected their fear. She stopped in front of Montgomery. His golden eyes still moved, and they held great sympathy.

"Emmeline told you?" she asked in a whisper.

Montgomery nodded his eyes up and down.

"I have to do it."

His eyes glowed with golden gratitude.

She knew he'd understand.

Kólasi's shadow simmered with golden sparks and His attention had returned to the sea.

<<*Do not fail me!*>> He shouted at the Marzans blindly crafting the black hole below.

Gemma exited the airship and climbed the side of the empty prison cell. Her uranium heart rattled within her silver ribcage and her skeletal feet against the titanium bars made a clinking rhythm with each step. Both sounds added a unique cadence to the music still blaring from the marble machine aboard the airship—with no one feeding it marbles or turning its levers, the tempo of the music machine slowed and the melody turned ominous.

Terrifying and inspiring—it was the song of her death march.

The monsters in the cages below were frozen in statuesque stages of turmoil. Fangs bared, eyes bulged, mid-roar—their futile unrest was locked in time.

Exhausted and weak, Gemma moved slowly across the top of the cage. When she reached the edge, she took a moment to collect her bravery.

"You're already dead," she reminded herself in a whisper.

The wind from the black hole leading to Deimos whipped her long silver hair across her face. It was so close, she could smell the damp, musty home of the Marzans.

She unfastened a section of the long, front-facing row of buttons on her Lunarian hospital gown. The flesh from her belly button down had been stripped during her last explosion. Gemma reached up and under the flesh still covering her chest and gently wrapped her fingers around her uranium heart. She closed her eyes and yanked.

No explosion.

Gemma opened her eyes, relieved.

Ripped free from the veins that held it in place, her heart now sat in her palm.

Kólasi's giant shadow turned to face her.

<<*What are you doing?*>> He barked.

Gemma lifted her heart and shook it violently, destabilizing the atoms within. When a low whistle sounded from the swelling interior, she clenched her fist and released a knuckle tool she had never retracted before—her uniquely shaped silver-tipped heart pick; its tip fit into the small hole at the bottom of her heart. She swiftly poked it into her heart, triggering the small interior detonation button.

She had half a minute before it exploded.

Kólasi's shadow multiplied in size as He tore toward her.

<<*What are you doing?*>> Kólasi repeated, His anger so potent it shook the sun.

Gemma lobbed her heart into the black hole before the furious god blanketed her in darkness.

As her heart crossed the threshold between Hydra and Deimos, Gemma fell to her knees from exhaustion and smiled.

"Summoning Solédon," she finally answered.

As the words left her mouth, her heart exploded in Deimos.

The nuclear detonation was so powerful, its burst wave traveled through the black hole and dismantled half of the detention center. The cages remained intact, but the tall beams they sat upon teetered and fell, sending the paralyzed monsters locked in those cages into the ocean.

The cage Gemma's lifeless body rested upon remained.

She was gone, soul lifted to Incarna where it would be evaluated and redistributed.

<<*Who dares to threaten my sun?*>> the voice of a new deity seethed.

With a mighty sweep of fire, Solédon arrived in Hydra. Fire swirled within His massive golden silhouette. Unlike Kólasi, who materialized as a sweeping shadow, Solédon took the form of a human male.

A brief scan of the scene intensified Solédon's fury.

<<*You?*>> He seethed, addressing Kólasi.

<<*It's always great to see family,*>> Kólasi replied, His terrifying energy diminishing as the size of His shadow shrank.

<<How dare you,>> Solédon accosted, noticing Gemma's lifeless body atop the cage near the black hole. <<You cannot kill my creations!>>

<<It wasn't me. She did that to herself.>>

Solédon furrowed His golden brow. He scanned Hydra, taking in every microscopic detail all at once. He lowered His left hand, scooped the air, and then closed His fist.

As He lifted His forearm, all of the blind Marzans were extracted from the sea. They hovered in the air, flailing helplessly.

<<Does Lunéss know that you've corrupted one of Her moons?>> Solédon asked.

<<She saved that punk girl from the brink of death, marking her with a protection symbol, all to thwart me ... so I suspect She knows,>> Kólasi replied. His furious energy had turned mischievous. He was caught and His plan was officially thwarted. Solédon was an elder god, one level below Kólasi who was a primordial, but their power was near equal. Facing a worthy rival, Kólasi's aura of menacing invincibility vanished and was replaced with casual acknowledgment of His disobedience.

<<You have to stop doing this,>> Solédon scolded Him. <<First, you instigate utter mayhem on Matrigaia's planet, which we had to help Her clean up. And while we were distracted helping Her, you infiltrated Lunéss's moons and my sun,>> Solédon said. <<Why?>>

<<Chaos is my sole purpose,>> Kólasi replied.

<<You're also supposed to help Mortacia and Incarna with death.>>

<<Mortacia has everything under control with the mortals. Incarna prefers working with Her over Me. Our sons of death call on Mortacia instead of me when they need something. All my lighthouses and edifices are in working order. I'm so bored. All I can think to do is cause chaos for Matrigaia.>>

<<Why do you taunt Her so much?>>

<<She is life and order; I am death and chaos. She is my opposite, my nemesis.>>

<<*The only reason She is your nemesis is because you've designed it that way,*>> Solédon reasoned.

<<*I find joy in little else.*>>

<<*Incarna has a backlog of souls, a few centuries worth. Help Her.*>>

<<*She refuses my help. Says I cause more problems than I fix.*>>

Solédon shook His head. <<*You're a nightmare. I'd refuse your help, too.*>>

<<*I guess that's that, then. I'll see you at the next family reunion.*>>

Kólasi's shadow thinned as He tried to escape.

Solédon used His free hand to grab Kólasi by the neck.

To the paralyzed Solarpunks watching in horrified awe, it appeared as though Solédon had reached into a black cloud and held it hostage with unexplainable precision, but from the gods' perspectives, they saw past the facades.

They saw each other as they truly were.

Montgomery was positioned perfectly aboard his ship to watch the entire exchange in the sky.

Solédon released a booming whistle sharp enough to pierce the heavens.

The presence of four other gods materialized in Hydra, each wearing their own unique forms in the presence of the Solarpunks.

<<*Lunéss, do whatever you wish with these corrupted moon beings, just remove them from my sun,*>> Solédon commanded of the goddess disguised in a colossal swirling trail of sparkling silver moon dust. She spiraled toward Her disobedient creations, collecting every Marzan in a single swoop—including King Helmer—and disappeared with them in tow.

<<*Why did you summon the rest of us?*>> a goddess swirling with cosmic greens and blues asked.

<<*Really, Matrigaia? I thought you, more than any of us, would want to see what new mischief Kólasi was cooking.*>>

<<He'd be drakkina food if it were up to me.>>

<<If He had obliterated this sun, it would have destroyed Earth,>> Solédon added.

<<I am aware. Another indirect attack on me,>> Matrigaia said, then moved in closer to Kólasi's shadow and seethed. <<Why are you so obsessed with me?>>

<<Your turmoil makes my heart happy,>> Kólasi replied, His voice choked by Solédon's firm grip.

Matrigaia spat at the shadow, then glared at Solédon.

<<I'm glad you saved this sun, but I need to return to the Avitus galaxy, as I have not yet remedied the destruction He caused there.>>

<<Yes, Namaté needs you. Check on Nebila while you're there; make sure He hasn't infiltrated that sun also.>>

<<Yeah, sure. Fine. As if I don't already have enough to do.>> Matrigaia vanished.

Still clutching Kólasi's shadow, Solédon turned to the deity camouflaged in a pearly orb of light.

<<Incarna,>> He said, His voice soft, <<I need a favor.>>

The glowing pearl expanded in size, and Incarna asked, <<How can I help?>>

<<See that girl there?>> Solédon asked, pointing to Gemma's lifeless body. <<She is the only reason I came. If I hadn't felt her heart explode, I never would have known this sun was in trouble. I never would have known to come. Her soul deserves great praise and high markings during its valuation.>>

<<I understand. I will take great care of her soul.>>

<<Perhaps, even, you can ask her soul what she most desires for her next life.>>

<<To honor her sacrifice, I will take her desires into consideration.>>

<<Thank you.>>

The fourth deity, yet to speak, had arrived in the shape of a falcon, but their form was not solid—they were a hole in the sky. Not a black hole, but one of foggy darkness. Black mist funneled over the edges, flowing smoothly in and out.

Solédon addressed Him. <<*Obscuro … you know what I need from you. Kólasi seems to think He is the god of darkness … remind Him that He is not.*>>

<<*He always finds His way out,*>> Obscuro warned.

Kólasi laughed. <<*I may not be the god of actual darkness, but I am one with the shadows. Death is darkness, in theory.*>>

<<*Then perhaps what you need is a prison of light,*>> Obscuro mused. <<*I'll recruit Lumine's assistance this time.*>>

He extended His giant wings and wrapped them around Kólasi's shadow. They both vanished within the hole that was Obscuro.

Only Solédon and Incarna remained.

<<*There are many souls for me to collect here,*>> She said.

<<*Let me free the survivors first,*>> Solédon suggested.

Solédon extended both arms and tilted His head upward.

Every golden fly released by Kólasi exited their Solarpunk host and flew into Solédon's fiery form, incinerating instantly. With a mighty breath, He cleared the Marzan poison from every Solarpunk who had yet to heal.

He then rotated His arms and swept them in a circular motion, lifting Kólasi's paralysis spell. All the Solarpunks and Lunarians were released.

Solédon faced the tired and beaten-up Solarpunks and Lunarians. Weary, ragged, exhausted, they looked to Him in equal parts awe and disappointment.

"How could You let this happen?" Montgomery shouted, mustering the courage to challenge their god. "We serve you loyally, and in return, we trust you to protect us."

<<*Kólasi is a menace. He has been on a tear infiltrating planets, suns, and moons all over the universe. I had no idea He was plotting this for Quintessence.*>>

"We have prayed to you for weeks."

<<*I was helping Matrigaia clean up one of Kólasi's messes in a different galaxy. I'm not sure if She'll be able to save Her mortals there. I left to intervene here when I felt the Terrapunk's heart explode.*>>

"If you hadn't, She'd have no mortals left to govern on Earth."

Solédon scanned the scene.

<<Ah, the Lunarians are here.>>

"We had to abandon the holy doctrine," Montgomery confessed. "Since we could not reach you, our only option was to align with the moon beings. Seems they aren't *all* as evil as you wrote into scripture."

<<You are mistaken. My scriptures instruct you to work with Lunéss's dimidivinus mortals. The sun and moon must work in harmony.>>

"No," Montgomery objected. "You specifically instructed us to keep the moon monsters as far from the sun as possible." Agitated, Montgomery scanned his crew. "Cyrus, please fetch the doctrine from my cabin."

Cyrus quickly retrieved the holy book for Montgomery, who then tossed it to Solédon.

Solédon caught the ancient book midair, never touching it with His hands of fire, and examined it closely, flipping each page with a light gust of wind.

<<This is not my handwriting,>> He stated. <<The black ink speckled all over these pages are the markings of Kólasi. His pen splatters as He writes.>>

"So you're telling me that we've been serving Kólasi all this time?"

<<From the standpoint of your rivalry with the moon, it appears so.>> Solédon incinerated the doctrine. Its golden ashes fluttered into the sea. <<I will return with the true doctrine. I apologize for my absence and oversight. We've been struggling to control Kólasi for eons.>>

Emmeline, Helix, and Avery stood atop the destroyed Marzan mooncraft. Oily tears stained their faces.

"Solédon," Emmeline shouted, garnering the deity's attention. "You cannot leave until you save my brother."

<<What happened to your brother?>> He asked.

"He and Luna of Mōnalene fell into a black hole made by King Helmer."

<<Show me the portal.>>

"It's right below us."

Emmeline, Helix, and Avery used their wings to lift into the sky, and Solédon carefully removed the roof from the mooncraft.

Two black holes swirled within.

"Helmer made the one by the command board for his own escape," Emmeline explained. "The other one in the middle of the room is the one Solís and Luna fell into."

<<Are you sure that Helmer made both of them?>> Solédon asked.

"Yes, why?"

<<Because the one your brother and friend disappeared into belongs to Kólasi.>>

Emmeline examined both black holes closer.

The one Helmer made for himself looked like the one they had entered through near the detention center—it had jagged edges clean of debris, cosmic colors pulsating within, and low, rumbling thunder echoing from its depths.

The black hole that Solís and Luna fell into had black thorns lining its edges, the interior was pitch black besides sporadic golden sparks, and its depths were silent.

"Where are they?" Emmeline demanded, voice raw with emotion.

Solédon moved closer, peering cautiously into the black hole. Before announcing His findings, He waved Incarna over to look as well.

<<How could a dimidivinus craft a primordial black hole?>> Incarna asked Solédon.

"Helmer wore some kind of black rock around his neck," Avery recalled. "It's how he summoned Kólasi here."

<<He must've been holding it when he made this black hole,>> Solédon realized. <<This leads to one of Kólasi's penitentiaries. There

are three of them: one for the mind, one for the body, and one for the spirit.>>

"Free them!"

<<I cannot interfere on Kólasi's prison planets. They are in His hands now.>>

"But they are your creations!"

<<Just as Kólasi could not smother the source flame Himself, I cannot free His prisoners. If Kólasi had tossed them in there, I'd be able to do more. But He didn't. They walked into the black hole without His force.>>

"They did not choose this fate! They were tricked!"

<<I am aware, but they entered on their own.>>

Incarna glowed brighter and suggested, *<<There might be a way.>>*

"How?" Emmeline pled.

Every Solarpunk in Hydra was listening intently.

<<They are trapped on the planet Corpeus. Their physical bodies are the only parts of them that are bound there. I can still access their souls.>>

Solédon cut in, *<<Ah, brilliant idea.>>*

Incarna continued, *<<They have two choices: endure eternity on that prison planet together, or have their souls stripped from their physical bodies and sent into the minds of mortals until new bodies can be constructed for them.>>*

"The second option!" Emmeline pled.

<<The decision is up to them,>> Incarna replied. *<<If they choose rebirth in new bodies, they will first have to serve the minimum requirement, which is one hundred mortal lifetimes.>>*

"Why so many?" Montgomery shouted up at them from the airship. "One hundred lifetimes is a punishment!"

<<When you remove a soul from a body prematurely, it is weakened. Their souls will need time to heal and strengthen. And there's no better place for that than nestled in the womb of a mortal mind.>>

<<*This is the only solution,*>> Solédon added. <<*Begin building their bodies, and if they choose rebirth, they will return to you in due time.*>>

Elongated silence filled the war-ridden space between the Solarpunks and the primordial gods.

<<*Do you forget yourselves?*>> Solédon bellowed, His soft nature rapidly morphing into terrifying rage. <<*Are you not grateful?*>>

"We are," Montgomery quickly corrected their collective error. "I'm still in shock that we survived. I can speak for everyone here when I say that I did not think we would live to see another tomorrow." Montgomery inhaled, collecting his composure. "I am grateful. We are all grateful."

Solédon's intensified fire simmered. <<*You will not see us again, but I will keep a closer ear on the celestial sound waves. I will hear your prayers next time.*>>

Solédon and Incarna vanished.

The sun was saved.

The Solarpunks and every living creature in this galaxy would live to see another day.

Chapter 47

The sky shifted from orange to pink as night blanketed Quintessence. The rosy hues complimented the trail of silver stardust marking Gemma's memorial service.

Every Solarpunk was in attendance.

The Aeropunks and Thermapunks lined the skies, and the Hydropunks were transported to Terra and stood among the Terrapunks, breathing the air above Hydra for the first time.

Gemma's small and broken body rested on a bed of soft clay in the back of an open golden carriage. Golden nets attached the vehicle to a giant white balloon that carried it through the sky.

Emmeline and Avery sat on the coach seat in the golden carriage carrying Gemma's body.

Cyrus and Helix guided the vessel through the sky while Regis and Willie Morrell adjusted the helium levels within the balloon.

Memorializing a low-level Terrapunk was unheard of, as was participation from every member of every Solarpunk faction during a funeral.

Emmeline had opened everyone's minds to the possibility of unifying, and Gemma's sacrifice opened their hearts.

No longer would Quintessence be divided.

No longer would fire, air, land, or sea indicate their individual worth.

Though she was heartbroken to lose her friend, Emmeline felt unsurmountable pride and gratitude. Gemma was a hero, and she'd be remembered forever.

The Thermapunks formed two lines that ran the circumference of the sun, which marked the path for the carriage. Collectively, they sang their hymnal of death and rebirth, illuminating the pink sky with fire flares and sparks to light Gemma's path.

Tears streaked Emmeline's face as she sang:

"Death becomes us

in the end.
No bells, no whistles, just hollowness.
I beg:
Lift this spirit, regift this soul.
Rebuild what was lost into something whole.
May the gods see worthy this love of mine;
forever grateful, forever entwined.
I'll see you soon.
In that, I trust.
Together again
when death becomes us."

The Aeropunks flew overhead, following the carriage at its leisurely speed and honoring Gemma in flight. They carried small chimes and bells, ringing them in synchronized patterns, as they would have for a fallen Aeropunk. The timing and melody matched perfectly with the Thermapunks' song, and as the Thermapunks ended the stanza and took a break before restarting, the Aeropunks vocalized the harmonious line that paired with their bells:

"Divine light, honor her and guide our sister home."

The Terrapunks stomped their feet and clapped their hands, creating a sun-shaking rhythm that enhanced the power of the song echoing from above. They mumbled their chant—a blessing normally reserved for the elite Terrapunks—fitting each line into wordless pauses in the song.

"May the body find new purpose.
May the mind rest with ease.
May the soul serve another in the quest for eternal peace."

The Hydropunks joined the chorus with smooth oohs and aahs. Like a chorale of sirens luring lost souls to sea, except in this case, they were releasing lost souls to the heavens. Their voices held the power of the ocean, and the rough nature of their raspy tone perfectly contrasted their enchanting melody. The closer one listened, the clearer the message became. Each bewitching hum was actually a word elongated and broken into far more syllables than normally required. Guide, protect, honor, repurpose—each word they sang harmonized with the music filtering across the sky.

This synchronized song of unity from the four factions blended with flawless precision, and the effect was so powerful, it brought many of the Solarpunks to tears.

Cyrus, Helix, Regis, and Willie guided Gemma's carriage around the circumference of Quintessence three times before slowing to a stop near the Pyro-Argo base. The song tinkered to a stop as well and the gathered Solarpunks returned to their homes.

They docked the balloon carriage.

Emmeline looked over her shoulder at Gemma, whose silver-hued flesh glowed in the pink light of night.

"Incarna has her soul now," Emmeline said. "She will be protected."

"What should we do with her parts?" Avery asked.

"They are so damaged," Emmeline noted. Gemma's silver bones donned deep scars and dents from all the damage inflicted upon them over the years.

"We shouldn't rebuild her with these broken parts," Helix offered.

"I'm not sure we should rebuild her at all," Emmeline said, shocking everyone gathered. She further explained, "I don't know that she would want to come back, and if she does, would she choose life as a Terrapunk again?" Emmeline shook her head. "I don't want to influence her decision. Plus, she has no parents. We have no way to make her new Terrapunk parts."

"We could just clean up her previous body so she has the option to repossess it if it's given to her," Avery suggested.

"If we do that, she might feel obligated to accept it."

"Let's sleep on it," Cyrus offered, lifting Gemma's lifeless body out of the carriage and carrying it to one of the spare rooms attached to the common area of the base.

Helix wrapped his arm around Emmeline.

"It's been a long, emotional day," he offered.

"More like year," she corrected him.

"Yeah, you're right," he agreed. "Everything will become clearer with time."

A week passed.

In a burst of fire, a golden book fell from the sky and landed on Montgomery's airship in Fyree.

Melora got to it first.

The edges were still on fire.

"The holy doctrine," she said as she lifted the book and patted down the lingering flames.

She opened the cover, and tucked inside was a note in golden ink that read:

They chose rebirth.

Melora fell to her knees, sobbing with relief.

In time, her son would come home to her.

Emmeline spent most of her time in Hydra with her father. With the threat of moon monsters mostly eradicated, their focus shifted to negotiating trade deals and alliances with the beings they used to capture and kill. They used portals provided by the Lunarians to travel to and from the other moons in their galaxy, and their newly formed friendship with the Lunarians as leverage to sway the others.

Their efforts were unsuccessful.

"It will take time," Cèla encouraged them after a failed meeting with the Unars of Umbriel, formerly known as the Behemoths of Fatigue.

Cèla departed, leaving Montgomery alone with his three children.

"We will try again tomorrow," he said.

Emmeline immediately turned her attention to the area of the airship reserved for Solís's rebuild—the Lunarians were working on Luna's on Mōnalene.

Before their meeting with the Unars, she had been working on Solís's left hand, and she resumed the project she had paused.

Her mother was there, as she always was, weaving Solís's beautiful golden-brown hair.

Though they said nothing, they found comfort working side by side.

Lost in the tinkering of gears, Emmeline was startled when a voice shook her concentration.

"I'm sorry."

Bifocals still set to their highest prescription, she wobbled where she sat from the dizzying change of focus. She flipped the levers on the sides of her goggles, lifting the magnifying lenses away from her eyes. Eyes still closed, she replied.

"For what?"

Louie knelt beside her.

"For taking my pain out on you. For adding more heartache to your life. For handling everything wrong."

Emmeline opened her eyes—they glimmered with oily tears.

"I forgive you," she said, then returned to the very important project of rebuilding Solís's body.

"Can we be together again?" Louie asked.

"In time, maybe," Emmeline answered with her gaze fixated on the nuts and bolts that held the golden finger bones together. "Right now, you need to focus on your mom. And I need to focus on Solís."

"You're right," Louie said. "Just know that I'll be here."

"I know."

Louie climbed over the gunwale and descended the rope ladder to his man-o-war pirate ship.

Emmeline exhaled.

The sun was saved, Louie was back to his old self, but so many new nightmares had unraveled. Gemma's body still sat in the Pyro-Argo base with no clear decision on what to do with her parts, and Solís and Luna were Kólasi's prisoners.

"We will build him as a man," Melora said, speaking for the first time all day. "His mature soul will have a mature body to reenter."

"It'll take longer to make enough gears and bones for an adult-sized body," Emmeline replied.

"Your father and I don't mind. Plus, we have plenty of time."

Emmeline nodded. "Solís will appreciate that."

"One hundred mortal lifetimes could last a few millenniums."

"Let's hope a few of those mortals live short lives."

"No," Melora countered, rejecting this notion. "We cannot wish brevity upon others when we want more time for ourselves. Equal exchanges keep the universe balanced."

"If you say so."

A month passed.

Between building a body for Solís and attempting to build alliances with the moon beings, Emmeline polished Gemma's damaged bones and gears. Avery helped her strip the rotting flesh from the top half of Gemma's deceased body, and together, they fixed what remained into tip-top shape. After some consideration, Emmeline decided it was best to have a body ready in case Gemma decided to come home.

Avery and Emmeline scoured the Terra junkyards for gears to rebuild Gemma's lost foot, and after two months of toiling, tinkering, and polishing, Gemma's geared silver skeleton was ready to house a soul.

Safely done in a spare room of the Pyro-Argo base, Emmeline and Avery examined their work.

"She's perfect," Emmeline stated.

"Where should we keep her?" Avery asked.

"I want to build her a monument," Emmeline said. "One that is based in Terra and rises into Fyree."

"And we will keep her body there?"

"Yes, in plain view, where everyone can see her. Her presence will serve as a daily reminder that we only live thanks to her. A monument to inspire gratitude and bravery."

"It will be a huge project."

"We need to stay busy."

"*You* need to stay busy," Avery corrected her.

"Maybe."

"Take a minute to breathe. We are all tired. It's okay to rest and process the trauma we all endured."

Emmeline shook her head. "I'd rather not. I'm not ready."

"The longer you avoid it, the bigger it will build, and sooner than later, the backlog will become unmanageable."

"I always manage."

Avery sighed. "I suppose you do."

"I'll recruit a team of Terrapunks and Thermapunks to build Gemma's monument."

Avery conceded. "Tell me how I can help as well."

For the following year, Emmeline was consumed by the monument build and the construction of Solís's new body, as well as negotiating alliances with the moon beings. With so many important distractions, her attention glazed over the efforts Louie continuously made to reconnect: sea flowers left in her cabin, volunteering for every mission Emmeline participated in, showing up and sitting beside her silently as she built Solís's parts.

Melora often scoffed and squirmed uncomfortably whenever Louie quietly sharpened his hooks and spears beside Emmeline. Though she never objected, and her disapproval wasn't enough to keep Louie away.

"I'm done for the evening," Melora said on a particularly peaceful night—the marble machine played a new delicate melody and the world was calm. She departed, leaving Emmeline and Louie alone with all of Solís's scattered pieces.

"Talk to me, please," he begged.

"How is your mother?" Emmeline asked, her attention fixated on the gears she tinkered with.

"She is great. She is back to a healthy weight and gearing up for her first dive since returning."

"That's wonderful," Emmeline said, but the emotion fell flat.

Louie ignored her lack of genuine enthusiasm.

"You should dive with us," he suggested.

"Oh, I would, but there's too much else to do. The monument build, Solís, the alliances—I'm so busy."

"Just an afternoon dive."

"I said I'm busy." Her tone was harsher than she intended.

"I'd rather you just tell me to stop trying," he replied.

"Stop trying what?"

"Are you truly that disconnected from reality? Don't you notice my efforts to reconnect?"

"Yeah, but why are you doing that?"

"Why wouldn't I?"

"Because everything is still a mess."

"We can help each other navigate the mess."

Emmeline shook her head. "I need the mess. It keeps me focused and organized."

"No, it keeps you busy and distracted. While you pine away for the lives lost, you're forgetting about everyone who survived, including yourself."

"I'm doing my best."

"I know," Louie said. He leaned in and kissed her forehead. "I'll be here when you're ready to talk."

He stood and left her where she sat.

Alone with her thoughts—a dangerous place to linger.

Unable to sit there a moment longer, she heated her heart, spread her wings, and rocketed toward the gates of Hydra.

She had a monument to build.

It took three years to complete Gemma's monument.

Made of silver, bronze, zinc, and gold bricks, the square pillar stood tall and represented unity, survival, bravery, and gratitude.

At the top of the massive column was a throne carved into the golden bricks. Gemma's geared skeleton was fastened there with steel buckles. A giant silver bell sat at the top of the monument, and a rope to the bell snaked down into Gemma's skeletal hand—a way for her to let everyone know if she decided to return.

Avoiding reality as thoroughly as possible, Emmeline hardly noticed those who stepped up to help with the monument build. Louie came and went with shiploads of zinc bricks. Helix, Cyrus, and Kiran helped the welders every day after long shifts traveling to and from the moons. Avery built a floating scaffolding system that kept the workers safe as they stacked and welded the bricks. Her parents donated a thousand gold bricks and rallied the other noble Thermapunks to do the same.

Though she expressed her gratitude daily, Emmeline was living in a haze. She was so hyper-focused on those who were lost that she was becoming lost, too.

"Where are you?"

The question ripped Emmeline from her work on Solís's toe gears.

She looked up to find Kiran.

"What do you mean? I'm right here," Emmeline scoffed.

"Physically, sure. But where is your mind?"

"That is none of your business."

"Do you even know?"

The truth was she didn't. She had silenced all of her terrifying thoughts and troubling feelings; she was existing in a state of anesthetized survival.

"I am productive—that's all that matters," she answered.

"You aren't healthy."

"Yes, I am."

"You're as skinny as ever," Kiran noted.

Emmeline looked down, genuinely shocked by his comment. Though she was mostly covered by the baggy work overalls she wore, the tank top she wore beneath did not hide her frail arms.

"I'm so busy, I forget to eat. It's not intentional," she swore.

"No one else will say it because of all you've gone through; they don't want to upset or trigger you … but I will say it—you can't control the world around you by controlling your appetite. The two aren't connected and never will be. It might feel like you have some sort of control when you deprive yourself, perhaps it's a temporary relief, but it can't last, and it's only making your problems worse."

"Wow," Emmeline scoffed. "Did Helix put you up to this?"

"No."

"How long have you been holding that in?"

"A while now, and you know I'm right."

"Are you trying to help? Or make me angry?"

"Help."

"Well, I already told you that when I forget to eat, it's accidental. So, if you want to help, maybe come with marbles next time."

Emmeline returned to the work she was doing on Solís's foot.

Kiran knelt beside her. "I care about you."

"So do a lot of people, but none of them attack me like that."

"You'd rather I say nothing?"

"I would."

Kiran huffed.

"I'll come with marbles next time," he offered as he stood to leave.

"Sure."

Emmeline had already checked out of reality and back into her hazy world of detachment.

Fierce, determined, and focused on progress for Quintessence, Emmeline lived like this for the next five years. Perfectly present when she had a task to perform, but absent otherwise.

Kiran kept a stash of marbles in a satchel attached to his waistband, and whenever he got the chance, he invited her to sit down with him for a meal. It wasn't often, but it was enough to add a bit of thickness to Emmeline's bones.

On their first lunch together, she made him promise not to ask unpleasant questions.

He obliged and proved he was capable of sitting and eating with her in silence.

A small gesture, but one that Emmeline appreciated immensely.

Louie came and went, too, but he refused to play Emmeline's game of disengagement.

One day after a meeting with the Unars of Umbriel—who were finally beginning to entertain the idea of working with the Solarpunks—Louie grabbed Emmeline by the bicep and pulled her to a corner of Montgomery's airship where they could speak in private.

"What are you doing?" Emmeline said, trying to shake free of him.

He let her go once they were alone.

"Talk to me," he insisted.

"About what?"

"You act like I don't exist!"

"That isn't true."

"Everything you said to me during the war—you seemed so sure of your love for me."

"I was."

"What changed?"

"Nothing, and everything."

"That isn't helpful," Louie griped.

"I know it isn't. I haven't quite figured it out myself."

"That's because you don't give yourself time to think about anything other than all your projects."

"It's been so long … I wouldn't even know where to even start." Emmeline sighed. "Avery warned me this might happen."

"First step is to acknowledge that you want to try."

"I don't know if I'm there yet, but maybe."

"Second step is to locate the root of the problem."

"How?"

"Ask yourself the tough questions."

Emmeline shook her head. "It's easier not to."

"Then I'll ask—what are you so afraid of? What are you trying to hide from?"

Emmeline knew the answer immediately, and for the first time in years, an explosive surge of emotion bubbled to the surface.

"It's not a what," she said. "It's a who."

"Then *who* are you afraid of? *Who* are you hiding from?"

Tears streamed down her face as she answered.

"Myself."

Louie wrapped his arms around her and Emmeline collapsed into his embrace as every emotion she had bottled up over the years finally surfaced.

It was time to heal.

Chapter 48

Luna and Solís

Forty-nine mortal lifetimes passed before Solís or Luna became aware of where they were. Their souls went through their assigned motions—helping the sun and moon rotate within each mortal mind—but it wasn't until their fiftieth mortal mind that their souls began to wake up.

"No," Solís said from within the mini-illusionary sun he was trapped inside. It helped mark time for the mortal; it helped distinguish the days of their short life.

He looked around—it was a familiar scene. Everything revolved around a giant sand clock situated at the center of the mortal's mind. Glowing orbs known as pockets hovered in the space around the clock, each representing different identifying emotions. They were shaped by real-life moments from the outside world. Fragments of the mortal host lived within each of these pockets, as each memory significantly defined who they were.

Around the center of the sandclock was the village of time. Here, little creatures counted the seconds, minutes, and hours, keeping perfect track of when the sun should rise and set.

Along the edge of the village was the ring of thrones. Each throne was a chair to a Face—Time, Night, Day, Joy, Anger, Fear, and Sorrow; every mortal started with these seven Faces and collected more as their life progressed. Like the pockets, the Faces were fragments of the mortal host incarnate, but they were marginally more aware of their purpose and surroundings than the creatures living within the pockets.

The dimidivinus souls placed into the illusionary sun and moon were the only beings who weren't directly part of the mortal host—their fates were not linked. The dimidivinus souls in any mortal mind were there to guide, observe, and learn. Or, in Solís and Luna's case—heal.

This sandclock and all its moving pieces defined the mortal, and when all the pockets and faces were looked at as a whole, they painted a full, comprehensive image of the mortal's identity.

Solís observed the inner world of this mortal mind with horror—everything was dripping with oozing black goo.

The Face of Day carried the sun through the sky, his wings stripped of their feathers and replaced with thorns.

"What happened here?" Solís asked.

The Face of Day glared down at him, his eyes empty sockets of darkness.

"He speaks," Day said, voice monotone.

"Why is everything smothered in that porous gook?"

"Why wouldn't it be?"

"Has it always been this way?" Solís asked.

"You tell me … you've been here since the start."

"So have you."

"I can only remember three yesterdays," Day confessed. "Then I forget."

"If I give you a message, could you deliver it to the moon?"

"I could deliver it to Night, who could then tell the moon." Day's expression tightened. "I can't promise your message will be delivered intact, though. Night is complicated."

"Let's try."

"What's your message?" Day asked.

"Let's start simple: find out the name of the creature living within the moon."

"That's all?"

"For now, yes."

Day finished his daily task of carrying the sun across the mortal's inner world sky, and set Solís and the sun in the Lunar Spire.

For the next twelve hours, the sun rotated the bottom half of the sandclock—also known as the Southern Abyss. This space was intended for processing hardships and letting them go, but this one was built differently.

What was normally a tranquil and serene section of a mortal mind clock had morphed into a brutal hellscape. Figments from the mortal's memories ran rampant here, ruthlessly killing one another while trying to reach a black marble propped high in the sky atop thousands of viciously maimed corpses. The marble was impossible to reach because every time any of the figments got close, one of the corpses in the pile would spring back to life and devour the figment.

The creation of figments was never-ending—they rematerialized at the base of the corpse pile after being defeated. It was a vile cycle of death and rebirth, and Solís had a front-row seat.

The hours passed slowly, and the longer he was forced to bear witness to the ruthless game being played in the Southern Abyss, the more he hoped Luna served a different mortal mind.

At the final hour of night, the sun entered the base of the Solar Citadel in preparation for sunrise.

"The being in the moon is named Luna," Day informed Solís as he lifted the sun into the sky.

Solís groaned, furious that he could not talk to Luna himself.

"This mortal's mind is a nightmare," Solís said.

"Is it?"

"Clearly!"

"It's all I know."

"Does anyone know what the mortal does in the outside world?"

"Not me," Day answered. "I lost my eyes."

Solís grumbled. Normally, the Face of Day was how he saw into the outside world, but perhaps he could peek through the eyes of a different Face.

"What about the other Faces?" Solís asked Day.

"Happiness got a glimpse once, but I don't remember what she saw."

"Where is Happiness?" Solís asked.

Day pointed to a throne made of rubies and daggers. Upon it sat a woman with blood pouring out of her eyes.

"*That* is the Face of Happiness?"

Day nodded. "She loves blood."

Solís retreated to the center of his sun.

Finding answers from these Faces was not an option—they were too immersed in this nightmare, too comfortable here. The clear signs of sociopathy and mental deterioration had become normal to them. They would be of no help to Solís.

As the day came to an end, Solís gave Day a new message to deliver to Night.

"Tell Luna that I love her. Tell her to hunker down and disassociate. Don't watch the horrors in the Southern Abyss. Don't engage with the corrupt Faces. All we can do is ride it out."

"That's a strange message," Day noted.

"Will you relay it?"

"Sure."

Night came and went.

Day carried Solís into the sky.

"Did you deliver my message?" Solís asked.

"I did."

"And what did Night say?"

"She laughed."

"Why did she laugh?"

"She finds humor in heartache."

"Did she relay the message?"

"I don't know … she told me to go away."

"And you listened to her?"

"I always listen to Night." He pointed to his empty eye sockets and shivered. "I can't afford to lose more."

Solís nodded, more aware than ever that getting a message to Luna in this mind would be impossible.

The murderous mortal lived for fifty-two years.

Finally caught after killing thirty-seven mortals in the outside world, he was sentenced to death by a jury of his peers. Strapped to a table with an onlooking viewing party, a doctor stuck a syringe into his arm and pumped poison into his veins.

The moment the poison killed the mortal, Solís and Luna were released into a black void.

"Where are you?" Luna sobbed.

"I am here," Solís answered.

<<*That was a tough one,*>> Incarna's voice echoed through the void. <<*I'm sorry your awareness returned inside of that mind.*>>

"Our souls are healed. We are ready to go home!" Solís said, his voice desperate.

<<*Your souls are still fractured from their premature extraction. You may not need to serve the full sentence, but you certainly need more time to mend. The illusionary suns and moons you reside within are healing pods. Take this time to rest and rejuvenate.*>>

"How are we supposed to relax when we're inside the mind of a serial killer?" Luna barked.

<<*I cannot predict the fates of the mortals I choose for you.*>>

"Please let us go home," Luna begged.

<<*Your souls would wither within the bodies your loved ones built for you. You need more time.*>>

Without warning, their souls lurched backward and were inserted into a new mortal mind.

Solís fell to his knees within his healing pod.

He would heal.

He would be ready to go home by the end of this mortal life.

Solís never left the center of the sun.

He rested and absorbed the healing energy of the sun.

When the mortal died at the age of eighty-three, Solís was certain his soul was ready.

<<*It's not,*>> Incarna informed him.

"How is that possible? I slept for eighty-three years!"

<<*You need more time.*>>

"No, I don't!"

<<*I can see your soul—it is severely fractured and fragile.*>>

"But I feel strong," Solís countered.

<<*Can you see Luna?*>>

He could hear her whimpering, but could not see her.

"No—you keep us in darkness."

<<*You are not in darkness; you are in a room filled with light.*>>

"Am I blind?"

<<*When you are healed, it will be clear.*>>

Eighteen mortal lives came and went since, none of which were as horrifying as the fiftieth, but plenty had their issues. Depression, narcissism, addiction, obsessive disorders—each was a nightmare in their own right. Living in these minds was exhausting, and while Solís did his best to pay little attention to their mortal woes, he was often dragged into their tribulations by the Face of Day. He participated when forced, but refused to learn their mortal names.

As the sixty-ninth mortal perished, his soul was transported into the black void.

Darkness prevailed.

Solís screamed.

"Solís, stop," Luna begged.

"I still can't see!"

"Take a deep breath and try again."

Solís swallowed his frustration and calmed his anger. As a flimsy wave of serenity washed over him, a faint silver glow shimmered in the darkness.

It moved slightly, taking the form of a woman.

"Luna?"

"Can you see me?" she asked.

"Just your silver outline. Can you see me?"

"Only your golden silhouette."

"We are healing," Solís said, his voice animated with cautious joy.

"Maybe we can go home now," Luna suggested.

She extended her silver hand toward him.

As he reached out to grab it, his soul was stripped away and he was inside the mind of a new mortal.

This was his seventieth mortal life.

"No!" he bellowed from within the phantom sun of an infantile mind.

He took his place at the center of the sun and prepared to never show his face.

It wasn't until the fifteenth cycle—the mortal's fifteenth year of life—that Solís took interest.

An unignorable blast colored the cosmic sky red. It sent every Face into a tizzy, and many of their pockets were contaminated.

"What was that?" Solís asked the Face of Day as she carried him through the sky.

"It's nice to finally meet you," she said, looking down at him with a smile.

Her confidence was unnerving—she reminded him of Emmeline.

"What was that blast?"

"Nothing we can't handle."

"I've seen mind terrors begin in similar ways," he warned.

"We will keep Jane safe," she promised.

It was the first time he had heard the name of the mortal he served.

Jane.

As the years passed, her similarities to Emmeline became more prominent. He saw bits of his sister in every Face and unintentionally became invested. When Jane's inner world spiraled into chaos, Solís did all he could to help the Face of Day survive the deadly invasion.

Oftentimes to his own detriment.

Each time the Face of Day failed and fell victim to the chaos, his heart broke a little more.

The heartache became so hard to bear, he found himself wishing for death upon Jane—a means to end the suffering—which ultimately broke his heart more because it felt like wishing death upon his sister.

Despite his efforts, he could not ease Jane's suffering, so instead, he tried to learn.

Maybe this knowledge could help Emmeline when he went home.

He shifted his perspective and found new purpose in Jane's sorrow.

Consumed by Jane's journey—one of great lows and highs—Solís lost track of time.

How many years went by?

He had never loved a mortal as dearly as he loved Jane.

When the day of Jane's passing arrived, Solís wept inside the sun.

The inner world beyond the sun went black, but Solís remained inside the illusionary sun, which had lost its glow.

<<*Are you ready to come out?*>> Incarna asked. It was the first time in seventy lifetimes that She gave him a choice.

"I am ready."

A gentle caress cradled Solís's soul and lifted him out of Jane's deceased mind.

He was in a bright room filled with grieving mortal faces.

Beneath him was a casket with an old lady lying inside.

"Is that Jane?"

<<*It is,*>> Incarna answered. <<*She was doomed for an early death, but your persistent love and presence helped her live a long life. As did yours, Luna.*>>

Solís was so bereaved, he hadn't noticed Luna floating on the other side of Incarna's pearly form.

He raced to hold her, and when their souls collided, they were sent home.

Solís gasped for air as his soul entered the new body built for him aboard Montgomery's airship.

Soul and bone, it took a moment for his golden flesh to form a protective layer encasing his fragile insides.

"He's back!" a familiar voice hollered.

Solís lay still, blinking his eyes repeatedly as they readjusted to the brightness of Quintessence.

When his vision cleared, the joyous faces hovering above him became clear. Montgomery, Melora, Cyrus, Helix, and Emmeline.

"How long was I gone?" Solís asked.

Emmeline smiled, then answered, "Long enough for us to make this world worth coming home to."

Thank you for reading *Rise of the Moon*—I hope you enjoyed the story! If you have a moment, please consider rating and reviewing it on Amazon and sharing your thoughts via social media. All feedback is greatly appreciated!

Amazon Author Account:
www.amazon.com/author/nicolineevans

Instagram:
@nicolinenovels

Facebook:
www.facebook.com/nicolinenovels

YouTube:
@nicolinenovels

Want to read more about where Solís and Luna went in Chapter 48?

<u>**Into the Foxhole**</u> is a separate novel that can be read as a standalone story or as an offshoot to this duology.
It is a deep dive into one of the mind's Solís and Luna serve.
(*Into the Foxhole* can be purchased on my website or Amazon)

To learn more about my other novels, please visit my official author website:

www.nicolineevans.com

www.ingramcontent.com/pod-product-compliance
Lightning Source LLC
Chambersburg PA
CBHW072022020726
47501CB00006B/1908